Readers

Greenw

Winner in the 2013 Rainbow Awards: First: Best LGBT Novel, Best B/T & LGBT Debut, Best B/T & LGBT Fantasy, Paranormal Romance & Sci-fi / Futuristic

"I loved this story for taking a legend and giving it a twist ... I have to recommend this to those who love folklore, mystical legends, historicals, fighting for a love against insurmountable odds, danger, betrayal and an ending that is devastating while giving you faint hope."

—MM Good Book Reviews

"This is a gutsy twist on a major classic that works."

—Gerry Bernie

"There is so much good about this book I'm not even sure where to start. ... This one is a highly recommended read. Just read it. It blew me away."

—Better Read Than Dead

"Greenwode is legend. It is epic storytelling. It is fantasy and history. It is religion and spirituality. It is a world in which faith is a weapon, faith is a tool, faith is the enemy, and faith is the last vestige of hope… when there seems nothing left to hope for. If you love epic fantasy, I can't recommend this book highly enough."

—The Novel Approach

"I can assure you the weaving of themes and legends in GREENWODE is mesmerizing. ... This novel will always be the one against which I will judge all the others."

—Christopher Hawthorne Moss

"…an interesting, spellbinding read."

—Rainbow Book Reviews

"I highly recommend this any fan of an epic fantasy with historical settings. It is long but worth it. I can't wait for the second book to come out."

—Hearts on Fire Reviews

J Tullos Hennig

DSP PUBLICATIONS

Published by
DSP PUBLICATIONS

5032 Capital Circle SW, Suite 2, PMB# 279, Tallahassee, FL 32305-7886 USA
http://www.dsppublications.com/

This is a work of fiction. Names, characters, places, and incidents either are the product of author imagination or are used fictitiously, and any resemblance to actual persons, living or dead, business establishments, events, or locales is entirely coincidental.

Greenwode
© 2014 J Tullos Hennig.

Cover Art
© 2013 Shobana Appavu.
bob@bob-artist.com
Cover content is for illustrative purposes only and any person depicted on the cover is a model.

All rights reserved. This book is licensed to the original purchaser only. Duplication or distribution via any means is illegal and a violation of international copyright law, subject to criminal prosecution and upon conviction, fines, and/or imprisonment. Any eBook format cannot be legally loaned or given to others. No part of this book may be reproduced or transmitted in any form or by any means, electronic or mechanical, including photocopying, recording, or by any information storage and retrieval system, without the written permission of the Publisher, except where permitted by law. To request permission and all other inquiries, contact DSP Publications, 5032 Capital Circle SW, Suite 2, PMB# 279, Tallahassee, FL 32305-7886, USA, or http://www.dsppublications.com/.

ISBN: 978-1-63216-437-7
Digital ISBN: 978-1-63216-438-4
Library of Congress Control Number: 2014944945
Second Edition October 2014
First Edition published by Dreamspinner Press, January 2013

Printed in the United States of America
♾
This paper meets the requirements of
ANSI/NISO Z39.48-1992 (Permanence of Paper).

For Kip
Bendith

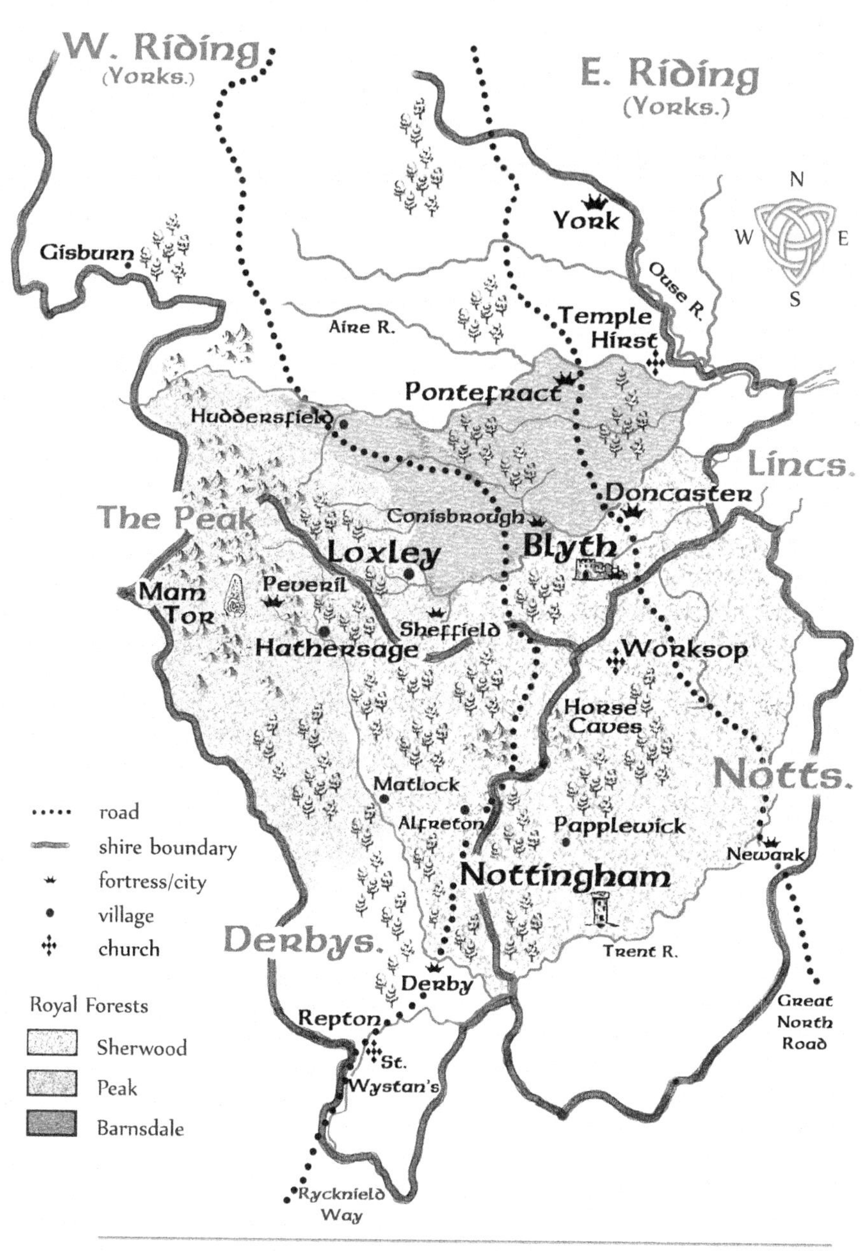

Map of the Shire Wode

☙ PRELUDE ❧

In the Deeps of the Shire Wode
1175 ACE

"WIND and water, stone and tree…."

Firelight flickered against rock, as if in time to the low melody. Both light and song wavered as they traveled into the depths. Not that the voice was not strong or the fire not warm—the caverns were that deep.

An old man, lean and crystal-eyed, stared into the fire. Every now and then the fire would jerk and start, as if some giant had spat upon it, but the cause was natural enough. Thunder rumbled in the forest above, sending puffs of wind through unknown entrances into the caverns. The old man could hear the stones embedded in the earth above him creak, almost in reply; he tuned his low voice as if in reverent time. Those rocks that formed the circle above him might be a tiny imitation of the ring stones on the plain of Salisbury far to the south, but no less eternal in their observance of the powers that he, too, had served for….

How long had it been? Stubble had scarce grown on his now leathern cheeks when he'd first taken up the mantle of the god. He had put aside his real name when, on a midsummer night not long after King Stephen had taken up another, more politic authority, a peasant gathering had crowned a young man with antlers and cried the god's name:

Cernunnos. Horned One. Green-Father. Hunter.

Cernun.

Stephen had relinquished his crown to his nephew Henry even as Cernun had groomed his own successor, moving from Hunter to Hermit's guise. It was the way of things. Shaking a twisted lock of silver from his eyes, Cernun grumbled to himself again, stirring at the fire with a long stick. He was old, but not infirm. The Sight was still strong in him, his body still hale and sound of limb; the forces of nature had rewarded him well for his service. Most men who had seen over fifty winters were bent and aged, senile from hard, miserable lives. The blood of the Barrow-lines ran strong. And he had been lucky.

He could only wish his successor such fortune.

The fire sparked. Cernun leaned closer, scrutinizing the writhing embers, watched them swell then flare white, reaching for the low limestone overhead. *Yes?* he asked, silent beneath the swell of power. *You speak, Lord?*

Images assaulted him. He saw what had been: the midsummer madness of dancing and singing, the rejoicing in rites, which, for a short, sweet time, took his people from the harsh reality of toil and hunger. Saw Horned Lord take Lady, clothed in Hunter and Maiden, horns and moon-crown.

Saw children born, Beltain-gotten, and the sweet green Wode prosper. As above, so below.

The fire damped, the vision strayed. Cernun spoke a low, guttural word, grabbed a handful of herbs from the cauldron at his side, and threw them onto the fire. The past was a given—to what future led this vision?

Scented smoke rose. It blossomed, damp cavern mists and heat writhing, tearing into wisps then coalescing.

A scream. The Mother's face reflecting flames and terror, the woods aflame, and the Horned One on the Hunt. Downed in snow, horns broken, wolves with blooded jaws snapping and snarling....

"No!" Cernun hissed. He caught his breath as more shapes danced in the smoke, dissolving then coalescing....

A cowled figure draws a freakishly long bow, the arrow's flight swift and sure, to split another arrow already in the black... a sister of the White Christ bends over a kneeling soldier... clad in the red and white of the Temple, he raises his fair head to let her make the sign of the Horns upon his brow... a booted foot stomps the long bow, shattering it....

Cernun blinked, shook his head. It made no sense, none of it. Smoke hissed, twisted into a pair of cowled figures locked in struggle....

One slams the other up against a tree, yanks his head back, and brings a drawn sword against the exposed artery, only to have the sword fall from his hands, to stagger back as if he has seen some demon... or ghost....

Another twist of smoke, and abruptly the flames flared high, gusting char against the old man's face. He didn't move, in fact bent forward.

A figure, crouching naked in the fire, a silhouette amidst burning ruins. The fire rises again, a spiral of sound and wind, and the figure rises with it, backlit, stepping barefoot over the coals and extending pale arms as if clothing itself in fire.

And, suddenly, it is. Flames whip, clad and cowl the figure in brilliant scarlet that ebbs to black... then gray-ash rags. Winter blows through, snow hissing in the coals and covering the figure. It walks back and forth, and in its footsteps ice crystals form. Green, sharp-edged leaves unfurl amidst the winter ice, revealing blood-red berries in their depths. The figure turns to him, eyes glowing within its cowl, still pacing, like to a wild animal caged.

Wolf, *it says, but does not speak.* Witch. Hawk.

Wind gusted through the cavern in a bank of noise and cold. The fire pitched down from copper into indigo, sparks flying, smoke rising.

Cernun did not bother to stir it. Instead he closed his eyes, tried to make sense of what he had seen.

Wolf. The most skilled of hunters, yet hunted throughout the land by another, even more treacherous predator. Or… outlaws were known as wolfshead. Perhaps? But not likely. Cernun would tolerate no outlaw within his covenant.

Witch. What the White Christ's followers called those who followed the old ways of the heath and Barrow-lines, a calling turned to hatred by outside forces, even as the Romans had done with another naming: *Pagani.*

Hawk. Proud birds, another hunter/predator forced to perform beneath nobleman's rule, barely tamed and kept from free flight, jessed, hooded.

"Hooded." It came out in a soft rush of breath. Not only the hawk but wolf and witch—predators cornered—the struggling figures, the flame-gotten one… all cowled. By fire, by ash, by blood. "Great Lord who lies incarnate in us. Has it come to this?"

He stared at the dying embers, not wanting to believe. But the image persisted.

The one to walk all worlds, to breathe the fates of dark and light and dusk between, male and female; the Arrow of the goddess and the Horns of the god. The champion of the old ways—and the beginning of their ending.

The Hooded One.

☙ I ❧

Near Loxley Village, Yorkshire
1185 ACE

"ROB!"

The weanling tensed, twitched long, wide ears. Blinked. Then greed overcame any start of panic. The deer crept closer, switching its buff-colored tail and chewing as if it could taste the goodies being offered. Its benefactor was kneeling in the fern and bracken, quiet as the mists hanging in the thick trees. It almost seemed he wasn't wholly there, a ghostly, hooded figure holding too still for mortal folk, offering a small measure of corn.

"*Rob*!" Then the sound, coming closer, of running feet.

This did penetrate. The fawn started and fled, tail flagged high. With a growl, the figure rose, revealing itself to be no forest sprite but a mere lad, lanky and unfinished as the weanling deer.

He'd almost *fed* the creature, almost felt whiskers and soft lips tickling against his palm. Almost touched the wild. Throwing back his hood from black hair and an even blacker expression, the lad rounded on the one who had broken his enchanted moment.

"Marion! You're noisy as a browsing cow!" She had slowed, picking her way through the copse, skirts tucked up to reveal sensible hose and worn leather boots.

She was not impressed, either by the considerable scowl or the inflammatory accusation. Her cinnabar hair was tucked beneath a kerchief, twining down her back with bits of bark clinging to it. The sopping edges of her skirts and boots slapped and squeaked as she walked. Her cheeks were pink, her breath steaming into the morning's chill; she'd run at least this far.

"Da wants you. He's an errand for you." Gray eyes took in Rob's clenched palm, the suspiciously bulging bag tied to his waist. "And if he finds you've been feeding deer again, you'll be in for it."

"He'll not find out unless you tell."

"And why shouldn't I?"

Rob grinned, crossed his arms, and leaned against a young oak. "We-elll, mayhap if I let slip—out of fear of punishment, mind—that I saw you in the fodder bin with Tom, the carter's son?"

"You treacherous little sod," Marion replied, but there was admiration in it. "All right, then. Pax. You waint tell about Tom, and I say nowt to *your* little assignation."

"Little what? Are you calling me an ass?"

Marion rolled her eyes, leaned forward, and grabbed him by one grass-stained woolsey sleeve. "As-sig-nation, y'fool. It means a meeting. Tryst."

"Well, why didna you just say that?" Rob protested as she began to propel him, hand still on his arm, toward home.

"I *did* just say that. Can I help it if you're a daft knob who canna be arsed to pay attention to his learning?"

"Parchments are a waste of time—ow!" He tried to pull from her grip; she just grabbed tighter and kept him on the march. "G'off me, I'm going, I'm going! And I've no need for smelly old tomes, I've my bow."

"I've a bow too. Sometimes I outshoot even you, lad. It doesna mean I've no need for my brain."

"You'll drive young Tom off, you will. Men dinna fancy clever women."

Marion snorted. "Like *you* would know, boy."

"I'm nearly a man!"

"Nearly only counts in quoits."

"Da married Mam when he was fifteen!"

"You're not even looking fifteen in the eye yet; I know 'cause I saw you born. How about we wait at least 'til your voice breaks to speak of it again?"

Rob tried to answer this, found "fuming" to be a word he *did* know.

"Anyway, you're assuming I ent clever enough to hide my cleverness. Not that I'm planning on marrying Tom."

"You keep on with what I saw you two about in the hay ricks and you might have to—Ow!" Bloody *hell*, but she had a fearful left cross. "I dinna know what you see in Tom."

"He's got nice eyes. And golden hair—"

"What's so special about *that*? He looks like corn that's been in the ground too long. He'd never have a chance in the forest; anyone would see him coming for miles." Rob shrugged free of Marion's grip only to have her grab him again. "'Tennyrate, the only reason Tom's so fair-haired is that he uses lime paste."

Marion shot him a look—clearly this was news to her. Unfortunately, it didn't stop her from continuing to propel him forward. "You'll understand soon enough. You'll see some girl that tilts your braies and then you'll want to be tilting into her."

"This is more than I really wanted to know about you, thanks awfully. I dinna like girls. Giggling, silly things, all sick-sweet flowers from their skirts to their empty heads."

A snort. "You like *me*."

"You ent a girl, then, are you? You're me sister."

☙

THE house was off to itself, really; close enough for convenience to Loxley village but set apart, right on the forest's edge, a proper location for land and chattels let to a king's forester. It was also sturdier than the wattle-and-daub siding of most dwellings near the forest's edge, a one-room cob cottage with a small loft. Rob liked to sleep on the little platform on wet nights, up next to the rafters and thatch, to hear the rain patter.

Not a bad place to call home, as such things went.

Marion started for the garden, but jerked her head toward the small barn; Rob turned to see their father walking from it. He was a brown man, from swart skin to curly hair and shaggy beard, with startling blue eyes. Rob often wondered if—hoped—he would ever grow to be as strong and statuesque as Adam of Loxley. In one hand Adam gripped a small folded parchment; the other held the reins to a sturdy little bay jennet.

"I need you to ride to Loxley, Rob." His father's speech, a deep, rounded dialect of the local-born, was clipped with impatience. "I would go, but there's still the nor'west section to cover before night. That poacher wants catching."

Rob nodded. Adam was known to the sheriff's guardsmen as an aloof and steady customer: hard to bribe, fair to a fault. The common folk knew him as their own: the one constant in a hard place. For them, Adam would overlook a kill amongst the king's deer during starving times, claim it beneath his own sparse yeoman's rights. Abandoned or senseless butchery, however, he would not tolerate. This latest transgressor had slain four deer already, taken their hearts and horns, and left the rest to rot. An outlaw, no doubt. Such waste infuriated Adam, and Rob himself was sickened by it. Everyone knew that if you held such disregard, it would fall back upon you threefold.

"What have you there, boy?"

Rob found his father's gaze fastened upon his clenched fist. Marion had hot-footed him so smartly home that Rob had forgotten what he held. With a grimace, he opened it, displaying the handful of grain.

Adam pressed his lips tight and shook his head. "Feeding animals again, when food's short enough for the village."

Rob looked down. "Sir, I—"

"Weren't thinkin'," Adam growled. "Son. You're getting to be of an age to understand such things. This harvest has been good so far, and one would think we'd eat for years, but it won't last forever. The only luxuries we can afford are our own beasts. You and your mother, you'd have the entire forest in our laps."

"I waint forget again," Rob murmured. As Adam held out his hand, Rob traded the grain sack for the jennet's rein.

"Rob?" another voice called. "Would you also take something for me?"

Rob turned to see his mother walking toward the barn, her tread mindful of the neat rows and beds of the east-facing garden. Marion was following, carrying a wood-and-hide pail—probably going to milk. Marion shrugged as she saw Adam holding the grain sack, but her lips betrayed a slight smirk.

Wanker, Rob mouthed at her.

I dinna have to, she mouthed back. *Wank, that is.*

"Did you say something?" his mother asked.

Rob shook his head. Eluned was clad for working, her gray overdress tied up at her waist for comfort, a wide, straw hat over her braided hair, and a basket spilling greenery hooked over one arm. She wasn't half as old as the wortwife who dwelt in Nottingham's fortress and tended to the sheriff and his retinue, but she was twice as skilled—and thrice as beautiful, Rob amended, thinking of Ness's craggy face. Surely the old white-bearded Christian god was not so ancient or scrawny as Ness. Not to mention that unlike Ness, Eluned still smiled with all her teeth, was small-boned and plump, with only a few silvered streaks in her black hair. It seemed that just the touch of her hands could cure a fever, that the least of simples and remedies prepared by her could cease any pain. Some of the villagers called her "The Maiden"—despite that she'd already had two healthy children and buried two—in tones of awe and respect. It was even said she had the Old Blood of the northern Barrows.

Looking at her, Rob could believe it.

She handed him a cloth packet. "Anna, the carter's wife, is sickening from her pregnancy. Tell her this should ease her."

"Ent that Tom's mam?" he asked easily.

From behind their parents, Marion shot him a look that, had it been an arrow from her bow, would have slain him instantly. Marion really was a fine shot.

"I do believe Tom is one of her children, aye." Eluned had been away from the Welsh borderlands for many a year, yet still had the singsong lilt to her voice—one both Marion and Rob seemed to fall into more often than not. She raised an eyebrow. "Why?"

He opened his mouth and watched with no little amusement as Marion's glare moved from *well-aimed death arrow* to *lop your bloody head off with a very shiny axe*. Rob grinned, merely said, "I was just asking."

Eluned peered at him, then slid her eyes to take in Marion, who suddenly found it imperative that she milk that cow, and the sooner the better. She started off for the barn, swinging her bucket with no little nonchalance.

His mother's eyes narrowed. Aye, Eluned of the March was as canny as her rumored people.

"Off with you, then." Adam grabbed at his son, boosted him onto the jennet's back. "No dawdling. Give Willow a good run, mind your business and be back before dark. And." He caught Rob's gaze, held it. "Mind you take no shortcuts through th' Wode. Go around."

Rob visibly deflated. This put a proper nick in his plans. "I was going to catch some fish. I thought you said outlaws only have the stomach to attack at night."

"This poacher's no reasonable outlaw. There's plenty fish to be had that dinna bide in forest pools." His father patted the furry bay neck, with the final justification, "You know good 'n' well mating season's to hand. Think of Willow's welfare—to a buck blind with rut, she might be no' but another challenge to take on. Be sensible, Rob."

The boy sighed and put heels to his mount's sides.

ଓଃ

ROB rode at a brisk trot, posting against Willow's short-legged gait, casting a longing eye upon the thick tangle of Loxley Chase. It was several miles via the plowed roads to Loxley village; it was barely a mile through the forest, and Rob knew every deer trace as well as the map of freckles on his narrow, sunburnt nose.

Even now, he saw a trail; faint, but unmistakably there if one knew how to look. Too many people didn't. The villagers were scared of the forest. Though Loxley Chase was just the tip of what became the great Shire Wode to the south, most of the farmers that lived in its shadow were convinced that all manner of h'ants and boggarts bided there. They told tales that put even the real dangers of wolves or boars to shame. Or the lord's men. For it was a fact that those men given leave to hunt—the few not scared of deep forest—tramped through it as if it were merely a woefully overgrown and tangled common, aiming their crossbows at anything that moved, peasant or game.

Crossbows. Rob's lip curled. Cheating, that was. A simple shortbow—aye, that was a man's weapon.

A quirk drawing between his dark brows, Rob considered that faint trail with no little longing. As if in answer, more distant than it sounded, the click and smack of antlers tangling stayed and reminded Rob of Adam's caution. He patted Willow's neck. She was too nice to get gored by some hey-go-mad buck thinking more with his balls than what little brain he had. Even better not to chance his father's ire two times in one day. Adam was already up in arms about something. As Rob had heard it, there was a new clutch of noble-born tenants in the castle sitting athwart the shire borders of York and Nottingham, rehashing some perpetual dispute over who should own the rents from Loxley and several other villages. Rob didn't understand half of it. The lords never came around, only sent others to do their dirty work, soldiers to threaten or sheriffs to bully. The villagers should just look to Adam as they always did; he was more thane of Loxley, it seemed, than the headman there who bore the title.

At least, that was the only explanation that Rob could come up with when the people of Loxley and its surroundings called his father "Lord."

He rode on, keeping to the road, quite chuffed with his own virtue. The air was nippy, pleasant and cool; Rob smiled as the little mare toyed with the bit. Mabon was drawing ever nearer, the equinox and harvest celebrations. There was excitement in the air even Willow could feel. The year had been prosperous, and the feasting would be good… and on the plowed road, they could make up time with speed. With a small yip, he dug his leather-clad feet into Willow's brown ribs.

"Go, Willow!"

The little bay leapt forward, eager, as if she had been waiting for Rob to ken that well-cleared roads equaled a good—and easy—run. Rob laughed and leaned forward; her black mane rose to slap his face, commingling with his own hair as he urged her on.

Over and down one hillock, then another, and as they came over the third and around a long curve, something exploded from the forest edge almost atop them.

Willow shied and rolled sideways on her muscular haunches as if some fire-breathing dragon had come roaring from the forest, primed for horseflesh. Rob was first tossed onto Willow's thick neck, then slid under her chest, then smacked heavily to the dirt. He made an instinctive snatch at the rein, but missed as Willow swerved at the last moment. She trotted off a few paces then halted with a jolt, head seemingly sucked against the earth as she set to a thick patch of grass.

Rob used a word for which his mother had once washed out his mouth with lye soap. Fingers full of dirt, he stood up, brushing at his tunic and leather breeks. His gaze darted about, quickly found the "dragon" that had leapt from the forest at them.

It was another horse. A gray stallion, pale as a thick-stacked thunderhead; tall and long-limbed, blowing and wide-eyed and ready to take to the hills if necessary. He was tacked with a saddle and bridle that together would have paid several years' worth of Loxley's taxes. One of the fancy, inlaid stirrups was flung over the seat and the saddle itself kinked to the left. A scabbard pointed skyward, its sword clinging only by the grace of being well laced in.

No commoner's mount, this. Rob smirked, considering that the stallion seemed quite the overbred noble set adrift, peering down his nose at having his day interrupted by some grubby peasant lad and his hairy jennet.

He also bore several telltale gashes along one ivory flank.

"Easy, lad." Rob held out a hand, soothing. "Did that buck get the better of you, then?"

The stallion stretched his neck and deigned to let Rob approach. Then, nostrils flaring, he promptly dropped his aloof pose, stuck out his knob, and pranced past Rob over to Willow, arching his neck and grunting and nickering.

Willow greeted this overture with an unearthly grunt, letting fly with a back hoof. She returned to grazing. Despite the pose of indifference, however, her black tail lifted; the roll of her eye was flirtatious.

Rob rolled his own eyes. "Bloody…. You too?"

He knew better than to get in the middle of the poncy stallion and his common paramour—at least, not until the mare had definitely said "aye" or "nay." Not to mention the possible spoils come eleven moons from now: a fine, if late-gotten, colt from a stallion whose fee they'd never otherwise approach. Rob shrugged and left them to it, once again scanning the terrain.

There had to have been a rider with that horse.

The trail was easily discerned, leading into the dusky canopy of green and fawn. The horse had been panicked, not terribly choosy about where he'd fled, leaving crushed bracken and rent branches and torn-up earth in his wake. He was just as noisy outside the confines of the forest; his loud dalliance with Willow could still be heard. Rob ignored it, ducking beneath branches and sidestepping thick bracken, treading the damp ground light as down and watchful as a priest on tithing day. His father and mother both had taught him well. He made no moves other than ones he intended, left no trace that couldn't be mistaken for animal spoor, was silent until he saw it, and then that, too, was a mere breath into the forest.

"Bloody *damn*."

A leather boot, worn but well made, was snagged against a gorse near Rob's eye level. Just beyond that was a bundle of fabric crumpled against the gnarled roots of an old oak.

Rob moved closer, cautious.

The bundle of fabric revealed itself, just as he'd figured, to be clothing. Unfortunately it was not empty, but again, just as he'd figured, was wrapped around what had to be the stallion's rider. The boot in his hand matched the one still worn; of course the other leg was bare, stocking yanked half off. More freckles than Rob himself had ever possessed sprayed across that pale calf.

Tale was as easily discerned as trail. Whoever this was had been riding, run across a buck deer looking for a scrap, the poncy stallion might have challenged the deer—probably not, those gashes were on his butt end, after all—and the likely as poncy rider had been thrown and then dragged a short ways before he met the oak.

Rob knelt, fingered the cape bunched and flung sideways. Fine stuff, all right, soft woven and well oiled to keep out the damp. Finer than the boots, even. Contrarily, the dark-blue tunic beneath it had seen better days, as had the woolen braies. What kind of lad—and it must be a lad, with that garb—wore such rich clothes until they wore out?

Grabbing the limp figure by his tunic, Rob gave a heave, turned him over. A pale shock of gingery hair spilled from the confines of the cape's hood. A lad, sure enough, and about Rob's own age. Rob grimaced as he saw the gash on the high freckled forehead.

Pure trouble, this was.

Tempting to just leave it all to lie, let this trouble find another target. Rob did, after all, have important business in the village. He could tell the headman there what he'd found….

Nay, he really couldn't. Because sure as crows flew with ill news, that gray stud would follow Willow home, and then wouldn't Rob have some explaining to do as to why he'd not gone looking for its owner.

Rob sighed, then reached out and tapped his fingers at the lad's shoulder. "Hoy. You, there. Wake up."

☙ II ❧

A HORRIFIC, grunting shriek, echoing over and over in his head, then the pounding of hoofs. The buck blasts defiance, charges; he is spit on the horns, thrown aside as if he is parchment ripped from a court ledger, set ablaze in a brazier... his head is burning from the fire, ground beneath the galloping hoofs.

He's going to die. He can feel the stag's breath heating and tugging his cape and he cannot even lift so much as his fingers to do anything about it.

Another shriek, wavering then trembling into a growl. The hoofs retreat, panicked and scattered. He groans, tries to turn over but cannot. Something shoves him, yanks him over and his eyes, fluttering and ill-focused, open to take in....

A wolf. Black pelt gleaming, dark eyes glittering with fire and shadows. Lean and dusty, the outlier moves toward him with another growl, soft threat. Hungry.

Consciousness roared back over him like waves against the white rocks of his mother's south coast home. He lurched upright, flailed, managed by some miracle to throw his cape back over his shoulder and grappled for his sword.

It wasn't there. Neither was his sword belt. He abruptly remembered hanging his sword on his saddle, which was with his horse, which was....

Gone. The nappy git had run like a bunny from that stag. Of course, it had been the biggest stag he'd ever seen. And it wasn't his horse, actually—it was his brother Otho's horse, and no matter that brother's liking for him, Otho was going to kick his arse for letting the stallion get away.

Of course, his head already felt like his arse would when he got back home. He gave up on grabbing the absent sword for protection, instead clutched his hands to his head and gave a sound that sounded distinctly like a mewl.

Buck up, Gamelyn, he told himself. *If you're about to be supper for a wolf, you can at least go down like a man.*

Gritting his teeth, he clenched his fists, opened his eyes again, and looked.

It wasn't a wolf. It was a lad about his own age, shaking a worn leathern hood back from a frowning face. That frown was a mighty one, dark brows drawn together over the blackest eyes Gamelyn had ever seen, with an even-blacker forelock nearly obscuring them. The lad didn't say anything, hadn't moved, just kept peering at Gamelyn, and for a panicked second, Gamelyn wondered if all those tales the old women told about the kitchen fires were true. If the forest here really was inhabited—not by mortal men but ghosts and demons who shifted their bodies to whatever shape they pleased.

After all, the lad still wasn't moving. Gamelyn wasn't sure that he was breathing, if it came to it, and in the half-lit forest gloom, his skin was white as the lead chalk some ladies used on their cheeks.

"Did the fall addle your head, or what?"

Gamelyn jumped as the demon/wolf/lad spoke, fell back against the tree, and went sprawling sideways.

"Bloody damn," the wolf/demon/lad swore. Reaching forward, he grasped Gamelyn by the tunic, and hauled him upright. Purely by instinct, Gamelyn grabbed the lad by his wrists, felt bones grind as he tried to fling him aside.

Now there was no doubt but the lad was surely some ghost or demon in boy disguise. He didn't even flinch at Gamelyn's hold, and Gamelyn had been told more than the once that he was quite strong for a lad whose voice hadn't even broken yet. The demon lad was surely of a height with Gamelyn, but his wrists were slim in Gamelyn's broad fingers, and his ragged tunic hung on a skinny, lanky frame.

The lad—wolf or demon or ghost, Gamelyn no longer knew what to think—gently but firmly extricated his wrists from what Gamelyn had thought quite the grip, then just as easily pushed Gamelyn down to a seated crouch against the massive roots of the oak. Nostrils flaring as if at some scent, he cocked his head not unlike a wolf.

"I think you have addled yourself," he ventured, very softly, and reached a hand to Gamelyn's forehead. Pressure, very light, but it stung like tens of bees.

"Hoy, that hurts!"

"I'll wager it does." The lad, or whatever he was, brought his fingers back to his face, sniffed them then shrugged. "I'm not me mam, I'm afraid. She does it all the time and can tell what it means by the smell of it."

Smelling blood. He *was* a demon, then, if his mother could tell if blood was fit just by the smell of it.

"What do you want of me?" Gamelyn tried to make his voice steady, succeeded after a fashion. Aye, he'd not go craven, even if unshriven.

A horrific screech echoed through the thick dim, reverberating off the trees. Gamelyn remembered that sound bringing and breaking the delirium of his fall. The buck had bowled them over and he'd gotten dragged a short ways, had lain for some indeterminate time, heard that horrible shriek. He regretted then and there he'd not just fallen in a faint like some tight-laced lass, wondered if the demon lad had called his kin to finish the job and crossed himself.

The demon lad did not, unfortunately, go up in flames at the fervent genuflection. Instead he merely blinked, as if puzzled. The shriek sounded again, this time with a definite *thud* at the end, and the demon lad suddenly laughed.

"Sounds as if they've had enough. I know you're a bit addled, but do you think you can walk? We'd better go and fetch them before they wander off, aye?"

Gamelyn blinked. "What?"

"Your stallion. My mare. I think she's tired of him for now." The narrow face bent closer to Gamelyn and said, very slowly, "Our horses. We have to catch them up. Ride home. Do you understand me? At that, do you even know where home is?"

He seemed exasperated.

It was Gamelyn's turn to frown. He was abruptly unsure he *did* know how to get back. It was this forest—it had twisted him all about until he was lost.

Not that he was sure he should tell a demon where he lived, anyway. Gamelyn craned his neck—subtly, he hoped—and peered at the demon lad's ears. If they were pointed, then he'd know for sure.

Wouldn't he?

Anyway, what if this demon's family went after his family? If demons had family. He should have paid better attention to the old priest back at Huntingdon. If this demon was a lad, and wasn't just appearing to be a lad, then it stood to reason that he was still growing and therefore had been birthed from *something*.

"What are you looking at?" The demon lad looked puzzled again, though Gamelyn wasn't sure he'd ever seen brows twist that way.

No pointed ears in that mass of black hair. And a good thing too, for Gamelyn realized he was lost. Perhaps he'd have to make some sort of bargain with this little demon; they could have his eldest brother, if it came to it, but he'd definitely miss the rest of his family.

"Bloody *damn*." The demon lad certainly flung about curses as freely as any spawn of Hell. "You *are* addled. I canna just leave you here like this." Another, somewhat aggrieved sigh. "Come on, then. Prop yourself against me. We can tie you to that fancy horse of yours, if we have to, and I'll take you to me mam. She'll see to you 'til you remember what's what."

Again, the amazingly strong hands grabbed him, hoisted him upright. Gamelyn's head spun and he nearly toppled over. The demon-lad swore, even more inventively, and Gamelyn had no choice but to lean on the skinny creature and accept his guidance to the forest's edge.

ঔ

GAMELYN was more and more convinced the demon lad was indeed that. He plunked Gamelyn down by a little grazing jennet, more shaggy dog than any respectable horse, and told the jennet to keep an eye on him. Then, striding over bold and self-assured as any tourney victor, the demon lad pinned sloe eyes on nappy gray Diamant and took hold of his bridle. Quick as that.

It would have taken Gamelyn loading up his tunic with swede to get within as much as snatching distance, and even then the stud might decide he wasn't hungry, ta!

As the demon lad came over, leading Diamant with one negligent hand—as if he just assumed the stallion would follow!—the little shaggy mare plucked her head from her grazing and approached him like a dog. Even a hopeful grunt from the stallion didn't distract her overlong; she merely made a sideswipe with pinned ears to put him in his place then nuzzled at the demon lad's breast. Gamelyn eyed her with a mixture of bemusement and disdain.

Surely demons didn't ride hairy little ponies.

His companion scowled. In the sunlight that frown was no less fierce than in the gloom of trees, even if the lad himself was not so daunting. He was looking more and more human; the death-pale skin proved, out of the forest gloom, to be just fair and freckled, sunburnt across the cheeks and nose. He had brown wrists and hands that didn't quite match the pale breastbone peeking from beneath the sideways drag of his hood against his rough-woven tunic. His hair was indeed black, unruly and too long, thick as his pony's mane.

And just like that, Gamelyn's head was spinning and his legs didn't seem to want to hold him up.

"Whups!" the demon lad said, and dropped the gray's rein to grab at Gamelyn just before he hit the ground.

"Not good," Gamelyn muttered. "Now you won't catch him again."

"Whatever are you on about?" the lad wondered, then, with a shrug, he muscled Gamelyn over to the pony. "Here. It waint be quite the climb, this way. Neither will she jump out from under you if the wind hits her ears. We need to get you to me mam, quicker's best. I'll ride yon Testicles."

Had he really meant it to sound like some ancient Roman general's name? Gamelyn shook his head, giving a tiny groan as it shook pain outward through his eyelids. "Nay, you can't… can't ride him." Merciful Heaven, was that really his voice, so faint and wobbly? "He won't let you."

"I daresay he will," was the answer. "There's nowt I canna ride. I can trust Willow to take care of you. Anyway." A sudden grin, like sun breaking over clouds. "I'm dying to step up in one of those fancy stirrups."

There was nothing for it; the lad was already starting to muscle him over to the pony, and again Gamelyn was startled at how much strength those scrawny arms had. "Wait," he said, then again, because it was a murmur and barely audible, "wait, wait… *wait.*"

The lad waited, again with that considerable frown. And waited. Finally, he said, "*What*?"

Gamelyn realized that he hadn't said what he meant to. In fact, he wasn't sure what he'd meant to say, so what came out was, "What's your name?"

The brows gave another massive squinch, perturbed to puzzled. "Rob. Rob of Loxley."

"I'm Gamelyn. Sir Ian's son." Somehow this last was particularly important, because he couldn't remember the name of the castle his father had recently been deeded holding to.

"Aye, Sir Ian's son Gamelyn," acknowledged Rob and then, after a pause, "Can we go now, then?"

*

HE BARELY remembered Rob half lifting, half pitching him into the saddle of the little bay pony, didn't remember much of the journey at all. But Gamelyn remembered, vividly, the look of dismay on Rob's face as Gamelyn had pitched out of the saddle and into the dirt just as they arrived at a squat, cob-bricked cottage.

He also remembered the feel of cool hands upon his forehead, and cooler water….

Lurching from fog and fugue, Gamelyn blinked, tried to focus, found a figure bent over him.

He also remembered *her*. Those hands were still cool, soothing upon him, and she had Rob's hair and eyes.

"So you're back with us, youngling," she said. "That's a fair-sized knot you've gathered on your pate, so lie still, aye?"

She even sounded a bit like Rob, but her accent was thicker, more musical. Which was aptly demonstrated as Rob's voice sounded from behind her.

"Hoy, Mam, is he back in the living? I didna kill him, did I?"

She smiled at Gamelyn, answered, "Nay, my Hob-Robyn. Not for lack of trying, though."

Gamelyn blinked. He'd heard that name before, but never applied to any human. His old nurse had told him stories of such things: fey forest sprites, trees that walked like wild, wanton girls, and wolf-men that ate naughty little boys. And all of them, led by their feral master, Jack o' th' Green, the Hob, the Robyn Greenfellow.

What kind of woman would name her child such a thing, even in jest?

"I just figured I'd get him here however I could and you'd put him right." Rob came into Gamelyn's view and crouched by the bed, peering at him. It was a bed Gamelyn lay in, curtains pulled back and frame piled high with rushes and furs, one of several in the cottage's back corner. Windows were flung open, letting in light and a cool breeze, and there was a hearth in the opposite corner. A girl—she looked to be nigh grown—was stirring something in a large kettle that hung in the hearth. A glint of setting sun caught her hair and it lit like fire, a fall of unruly copper twisting down her back.

Gamelyn had been told once that his own mother had been red-haired. It was a continual disappointment to him that his own hair seemed more rosy straw than honest red, even if the old priest at Huntingdon told him he'd enough red to be wary of. Red-haired children were Satan's spawn, no question. It had been the first time he'd questioned the priest, but not the last—and the punishment had been worth it. His mother was in Heaven, in God's grace, and had *not* been of any devil!

Now that he considered it, he'd like to hear that priest say such a thing to this peasant girl's face. Or her mother, seated all poised in her chair. Both of them looked like they'd have something to say back.

Setting sun? It hit him, abruptly. Had he been out so long?

"Will he be all right, then?" Rob peered at him, and Gamelyn wasn't sure it was as friendly as the query seemed. Rob's mother reached out and gave a tug, fond but purposeful, at his tangled hair.

"Son, I've seen wolves with less baleful stares than you." Rob shrugged, but lowered his gaze as she continued, to Gamelyn, "I'm Eluned, wife to Adam of Loxley. My bold Rob here," she said as she reached out and gave another tug, "said only that you were Sir Ian's son Gamelyn."

"Would that be Sir Ian Boundys, newly granted mesne lord of Blyth Castle?" A deeper voice, male, and a tall, broad figure striding through the door. "I see our young guest is awake. Welcome to our home, lad."

This, then, must be Adam of Loxley.

"Here you go, young sirrah." This from the girl who, as she approached, was revealed to have a bowl in her hands that steamed and smelled positively mouthwatering.

"You never let *me* eat in bed," Rob protested.

"You ent as handsome as our visitor," the girl quipped.

"Bugger, she's off *again*—" Rob rolled his eyes.

"*Rob.*" His mother, stern.

"Dinna mind him, he's a mouth like a piss pot," the girl told Gamelyn, almost at the same time.

"*Marion.*" Eluned's tone had not changed.

"Well, he does, Mam." The girl—Marion—shrugged. "Can you sit up, then, Sir Gamelyn?"

"Nor is he a 'sir', just son to one—"

Adam calmly went over, wrapped a beefy arm about Rob's head, and clapped a hand over his mouth. Rob struggled; Gamelyn watched in abrupt anxiety until he saw Rob's eyes were crinkling with laughter.

Gamelyn sat up, was surprised that he no longer felt as if a rabid warhorse was tromping through his head, and then was further surprised when Marion sat next to him—on the bed. She began to shovel up spoonfuls of whatever it was toward his face. Gamelyn opened his mouth out of self-defense.

The pottage was as delicious as it smelled.

"Da," Rob was whinging, "dinna I get to eat too?"

He had seemed so *mature*, out in the forest. It was passing strange to see that Rob might be younger than Gamelyn himself.

"Have you seen to the horses?"

Rob looked affronted. "Of course."

"Then, aye."

A good tilting horse didn't have a quicker start than Rob toward the cauldron. It was beyond passing strange to see him not get clobbered for whinging. Otho didn't mind the occasional whinge, and their father ignored it. But Gamelyn's eldest brother, Johan, was not so forgiving.

Adam was speaking, a low, unflappable voice that seemed to radiate calm. "I've business east; no bother to see you home proper, help you make your apologies for worrying your folk."

"My brothers won't miss me, they'll worry more after the horse," Gamelyn muttered. Then, as Adam and Eluned exchanged a meaningful look and Marion cocked her head and stopped shoveling food at him, Gamelyn furthered, "My father's away to York, doing the pretty as guest of the sheriff."

Eluned's eyebrows arched upward, altogether too canny for Gamelyn's peace of mind.

"Doing the what?" Rob inserted from over the cauldron, huddled over a bowl. He abruptly gave a hiss and sucked at his thumb like he'd singed it. "No wonder our visitor is so quiet. You've burned his mouth shut, Marion."

"Eat, then. Maybe it'll work on *you*."

"You canna be traveling in the dark, at any rate," Eluned told Gamelyn. "You'll stay here with us 'til the morrow."

ᴄᴙᴆ

"I DINNA like him."

"I do. Nay, really, Rob. He's nice."

A snort in the dim, quickly muffled into the bedclothes—or by Marion's cushion over Rob's face, Gamelyn discovered when he peeked.

Gamelyn, as he'd found out, was in Rob's bed. Rob was tucked in with Marion. They'd been quiet for so long that Gamelyn was sure they slept. But no, perhaps they were just making sure their parents were sleeping.

He couldn't sleep. His head was throbbing despite the potion Mistress Eluned had given him. The moon was full and overbright, the illumination coming directly over the bed in a manner he wasn't at all accustomed to. And the bed was nothing like he was accustomed to, either. It smelled of horse, boy sweat, and deer must.

"He's one of *them*."

"Everything with you is 'us' and 'them'. What about 'we'?"

Another snort, softer, and Rob hissed, "You know the only 'we' that matters to his kind are those born on the proper side of the blanket."

"You've been listening to Will Scathelock too much—"

"Will's mam was killed, after they—"

"I know what happened to her." Marion's whisper was suddenly odd and flat. "They're surely all not like that. You canna hem people into one garment, little brother. This one, this Gamelyn Boundys. He's seen some hurt, too."

"Did the fae tell y' so?"

"So you're the only one allowed to travel along the Barrow-lines?"

Barrow-lines? Fae? What an extraordinary way of speaking. It might have been another language for all the sense it made.

"Aye, me and Mam. Your hair's too red."

There was another *whump* of cushion against flesh, and Rob was… giggling?

"You just like that lad," this between giggles, "because he's towheaded."

"I'll pitch you from this bed, see if I don't."

"Pax, then." A loud creak of leather and cord; through slit eyes Gamelyn saw Rob sit up. "You kick like a jenny ass even when you're *not* set t' boot me. I'll go up top."

Marion merely said, "Take a fur, then," and rolled over. The moon's light glinted over her like cold forge fire.

Rob, on the other hand, seemed to swallow the moonlight. He was a shadow, silent once off his sister's cot; so silent that Gamelyn, closing his eyes against the moonlight and discovery, didn't hear Rob until he was close enough so his breath stirred Gamelyn's hair.

"I know you're awake," Rob whispered against his ear. It gave Gamelyn a sudden, deep-set shiver. "Spyin' on people's no way to make 'em trust you, neither."

Gamelyn opened his eyes wide, affronted. Rob's narrow face wasn't a handsbreadth from his, a thin skim of moon frost on his cheeks and a tiny glitter in those dark eyes.

"I know your kind," he murmured. "Stay away from my sister."

A frown gathered at Gamelyn's brow. The expression stung his injured skull, but not half as much as Rob's words had. "Grotty *peasant*," Gamelyn growled, *sotto voce*, before he had a chance to rethink the wisdom of brassing off someone whose bed he occupied. "I'm not 'after' your sister."

The dark eyes widened.

"And I'd *not* be so ill-mannered as to take advantage in a house where I'm guest!"

Rob blinked. Then inexplicably grinned, a flash of white teeth in the dim. "Aye. Well. All right, then."

And, still silent, Rob backed away from the bed and mounted the rope ladder leading to the loft.

☙ III ❧

"WHEN'S that one leaving, then?"

Marion peered at her brother. He had flung the question all nonchalant, but seemed preoccupied. Rob bent the yew bow skyward instead of in line with the target, rolling his shoulders in their sockets as if they were stiff. "You *did* get tossed yesterday," she insisted.

"'M always hopin' for a good toss," Rob smirked. "*Ow*!"

"You know what I mean, you little… *tosser*! Willow *dumped* you. On your arse."

Rob flipped the forelock from his face and took steady aim. A small waft of wind played at his nape hair; he waited until it had stilled then let fly.

Their target, a small drinking skin hung by a narrow rope some ells away, jerked and fetched as the arrow hit it square.

"Good shot."

"Aw." Rob gave a forbidding squint at his string, plucked at it with his fingers. "I was aiming for the rope."

They had tried to get him to draw with his right arm, but it had been disastrous. From the moment he had aimed a bow, the ease with which he drew to the left was only matched by the clumsiness of trying to achieve a proper right-armed draw.

Their father said it simply meant he sighted stronger with his left eye, but then Rob was left-handed as well. Neither were good omens to Christian or Heathen; Eluned was not altogether happy with her son's leanings. Marion was more pragmatic. Her father had a point—what mattered was accuracy and speed. Rob's ability with the bow was already prodigious for his age; if he could put people off with an uncanny technique, then the advantage was his, surely.

Another advantage—or maybe not, Marion considered, since she often bore the brunt of it—her baby brother didn't give up easily. "So," Rob persisted. "When's His Lordship taking his leave?"

"As soon as Da returns. You were awake, you saw old Gareth come for him and Mam." Marion nudged him over, took an arrow from the quiver at their feet, and inspected the fletching out of pure habit. "We're to tell our guest Da will see him home after lunch. 'Twill give him a bit more time to get his head back on his shoulders. And he's named Gamelyn, y'know."

"I know what he's called, the way you carried on over him." Rob pitched his voice even higher. "'*Sir* Gamelyn'—"

"Oh, belt up. I'm carrying on over nowt. He's too young for me and you look ridiculous all puffed up like that. Like a cornered badger, all full of air." Marion gave a hard poke to Rob's solar plexus; predictably, the breath huffed from him. "You surely have your braies twisted this morn."

He gave a small scowl, looked aside. "I didna sleep much."

Marion peered at him. "Are you having those nightmares again?"

A shrug. Marion gave a narrow look; Rob returned it with a rather forlorn twist of brow and another shrug.

"Have you told Mam and Da?"

Yet another lift of the bony shoulders, with a twirl of his bow end in the moist grass as punctuation.

"Mm." Marion stepped to the mark. This was happening more and more to her brother. She remembered the feeling all too well. Over three years ago, it had been, when it started in on her. He didn't look as though he was starting his time, but then lads surely showed it different than the lasses. A girl became a woman with her own blood; boys often approached manhood upon the blood of others.

"I got the horses fed." Rob gave a flicker of a grin. "A good thing too, since Da and Mam had to leave so early. And Testicles has bred Willow thrice already this morn."

Marion chuckled, put arrow to string. "I'm sure that stud also has a proper name."

"Mayhap we should let His Lordship sleep the day away to see she's properly caught.… Hoy, Marion, that was brilliant!"

The arrow loosed, a mere half second later the bag had fallen to the ground, its rope severed.

"Merciful Heavens!"

The new voice made them both start and whirl about to see Gamelyn standing several lengths behind them. His pale hair was sticking at odd angles from the bandage still wrapped about his head, but he looked better. Had a lot more color, certainly, than when Rob had brought him in, half wilted over Willow's withers. "That was… amazing," Gamelyn said, eyes still on the arrow's path.

"Hullo, Sir Gamelyn!" Marion greeted, letting the smooth wood slide through her hands to rest on her boot. "You step quiet for someone still not too steady on his pins."

He had a nice smile, rather shy. And eyes green as grass—she wasn't sure she'd seen anyone with eyes that green. Or maybe it was the flush in his cheeks that played them up.

Cute lad. If he was older than her brother, it wasn't by much. "Me da said to tell you he and me mam had to deal with a wee predicament this morn," Marion offered. "But he'll be back to see you home."

"I know," Gamelyn said, sliding his gaze to take in Rob. "I heard."

Rob had the grace to flush. Marion smirked.

"Your turn," she pointed out. "I'll go reattach our target, shall I?"

She noted that Gamelyn was creeping closer, interested. Quickly Marion retied the bag's knot, then grinned. Gave it a push.

At the end of the sight line, Rob's eyes had gone wide. Gamelyn's mouth had dropped open.

"You *must* be good," he said to Rob.

The edge on the glare Rob shot Marion could have cut steel. She kept grinning, sauntered over, and grandly flipped her hand toward the bag.

"*Sod* you," Rob hissed her direction.

The thing was, she knew he could do it. He just didn't know it yet.

Having an audience had never put Rob off; now was no exception, save that this time he didn't pull skyward. Marion saw the whipcord muscles in his arms and back quiver protest.

"Willow dumped you," she whispered.

Black eyes slid her way, promising damage, settled instead for sighting down the arrow and loosing it with a tiny snarl of breath.

The sack wobbled mid-swing, then dropped to the ground.

"Holy Mother of—" was Gamelyn's truncated exclamation.

"You did it!" Marion let out a whoop and leapt into the air, came down pummeling Rob's shoulder. He gave a hiss and leapt aside, rubbing his shoulder and eyeing her reproachfully. Then he grinned.

"I did, aye?"

Marion gave another grin at the way her brother flashed their flabbergasted visitor a self-satisfied look. Well, all right, then, he was entitled.

But it was still funny.

"Set it up again!" Rob demanded suddenly.

"You couldn't do that again!" Gamelyn yipped. Then, hesitantly, "Could you?"

Marion laughed and went to repair their target. She was fairly sure she wasn't meant to hear what Gamelyn said as he sidled closer to Rob, but she did.

"I won't go near your sister," Gamelyn swore softly. "I'm not interested in her, I swear to you."

Rob didn't move, plucking once more at his bowstring. "Then what are you interested in, nobleman?"

The answer surprised her as much as Rob.

"I want to learn *that*." Gamelyn pointed at Rob's bow. "I've never seen anyone shoot like you and Marion can."

"G'wan home, then. 'Ave your villeins t' teach you."

The quicker clip and pace of Rob's speech revealed, as always, his agitation, but Marion wasn't about to let this go, twisted braies or no. "Rob! Mind yourself!"

"They aren't my villeins," Gamelyn said, quietly reasonable. "They're my father's."

"An' no doubt they'll be yours when you take his place. People bought and sold like cattle."

Marion came back over, arms crossed. She would like to hear this one, truth be told.

Gamelyn's eyes narrowed, went hard. "So you've never had people work your fields, or graze your beasts when you can't?"

"We're freemen, but we own nowt *but* our freedom!" Rob retorted. "An' precious little of that! We dinna own people, or claim their work is ours!"

Gamelyn was frowning. "But villeins live off their lord's work, just as he does theirs. If my father hadn't fought on Crusade, got rewarded for his service to the king with his lands, then there would be no food grown for any tables, serf or nobleman."

"And just because it's the way it is, we shouldna try to make it otherwise?"

Gamelyn had a half smile on his face; Marion didn't think it was patronizing, but she wasn't sure her brother would stop to consider otherwise.

"You sound like someone I quite admire," Gamelyn said softly. "Jesus was quite known for trouting people who lived off the backs of others until those backs bled."

Rob blinked. Marion wasn't sure how to answer that one, either. The White Christ was known for humility and charity; few of his followers were so inclined.

Gamelyn looked away, crossing his arms and peering toward the sack target. "I don't think I could hit that if I tried."

"My da taught us." Rob shrugged. "From when we were weans. But I ent sure I could teach you all of it. These sorts of things… they're gifts. From the Lady. Y'see?"

"The Lady? Mary?"

Rob fell silent, looking at Marion. She answered, "Aye, that's one of her names."

Gamelyn seemed confused.

"You can only be as good as your heart," Rob said, softly. "If your heart's an archer's heart, then…." He shrugged.

Gamelyn still looked confused. But he also looked determined. "I *want* you to teach me. Both of you," Gamelyn added, smiling at Marion. Because Rob was certainly not inviting any smiles.

And then, conversely, Rob offered one up. "That means you'll have to come back. We canna teach nowt in a morn's time."

"Can you come back?" Marion prompted.

The sunburnt-and-freckled face went even more determined. "I can."

ঊঋ

THE two riders took their time, no shortcuts through the green Wode. Adam explained the poaching incidents to Gamelyn with a soft anger in his voice that reminded Gamelyn of his own father.

Sir Ian was a quiet-spoken, reasonable man. But he would still be away south, so Gamelyn could only hope they could find the old stableman, Brand, and through him gain the attention of Otho. Otho had inherited more of their sire's reasonable temperament than Johan. And maybe Johan, in charge of the daily business with their father away, was too busy to bother with his youngest brother.

Diamant was quieter than usual, no doubt due to his dalliance with the bay pony. He walked beside Adam's chestnut gelding—a rouncey much better bred than Rob's little jennet, Gamelyn noted—as quietly as if he were dozing. When Diamant did tug at the bit, his eagerness was not so much for a thumping good gallop but the roomy comfort of his box, a good curry, and a generous graining.

The clouds were low and ducking lower, shivering the first layer off their fluffy gray coats and letting fall a soft not-quite rain. A normal state of affairs for early autumn. Neither Adam nor Gamelyn even bothered with their hoods; in fact Gamelyn turned his face up to the mists, enjoying the tiny drafts across his cheeks.

Adam talked, some. What questions he had were not overly personal, yet Gamelyn found himself volunteering more information than was truly asked for. Adam didn't seem to mind. He merely nodded, taking it all in. By the time they crested the hill leading to Blyth Castle, Adam knew Sir Ian was a Norman who had been in the Second Crusade, had been awarded lands in Huntingdonshire from the earl, had buried his wife there after Gamelyn's birth. Knew they had lived there until Gamelyn's eleventh birthday, when Sir Ian had been awarded Blyth, then had removed here. Knew Gamelyn was to receive his own riding horse upon his next birthday, had two brothers older than he, and lit candles for his mother's soul every seventh Compline in the chapel.

When they finally did arrive at Blyth, the clouds had dipped down to wreath the crenulated stone of the towers, and their presence seemed to mute the horses' hoofs against the paving stones.

As if whistled from the mists, a young stable lad came and took their horses, followed by a middle-aged, thick-fingered man. He eyed up the horses and gave a grunt at the gashes on Diamant's hindquarters, well medicated with some balm from Mistress Eluned's kit. Brand had forgotten more about horses than Gamelyn could ever hope to know. Eyeing then sniffing the balm, Brand gave another grunt, this one approving. Only then did he address people.

"Good day t' ye, young marster." His faded blue eyes flickered a question upon Adam, narrowed, then fastened upon a pendant lying on Adam's breast. It was plain silver, shaped and curved into horns. Gamelyn hadn't noticed it before.

"And to you, milord." Brand's basso went even lower, in a soft respect Gamelyn had only heard given to Sir Ian. "Is your guest staying, then, young marster?"

Gamelyn shot a hopeful look at Adam, who shook his head.

"Nay, I've duties waiting. But thank you, lad, mayhap another time."

Brand jerked his head at the stable lad. "Take the stud, grain 'im light and pitch some fodder."

"Gamelyn!" Otho's voice cut through the misted courtyard; his boots rang on the wet cobbles, quick and heavy. "I was looking for you to return before yester even." He slowed as he came closer, eyeing Adam with some suspicion.

Adam quickly stepped forward and gave a quick bow, hand to his breast. "I'm Adam of Loxley, forester to the king's Wode."

"I am Otho, now of Blyth, second son to Sir Ian Boundys." Just as quickly as the introduction, Otho dismissed Adam, turned to Gamelyn. "What have you done now, little brother?" There was a slight quiver of humor at Otho's upper lip; otherwise he seemed less than pleased. He brushed a lock of sand-colored hair back from the gloss of his wool cape—burgundy and gold, Huntingdon's colors—and calmly crossed his arms over a barrel chest.

"Diamant ran like a scared rabbit from a buck and dumped me."

Otho's brown eyes flickered as he took note of the finger-long gash on Gamelyn's forehead; otherwise he still radiated that stonelike composure.

"The buck was likely in rut. Not an easy opponent," Adam offered. "'Twas my son who found your young brother with his head laid open. Rob brought him to our home nigh to Loxley Chase. My wife is skilled with herbs; her salves did the trick, but he was a wee addled. 'Twasn't safe to bring him back until now."

"You have my thanks." Otho still seemed unruffled, and Gamelyn felt a surge of irritation. He could at least show a bit more gratitude to Adam! And neither did he offer any hospitality; at least Brand had hinted at it.

Well, then, Gamelyn would. "Are you sure, messire Forester, that you will not stay to sup with us?"

Otho's gaze slid his way, surprised.

Adam smiled, but his gaze moved to Otho's, gauging, before he gave careful answer. "Nay, young Master. 'Tis well of you to think of me so, but as I said, I've business not far from here before I turn my horse's nose home, and the days grow shorter since midsummer's fires dimmed."

Otho frowned slightly.

Adam bowed, very low, to them both. "I bid you fare well. Gamelyn Boundys, you are welcome to sit to my board at any time." A wink. "I think Rob and Marion would agree."

Gamelyn grinned, and didn't stop grinning until Adam had mounted and ridden out the gates.

Then a swat to the back of his head—toned down, no doubt in consideration of his injury—brought him back to full consideration. "Riding alone again—and halfway across the shire," Otho grumbled. "You're just lucky Johan isn't here for several days. He won't even know you were gone. Unless you do something even more asinine and force me to tell him." It was definitely a threat; Otho was easygoing, but he wasn't about to get himself in hot water over a younger sibling's foolishness. "Come, show me what you've done to my horse."

"If he hadn't run—"

"I heard you, 'like a scared rabbit'." Otho still sounded less than pleased, but whether it was toward Gamelyn or the horse, Gamelyn wasn't sure. Didn't ask.

They went into the gloom of the stable, a block of stone and wood jutting just out of the back fortifications. Diamant had his head stuck in his grain bucket; Otho chirruped to him before climbing over the wooden bars and into his box. Brand was in the box beside, wisping Otho's other mount clean.

"Do you have to ride out today?"

"Later." Otho ran his fingers along the ivory flank. Diamant didn't bother to raise his nose from his feed, but one ear twitched backward. "It looks very well-tended."

"Milady Eluned knows her art, my lord," Brand put in from the next box. "Milord Adam surely has a—"

"The man's a forester, Brand, a commoner at that." Otho was curt. "Mind who you give honor to."

Brand fell silent, resumed his currying of Diamant's stall mate. Gamelyn frowned. Neither he nor Adam had mentioned Eluned's name. And it seemed that Brand had *recognized* Adam.

"Gamelyn." Otho drew him from the barn with an arm about his shoulders. "I know the man did you a service, but that's his duty. He's our father's vassal, now—"

"I thought foresters answered to the king."

"They do. And our father is the good right hand of the earl, who through writ of the king administrates the land that the forester sees to. So Loxley and his son did their duty by you, their lord's son; nothing more and nothing less. I know he said you were welcome at his table." Otho shook his head. "He was just reaching beyond himself and calling it politeness."

Gamelyn could feel his chest puffing up with outrage. "Otho, he has treated me with nothing but courtesy. You wrong him."

Otho chuckled, and it stung. When would they ever take him seriously? "When you get riled you remind me so of our mother—"

"I wouldn't know, would I?" Curt.

Otho sighed. "Listen, little brother. You've no business going back there, breaking bread with commoners. He might be freeman, but all that means is that he has reason to think himself a cut above what peasant stock he truly is. You're not to accept his invitation."

This was beyond unfair. "But I—"

Otho's arm grew stone heavy across his shoulders. "I told you I wouldn't mention any of this to Johan. It's up to you whether you tell Father or no. But if you fuss me on this, I'll have no choice but to tell Johan to tell Papa."

"I'll tell Papa, if I must."

"Papa's not here right now, and you know what that means." Otho released him. "Just be reasonable, Gamelyn. Do as you're told and none of it will come to anything."

ENTR'ACTE

POACHERS or no, Adam was not afraid of nightfallen woodlands as were most. Lover and nemesis, companion and adversary; Adam knew his forest as only the green Wode's true lord could. He had done his best to pass that on to his children; had succeeded in many ways, yet still too many things had passed, unacted upon.

Like the mesne lord's son, Gamelyn. There was something about him. Some fate hovering above his fire-flax head.

In their desire to be sure that Rob's talents would not take him too soon, they had left him in ignorance of much of what they did. It seemed Gamelyn walked in ignorance as well, and Adam hoped that the lad would take an offered hand despite a brother's disapproval.

He felt it before he saw it: a giant, pale stag, quiet. Standing on the rise, enormous tines glinting, framed by bracken fern and yellowing leaves. Waiting.

No ordinary stag, this time of year.

He took a deep breath, dismounted, and in the time his line of sight was blocked the stag had disappeared. In its place was a man, white hair gleaming in the dapples of setting sun slatting through the trees. His approach was slow, measured.

It was Adam's, this time, to wait.

"Cernun." Adam bowed, and the old man halted before him, returned the bow.

"Lord."

Adam had never quite gotten used to it; for so long had Cernun been Lord of the forest, worn the horns. And now that the old man did not wear the horns, he was no less Adam's master and mentor.

The name said it all. *Cernun.*

"Walk with me," Cernun said.

"I'D NOT expected to find you here."

They paced slowly the shores of a deep forest pool. Adam had tethered his gelding to a stout tree; he could see the silhouette of him, hip-shot in the setting sun.

"I followed a dream."

Quiet steps in the moist loam, breath hanging against the misting rain. Adam did not ask. Cernun might elaborate, or he might not.

"That pale nobleman's son, he was part of it."

Adam slid him a puzzled glance.

"I cannot see all of what he will be. But he will be something."

"As will we all," Adam easily agreed; often the old man was more cipher than companion.

"*Tynged*." Cernun oft used the old Barrow tongue for concepts that were wider than Anglic dialect could easily encompass. "But when that magic and chance of fate calls divergent paths to conjoin, it is to ruin or ecstasy. Oak and Holly ever seek, in enmity or fellowship, the balance of the Arrow. And the Lord of the Dance of Life knows His ways too well to leave *all* to the chaos of chance."

Cernun had the look to him of one who has just clawed himself back from the depths, and his speech confirmed it: lucid yet slow, filled with myths, dreamings. And when deciphered, those dreamings were frighteningly prophetic. Adam had, as a youth, wished he had a tenth of Cernun's Sight. Now he was more than content to be as he was: gifted, but not in constant danger of a final tilt and slide into the madness.

"The little acorn of noblemen is Christian. Not… preferable. But," A shrug. "The followers of the White Christ would, despite his teachings, see our kind destroyed. They have almost succeeded. Perhaps he will, also." Cernun looked away, and Adam contemplated what he had said, stored it for later musings.

Again, silence, and steps through the green. Cernun squinted in a patch of sun. "You will find the poacher anon."

Adam nodded. "He'll slip. They always do."

"This one already has. His took him to the bottom of Ceryth Fall. The wolves have taken much of him—and the deer he left slain. Men come to our green Wode, searching, always seeking the heart of our demesne. Instead they find their own, shadows and mists. You will have most of a skull, another bargain made to keep what is ours *as* ours. Proof to the conquerors that we remain conquered. It is good they think this. So must it be."

"So must it be," Adam repeated softly. Ceryth Fall. A rocky promontory that, in heavy rains, swelled into a frothing torrent that roared to a just as rocky conclusion an arrow's flight below. Well. It was a certainty that Cernun wandered the Wode more than even Adam—even more a certainty that no predator would stay him. He had that gift, one that Adam did not have but, when the Horned Lord possessed him, could mimic.

He spoke what came to his heart. "I think Rob—"

"Aye, my son. Your boy could also walk up to feasting wolves and walk away with nary a mark on him. It is but one of the Lady's signs upon him." Cernun halted, considered the shining expanse of water that lay next to them.

"You have been twice saddened, but those lost souls have returned, enriched. You now are blessed fourfold in the two children that have come to you. First your daughter, her soul pierced with the gold of the Goddess's Arrow. And your son shall one day wear the Horns, lord of winter's passage. Be the one to bear th…." He trailed off, seemed to be in pain.

Adam bent closer. "Cernun?"

Cernun straightened, held up a hand. Looked out over the water. "Time draws near. Bring the boy to me when the moon calls winter's solstice."

Nodding, Adam sighed.

☙ IV ❧

Near Loxley, 1190 ACE

"ROB'S not here."

Surely he shouldn't feel this disappointed. Gamelyn mustered up a smile for Eluned. Not that it fooled her. If Gamelyn had learned anything in his infrequent visitations over the past several years, it was that Eluned had an uncanny ability to ferret out just about any truth.

There was a smile ghosting about Eluned's mouth. "I know you've come a long way, but surely sitting to sup with me isn't that horrific?"

Gamelyn's eyes widened and he started to protest. Eluned shook her head.

"Never you mind, lad; I should know better than to tease you about such things. Of course you're disappointed. But come in, at least have something to eat." Her eyes glinted with amusement. "Rob's gone for several days, but Marion should be back anytime."

Gamelyn's broad smile coaxed a chuckle from Eluned, and he didn't care. Suddenly prospects were not so bleak.

☙❧

"CONCENTRATE."

Marion's voice was soft, full of a confidence that Gamelyn did not himself feel.

"Check your wind. It's chancy, about now."

Gamelyn gave her a frown; Marion didn't answer it, merely crossed her arms, waited. He bent, plucked a tuft of summer-dry grass tops and let them flutter from his fingers. Frowned again.

"Aye." Marion nodded. "I told you."

Eluned had shooed Gamelyn and Marion out of her cottage sometime back. It was no hardship, despite the steady patter of rain; Eluned was boiling some concoction that smelled just this side of disgusting. Marion had already expressed thanks—more than once—for rescue from a sweaty, smelly afternoon with a kerchief over her face. The forest smells, redolent with rainfall and summer blooms, were a welcome relief.

"Breathe in. Scent the wind. Then let it out, and let fly."

Gamelyn did it all, in painstaking order. The moment his fingers loosed the string, a gust of wind tickled the arrow and sent it to the right. He still hit the clout, but his huffed-out breath was exasperated.

"Not a bad shot," Marion sympathized. "See, you always focus more on your bow than the arrow. Holding your bow's sovereign, no doubt, but you canna forget the arrow is what comes of it. Not like a sword. More like the breath from your lungs."

He let the bow slide through his hands and to the damp earth. "I really don't have an archer's heart, do I?"

"You shoot better when Rob's haranguing you, 'tis true," Marion admitted, a hint of amusement tucking one corner of her mouth. "If I give you a good whack with my staff here when you miss, will you shoot better for me?"

Gamelyn had to laugh. It was true; the one time he'd brought down anything that Rob or Marion hadn't had to finish off for him was when Rob had hauled off and whacked him one. Granted, they'd been hunting that wily red old-timer for hours, and Rob's string had split when they finally did reach him—Rob would never have let him shoot first otherwise—but surely a smack across the pate with Rob's bow had been uncalled for.

Yet Gamelyn had sprinted after the wounded deer and finished him with a shot to the heart. He'd been that angry. Not to mention the spectacular row after that, which left Rob with a black eye and Gamelyn with a split lip.

And the dressing-down that Gamelyn wasn't meant to hear, with Rob sullen and Adam resolute upon the consequences of a peasant visibly marking a nobleman's son.

Gamelyn had also heard the wily tone in Rob's voice when he'd asked about marks that *didn't* show.

"He hasn't forgiven me yet, has he?" Gamelyn asked, and though he tried, he couldn't help the wistful tone to his voice. "That's why he's gone."

"'Tisn't that at all." Leaning on her staff, Marion raised a leathern skin to her mouth—cool water, from the stream several ells beyond. She drank and offered him the same. "It's nowt to do with you. He and Da do have other duties than just waiting for you to come visit us."

There was a chide in it; Gamelyn shrugged and accepted the skin, tipped it gratefully. "I'm just sorry to miss him, is all."

"Next time." Any chide was gone from Marion's gaze, but the tiny grin had returned. "You'll just have to make do with me."

Making do with Marion, Gamelyn had long ago decided, was no hardship. It seemed a forester's son had more duties than a lord's late-gotten lad whose beard was barely scruffing at his chin. Still, he was not exactly free… and it seemed to him, more and more, that these friends of his, children of two conquered races, somehow were.

With stark embarrassment, Gamelyn realized his cheeks were warming. He covered it with a long stretch, then bent over and took up an arrow from Marion's quiver.

She made a snatch at it; surprised, he held to it when she would have taken it from him. Eyes dropping to their hands, his gaze lingered on the arrow, blinked. It seemed normal. The straight, pale shaft was new-made, the feathers split and glued with a precision he had come to take for granted with the arrows of Adam's household—but there was an addition. Several tufts of cerulean and emerald, set snug against gray.

"You know," Marion chided softly, "it's almost as bad a manners to go through someone's quiver as it is their purse."

Cheeks stinging and—he was sure—red, Gamelyn released his grip on the arrow. Marion twirled it in her hands, seemed to reconsider… something. "I'm sorry. It's nowt, truly. I shouldn't have snapped at you so."

The sincerity of her apology allowed curiosity to peek from beneath the fear—unwarranted, surely—that he'd offended her past reason. "It's just so… different. Is that a peacock's tail placed amongst the goose feathers?"

Marion was silent, seeming to consider him, but before he could start to worry again, she smiled. "Aye. A luck charm for our people, more than anything, but also something special." She shrugged. "You know how it is. Fletchers are always looking for the best ways to tout their own making."

"Surely such a thing wouldn't easily fly."

"In the right hands, it will." Another smile, quick and reckless as Rob could display. "Watch."

Marion put the arrow to string; its fletching set off tiny glimmers that were rather pretty.

Pretty—but still deadly accurate. The arrow loosed like a thousand angry bees and hit the clout's black center, quivering.

Gamelyn shook his head. "I will never," he said, rueful, "shoot as well as you."

"And why should you?" Marion was as practical about shortcomings as Rob was challenging. "I've been doing this since I could hold a bow. No doubt you'd have a bit to teach me about that bloody great sword you carry, eh?"

He grinned. "I'd love to teach you."

"Get away!" Marion grinned back. "I'd like to see you sneaking two swords from that armory of yours."

"Is that a challenge?"

A snort. "Boys. Always on with the 'mine's biggest', all of you." Slinging her quiver over one arm, Marion strode over to the clout and began pulling arrows.

Gamelyn decided, then and there, he would find some kind of sword. It would be worth it to see Marion wielding a sword like some fierce, crimson-haired Boudicca.

It would also be worth it to see Rob clumsy at something. Gamelyn smirked. Aye, more than worth it.

But he had other things, for now. "I brought you something, you must know."

"Did you, then?" Marion slid gray eyes to him. "Did you bring me another book?"

He grinned and tossed her his bow. "It's in Diamant's pack. Let's go fetch it. You've endured enough torture from me for one day."

ᴓᴥᴓ

IF MARION didn't know better, she'd swear they were being followed.

Not into the forest. But before, when they'd escaped the cottage. And now, oddly enough. She saw nothing, but the sense remained, as if eyes were steady upon her. Not overt danger, not anything that would make her worry her companion. But a… curiosity. Several times she thought she'd seen someone—a hooded figure watching, marking time. Waiting.

Maybe Rob's dreams were straying, catching her up. Maybe she was just concerned about him. Marion herself had endured time in the dreaming—Seeking, as their people called it—and they could be dangerous. The drug itself was chancy and then there was the reaction to the drug, or the dosage, and amidst all of it was the possibility of the magic taking you from your body and never letting you return, did any of the former go awry….

Ach, and she didn't need to be thinking on that, not now. The day was turning out promising. The rain had let up as they'd returned, but Eluned's herb preparations were still ongoing, from the thick and pungent mist drifting out the opened cottage. She and Gamelyn had taken the animals for grazing on the hillock a furlong away, a field planted last year but fallow with grass this season. The cow was lying down, having a second go at her forage. Willow's latest foal, a filly who was shedding her dark foal coat into gray about her muzzle and eyes, ran circuitous riot around Diamant and her dam. The latter two had, after an exchange equally comprised of flirtation and irritation, settled in to the real business of life, which was grazing.

It seemed that Gamelyn and Diamant had also come to some accord. The gangly boy who'd barely fit the saddle of his brother's warhorse now rode in his own well-accoutered saddle, had also grown to fit the temperamental stallion. It seemed that Diamant had, all along, been meant to be Gamelyn's, a gift from his father, Sir Ian. Who sounded a nice fellow, true enough. For a lord. It was easy, most times, to forget Gamelyn was a lord's son. Not that Rob ever let him forget it.

Marion smirked, remembering one time she'd had it shoved in her own face. Gamelyn had been amazed that she could read—*loved* to read, unlike Rob—and not only Welsh, but Latin, and some Anglic as well. Only he called it Norman-Anglic—*langue d'oc*—and had gotten a funny look on his face when she'd objected. He'd been even further set on his heels when she'd explained her reasons: that she'd always honored the oral traditions of her ancestors, but more and more it seemed to her the only history that was being remembered was what the conquerors were writing, with their pens and parchments.

Aye, Gamelyn had left quite chastened, that time. But he'd returned bearing gifts. It seemed Blyth had a well-stocked library, and the household priest, Brother Dolfin, was so glad to find a like-minded scholar that he willingly lent Gamelyn whatever he asked. Gifts? Treasure, more like, and a more welcome apology she'd never seen. Apology had become habit, habit had become another small and tight-spun thread drawing them together… and here they were.

The ground was sopping, threatening to wick through the oilcloth they'd spread, and Marion's copper head was bent over the old tome—a rather barbarous thing, in her eyes, full of "medicine" that had more to do with hocus-pocus and sharp instruments of torture than a wortwife's herb lore and common sense.

Aye, and Gamelyn brought all kinds: scientific texts, puffed-up treatises, even once a romance so blue and torrid it had put a heat in Marion's loins, a blush on Gamelyn's fair cheek, and a rather-horrified light in Rob's dark eyes.

Marion smirked, sliding a look at Gamelyn, who was trying to coax the filly, Jewel, to let him scratch her neck. Both Gamelyn and Rob were nigh grown in length, mayhap, but still altogether young. Particularly Rob, who didn't seem the least bit interested in lifting a kirtle if one was twitched in front of him. Even Calla—as fair a hussy as Willow over there, and not so choosy—couldn't budge him. Calla had even once teased Marion into a quick go against the back of Loxley's alehouse, and while Marion preferred lads, there had been no doubt that Calla had known precisely what she was about….

And neither did her thoughts have any business taking that turn, not now. She turned the page, found her stomach lurching for an entirely different reason as she read a graphic description of tooth extraction.

"Are you all right?"

She looked up to see Gamelyn had left off coaxing the filly. He came over, a frown on his face, and knelt behind her, leaning over her shoulder. "Whatever is… hoy. Never mind." He reached out and snapped the book closed. "I should be a bit more careful about the subject of what books I set before you."

Irritation rose, despite that his attitude was no doubt stemming from that other too descriptive book she'd just been remembering. With a warning frown his way, she reopened the book. "No doubt I'll learn a bit from this one, I will. It's a good lesson in why Mam's so popular, if this is all a leech has to offer."

Gamelyn gave her a glance that also seemed to mix irritation and humor. "Otho's wife says the same thing. Johan says she's full of shit."

"And what does Sir Gamelyn say?"

A tiny smile at the appellation, then his green eyes flickered away. Gamelyn was too fond of taking everyone's thoughts at face value… except, unfortunately and far too often, his own. "I like Otho's wife," he answered, almost musing.

"And how is your da doing?" The moment she voiced it, she wished it back. Gamelyn's expression tightened.

"He is well." It was careful, neutral. Bloodless.

"You know you only have to ask me mam and she'd no doubt—"

He stood. "I have to go, anon."

Marion peered up at him; instead of saying anything more, she smiled and nodded. "I know. But you've still a while, aye?"

Every time he would think to pull away, some mysterious something would pull him back, as sure and oddly natural as the filly to her dam's side, seeking sustenance she could get nowhere else. Not for the first time, Marion found herself wondering why he kept coming back. One of the more appealing—and frustrating—aspects of his visits.

His smile was grave, but warm. "As long as I dare."

ↄ℘ɛↄ

LATER, after he'd ridden away on Diamant, Marion had spoken to her mother.

Perhaps Eluned was worried after Rob as well, or irritable from being in the heat and stink for much of the day, but she was curt. And final.

"Marion, you must have a care in what you say to that lad. Don't make any promises you canna keep, don't offer what might put you in harm's way."

"But his da's ill, Mam. I only thought—"

"Gamelyn's father is a Frankish knight. A *Christian.* They've gotten quite specialized in killing our kind."

"Mam, surely, though, *Gamelyn*—"

"I know the lad is dear to you. He's dear to me as well. But you must never forget what he comes from."

"Da says that was exactly why we *should* keep him close. *Because* of what he comes from."

Eluned peered at Marion from the wide wooden table, hands damp and stained, holding a deep pottery bowl filled with limp plant matter. Both table and those telltale stains upon the fine, square hands had been a part of her mother for as long as Marion could remember. But the expression on Eluned's face was unfamiliar. Strange. Wary, even.

"Marion," Eluned finally said. "I'm sure Gamelyn's father has the finest of physicians looking after him."

"I've seen their handiwork," Marion protested, "and it surely ent a good thing."

"Nay," Eluned agreed. "But they're his kind, see if they're not, and…." She trailed off, set herself to her task for a few more moments, hesitated. "Can it be possible you care for that lad more than you should?"

It startled Marion; both that her mother would think it and that she knew the answer without so much as a qualm of indecision. "Nay, Mam. Not like that. I care for him, but he's… well. He's like Rob."

At Rob's name, Eluned's lips tightened. Coming forward, Marion took the bowl from her mother's hands and said, softly, "I'm sorry I left all this to you. I should have helped, not gone off larking with Gamelyn."

Eluned peered at her, then leaned forward and kissed Marion's cheek. "I know. I'm worried after Rob, too."

ଓଃ

THE earth had her own pulse point, he had been told; one deep, one only those children who truly opened themselves to the listening would hear.

He was listening, every sense attuned, yet he heard only the echo of his own heartbeat.

Rob lay, naked against rock and earth. Arms spread like a hawk a-wing, fingers spread like pinions flared, he seemed to seek air, yet… still, grounded. Down. Flesh made small, flattened face down from cheek to breast to thigh to toes, a thousand-weight of stone overhead, looming. The caverns were dark, chill despite the summering's presence. The fire's light, crackling and setting the drawings against limestone walls to dancing, was vanquished mere cloth yards away by the pervasive, heavy presence of burial. Even the runes and art describing graceful lines against the chalk-pale walls—some faded with time, some vibrant—were no more than mere scratches in a vast expanse of Existence.

Rob's hair had been washed and flung up over his face, ringlets of ink that lifted with his breath and spilled over the stone. An old man hunched over him, his only garb a red deer hide over his shoulders, a crown of horn and holly, a belt of woven ivy. As he moved, acorns and dried berries rustled. Every gesture laid thick, liquid tracks across Rob's skin. Runes and sigils, formed with a steady hand and a mix of woad, indigo, and walnut.

It smelled… brown. Like mud and meal, with a hint of sap and greenstick bruising. The brush tickled, cool and wet, and this time when it left him it did not return.

Instead, a bony knee pressed against his left shoulder, pinning it, and fingers stroked his nape. "What do you hear?" It was a bare whisper against his ear, swallowed beneath the caverns.

Rob didn't want to say, but there was no escape, either from the looming rock and earth, or the old man's demand. "I hear… nowt. Only my own heart."

A grunt, then pressure lifted. "Rise."

Rob obeyed, slowly, as the blood tingled in starved limbs, as the thick markings on his backside pulled taut, drying. He left faint outlines of his body upon the stone, flakes of what had already been traced on his front, and raised his face to a held-out bowl.

"Drink," Cernun bade, when he would hesitate.

Rob took the bowl and drank. Sour and sweet and strong, sending fumes into every orifice from the neck up. Rob swallowed, loud into the silence, and thought to hand the bowl back.

Cernun pushed it to his mouth, said again, "Drink."

This time the fumes spread through his entire body, drawing up every follicle, every other orifice, every limb. As if in defense, or rejection.

He would not reject this.

His father stood at the curved, black entrance to the cavern womb, unmoving and silent, a shadow with fire-lit tongues gilding him in fits and starts. His brawny arms held a staff. Rob blinked, then blinked again as his eyes filmed, went scratchy. Adam's figure wavered, from sturdy to shadowed, from mortal guardian to horned, evergreen watcher.

His eyes glowed.

And suddenly, everything slowed.

Cernun backed away, the movement sluggish, drawn out. Rob blinked, and even that was strung lengthwise, the time between eyes open and shut lingering, and when Rob could focus again, he saw Cernun, still retreating.

But the bowl stayed there, hovering midair.

Another blink, lasting several breaths… nay. One breath, one half a breath, the inhalation lasting. The bowl, hanging.

Then exhalation, and eyes closing, Rob fell.

Falling….

With some part of his consciousness, he felt the hard, boneless impact against the stone, but it had nothing to do with him. He was already gone.

Free….

He slides from his body like a snake gliding from old skin. What tethers remain, he untangles with a gesture and a single word that fills the cavern… then hesitates at one, pulsing and gleaming, reaching outward from his heart.

He follows the line of it, sees a pale, mortal creature lying homely and senseless amidst the cavern rock of Mother's womb. Skinny limbs splayed like a doll of braided rags, long black tangle-locks sucking into the slack mouth with every rasped moan of breath, fair skin scrimshawed with earth-hued knotwork and sigils.

Something in him recognizes that creature, is glad of the vein of light—heart line, soul tether—connecting him to it. Something else within, something hot and dark and growing stronger, sees it for what it is: merely a shell, a frail husk lying on the ground, binding him down. It twitches, raises a hand to its breast, and he starts to speak again, to sever it from him so he can *fly*.

"Byddwch chwithau yn dal i!" It tolls from the dark, vibrates through his being. Another voice follows it, deep and warming; a familiar caress: "Be ye still."

Around the edges they wait, father-guardian and fulcrum-gatekeeper, and in this moment they have more power than he.

Snared, stayed, he watches. And as he does so, the markings upon the creature's skin begin to twitch then writhe, smoke from ivory-pale ash. From the edges comes the caress of words—ones he does not know, a gesture he cannot see—then the earth-marks begin to runnel, brown as earth, brown as old blood, onto the stone. Bleeding, gathering and forming into veins of light. Three, leading into the darkness, one arching up—like a whip, like a serpent—then arching forward, skimming up the line toward his heart and sending him hurtling.

Falling. Only this time there is no impact, he is hurtling outward, shards of light and shadow flickering about him.

Time was. Time is. *Time could be.*

The bits of color coalesce into shapes, then images, flaring then… stretching, somehow, sucking past him into the black.

Dancing…. Fire…. a man running through the Wode… leaping… changing... *and a stag leaps through the flames….*

*Hanging... panicked breath hot upon his neck... Marion! Clinging to him... both hanging above a chasm so deep and dark... his arms weakening and a voice... familiar voice—*take my hand!—*and he lurches...* reaches... *feels a hand in his, looks up to see a cowled, mailed figure holding him, and the hood blows back to reveal Gamelyn's face….*

Flames in his mind... brilliant-hot reflections blinding him... a jeweled cross dangling above him from a silver chain, swaying to the beating of his heart, shivering with his breath, and it seems so... beautiful... *but it is as treacherous as lovely….*

Heat. Blood. Fire. Blinding.

It is over.

It is blood, drip-drip-dripping onto the stones—his own blood draining from him and bringing the sweet, numbing nothingness of a sleep from which he will never wake, and there are arms clutched tight around him, a tear-soaked voice trying to stir him.

It is fear, rending into his mind

It is pain, clotting his lungs, a shard of agony stabbing fire into his ribs with every breath, the arrow swelling shock with every shudder of his flesh.

Falling.

Emptiness. Blackness, then breath, as if some massive winged wyvern from legend is venting in the darkness. Then something in the darkness… moves.

Eyes glimmer, horn gleams, and it rises, black from the waves: animal, yet not, human, yet not. That it is male is unmistakable, naked and erect, muscles taut, issuing challenge with toss of horns and blast of defiance. It demands reverence. Submission.

He knows he can give only one and hope to survive. He dips his chin and extends his hands, palm up, but does not drop his eyes. Stands his ground.

Breath escapes the Horned Lord in a long, low hiss. Eyes, glowing fire red, bank to orange embers.

I know you. The voice is deep, a growl. *Have known. Will know. But you are not* dryw, *not in this now.... How is it you can call me? How do they call you, now?*

They? He searches, tries to find his name. He knew it, once. That skinny, emptied shell his heart would tie him to must know it, surely.

Ah. He remembers. Tries to speak it. His tongue does not work, his mouth cannot shape the word, but nevertheless it comes from him. *Rob.* It echoes, tiny into the void, not enough, not true. He brings forth another, stronger one. *My dam calls me Hob-Robyn.*

A sound like purling thunder escapes the beast-man; Rob realizes it is laughter, low and not terribly friendly. *Even so. You are that, and more, little* pwca. *You are small, barely come to your power, yet that you have power is unmistakable. Otherwise you would not see me thus.*

Thus? His "voice" sounds thin, unfinished next to the Horned Lord's thunder, yet is gathering strength with every echo.

He who sired you sees the old man's image, and the old man sees this. A shift, a glimmer, and a beautiful, pale stag-man stands before him. No less male than the dark one, no less potent and awe-full, but old; older than many an oak in the Shire Wode, and wise, and shining fair.

It is my other aspect. I have many faces, each as powerful as the other. It is... interesting, that a stripling such as you would see not innocence, but awareness. Again, the blur, the shift and slide sideways into something Rob had no words for, and the light that had blazed forth then steadied sucked itself in, shaded ebon, gleamed along horns and lighting golden eyes with menace as well as wisdom. *Of course. What else would* you *envision, o Hob-Robyn, darkling King of Shire Wode, one of few now walking the* Ceugant *who could so easily bear the cowl of death and vengeance?*

I... don't understand.

You must listen, little pwca. *You must hear the breath beneath the words. The last, dying rattle of death, and rebirth.*

The Horned Lord charges. Rob has no chance to so much as throw his arms up in defense before he is picked up in the rack. Horns rake his flesh then he is flying, thrown aside… and just in time. Fire explodes upward from where he had stood. He cries warning but the Horned Lord merely smiles.

Stay, young King. Stay, and watch the King die. Do you not know the true meaning of sacrifice?

The flames burn hotter, higher, swifter than any mortal flame. The Horned Lord falls, screaming, writhing… *changing.*

Silence. Darkness. Only a charred lump of ash remains… and the horns, blackened. Then the lump… moves. Rises. Covered in ash, dark as the Horned Lord had been, the figure is tall, and hooded, and it reaches for him….

Somewhere in a cavern deep beneath the ring stones and the forest, his body convulses. Rob knows it, feels the waver of life pulsing from the heart line sunk into his breast. Hears the musical, polysyllabic language of the Barrow People, curling about the edges of the dream. It rings with power, with command: calling him back.

He cannot go, yet. He has not *heard.*

Instead, he reaches for those extended hands. There are runes scrawled over them, backs and palms, whispers of forgotten lore. *Tell me*, he implores the cowled figure. *I must know.*

There is a flash of white teeth beneath the hood, smile or snarl, he knows not which. Within those outstretched hands appear the antlers of the Horned Lord. Another smile, another murmur, this one resonating into the black, and now it is the horns that shimmer and shift before Rob's eyes, the rune-marked hands shaping them into the longest bow he has ever seen… one to rival the power and grace that make the weapons of his mother's archer-kin.

Anadl tynged, the Hooded One says, taking aim. *Anadlu eich tynged.*

And lets fly.

It hits Rob square in the chest. He puts both hands to it, in almost the same instant takes in a huge breath, a gasp and swallow that rattles as the agony strikes.

It is pain, clotting his lungs, a shard of agony stabbing fire into his ribs with every breath, the arrow swelling shock with every shudder of his flesh as he falls.

Falling….

He hears Marion, weeping as though her heart would break… hears frantic murmurs, spelling him from the void: his father, Cernun.

Sees. Hears.

Dies.

Fading, falling, into blackness and the infinite, soul chilling as body shudders its last, stills.

Then a hand clutches at his hair, and another splays flat upon his breast, burning. Twists. *Pulls*—to remove the arrow, arrow become heart line become real, solid against his breast—and yanks him upward.

His body convulses, jerks against stone.

His spirit, wings fouled, warms.

No, Gamelyn says. *No, not yet.*

Then the heart line wraps about his throat and pulls him from the black.

ଔଓ

WHEN Rob woke, hours later, spread-eagled upon the cavern floor, dry-mouthed and itching from the dried matter on his bare skin, he heard it.

Like a breath, deep within a gravid belly. Like a heavy, slick-slow movement made underwater. Like a hum, deep and primal and almost inaudible, at the base of his neck and down his spine.

Like the last, rattling gasp before the black, spilling secrets unto death.

Like all of those, and none of them.

"What do you hear?" Cernun asked him, and Rob lifted his head to see the old man sitting across the fire. He tried to push up, but failed. Instead he rolled over, clumsy with chill, shivering.

"Nothing," he whispered to the ceiling, his tongue thick and slow. "Everything."

From the shadows his father came, and covered Rob up with several furs. Cernun nodded, then leaned forward and fed up the fire.

ଔଓ

PAIN. Pain, *seizing his lungs, and the breath leaving him with a last, rattling gasp into the black….*

Gamelyn heaved up from the bedclothes with a muffled shriek. For a stuttered, shattered time he was unable to draw any breath back in, staggering up to his knees and clawing at the agony in his breast.

Then, so abruptly he fell forward, both pain and the band about his ribs snapped free. Gamelyn sucked in a huge, grateful breath, then another. And yet another, his fingers digging into the woolen coverlets….

Coverlets. He was in bed. His harsh gasps, punctuated by a slight wheeze, echoed against stone walls. His bed. His chambers. He dropped his head, still panting. The muslin bedclothes clung, damp and cloying, and his forearms, stretched out before him taut as weighted rigging rope, were wet with sweat.

It had been a nightmare, nothing more, and the knowledge soothed him as his head began to clear, its pounding beginning to subside.

His ribs felt as if he'd fallen from Diamant onto rock. Or as if Johan had been too assiduous in sparring practice.

Gamelyn put his head in shaking hands. The nightmare must have been… spectacular. All the more because he didn't dream. Well, not ones that he could remember, anyway. Nor, truly, could he remember this one. Except for the pain, striking his chest, and the breath caught within the pain… impossible to draw or release, as if it were not truly his own.

A breeze riffled the curtains tied to his bedposts, skated across his heated, sweated skin. He looked up, found the full moon framed in his window, clearly lighting up the dormer room—in pale frost, though, instead of warm sunlit fire. Beautiful. And the breeze… it whiffled through his damp hair as if teasing breath back to him. His gasps had subsided to smaller pants, and it beckoned: cool, green, soothing.

Lurching up from bed, Gamelyn made it two steps before vertigo made him clutch at the footer bedpost, tangling his fingers in the draperies there. His heart still hammered, his skin was still crawling with sweat, and the breeze from the window still beckoned. With a slight shake of his head and a small growl, he regained his equilibrium and tottered naked and unsteady over to the window. Leaning against the cool stone, he took in and then let out a huge, gusty sigh.

Christ have mercy, but he never thought he would be so grateful for the mere act of *breathing.*

The fields around Blyth were skimmed with the pale light, the tree line to the west and south black with shadow. The beginnings of the woodlands leading farther south, into the Shire Wode of Nottingham, and west toward Loxley.

He wondered where Rob was, about now. If he was home, he and his father, from whatever business they'd had, or if Marion and Eluned were still snug in their cottage, tending to the upkeep while their men were away.

His breath cramped within his ribs again, so savagely that he hunched over, eyes darkening. And against his closed eyes a shattered fragment showed itself….

A figure on the forest's edge, beckoning as he follows, and as he glides into the thick green Wode the figure is waiting. He has no face… nay, it is hidden, shadowed beneath a cowl, and as Gamelyn watches, the figure extends a hand to him.

Only the hand is pushing against a great bow, taller than the hooded figure who wields it, and he draws back, releases, and the peacock-fletched arrow drives through Gamelyn's chest and out his back, to lodge in the tree behind him as he falls....

Sick—he feels sick not only with pain but sorrow, enough sorrow to end the world. Hunched over the windowsill, clenching his eyes and his teeth until pain throbs through his skull and the breath, once again, releases him....

Gamelyn staggered, clung to the stone, and murmured a small litany into the darkness—a paean to Mary, first, then Her son, until the bleak, alien sorrow loosened its grip. He took in deep the cool air, let the moon-silver bathe him, remote and watchful.

It was then he saw it.

He blinked, several times, unsure that it was not another phantasm of nightmare hanging over him from sleep. Yet it did not waver. It stepped forward.

It was the largest stag he had ever seen, with a spread of antlers that would seat a full-grown man. Its hide was uncanny pale, and the stag's horns seemed dark in contrast, nearly black. It stood there, gleaming in the shadows of the tree line, then with a mind-bending grace stepped fully from the tree cover, pale fur casting from gleam to a glow that rivaled the moon's silver light. It scented the wind, then let out a call—a note of longing, and hopeful recognition.

Gamelyn's heart lurched in his chest. He had never witnessed anything so beautiful, so wild, and so pure.

Closing his eyes, he savored the image, then opened his eyes again, eager to take the loveliness in again, to feel the surge of… whatever it made him feel.

But the stag was gone.

☙ V ❧

THE very next night, they blooded Rob into a copper goblet, bound him, eyes and hands, and took him to the flat bluestone altar of the standing stones ringed above the caverns. Uncovered his eyes to a full moon, and the fires blazing, before not only the covenant but a gathering of the common folk bound to their protection.

Bright, it was, almost bright as day, but dim compared to the light in Marion's eyes as she put the wreath of vine and mistletoe upon Rob's black hair and called him, not novitiate, but *drywydd.*

Drywydd. The word teased at memory, and as Rob listened for it, the knowing came to him in a flash: the Horned Lord, gleaming ebony, had called him like to that, had called him….

Dryw. It means "Seer," in the old tongue of your dam's blood. The voice sounded in his skull, deep and thick, and Rob beheld sudden movement over by one of the guardian stones, the south-most one. The mist of hot breath in the night, the gleam of horn and teeth, the glitter of golden eyes….

Rob blinked, shook his head, and in that distraction, He vanished.

The people murmured approval around him, almost a sigh, but Rob could nevertheless hear the ebb and rise, the echoes of something in truth beyond hearing. Could feel it, pulsing up through the stone beneath his bare feet.

"Attend!" Adam's command was instantly heeded, the gatherers falling silent. His brown head was oddly bare to the moonlight—no crown of horn and green this night—and as he walked toward Rob, the reason became clear. The horn-crown was held, outstretched, in his hands.

Like the cowled archer in his Seeking, the one who had... killed him.

For one ragged breath, Rob's knees quavered and the need to flee possessed him. Spreading his feet wider, he set himself against the rock—with the rock—and reminded himself this mortal clad in the Horned Lord's power was his father.

Aye, little pwca, *that I am.* Another flit of horn and shadow near the south dolman, then, again, merely the hint, the breath and beat beneath Rob's bare toes. It thrummed heavy, meeting and matching the sudden thump of his own heart against his ribs as Adam placed the horn-crown at his feet.

"Your Maiden is now Mother." Adam rose, his voice pitched quiet. Nevertheless it carried across the gatherers, sending them swaying like corn in a soft breeze. "She has given not only a daughter but a son to the Horned One."

Eluned came forward, bearing the copper goblet. And if Rob had thought the grounding of the horn-crown to set him sideways, it was nothing next to what surged forth. His mother held up the copper goblet and poured it over the stone beneath his feet. Nay, surge was not the word for it; it was as if there truly was a great and couchant wyvern coiled within the earth, taking in a great, heated breath then releasing it, mist to cover the crimson-dark that runneled over stone and into the fecund soil. Rob drew in another breath, could taste it, on the back of his tongue, thick and heavy and present, the beating, pulsing heart of the forest and the breath of it, shifting and ebbing, filling him. *Filling….*

"Let it out." Marion's voice just behind him, soothing, and Marion's hands in the small of his back, curling comfort about his ribs. "Let it pass through. It's strong, so you canna hold it long."

As if her voice had been his gaze upon a jittery, spooked horse, calm feathered down his spine and he exhaled, letting it go.

ↀↂ

"WHAT was it?" Rob mumbled around a thick bite of venison.

The ritual had unnerved Rob, that much was obvious. But now that the circle was finished and opened, he was even more perturbed by how people kept passing close to him, just for the chance to touch fingertips to his hair or sleeve.

He'd finally retreated to a small stand of gorse, put it to his back, and begged Marion to sit beside him. It didn't stop them from looking, probably wouldn't keep them from coming over by and by, but for now?

For now they'd let their young Hunter eat, and Marion could steer away the ones who were thoughtless. She had brought a manchet heaped with enough meat for both of them—there were several deer roasting on the cook-fires, taken under Adam's rights. After all, Rob hadn't eaten in… three days, was it?

"What *was* it?" he repeated. "Why won't you tell me?"

"I was letting you eat. If you talk with your gob crammed like that, you waint have to worry at giving blessing luck to anyone. You'll choke."

He scowled at her, purposefully biting off a hunk of the manchet bread. "'M *hungry*."

She slid gray eyes at him, then chuckled and handed him another slab of meat.

"I love you, you know," he said, fervent, as he chewed.

"As long as I keep food in front of you," she smirked, then sobered. "I've never seen it so strong as it took you. Are you all right?"

The question obviously made him uncomfortable, even coming from her. He stopped chewing, swallowed, and took a hefty swallow of the mead she'd brought. "Then you *did* feel it. Aye?" It was a plea more than question.

"I did. But it's...." Marion paused, trying to come up with the proper words. "My *tynged* breathes diff—"

"What did you say?" It was a sharp gasp.

She blinked. "I meant the making, the spun threads of fate. *Tynged.* You've heard it before, surely—"

"He said that." Rob lowered his voice to a bare murmur. "But it sounded different." His eyes grew dim, then lit, and he uttered his next words, curling all sibilant and soft, "*Anadlu eich tyn*—"

Marion felt the power of it behind her ears even as she clapped her fingers against his mouth.

It was not so much that he'd said it, but *how*.

Neither did she have to tell him why he shouldn't; his eyes had dimmed, and no doubt he'd felt the same thing she had, rising.

His eyes flitted over to the south dolman; Marion followed his gaze, saw Cernun there, watching them.

"Do you see him?" Rob breathed, and it was clear that he wasn't just talking about Cernun.

Marion peered closer. Half shutting her eyes, she tilted her head, thought for a moment she *could* see something. A shadow behind the old hermit, black as starless night, with gleaming eyes. It was more a sensation, heat that flushed her cheeks and dropped down into her loins.

Taking in a deep breath, she turned away.

"Marion?"

She nodded, hazarded a glance at Rob. There was sweat on his upper lip and his breath was shallow, quick.

"He means us no harm," Rob whispered. "But he could. He's dangerous, I think."

Dangerous. Aye, that and more.

"What does it mean, Marion? What I said. Tried to say?"

"It means, 'breathe your destiny'. Somewhat. But... more."

He bit his lip, peered at her. Marion didn't like the trepidation in his face.

"So, Hob-Robyn! Are y' all too jumped up to share a mead sack with the likes of me?"

Surely the mere sound of a friendly voice shouldn't send Rob nearly to jumping out of his boots. He covered it well, however, and the familiar cheek had returned to his expression as he greeted Will Scathelock.

"That I am. So piss off."

Will—being Will—of course did the exact opposite. He flashed a heart-stopping smile at Marion, who just as adamantly refused to stop her heart or even move over and give him room. It gave her great satisfaction to see Will's charming façade falter, even if slightly.

Served him right, the wanker. He had every other girl falling over him *and* managed to scoop up what ones who were first intrigued then disappointed by Rob's aloof indifference.

Instead, he knelt beside Rob and rallied with, "I'll kick your arse between your ears if you're too full of y'rself to make it to the pub tomorrow."

"You and who else?"

Will snorted, then grinned evilly. "How about Simon?"

Rob actually flushed to the tips of his ears. Marion blinked, watched him duck his head, saw that his nape was just as red.

"M-hmm. Thought you might like that. You sure had nowt against Simon wrestling you up against the back wall last time we went to Loxley—"

"*Will*!" The protest was vehement, full of *shut your bloody gob before I shut it for you!* and a quick, panicked glance toward Marion. While Marion suddenly *saw*, with a twitch and a dropped-open mouth, what she surely should have seen before and somehow hadn't.

Will's mouth had also dropped open; his gaze flitted from Rob to Marion, then back to Rob again. "Um… sorry? I was sure *she'd*…." He trailed off, for the first in a long time seemed out of his depth. "Shall I wait for you, then? On the road to Loxley?"

"Aye!" Rob gritted out, slightly squeaky. "Go on!"

Will beat a hasty, subdued retreat.

Silence. Rob resumed eating, albeit with less gusto.

Marion decided, right then, to take the Hunter by His newfound horns. "Simon, is it? The fletcher's son?"

Rob stiffened.

"He's quite nice to look at. No wonder I couldna get him to look at *me*."

Grabbing for another piece of venison, Rob took a small bite.

"He'd better be nice to you, or I'll have his bits in my sights."

Ah—at last. A tiny quirk was twitching at one corner of Rob's mouth. "I'd—um—rather you leave his bits where they are."

"All right, then. But if he breaks my little brother's heart—"

"Honestly, Marion, it ent like that at all!" Rob protested. "I mean, I don't *love* him, or anything like. He's just—"

"Good at it?"

"Um." The quirk became a rather goofy grin. "Very."

Marion had to restrain herself from leaning forward and pinching his cheeks. "At least it ent *Will*."

"Not likely." A short laugh, purposefully casual. Instead it suggested that he might have hoped. Marion abruptly wanted—really, really *wanted*—to go hunt

Charming William and give him an eyeful of her good right fist. "Anyway," Rob continued, "Will fancies lasses."

"I've noticed. Any lass, anytime, anywhere. I dinna see how you stand him for longer than you can hold your breath underwater."

"Aw, Will ent that bad." The sweet, slightly goofy smile was back. "I can hold my breath pretty well, y'know."

"He's *insufferable*," she retorted.

"Not to me. Nor to you, if you'd let him. He quite fancies you, you must know."

"He only fancies me because he's not had me yet—"

"Yet?" Rob's grin got bigger.

"And won't *ever*, if I've anything—"

"Maiden. Hunter. *Bendith y Mamau*." An old woman stopped by them and crouched, hands at her heart. Rob peered at her as though she might set him on fire. Marion was well used to what was expected at the rituals and reached out, returned the blessing by tracing the moon-horns on the old woman's brow. The woman took her hand, kissed it, then gave a fleeting touch to Rob's sleeve and departed.

"I always wondered," Rob said, looking after her, a mix of wonder and dread in his voice, "what it would be like. To have someone look at you as though you'd hung the moon and stars. I figured that would be what it would be like to be in love. But this, it ent love—"

"Aye, 'tis," Marion told him. "Not the same kind of love, I'll wager, but love. It's overwhelming, sometimes. But everyone needs something, or someone… well, to believe. To trust in."

"So it is like, after all?"

She wished she knew, could say she'd grasped it for herself, if only to answer the troubled questions in his eyes. But she could only say what she'd seen, from others. From their parents, who loved each other so hard and fine. "I guess falling in love would mean you believed in something. And Mam and Da are worth that belief, surely; along with Cernun, they walk the *Ceugant*—"

"The trine of all worlds," Rob whispered.

"Aye. And make it strong."

He fell silent, went back to eating. He looked, suddenly, so… lost. Not that his stillness was odd. As surely as he would fling himself about with too much energy, he also could be very quiet, and patient.

Of course, he'd just gone into the Seeking. He would be floundering, surely, for the while until he had a chance to sort it out. She had done, herself.

Still, she hated to see him so somber. "Gamelyn came while you were gone."

He looked over to her, eyebrows raised.

"He was much put out that you weren't here, I think."

"More like he was glad I was out of his way," Rob snorted. "That one also fancies you." Then, black eyes sliding her way, "D'you fancy him?"

It was Marion's turn to smirk. "You and Mam are convinced, aren't you?"

"Mam?"

"She's got it in her head that I do fancy him. No question that Gamelyn's a sweet lad, but he's… well, he's a lord's son. There'd be no good future for such as me with one like that."

"Such as you?"

"We are what we are, little brother. Mam's right. You've said it yourself—he's a noble's son, and one day he'll tire of us, no doubt."

Rob frowned, looked as if he was going to speak, then took another bite of the dwindling mound of food on his manchet.

"We're all getting to an age where we have to start making things happen," Marion went on. "As opposed to things happening to us. If Gamelyn has to make a choice? Well, we've had our fun."

Rob gave her a thoughtful look, then waved his hand, encompassing… well… everything around them. Then said, very quiet, "And what d'you think he'd make of all this, then?"

❧

"AGAIN."

Perhaps it was indeed true that he learned best in anger, or from pain, because Jesus *wept* but he felt both in full measure when his elder brother instructed him in swordplay.

Gamelyn brought up the sword—a plain learner's instrument of black-pitted steel—and rocked, back and forth, on the balls of his feet. He and Johan were alone in the practice lobby of the weapons hall, sweating and stripped to braies. The air was torpid, heavy with the damp rain falling outside. What light there was came from the two narrow windows along the outside wall, as well as pitch torches set into sconces three strides apart, some on the wall and some free-standing. The earthen floor was smooth-swept, hard as any stone beneath their feet. Gamelyn spread his toes within the confines of his boots, trying to further read the chancy footing. It was slimy, almost, thick as the air they labored to breathe.

He hadn't been sleeping well, either.

Not that any of that mattered. Every other day, after the chapel bell rang the end of Matins and the opening of the courtyard markets, he was to be here, learning.

"Parry forward, step and step, *dedans*, *dehors*, right-left-right, *de côté*," Johan repeated, outlining their drill in broad shapes.

Gamelyn nodded.

Johan twirled his blade in a thick, noisy sculpt of air, then attacked. Sidestep, five monstrous-quick slashes, disengage. Then again: repeat steps, slashes and release, again and again like steps in a dance. Soon there was hardly a pause between, drill lengthening into a long, never-ending combination of like motions.

Gamelyn parried every blow, moves practiced, nigh effortless.

"Papa is watching, from the upper gallery," Johan murmured. Gamelyn snuck a glance upward, saw the familiar silhouette. "Shall we show him what you have learned, *petit lapin*?"

It was not the worst thing Johan had ever dared to call him, but nevertheless Gamelyn felt every nerve ending on his body draw up, angry. Johan smirked as if he sensed it, and lunged forward. To the inside, to the outside, right then left and right, one to the flank.

Then one to his head, a heavy swing from Johan's right. Gamelyn sucked in a quick, surprised breath, managed to parry the move by sheer luck.

Drill was, obviously, over.

Steel clanked, locked and slid. Johan lunged forward, raining blow after blow. Gamelyn blocked each one—it was not pretty, nor practiced, but it was effective. Unfortunately, it was also merely a defense. He couldn't so much as gather a single blow, and Johan kept advancing, driving him backward with every third step.

Then the wall appeared, somehow, behind Gamelyn, and he had nowhere left to go. So Gamelyn lunged sideways.

Johan merely blocked him with the flat of his blade, pressed him harder against the wall. "How many times must I tell you to *watch* where you're going?"

"And take my eyes off my opponent?" Gamelyn challenged. He brought his blade under and inside, locked guards with Johan's sword and shoved. Johan gave, almost too easily, it seemed.

A blur of movement off to his right, and before Gamelyn could so much as duck, something smashed into the right side of his jaw with all the force of a charging destrier. Metal rang and flesh gave; there was the tang of copper-salt on his tongue and white-hot lanterns popped behind his eyes. Johan's mailed fist sent Gamelyn spinning then staggering against the rough stones of the wall.

"Better still, *petit lapin,* to grow eyes in the back of your head." Johan laughed, backed away with arms at his side, no more threat. Raised his voice. "Eh, Papa, this one is no goodly squire. He would do best to stay hunched over his books. Brother Gamelyn, anon, all properly draped with prayer and skirts."

Gamelyn's knees were wobbly; nevertheless he gave a small growl and lurched off the wall. He was stopped, not only by the shards that flared anew from his jaw and up against his temples, but the glare of flat warning that Johan leveled upon him.

Like it or not, the truth still remained: Johan was quite capable of wiping the floor with him.

The sudden movement also made Gamelyn's stomach rebel. He bit down on his tongue, let one bloody ache sift through the other and, thankfully, overcame the sudden wish of his gorge to spill over. He hawked, felt a small, hard bit gather on his tongue, and spat. Likely part of a tooth.

Their father's voice floated down from the window arch. "Well. He's young yet."

Johan reached out; Gamelyn almost flinched—*almost*—but kept iron about his being and let those mailed fingers brush his jaw. "Enough fuzz on this cheek to liken near a man. At his age, I'd already several sorties beneath my belt. And more than a few missing teeth."

Gamelyn lifted his chin and glared at his brother. Johan smirked and tapped his fingers. They sent a dull throb, like the hotspot of a bee sting, up the side of Gamelyn's face.

"You had Roberto teaching you." Sir Ian's voice was testy, but his next words proved it was not toward Gamelyn's efforts. "Perhaps it is time Roberto took over Gamelyn's education as well. You are excellent with that sword, Johan, but you are proving no teacher."

Johan's smirk soured, and an unbecoming flush lit him, neck to cheeks.

"See to it, Johan. And Gamelyn, you are quite ready for Roberto's expertise. Heed him well and you'll find yourself ready for much."

"Yes, Papa," Gamelyn said, heartened by Sir Ian's smile.

"Come to the hall later, boy. Read to me a bit."

"Yes, Papa."

"A storm is coming," Sir Ian continued after a small pause. "The air is too heavy. There is a big bank of clouds gathering to the north. We need to close everything down, I think."

"I'll see to it, Papa." Johan was still looking away.

"I've already sent Otho to do so. Finish up here, then go and make sure he's on track. You know how he can be."

"I know." It was quiet.

As their father nodded and moved away, Gamelyn watched him go.

It was a mistake. Almost before he could draw another breath, Johan had grabbed him, spun him around, and slammed him back against the wall.

White-hot bits once again danced behind Gamelyn's eyes. It was by sheer will and the dubious fortune of Johan's grip upon him that Gamelyn kept his knees straight. When he could focus, Johan was close. Watching him.

"What did I tell you, *ma petit lapin*, about growing eyes in the back of your head?"

"I," Gamelyn hissed back, "am not your 'little rabbit'."

"You are whatever I say you will be." It was quiet, almost musing. "But yes, you are not so little anymore."

Suddenly, inexplicably, Gamelyn was released. He wanted to cradle his aching jaw, but he wasn't about to acknowledge any discomfort. Not under Johan's critical gaze.

"Where have you been going as you ride, brother?"

Gamelyn frowned, felt a tiny thrill of apprehension beginning to nudge aside any pain. "What do you mean?"

"Brand says that you are putting wind-work on your mount. But what for? What use will you have for a horse's endurance when you are buried in a monastery with all your books and papers?"

Apprehension was niggling its way into alarm. "I like to ride alone."

"Do you, now?" The smirk had returned to Johan's face. "That's not what young Much tells me."

Much was the newest addition to their retinue. Eager to advance himself, he was youngest of five sons to the local miller, adequately explaining the change of trade. What could that one have to say?

"I had him follow you yester's morn. You went north, took your ease at a serf's cottage—"

They aren't serfs, Gamelyn's mind gave foolish protest even as every nerve ending shrieked, *I'm caught. Bugger and piss, I'm* caught.

He'd learned, quite well, how to swear under Rob's tutelage. He had also learned, beneath Johan's tutelage, that to give away any reaction whatsoever was to court further penalty. Nevertheless, Gamelyn nearly fell over in sheer surprise as Johan gave a sudden bark of laughter and gave him a clout on the shoulder.

It seemed almost—friendly.

"So you've a slut on the side!" Johan was still chuckling. "Frankly, lad, I didn't think you had it in you."

Several conflicts reared themselves within Gamelyn. One was, *Slut? What in hell are you talking about?* Then, *He had me followed,* followed, *and what all did they see?* Then, a slow burn of anger: *Merciful Heaven, he's talking about Marion.*

"She is *not* a—!" Just in time, Gamelyn throttled the words down in his chest where they roiled, burning.

"Of course. They never are," Johan agreed with a smirk. "Even when they are." With a sudden, swift motion, Johan moved close and laid a heavy arm across his shoulders. Control or no, Gamelyn couldn't help but tense.

"We were worried after you, wandering about," Johan said, eminently reasonable. "But don't worry, I didn't tell Papa about the girl. He's old-fashioned, he won't understand. At least you're occupying yourself with a man's business for a change, and not mooning about the chapel. All that praying only makes for sore knees and a foul temper. Better you sore your knees in another fashion, eh?" Another laugh, and Johan snugged him closer, all man-to-man solidarity. It almost made Gamelyn want to respond.

Almost.

His instincts were proven right mere seconds later. Johan leaned in.

"But if she comes to our gates with any bastards?" Johan's voice tickled his ear, went very soft. Dangerous. "She'll wish the little worm had never been born." Another snug, this one cruelly tight, and Johan's breath tickled his ear, humid threat. "Mind that, *petit lapin*."

And Gamelyn was released, hot and cold all over, and Johan was striding from his chambers, boot heels clicking against the stones.

"I'll send Ricardo to you here on the morrow." Johan's voice drifted back. "As Papa wishes. I suggest you take this opportunity seriously."

The wooden door slammed, echoing into the hallway with the sound of those boots. They faded into the heavy silence of the armaments lobby.

Gamelyn took his practice sword over to the wall, hung it in its place. As he drew his hands back, he realized he was shaking. Wondered if he was going to be sick.

He turned on one heel, went to the narrow, open window against the far wall. The wind had indeed risen, sending small spatters of rain against his burning cheeks. He took a small, shallow breath, then another, deeper. He sought out the thick buttress of Blyth, glowered at the wall as if it was the slimed and filthy wall of a gaol.

You coward! some tiny, furious voice behind his eyes lashed out. *You should have… should have….*

Should have what? Protested? Told the truth? Given Johan a right hook?

You should have at least defended Marion!

Fear abruptly crystallized into a rage so abrupt and fierce that he thought he was going to hurl his guts out onto the cobbles below. Instead Gamelyn gripped the stones of the sill, clenching his teeth until angry white flares throbbed at his temples. He winced, put a questing hand to where Johan had backhanded him. Sticky, and when he pulled his hand back, blood smeared his fingertips.

And more blood in his mouth. Running an experimental tongue across his teeth, Gamelyn found a jagged corner off one molar. Aye, and it could have been worse. He'd need to find some wood spirit and myrrh, pack it well to ensure it wouldn't grow angry with any rot. He was no more impressed with a barber-surgeon's tools than Marion had been.

He closed up the shutters against the gathering clouds and retreated to the opposite corner, where there was always a hogshead filled with water. Gamelyn grimaced at the scum floating on the surface—more to blame on the warm, humid weather—and instead turned to peer in the polished surface of a shield hanging on the wall. Johan's mailed fist had done adequate damage. Gamelyn's face was abraded from his chin to up over his cheekbone, and his face was already beginning to swell. Particularly his jaw, which sported an ugly, finger-long slash.

With a resigned sigh, Gamelyn went to the hogshead, dunked his entire head, and came up sputtering.

Defending Marion would have betrayed her. If Johan thought that Gamelyn was keeping company with a family of peasants for any other reason than having his "rights" with that family's daughter?

He would suffer, yes. But he had seen, since his father's illness, how those with much less power than Gamelyn himself held could suffer if they crossed Johan.

Gamelyn turned, put his back to the stone walls. A shiver, not altogether from the cool, damp stone, claimed him.

He'd never fully considered the gravity of what he'd been doing. Never considered that the consequences of discovery could reach out beyond himself. It had been a lark, nothing more.

No, that wasn't true. It had been much, much more. An escape from an ill father, a brother's intimidations, a tiny chapel that was the only connection, cold and empty, with a mother he had never known. A dream, really: a never-ending summer's warmth of simple dreams, aspirations, *approval.*

And now, at the thought of those things in danger?

He should not return to Loxley.

The thought rent a slow, desolate fissure in his chest. Gamelyn put a hand to his breastbone, almost expecting to feel the warmth of laid-open flesh and blood set to seep.

The hot spurt of tears behind his eyes was real enough.

It had been over a month since he'd been able to visit Loxley, and it was passing strange how the previous day's visit had felt incomplete, somehow, without Adam's calm presence, or Rob's… well, whatever it was that Rob had.

Perhaps it was fear, again. Neither Adam nor Eluned were serfs. Adam was a king's forester, a skilled archer, a yeoman with more rights than many.

"No fear, Gamelyn," he whispered. But it was Rob's voice he echoed, Rob whom he heard in his mind. A much lower register than it had been the first time they'd met, but still with that lilt and brass, shiny as polished metal. *Fear does y' no good. You show throat, they'll only sense it, and then you're nowt to 'em.*

Rob had been talking about the outlier wolf they had run across on one of their forest jaunts. Gamelyn had started to back away—surely a sensible move, when faced with a wolf with his jaws full of fresh-killed rabbit—but Rob's slender, callused hand had shot out, tangled in Gamelyn's tunic, stayed him. And damned if Rob hadn't just stood there, shoulders squared, nostrils flared, peering with flat eyes from beneath his brows. The wolf had bristled, growled, and stared back. Then, after the longest moments of Gamelyn's life, the wolf had snarled, relinquished the rabbit, and slunk away.

Fine, then. No fear. He'd just been given the best excuse of all to continue his journeys: a dalliance with a peasant girl, expected for someone of his age and status.

And even more, reason to heed the utmost of cautions.

☙ VI ❧

THE forest seemed to moan around them as they emerged from it and onto the main road, a pitch of not-quite-sorrow that echoed the wind. Adam straightened in his saddle and halted just past the crossroads. He cocked his bare, brown head this way and that, as if testing the wind, the foothills, and the fens.

Beside Adam, his lieutenant, George Scathelock, took the rein in his teeth and unbuckled his crossbow from its harness. Rob, mounted beside Will, exchanged uncomfortable glances with his friend.

"Da?" Will put hand to his own shortbow, athwart his back.

"No worries, lads," George said easily, hefting his crossbow and watching Adam as he knelt and put ear to the ground.

A gust of wind tugged at Rob's dark curls and fluttered at the fur over his father's shoulders.

"Brr," George said. "From muggy enough to sweat yourself sick to *this*. The wind's turned all chill t' sudden, eh, lads?" Then, as Adam stood: "Is sommat wrong?"

"Nay."

But they all heard the unspoken: *Not that I can put my finger to.*

Rob watched his father, frowning. They were here as courtesy, a forester's escort to see a cavalcade through their territory of Barnsdale and the Peak Forest. Many travelers chose to have a good man of the forest as traveling companion. And no doubt Adam would receive a goodly tip to share with his companions. It was a normal and easy enough obligation, yet Adam seemed ill at ease.

Aye, very strange. Rob was starting to sense it as well. It sent prickles over his arms and a hum… nay, more a vibration… was shimmying its way all slow up the back of Rob's neck. Between his legs, black Arawn crabstepped, as if also feeling it. Not for the first time, Rob missed Willow's steadfast presence. Arawn was more fit for both Rob's leggy height and new station, but was young and often lived up to his name—not necessarily bad by nature but aloof, and sometime unpredictable as any lord of the otherworld's darkling realm.

And Adam watched Rob—when he thought Rob wasn't heeding him. Adam had always kept a careful eye upon Rob, in truth, but since Rob had ventured into Cernun's caverns and come out to be crowned with the Hunter's wreath, it had turned even more piercing, more… apprehensive. As if when Rob had gone down into the Seeking and taken hold of things he still was fighting to grasp, Adam too had found existence tenuous. His father had taken on a weight, somehow, and Rob couldn't help the wondering: was it a weight that was meant to be his own?

There was fear, now, in Adam. Rob could all but scent it. Yet he didn't know how to classify it, what to do with it other than turn his head from it, discomfited.

"They're coming. The ground echoes. It's quite a body of horse, for a church retinue." Adam's frown swept over his companions as he remounted.

"And the other?" George pressed. He was Adam's assistant forester, but he was also of the covenant; he knew something was… off.

Adam shrugged. "Probably the coming storm, nowt more."

The words grated, somehow, opened within Rob a fissure of that deep, ancient place—the one that could issue the same tiny tendril of fear in his own heart that had taken root in his father's soul.

The coming storm. Nothing more, and nothing less.

They unslung their bows, mere show if that approaching company was indeed large and heavily armed, and set themselves to the wait. Soon a group of blue-clad soldiers, some on foot and some a-horse, straggled over the north-most rise and spilled down the dirt road. They were followed by two wagons and more soldiers. Bannermen marched fore and aft—or in this case, bannerwomen. Nuns in black gowns, dusty from the road, in a dutiful and grim march amidst the sheriff's soldiers, carrying the colors of their allegiance—a crimson so black it looked like old blood. The first wagon was overlarge, pulled by a team of cold-bred horses, while the other was drawn by a light team.

"Prosperous," remarked George.

"You don't invest a new abbess with sackcloth," Adam said, wry, then rode forward, hand held up in greeting.

The soldiers had already grouped together in defense. One, obviously the captain, rode forward on his high-mettled horse, sword prominent at his hip and head defiantly bare. Several others flanked him, helmeted and a-horse, to surround the party of foresters. George and Will went rigid, both ready. The tension was sudden, palpable.

One never knew what would happen when strangers collided upon the roads. Friend—or foe? Outlaw—or gamekeeper?

"I demand recognition," the captain demanded, "in the name of Her Most Reverend Lady Elizabeth, Abbess of Worksop."

Adam inclined his head courteously, but did not relax his guard for a second. "I am Adam of Loxley, king's forester. We were requested by the Lord High Sheriff of Yorkshire, Brian de Lisle, to provide escort through our territories of Barnsdale and t' Peak Wode. It is my honor to serve."

"And mine to take your service." The captain also gave an amiable tilt of his head. "Please, ride with us. We were expecting you and welcome your knowledge of this place. I am Colin Stutely, guard-captain to Sheriff de Lisle."

"Has manners," George murmured to Rob and Will. "Must be English."

Will smirked at Rob, who wanted to smile but couldn't. The odd drone purling beneath the wind had gotten louder with every step the party had taken, ramping up into a throb behind his ears. He was desperately afraid he was going to be sick, and this only his third foray at his father's side for something so important.

Behind the mannerly guard captain, the soldiers parted, revealing a black-veiled rider. The Abbess—it must be—was dressed like to the lesser nuns afoot, her voluminous skirts made of the same wool serge. Her veil, however, drifted on the wind in the manner only silk had, and her pectoral cross was large and set with gems. It winked against black, off and on catching the wind-tossed light.

Adam ducked his head respectfully, as did Will and George in quick secondary tandem. Rob disguised a heavy lean against Arawn's neck as obeisance, but his eyes did not give way. They were snared to the Abbess.

Or rather, to the cross upon her breast. It was a lavish thing, unique, inlaid with enamel, set with sapphires and rubies in gold and hanging from links of finest silver.

He had seen it before.

Dreamed it before, dangling over his head while he lay bleeding, breathing sharp and shallow, *dying*....

"Lower your gaze, boy!" A sudden, sharp blow to his temple knocked Rob sideways in his saddle. Head ringing, eyes watering, he yanked himself back upward and flung a flat, furious snarl at the soldier who had ridden up and struck him.

"Don't you dare raise that insolent look to me, you—!" And the next blow knocked Rob out of the saddle and to the ground.

It had all happened so quick and brutal, in a furious almost-silence, and Rob was unable to hear anything further for a smattering of seconds. He half lay, sprawled on the ground with ears ringing and head spinning, hoofs dancing altogether close to his head.

Suddenly, he heard shouts, saw another body hit the ground on the other side of his horse. He barely rolled aside in time to avoid Arawn's sideways spook.

"Will!"

"Stop him!"

A feminine voice, imperious. "Stop it, stop it this instant!"

Then his father's voice, rising above the rest and setting the earth beneath Rob pulsing with its power. "Enough of this! *Captain*!"

And the captain's voice, shouting orders.

Arawn had settled down; Rob reached up, grabbed at his stirrup and dragged himself gingerly to his feet. Thankfully, Arawn stood like a rock, for Rob still felt as if sparks from a very large fire were scattering and popping off the inside of his skull. He peered over Arawn's withers to see a soldier holding one of their own—Rob assumed it was the one who'd struck him—they all looked alike in their ridiculous helmets. George was holding back Will, who was snarling silent curses toward their antagonist, and several soldiers were ringed around them.

Adam was still mounted, and while Rob knew his father would never entangle himself with the authorities for any reason, this time it bit deep and bitter.

After all, his son had just been whacked off his horse, and his underforesters were cornered.

"What in *Hell* is going on here?" The captain had dismounted, was stalking over. To Rob's surprise, he vented his ire not on Will or George, but the soldier who had struck Rob down. "You there! By what rights do you abuse our escort?"

"That boy villein"—a gesture over to where Rob was still clinging to his saddle—"gave my lady an unseemly gaze, Captain!" Neither was the soldier backing down.

"You pu—!" Will's growl turned into a muffled snort as George clapped a hand over his mouth, gave a terse order into his son's ear.

The Abbess, meanwhile, had dismounted and come forward. Her eyes were as a burning brand into Rob's skin. Blood pounding in his ears, he met her gaze, unable to help himself. A hand came heavily onto his shoulder, and his father's voice murmured in his ear.

Gritting his teeth, Rob looked away. Pulled away. His father's breath hitched, troubled; it seemed another, deeper breath exhaled about them. As if something had been avoided, just barely, but not averted.

"Rob, are you all right?"

No thanks to you, it was on his tongue to say, his own disappointment raw and angry. Instead he murmured, "Aye. I'll live."

"Let me help you back up—"

"I'll do it m'self—"

The Abbess's voice broke the silence, soft but underlain with steel. "Joubert. Your diligence is valued, but you misconstrue. He is but a boy and needs forbearance, not harsh admonition. Come away."

Rob looked up to see the soldier—Joubert—nod curtly. He obeyed his mistress without another word.

"And as to that lad, he merely rose to the defense of his friend. An honorable trait in any man or woman. Release him."

The Abbess had charm—and Will was, as always, susceptible to a lovely woman. The fact that this particular one was a professional virgin merely roused his spirit. He bowed, very low, and her lips quirked, as if she knew exactly what he was about. "He is your son?" This to George.

"Aye, Reverend Lady. And more temper than brains, most days."

She smiled, dipped her head, and turned from them. Arawn shifted; Rob hissed a hoarse-slurred, “Be still, you nappy bugger,” and the gelding quieted.

The Abbess looked his way, as if she’d heard, and her smile wavered. She seemed… puzzled. His gaze met hers and held; the persistent ringing of his ears reminded him he’d be better off with his eyes to the ground and he lowered them. Nevertheless, it was hard to remain unaware of her notice as she walked over to where he and his father stood.

“Good yeomen, both of you must accept my apologies.” Her words were truly directed to Adam, though her eyes remained upon Rob. “My retinue is from York proper, and the ways of such cities are different than country customs.”

“The apology is ours, Lady.”

How is it yours, then? Rob’s somewhat-still-addled brain protested, while another, more cogent reminder rose: *You’re a peasant, remember? You might be the Horned One’s Son in the green Wode, but elsewhere you’re nowt, and neither is your da.*

“My son meant no disrespect, I assure you,” Adam was saying, very polite. “In this shire, we consider curiosity as ever a virtue as vice. Shall we make our way on to Worksop? The weather grows chancy.”

“It does indeed,” the Abbess said. “But I shall ask for your guidance to the castle of Blyth, if you please. I and my closest retainers have been offered a fine welcome feast there, from my mother’s brother, Sir Ian Boundys. Do you know of him?”

Blyth? Sir Ian. Gamelyn’s father. Ringing ears were numbed, if not totally overcome, as Rob’s mouth tucked in a slight grin.

Adam nodded. “I have had fair dealings with Sir Ian since his arrival to our shire. I will be happy to take you there, and if you like, I can detail George Scathelock and his son to escort those who’ve need to continue on to the abbey.” He seemed to hesitate, then continued, “If I c’n be bold enough to suggest, Reverend Lady, that the soldier who—?”

“He must go on,” the Abbess said. “But I give you my word that he will not interfere any more with your party. And your plans are more than suitable. You have my thanks and blessings.”

She gave a brief nod, more polite dismissal than any pleasantry, and walked back to her horse.

Adam again made as if to help Rob onto his horse; Rob shook his head, all too aware of his father’s concern as he mounted, somewhat painful and slow. And then there was Will. George was speaking to Will, who kept looking at the soldier who’d struck Rob. Will looked angry, almost. Nay, confused. And that soldier continued to glare through the slits of his helmet at Rob, alert for any further transgressions.

Rob's anticipation of a chance to see Gamelyn was inexorably giving way to a return of the odd queasiness that had plagued him for half the journey. He felt his stomach sink even more as his father mounted his horse, then sidled close.

"Suppose you tell me what was that all about?" Adam murmured.

Rob shrugged.

"I keep telling you, son, you canna be insolent to such folk."

"I didna *do* owt but look at t' bloody cross!" Rob hissed back. "Ent that what her like is wanting, for us poor Heathen filth to see the light?"

"We'll discuss this later," Adam said, terse. "For now I'm thinking I should send you home—"

"Da!" Rob protested.

"If there's no trusting you to keep yourself in hand on the road, can I trust that you'll do so around your friend? Your *nobleman's son* of a friend?"

This was plainly unfair. "I'm t' one as got whacked, Da. I didna do *owt*!"

And neither did you. Again, it lay between them, unspoken but nonetheless heard. And Rob knew why, *knew why*, but still he wanted to lash out.

His father's flinch gave him no satisfaction, though. So he blurted the truth. "I'd Seen it, Da. The cross. *Seen* it."

But Rob was sorry the moment he'd said that, too, for the strange apprehension once again crawled behind his father's expression and burrowed in.

"Loxley?"

Adam plainly wanted to ignore the summons and further question Rob, but the captain came riding up to them, determined. "Loxley, please accept my apologies. That one isn't one of my men, and the Abbess's paxmen have proven, well, overzealous as to her sanctity. I'll see that it doesn't happen again."

"My thanks," Adam replied.

The captain turned his affable gaze to Rob. "Are you all right, lad? He treated you ill for no good reason; if he was in my guard, I'd throw him in the stocks."

Rob nodded, albeit carefully. His skull was still tender. "I thank you, milord Captain."

"Just Captain, lad. I was born a yeoman like yourself. In fact, your friend over there"—he tilted his head to Will—"is quite the scrapper. If he decides he'd like to give the shire guardsmen a try, have him come apply to me, aye?"

Rob's mouth quirked despite the underlying dismissal. Will's muscular frame was certainly more the fighter's ideal than some skinny lath of a lad who had but recently won over the predilection for tripping over his own big feet.

It was certainly what Rob liked. But Will was, unfortunately and resolutely, disinterested in anything that didn't have breasts.

The captain grinned back, dipped his chin to Rob, and turned to Adam. "Then if your boy is well, can I request your presence, Loxley? Discuss the detour?" Adam returned the polite overture with a remark of his own, and rode off with the captain as the cavalcade began to move again. It was slow, as such things often were, but soon they were traveling, backs to the wind, Adam and George at point with the captain.

Will fell in beside Rob. He was quiet, too quiet. With Will, it usually meant trouble. Soon they had fallen to the back of party, both eager to be as far away from the Abbess and her overzealous guards as possible.

"You all right?" Will's voice was low.

Rob shrugged. "No blood, no bones. Well enough."

"I'll warrant your head's still ringing. That bloody-minded turd knocked you good." A strange, sick-seeming quaver threaded Will's voice.

Rob peered at him. Will was grinding his teeth, slow and steady, and staring at the back of the soldier who'd struck Rob. He looked unsteady, unsure.

"Will?"

"I know his voice," Will said. "I know it somewhere, and I ent placin' it. But it's—"

"It's what?" Again, Rob was struck by the… the *strangeness* of it all. The ill-seeming wind, his father's wariness, the Abbess, *the cross.*

And now, Will.

Was this what Marion had meant by *tynged*, then? This feeling, this sensation, as if someone… something… was breathing down your neck with possibilities?

"It's important," Will said, flat. "I know that much." Then, quick and capricious as ever, he smiled. "Blyth Castle, aye? Ent that where your poncy ginger paramour lives?"

"My… what?" Sometimes there was no accounting for Will's turns of thought. "Who says he's my… bloody hell, Scathelock, you tosser, I'm not even going to *say* it."

"Or does he like Marion?" A snort. "Of course he likes Marion better. Who wouldn't? She's lots prettier than *you.*"

Rob couldn't argue with that, in fact wouldn't, because Will would just twist it back around, probably tell Marion some nonsense like Rob thought he was prettier than she. Which was preposterous. Not that Marion would listen to Will.

But maybe Gamelyn did like Marion better. Which was also irritating, and for no good reason.

"Aye, well then," Will murmured with a wink. "*Simon* thinks you're prettier. But he's a tunic lifter, just like you—"

"*Sod* you, Scathelock."

☙ VII ❧

BLYTH CASTLE was huge. Perhaps it made sense—it was, after all, a main stop along the main road from Nottingham to Doncaster. Still, it sprawled out to twice the size of the keep at Sheffield—the only other one Rob had ever seen. Stone walls as tall as an arrow's flight greeted them, a persuasive carapace marred only slightly by a solid and misshapen outcrop on one side. Like many of its kind, the inner keep was set up on a mound, the trees scalped from the surround to let grass grow, lush and verdant.

Arawn was very happy with that last. He was taking full advantage of the brief stop by stuffing his muzzle with as much green as he could take. He wasn't the only one—all the horses were grazing fast as they could.

A bell rang from inside the stones, one of the men standing watch atop the gatehouse having shouted down warning of their approach. No doubt that was why the captain had ordered a stop, here in full view, to prove themselves friend and not foe. As the bell echoed across the sward, they started to move again. Which did not best please Arawn.

Rob let him snatch a few mouthfuls, here and there, as they advanced.

Details became more visible. The odd misshapen lump on the side of the castle proved to be construction along the far side, a puzzle of ladders and scaffolding, with stone bricking piled hither and yon. There were more figures on the wall, and down by the gatehouse entry—a fortified bridge, over a moat. There were dark, moving blobs to either side of the entry. They took form: cages, hanging, with carrion birds fluttering, pecking at the corpses hung in those cages.

Outlaws, no doubt. Rob had heard of such things, like gallows poles, left as warning to others; in Sheffield he'd seen a brace of severed heads over the gatepost.

It was sobering; Rob had always thought of Gamelyn with the label "lord" despite any protests to the contrary, but this? It was hard to process. The same ginger-haired lad who couldn't shoot straight unless he was pissing mad, who wore hand-me-down clothes and read too many books… *Gamelyn* came from such state.

"Lady's paps!" Will exclaimed as they arrived to the massive wooden gates, flung open as if by some giant's hand. "Each of those timbers'd hold up a house on its own!"

Rob shrugged, wondering if Gamelyn was on the other side of those gates. Might he see him? What to do if he did? After all, his visits to the forester's house in Loxley were supposed to be a secret.

Will bumped shoulders with him, roughly. "See you in a few, then?"

"A few?" Rob's snarled senses had, on the ride, eased and untangled somewhat, but he still felt as if he was that much too slow. As if his mind had been unhinged to some speed that his body couldn't quite catch. Cernun claimed he'd find a balance. Someday. It couldn't come a day too soon as far as Rob was concerned.

"You've put me off long enough. The alehouse, remember?" Will gave him a look that was just that much too mild. "Thursday?"

Ah. Now he remembered. They'd been unable to keep their last plans—this journey had interfered—so they had made others, for later this se'nnight.

The horses were milling just outside the gatehouse, some crossing the bridge and others halting. People of all sorts were gathering up on the parapets, peering down at them. The captain's voice was singing out orders. Rob snuck a look to where the Abbess's horse stood, still chewing—no doubt at a quid of grass that had stuck in its bits. A grey-clad novice was holding the cheekstrap, and the Abbess was leaning on the sidesaddle's horn, speaking to several nuns gathered at her stirrup. Instructions, no doubt.

"What a waste of a good woman," Will sighed, and Rob looked sideways at him, snorted.

"Is it all you ever think about, Scathelock?"

"What else is there?" Will cocked his head, sly. "Are you 'n' Simon going to partner up again, then? Or mayhap you're hoping to bring the poncy ginger paramour?"

Rob rolled his eyes, pretended to look off and down the valley.

"I wonder if such as lives here has ever seen the inside of an alehouse like to ours."

"'M *not*," Rob growled, "answering you."

Will fell silent. Rob slid curious eyes back to him, found him studying the soldiers with an odd frown.

"The captain said you were quite the scrapper," Rob put forth. "That should you want to be a soldier, you should apply to him."

"Not likely." There was a low contempt in the words, and then Will grinned again and kneed his gelding closer. Arawn exchanged a few breaths with the gelding, then let out a short grunt and nipped at him. "Look, I only want to know because of Calla. She fancies you, and if you're off in the hay with Simon, then she'll fancy *me*."

Rob had to grin. "You'd best be careful, or your bits'll be scarlet as Calla's knees."

Arawn's nip was raised and seconded by Will's gelding.

"Will?" George's voice rose. "Time, boy!"

"You don't know how nice it is, t' have mates that waint compete with you for a lass." Will's murmur was almost reverent.

"So that's why you like me. And why you introduced me to Simon."

Will's grin was impenitent. "Well, you weren't mindin'."

Rob didn't mind. Simon was a lighthearted fellow, not one to be breaking a heart over, but quite skilled at the types of things two lads could get up to in a dark corner.

"Now, if you could just see your way clear to talking your sister into letting me court her… aye, then life would be heaven."

The nipping was becoming a contest, necks snaking back and forth.

Rob shrugged. "As long as you keep on like you do, Marion's going to give you no more than the back of her hand. Canna blame her."

"If I had her, I there'd be no others," Will said, so oddly earnest that Rob blinked and started to speak.

"Will!" George, again.

At the same time, Arawn rose up lightly on his hind legs and Will's gelding bent down to nip at his shoulder. Rob laughed

"Hoy!" Will smacked at his gelding's neck lightheartedly. "Leave off, you two!"

"Boys will be—" Rob waggled his eyebrows suggestively.

"You'd know, tunic-lifter!" Will snorted, and pulled his horse away. "Be seeing you."

"In two days," Rob smirked after him. After the past se'nnight, Will was a breath of fresh air. Lasses, ale and lasses, with an occasional bout of archery practice, merely enough to keep his hand in before he went back to ale and lasses. Perhaps Marion had no use for him, but Will was so wonderfully… *uncomplicated.*

The Abbess's retinue was separating into two parties, the smaller one riding forward, hoofs ringing on thick planks as they went through the gatehouse arch. Adam hung back and held up a hand when Rob would have followed the smaller group—which included the good-natured guard captain.

"Ent we staying?" Rob wasn't sure how he felt about it as he asked.

"They owe us a meal and a bed for our service, right enough, at Worksop." Adam seemed uncertain. "But we've no true claim on Blyth. Might be best if we went on home."

"I'd like to see Gamelyn." Rob said it before he thought.

"And aye, that too." It didn't seem an agreement as much as a pondering, and Adam not much liking the direction of said pondering.

"Loxley!" It was Stutely, the guard captain, riding back through the gate. "You are polite to hang back, but Blyth owes you what courtesy you would expect at Worksop. I spoke with the Abbess, and she too insists. See, even now she speaks to Sir Ian."

The Abbess had dismounted and was indeed speaking to a man who must be Sir Ian. He was not very tall, hunched over a staff, and frail-seeming beneath the bulk of a fur-trimmed cape. But his eyes were sharp, missing nothing as he turned them to the foresters outside his gate.

With Sir Ian were three figures, two unrecognizable to Rob but the third immediately so.

As if he'd spoken Gamelyn's name, the lad's eyes rose to Rob's. There was a flash of a smile, gone as one of the others turned to him, said something. Rob watched as Gamelyn nodded then turned away, heading somewhere with no little purpose. He didn't look back, disappeared behind the walls.

Surely it wasn't disappointment Rob felt.

"Son!" The sharp tone to Adam's voice suggested it wasn't the first time he'd so summoned Rob. "Take the horses, I tell you. Go with this lad"—he nodded to a slight, brown-haired lad who held the captain's rouncey—"and see to them. I'll come to the stables for you when food is served."

"You'll both eat with me and my men, no doubt," the captain said, and he gave a friendly clout to Adam's shoulder. "This way."

Rob watched the two men stride away, then noticed the lad was watching him with a soft, tolerant gaze. As if waiting for just that notice, the lad dipped his head and started off.

Hoofs clattered over the cobbled walk as they progressed. Rob's eyes were widening with every step. Gamelyn's people were bloody *rich.* The interior of the castle was even grander than the outside, hung with banners and draperies over the bailey walls, the wide bailey itself still grassy in spots, with fine-dressed people taking their leisure. It must be a market day, for there were a lot of people lining upper walkways and doorways—some watching the newcomers, others simply going about their business. One stall in particular caught Rob's eye, festooned with cloth hangings and yarns—they looked like market displays until he saw the women behind them, working with more in large vats. It was the largest dye operation he'd yet seen. People in carts and stalls, horses and cattle, meat on the hoof and already butchered, implements and weapons and tools; all of it a mass of sound and smells and colors to send the senses spinning.

It was grand. Amazing. But for all that, he didn't much care for it. Despite their festive adornments, the stone walls seemed to loom overhead, oppressive, punishment instead of stronghold and guerdon.

So gawking, Rob nearly ran into a man carrying a huge wooden tray of bread loaves. The stable lad yanked him aside just in time. Arawn balked as the maneuver accidentally snatched at his rein; Adam's gelding merely sighed. Rob gave them both an apologetic pat, gave the stable lad a shrug.

As if in answer, the stable lad touched his sleeve, then made a gesture that Rob recognized, one kept amongst those of the heath and forest.

Rob gave polite, nigh silent answer. "*Bendith y Mamau.*"

The stable lad tucked a tiny smile into the corner of his mouth and started off again. This time Rob stuck close upon his heels. The way the lad navigated the throng with such quick efficiency was impressive; before long they had reached the far side of the bailey. The stable was there, amidst several blocks of stone and mortar, outbuildings that backed up against the hill where the main keep stood.

The stable lad led them in, turned as if to say something else to Rob, then, eyes going wide, he turned and hurried off, leading the captain's horse with him.

Unsure, Rob started to follow; then a familiar voice called his name.

"Rob?"

Rob abruptly understood the stable lad's caution. It was one thing to rough about with Gamelyn in the green Wode. It was another altogether to greet him *here*.

Rob suddenly felt as he had done standing before the Horned Lord, knowing that he could neither bend the knee nor show throat; that either could be construed as weakness....

"*Rob*!"

So he plastered on the cocky smirk that had more than once earned him an arse-thump from his mother's besom, and turned around.

Gamelyn was striding across the cobbles, an irrepressible grin scrawled over his face. "You're still here! I was hoping you wouldn't get away before I finished my errand, and then Brand said he'd sent his lad to help the captain and the forester, so I knew you must be staying." He was laughing, and seemed no different, really, than the lad in the forest.

Except for the clothes. Worn tunic and leather breeks had given way to a fine woolen tunic trimmed with silk threads, soft linen braies, and a cape almost the same green as his eyes. It all made Gamelyn look... older, somehow. As if he'd all to the sudden grown to fit them.

"You're tarted up a bit nicer than usual," Rob drawled. He was not about to admit to the trepidation writhing in the pit of his belly. Not.

Gamelyn snorted. "You're not."

"We canna all afford fancy threads, can we? I'll have you know this is me best tunic!"

"I meant your hair, not your clothes. Do you never take a comb to it?"

"It's windy," Rob defended. Then growled, "Watch it, now!" as Gamelyn started to grab his arms.

"Aye, sure enough. Come on." Gamelyn looked around, shrugged, then led deeper into the stable's deep-hewn cool. Rob followed as Gamelyn took an abrupt left then halted. "The boxes are full, but you can tie up here, near Diamant."

A row of horse boxes, all occupied, spanned beyond them. Motioning to several metal tie rings attached just above their heads, Gamelyn took Arawn's rein. "Who's this, then? Wait... Willow's all right, isn't she?"

Rob nodded, tying his father's chestnut to a free ring. "She's just not fast enough for the long rides me and Da take for forestry duties, but her foals meant Da could do some horse tradin' for Arawn. *And* the extra fodder for him." Rob grinned and walked over to Diamant, giving his rump a fond slap. "Thanks to you, old fellow."

Diamant gave a grunt and sidled his rump closer for a scratch. Rob obliged.

"It's good to see you!" Gamelyn tied Arawn, then skipped over and grabbed Rob's arms once again, looking him up and down. "This is brilliant, you know. We shan't be bothered here, save by Brand, and he and his lad think your father has hung the moon or something."

"Or something," Rob agreed, and raised a palm to lightly smack Gamelyn's cheek. To his surprise, Gamelyn gave a pained hiss. As he recoiled, Rob could see the nasty gashes along cheek and jaw.

"I'm sorry... but bloody hell, whatever happened to you?"

Gamelyn shrugged it away. "I was sparring. With my brother—"

"Your brother?" The slow burn of ill will that rose in Rob's chest surprised him.

Gamelyn twitched his shoulders again, which just made Rob angrier. "No doubt when I am a better swordsman, I'll avoid the consequences."

All Rob could think of, suddenly, was that knob of a soldier who had knocked him off his horse. Surely a nobleman's son didn't have to put up with such a thing. "What kind of brother sets himself to beat shit from you?"

The green eyes swiveled his way. "Are you angry on my account, Rob Loxley?"

The question, stated so baldly, threw him. Rob opened his mouth, but those eyes, still leveled upon him, made his tongue stick behind his teeth, mute. Then Gamelyn gave a tiny, one-sided smile that, for some reason, further silenced Rob, and asked, "Does that mean you forgive me for almost losing the buck, last time I visited?"

Well, didn't that figure. Exasperation freed Rob's tongue, quite abruptly. "I dinna carry grudges like a nobleman," he huffed. "We had it out then, all good and proper. It's done."

The smile had broadened. "So you giving me a split lip is different than my brother giving it to me?"

Now this was absolutely unfair. "I didna knock you with a mailed fist, did I?"

Gamelyn's grin slipped. "I didn't tell you that."

"Aye, well, I know what a slap from a mailed fist looks like, don't I?"

The grin was truly gone, now. "But… you haven't any mail—"

"Of course I've no mail, you great prat; happens I've likely been on the receiving end."

Gamelyn had a very strange look on his face. "And your father didn't stop it?"

"Like your father didn't?" This line of questioning was just brassing Rob off, truth be told.

"That's… different."

"Aye. It is. Quite."

Gamelyn just kept peering at him, in that odd, passive but insistent *I'm not forcing any truths from you but... tell me* way he had. And what was Rob supposed to say? Adam had power—real power, the kind that could change hearts and minds—but it wasn't enough to stop an angry soldier from knocking his son about? That Sir Ian obviously had the power that counted—his own castle and spoils, people who had to bow and scrape, serve him and his family—yet thought that holding that power meant he had to encourage his own sons to fight like dogs? Not wolves; there was sense in their order, in the strongest holding the pack with his will and strength. Dogs were too like people, the weak ones often ruling just because they played dirty.

"Here." Rob started digging in his pouch. He had to *do* something—either to cover up his own sudden awkwardness, or Gamelyn's, he wasn't sure—but once his fingers met with the small pot jar, he knew what he was looking for. It was the perfect out.

Out from what? He wasn't sure, and he still wasn't sure as he grabbed Gamelyn's tunic and strong-armed him over to Diamant's manger, sat him against it. Diamant was, naturally, eating there, but when he thought to protest, Rob gave him a pat and a soft word. Diamant nuzzled down his front, gave Gamelyn a sigh just for good measure, then bent back to the corner of the manger that wasn't occupied by Gamelyn's behind.

"How do you do that?" Gamelyn always asked it, and Rob could have answered, but knew he shouldn't.

It's magic, don't you know? I'm son to what your Church claims is a demon, see, and I can speak the language of things that really ent got language, and if I was to tell you, would you pour pitch over me and set me afire, like me mam says your kind does?

"I just do. Belt up, and let me put some of this on your face."

Gamelyn smiled as Rob pulled the stopper from the pot jar and the familiar smell wafted out. Eluned's arnica ointment, infused with all sorts of other things that Marion knew but Rob didn't want to. It smelled well enough now, but not when it was being boiled up. Rob considered his target, reached out, and tilted

Gamelyn's face up to the light. Despite the lack of sun and the wind's force, the day was bright. The gash was clotted up, nasty with pus and swollen.

"Bloody hell, did you even bother to clean this?"

"I—"

"I didna realize your god told you bathing was a sin, too."

"It's not…. I… I bathe!" Gamelyn protested. "What do you mean, 'my' God? He's yours too, you know."

"Is he, then?" Rob restoppered the ointment.

"What?"

Rob didn't answer, simply went looking. If this was a proper stable, there'd be medicaments, fresh water.

"*What*?"

Well, and that was typical. If Gamelyn didn't know what was going on every moment…. "I need water."

A pause, then Gamelyn said, "There's a kettle always over the fire pit just outside."

"Hot water in a stable? I'll wager you even get hot water when you do bother with a bath." Rob's face went euphoric. "Hot water. What I'd give!"

"You've a hearth," Gamelyn pointed out.

"And we're only allowed to take so much wood from the forest," Rob said, still rummaging about. Surely there were rags, or something. "Hot water's sommat *we* canna afford. Where's the groom's box? Eh, never mind, you probably don't even know—"

"It's over against the wall, by the bridles." Gamelyn was curt.

Well, fine, then. Surely the grooms wouldn't get too arsy at him going through it for the benefit of their lord and master. Lord and master's son. Rob considered saying this out loud, snuck a look at Gamelyn, and decided he'd probably been bashed enough as it was.

Rob found a shallow burl bowl, went to the fire pit for warm water. There were several of the Abbess's soldiers taking their meal next to the fire pit. They shot a narrow look at Rob; he kept his eyes down and did his business quickly.

Finally he returned to the manger with a shallow wooden bowl of water and a reasonably clean stable rubber. Gamelyn's eyebrows were drawing together rather thunderously. Rob nudged Diamant with one shoulder and the stallion readily sidestepped. "We're cleaning up that cut. I ent putting Mam's good ointment on filth. Won't do any good that way, and she'd clout me for not doing m'job right."

"It's not 'your' job," Gamelyn murmured, rebellious. "I can do—"

"Aye, and you've done so well this far. Shut up and let me get on with it."

Gamelyn shut up. Not, however, without a roll of his green eyes.

And green as juniper needles, they were, even to the tiny hint of blue around the edges….

Juniper needles? Rob snorted at himself. Next he would be spouting girly poetry like his mam did on his da's birthing morning. Not that he knew any poetry, and whatever was possessing him?

The poncy ginger paramour….

Sod you, Scathelock, Rob thought, then Gamelyn closed those juniper-green eyes and held his face up with a compliance that hit Rob like a hundred-weight of sacked corn. Truly, it was all a massive *thud* in the chest, with the slip-slide-trickle of spillover rustling about his ribcage.

Gamelyn's eyelashes were tipped all pale on freckled cheeks, and strands of rose-gold hair caught against the damp of slightly parted lips with the rest scattering down, settling across the hard, skin-and-sinew bow of that neck. And the worst—the best?—was how Rob could see/smell/*feel* the pulse beating in that throat….

Oh. *Oh.*

Gamelyn opened his eyes, narrowed them on Rob. "What are you on about?"

You. I'm on about you, *Lady Huntress save me.* The bowl tottered, nearly slipped from the sudden laxness of Rob's fingers. That was the only thing lax, though—he was abruptly glad his mam had always insisted her offspring wear a snug linsey loin-wrap beneath their clothes instead of naught, because otherwise it would be pretty flaming obvious that his knob was about as blind-stupid and subtle as Diamant, there.

"Ha. Caught you, Hob-Robyn." Even Gamelyn using Eluned's nickname for him didn't blunt the edge of sudden want. "You were about to tup that on my head, weren't you?"

Nay, Rob thought, leaden-dull and shaken. *That ent what I was thinking of tupping.*

Perhaps he should tup the bowl, but over his own head. Perhaps it would help.

And chance would be a fine thing, at that. The perfect out? Nay, this was sinking him deeper in, somehow.

Gamelyn was bemused, still watching him. That didn't help, either. Gamelyn bemused was, all to the sudden, as subtly sexed up as….

As Diamant, there.

With a small growl, Rob tugged the cloth from about his neck and dunked it, then took it all dripping and laved it over Gamelyn's face.

"Hoy… ow… that's *hot*!"

"Better than cold. Dinna be such a bairn. I'd wager there was no whinging when you got that whack in the face."

"Whinging in front of Johan just makes him want to hear more of it."

"One of those that gets hot on a blood trail, eh?" Aye, just like the soldier. Noblemen were dogs, all right.

"That's—ow… *ow*… stop *digging*, will you?—that's one way to put it. Eh," Gamelyn twisted his face as Rob kept scrubbing, "Johan's all right. Just trying to knock some sense into my thick skull."

Thick… aye, that about described the predicament Rob found himself in; mesmerized by nothing more than the trickles of water runneling down the cords of Gamelyn's neck and beneath his tunic. Gamelyn twitched and gave a yank at the embroidered collar, canting it sideways and exposing a surprisingly substantial pad of pectoral muscle dusted with copper freckles. That led into a shallow dip of breastbone, and the smattering of gilt hair was shivering and lifting at the wet.

Bloody fucking hell. Gritting his teeth, Rob focused on the clotted gash on Gamelyn's jaw. "This is going to hurt more," he warned, though the gash wasn't as bad as he'd first thought. It was obviously painful; Gamelyn grimaced again and swore, low and inventive, beneath his breath.

"The priests would have at you for that, wouldn't they?" Rob quipped. "You've been listening to me far and away too much."

Gamelyn slid him a look, rolled his eyes once more then closed them. "Just have it done, will you?"

And bloody damn, not only did he have a rod in his loin-wrap that would make the Horned Lord proud, but it was back—the sense of… too much sensing, too much of… everything. It set him on edge, buzzing like a jiggered wasp behind his ears. His hands were shaking, again. Mayhap he should just hand over the arnica and whatsis, let Gamelyn apply it himself.

Mayhap he was a big coward.

Rob took his time at opening and dipping his fingers into the pot, reached out, and dabbed salve over the cut. And, since arnica was good for bruising, he started working up the rest of Gamelyn's face, all the while wondering if he had a liking for peculiar self-torture. Or was just plain daft.

Because that's what it was. Daft and gormless, to boot. It was also sharp as the knife along his hip, the realization that this was the first time he'd really ever touched Gamelyn. Oh, he'd touched lads before—Simon wasn't the first nor would he be the last—and it had been with much more direction and intent than a trail of fingers across a cheekbone. Rob knew what he liked and how to share that liking; he had nimble hands and a growing appreciation of what might be technique in a few more years. Will's teasings were simply that, and there had never been much need to take care because his own kind didn't have reason to take care. Sex was what nature was—making and bleeding, birth and dying. All to be venerated, not disparaged. Let the conquerors be damned in their contempt for such sacred things.

And that was the daftest of all, ill-advised beyond any sense or sanity. Gamelyn was *of* those conquerors. Of their religion. He even smelled of it: the heavy, thick incense Rob ever only caught wind of in the folds of the monk from Beauchief Abbey who visited Loxley for tithe and little else. And something else, too, besides sweat and horse… was it myrrh?

"He's your God, too."

Nay, he really ent.

It was foolish to keep at this. More than foolish… dangerous. Yet Rob couldn't pull away. A tiny ghost of a smile had begun quivering at the corner of Gamelyn's mouth, and Rob's fingertips were leaving slick tracks across the freckles on Gamelyn's cheek, riffling the fine down shading his jaw. Rob found himself leaning in—close, ever so close—found his breath turning to mist upon the balm skimming that upturned throat. Gamelyn gave a tiny, unconscious shiver, and his lower lip dropped in an outward sigh. Then those green eyes opened, slowly, angling toward him. There was puzzlement, and curiosity, and more than a little of *What in bloody hell?* But there was also an artless, deep-set *knowing,* a recognition of something being spoken, ever-so-silent.

"Gamelyn? Gamelyn!"

And just like that, the moment broke itself in twain. That hundredweight sack pressing Rob's breath tight in his chest had its underside sliced, and all the grain went funneling out to scatter about his feet.

Rob turned away, tapping the cork back into the mouth of the jar just as Sir Ian, trailed by several liveried men, came hobbling in.

"Gamelyn, where *are* you, boy? I need you to—" He stopped. "There you are. What in the devil are you…. Who is this?"

Rob turned to the lord, dipped his head, was careful to make no eye contact with anyone. Including Gamelyn. "Milord, I'm Rob of Loxley, son to—"

"Son to the forester, are you?" Like many of his kind, Sir Ian spoke with a firm haste, a for-granted authority. "I see."

"I was seeing to our horses, milord."

"Looks as if you were seeing more to my son." It was a drawl, and one Rob had no idea how to interpret. Yet he did not make the mistake of raising his gaze, even in curiosity.

"'Tis n-nothing," Gamelyn's voice was a tight stammer. Rob cut him a swift look beneath his brows, trying to decide what that stammer was founded on. "I was showing him a free spot for his horses and he saw that I'd cut my face, and thought to help. His mother is a healer."

"A healer, eh?" As Sir Ian came closer, Rob dropped his eyes. "You're the one who found Gamelyn in the Peak Forest, aren't you?"

"Aye, milord. 'Twas Loxley Chase, actually, the woodland there."

There was a silence. Rob held to it for as long as he could stand, then peeked at Gamelyn, who was staring at his father with quirked brows. Rob followed that gaze to Sir Ian, who was standing with his hand outstretched.

"Well, young man," Sir Ian fussed. "Obviously you know my son, by chance or design. Am I allowed to know what concoction you have there?"

Rob flicked a glance toward the two guards behind Sir Ian. One was scratching at Diamant's rump, and the other watching with only minimal interest. With a sidelong glance to Gamelyn—no help there—Rob handed over the pot jar of ointment.

Sir Ian uncorked it, took a light sniff. "Did your mother the healer make this, then?"

Rob gave a tight nod.

Sir Ian's nostrils flared. "I see. And did your mother—"

"Milord?" This time it was Adam who came through the barn entry, at a quickened pace, his expression troubled. "My lord, I hope my son has not been a trouble to you—"

"Indeed, Loxley." Sir Ian plied the stopper almost thoughtfully, then gave Rob a wink. "Your son is no trouble at all; he was merely tending mine in a goodly enough fashion. I understand your wife is a healer?"

Adam quirked his brows at Rob; Rob shrugged and jerked his head toward Gamelyn. Adam took a breath, said, slow, "Aye, milord, she knows some herb lore. This and that."

"I was about to tell your lad that my old nurse was a wortwife." Sir Ian was nodding. "Quite a talented woman, and this ointment of your wife's takes me right back. Which is a long way, mind you. The smell, you know, honey and all the herbs. I'd no idea there was a wise woman in these parts."

"They're about, my lord," Adam said carefully.

"The surgeons would see them gone, no doubt," Rob murmured to Gamelyn—quietly, he thought, but Adam turned.

"Rob." The warning was unmistakable.

Sir Ian laughed suddenly. "I've no doubt you're right, boy. But your father is in the right, even more, to heed some caution. Not every castle's keeper would hear of a woman brewing potions and think 'healer' instead of 'witch'."

Abruptly Rob could hear… sense… *whatever*… that soft-thick hum again. He twitched his shoulders, exchanged grave glances with his father, then saw Gamelyn eyeing him with sudden trepidation.

"Perhaps," Sir Ian mused, peering at the pot jar in his hand, "she might have some aid for an old, ill man?"

"Milord?" Adam's face had gone blank.

Sir Ian straightened, looked Adam in the eye. "As you no doubt can see, my health is… questionable. Would your wife be willing to set her skill to it?" Sir Ian peered over at Gamelyn, a tiny smile quirking his stern mouth. "You're a father, Loxley, surely you can understand. Perhaps it is base of me, but there are many things I would prefer to see in this life before I go to meet the next."

"It ent base at all, milord," Adam said, very soft. "Surely Eluned can aid you."

Sir Ian nodded. "She is welcome here. You all are welcome, and I hope you will at least sup with us and rest for the night, as you would have done in Worksop."

A foot nudged the back of Rob's thigh; he turned to see Gamelyn grinning. As for Rob himself, he was not so sure, considering, that staying overnight was a good idea.

Adam bowed very low. "You honor me and my son, milord of Blyth."

Sir Ian tipped his chin then, the half smile still upon his lips, limped from the barn. His two paxmen followed, with care for their lord's pace.

"Perhaps you could stay with me?" Gamelyn offered.

Rob threw his father a look, hardly understanding what it was he pled for, only that… that….

Bloody hell, he was in for it.

"That ent fitting, lad," Adam said, his mien stern. "Moreover, you two must take care. You've already had one lesson in minding your place, Rob; don't court another, aye?"

Ire, hot and sour as bile, rose in Rob's throat. The look he threw his father turned captious.

"I mean it. Both of you heed me, now. We ent in t' Wode, here."

Gamelyn was the one who answered, soft and somewhat downcast. "I understand."

Adam's gaze flickered to his bruised face. "I'll wager you do, lad."

Then he was gone, following the others.

☙ VIII ❧

"ARE you sure you want to sleep here?" Adam crossed his arms and peered down the stone aisleway of the stable. "Captain's been instructed to offer us both a place in the guard officers' quarters."

Rob shook his head. If he had to sleep, trammeled and nigh smothered, amongst stones that had been built with the sweat and blood of people who'd had no choice but to raise them? Better to hear the soft, homey sounds of munching fodder, the groans and sighs of creatures that had little more say in life than he did, and were more pleasant to be around than any soldier. Even that friendly captain.

"All right, then. I need to accept his courtesy, you understand?"

Rob nodded. Just as well. He wanted… no, *needed*… to be alone.

No, he needed to get out of these walls, take Arawn and thunder off over the land, running the night like the Horned Lord upon His Hunt….

Adam put firm hands on Rob's shoulders, gave him a shake. "No wandering, mind."

"I waint, Da!" It came out sharper than Rob had intended.

His father's grip tightened further, then went lax. Adam looked as if he wanted to say something, then shook his head. Leaning forward, he brushed a kiss to Rob's forelock and then departed, the soles of his boots a heavy, almost resigned cadence against the stones. There was an upheaval of voices, laughter, and light as he opened the heavy door across the way—the guardsmen's quarters—then it muffled again as he closed it behind him.

Silence. Finally.

Rob breathed it in like burning sandalwood flung into the need-fires, let the soft background of stable noises lull him. He hadn't allowed himself to realize how inwardly keyed up he was, between the day's happenings and Gamelyn….

And. Gamelyn.

The moon was rising, just visible over the thick walls. Despite what his father thought, Rob knew better than to wander a fortified and fancy gaol without leave, so he stayed put. He did, however, step out into the moonlight, asking….

What? What exactly *did* he want?

It was usually so simple. To want, to reach out, ask. Be disappointed or rewarded.

"We ent in t' Wode, here."

This wasn't… simple.

He couldn't believe it, anyway. He'd never imagined… never even thought to look to Gamelyn in such a way. But now?

Now, his imagination was whirling him widdershins about a fire he couldn't quench.

The moon wasn't helping. She touched him, smoothed cool, silver fire over the heat of his cheeks and promised… well, the moon. The sight of his own skin hinted at what Gamelyn's might look like, all fair and bare….

Nay, not helping. Not at all.

Boots, clicking against hard ground, a slow rhythm that suggested purpose—the guard, no doubt. Patrolling the castle for peasants who were wandering where they didn't belong, for Heathen scum bathing in the moon, for anything they could bully, like.

Rob vanished back into the shadows, watched a brace of soldiers move past, alert. He made no sound, not even a breath, and found himself sweating with relief as they didn't turn to see him, and then despised himself for the fear.

"'Tis well t' not be seen."

A whisper from beside him, and bloody hell, but how had the stable lad snuck up on him like that? He was being a proper git, no question, literally mooning after something he couldn't have and heeding only the lurchings of his knob! Idiot!

He started to speak; the stable lad put a finger to his lips, jerked his head to bid Rob follow him.

Slightly mystified, Rob did.

They wound back through to the back of the stables, to a small alcove where the lad obviously slept, around the corner from a turret leading, it would seem, into the bowels of the keep. It was a nice little cot, as such things went: partitioned with wood, so likely a stall at one time, dry and warm from the body heat of the animals, and convenient to their care. Lots of straw to pad a bed, and the lad looked as if he'd just come from there, straw in his brown hair. There was the smell, all about them, of corn and chaff, urine and dung; the lad smelled more horse than human, and it was lovely. Walking over to the head of it, the lad reached under the pad of skins he used to cushion his head, then rose, holding his hand out to Rob.

From his fingers dangled a leathern cord, and in his palm was a tiny carving: a wooden stag's head, horned and polished until it gleamed in the faint light.

The lad nodded, his eyes lustrous, and motioned to Rob with the necklet, offering.

"I… Nay. It's too—"

Again the lad put his finger to his lips, requesting silence, and instead of trying to get Rob to take the necklet, stepped close and threaded it over his dark head. The lad's breath misted Rob's ear as he pulled back; Rob reached out, took several wisps of straw from that mop of hair and held them up, smiling. Let them flutter to the ground.

The lad looked into Rob's eyes, smiled. Bent down and put his lips to the amulet—and that was what it was, of that Rob had no doubt. He could feel the little tremors of power within it.

The lad was also leaving no doubt about what else he thought to offer. His hands had flattened against Rob's chest, his pelvis starting to sway against Rob's, with a knot in his loose braies to rival Rob's own already substantial erection. The lad's mouth had returned to his ear, tongue darting. As he slid one hand from Rob's chest downward, seeking then finding, Rob sucked in a sharp breath, started to speak again.

Again, the stable lad covered his words, only this time with his mouth.

It was gentle, asking. Rob answered it with his tongue, probing, and the lad whimpered into his mouth, pressed closer. Slim, agile fingers made quick work of unlacing his leather breeks, bared him, curled about him, began to tug. Neither were Rob's hands idle; it was a mere matter of one tie, at the top of the lad's thin-worn braies, then Rob was fisting him, slow and firm, and the lad was kicking his braies aside, pushing into Rob's hand even as he coaxed Rob likewise.

No words, just need. Hands stroking, lips and tongues tangling, quick and growing frantic, the lad giving tiny whimpers against Rob's collarbone as he shuddered and spilled into Rob's hand. Rob gave his own whimper, first as the lad's hand left him, then a gasp as the lad pushed him against the partition behind them and knelt down, unlaced Rob's boots and pulled them, peeled him from his breeks. The lad knelt lower; there was the quick touch of a tongue to first one instep, then the other, then the brown head came back up. Paused at the level of Rob's hips. Leaned forward, covered him, took him in.

It didn't take much, not with this, not as keyed up as he was. Just a hint of teeth, and wet nap of a very agile tongue, and a hand stroking and cupping his testicles, and Rob was driving forward, clutching hay-strewn brown hair with one hand and smothering his groans into the other, finally biting down so the silence… heady, sacred silence… would not be supplanted.

The lad was peering up at him, expectant, and more by instinct than anything, Rob took the lad's hands and pulled him to his feet, laid kisses into those palms. Knelt and ran his lips along the lad's feet, then his belly, then rose and kissed his mouth. Lingered there, savoring the sweet-salt still lingering on the lad's tongue.

The lad stepped back, knelt to grab up his braies, then gestured to his bed. Rob frowned, started to shake his head, but the lad merely smiled, gestured again, making it very plain that Rob was to stay there. Then he bowed, murmured, "*Bendith*, lord."

And disappeared into the shadows.

cs৪০

GAMELYN spent the first quarter of the night wishing he was elsewhere. He didn't even climb into bed; instead, he clambered up into his window and watched the wind whip the tree line into sinuous shapes across the rise of the waning moon.

His jaw had subsided from sullen throb to pleasant buzz.

And he wanted to see the stag again.

But again, he didn't, for reasons he wasn't even sure how to elucidate. Gamelyn had never before questioned the need to hunt anything, but had found himself secretly hoping the white stag would stay wily, free and alive.

No stag. But his breath caught in his throat as someone inched out into the courtyard below.

Rob. He obviously wasn't sleeping, either, as he trod carefully out from the stable block, looking either way, cautious. He looked as if he was about to do something wayward, or devious.

He did neither. He tossed the pitch of hair back from his face, lifted it up to the sky, extended his arms above him as if warming himself in sunlight. Only it was moonlight, streaming down on Rob as the thick three-quarter face of the moon cleared the trees. Gamelyn watched, a bemused smile tickling at his mouth.

Well. If Rob was up, maybe he should go down. At least, if neither of them were going to sleep, they could spend the time in something of interest.

He'd not undressed, so he waited only long enough to pull on his boots. On his way out, he grabbed up a small bag and put some fruit in it—Rob was always hungry.

His door would groan, but not if he yanked it quickly in the last quarter of the swing inward. This time of night, with guards detailed particularly to the guest chambers in the south wing, there would likely only be one guard making his rounds. He peered both ways down the hall, listening carefully, was merely treated to the sound of Otho snoring several doors down and across. Or maybe it was Otho's wife, Alais—he truly couldn't be sure.

Careful, Gamelyn closed his door behind him. His teachers from Loxley Chase had been thorough—he didn't make a sound, hardly even breathed. He tiptoed down the passage, passing his father's massive solar with a fond touch to the wooden door, then carefully past Johan's door. Johan was as much a night owl as Gamelyn himself, and though Johan spent his sleeplessness in a different fashion, it was never wise to trust he was so occupied he'd not emerge.

However, emergence was unlikely at this point. There was a rhythmic creaking and grunting coming from beyond the door. Gamelyn slowed, stopped. He knew he shouldn't, but the illicit lure of such a thing merely made it all the more mesmerizing. Johan had a lot to confess when it came to what he did in his bedchamber—several serving girls in particular seemed to attract his attentions. But if Johan was going to spend time in Purgatory, then so was Gamelyn, since he had an unfortunate vividness of imagination. Recreating what was likely going on behind Johan's door when the bedstrings popped so was all too easy, fantasy unencumbered by what expertise Gamelyn didn't have.

Another dull sound, rhythmic and slow, rived Gamelyn from erotic fascination; he turned toward the main hall entry, identified it as the tread of the guard. He sped the rest of the way and down the back stair just as the guard came walking through.

A strong draft sucked up the black stair as he disappeared downward, sending welcome cool over the sudden flush of his cheeks. Then it wafted back downward, feathering his hair into his eyes, and Gamelyn smiled. It was comforting, in an odd way—as if the castle was a breathing entity. Not so fine in winter, though. They had to shut off this tunnel and get to the stable from a much less direct route. Putting a careful hand to the wall, Gamelyn kept going.

His grin widened. Perhaps he could sneak up on Rob! What a triumph that would be. He'd never managed it before, but this was his territory, *his* place, and one that he knew like the backs of his sword-callused hands. As well as Rob knew his forest.

He alighted on the bottom stair as noiseless as any ghost, blinked in the dim to catch his bearings. He could hear the lovely rhythm of horses chewing their fodder, an occasional snort, a shift of shod feet against straw and hard-packed dirt. He would have to be mindful making his way through; this stairwell was used by a very few, so sometimes things got moved here and there, and what with the extra horses….

He froze in place as a soft groan sounded to his left. Then a gasp of breath, then a rustle. Not horse, but human. Reminding himself that the stable lad's cot was just on the other side of the wall he now leaned on, Gamelyn forced his muscles to relax. Likely the lad was murmuring in his sleep.

Better to check, though. Using the wall as prop and concealment, he peeked around it just to check.

His breath staggered, slipped, then nearly choked him.

The stable lad wasn't asleep.

And Rob wasn't out in the moonlight anymore.

But it was as if he was still basking in it, neck arched, head flung back against the partition, mouth parted in an aching, endless gasp. Gamelyn found himself echoing it, clinging to the cool stone of the wall, staring mindlessly while the stable lad ran his hands and mouth over Rob's body as if he were performing some sacrament.

It couldn't have been more than a moment, but it felt like forever, with something strange… foreign… *painful*… coursing through Gamelyn's own limbs, pulsing as if to match the beating of his heart, stiffening him from nape to knees.

Gamelyn wasn't sure how he got up the stair without being seen or somehow heard. But he did, and he closed the door behind him, leaned up against it and panted like a mad dog, eyes wide into the darkness.

He spent the second quarter of the night squirming and aching hard. He spent the third quarter easing that ache—not just once, but thrice.

Then he crawled from bed and spent the remainder of the night on his knees.

ᴄᴙᴚᴐ

"ALWAYS, you must ask before you take. Seek the enaid*—the soul—of the mere, for sympathy and benison, so that you shall See true in its waters."*

Marion had done as instructed; asked of the mere, then gathered the fresh water just below where the upper rivulets fed in and not where it drained out into the stream leading toward the village. Beginnings were easier to parse than endings—too many paths between here and there, too many things that could be set in motion to ken a reliable future.

And she was still learning.

Now Marion was on her knees, hands cupped over the bowl. Dew shimmered in the grass about her, the silver bowl of lake water glinted on the small, woven wicker stand before her. It was predawn, that time when the sun's radiance was just beginning to light the horizon of the distant hill leading to Loxley; that quiet-calm stillness when day held its breath, as if waiting to see what would come with the sun.

About her, Eluned circled deosil, almost gliding with bare feet and skirts brushing the grass. "Close your eyes, now. Feel the breath of Her seeping in—"

"Right now all I feel seeping is the damp," Marion answered, unable to halt a grin.

"That too is part of Her," Eluned chided. "Discomfort can bring connection."

Marion nodded and closed her eyes. But the more she tried to disregard the cool, heavy soak against her shins, the more it seemed to prey upon her attention. Her right knee, in particular, was not only wet but had a small stone lodged against the outside of it, a tiny edge of irritation. And the damp was wicking its way up the thick weave of her skirts, encroaching where thigh met calf….

Cool, dry hands cupped her cheeks, gave her skull a tiny shake. "Lass, lass. Where is your concentration lately?"

Marion spoke before she thought. "It seems the more I try, the less it comes."

"Does it, then?" The firm grip softened, Eluned's strong fingers stroking gentle at her temples. Her voice dropped to a murmur. "As a bairn must learn the walking, from creep to crawl to careful steps, so must we learn the ways of the Wise, handed down since the first woman squatted to birth a girl child."

"Rob never crawled," Marion said. "He rolled everywhere. And watched us like a hawk in a meadow. Then he grabbed my skirts and pulled himself up to walk."

"Aye. That one," Eluned said, "has been a riddle his entire existence. Even as the Horned Lord rides a reckless Hunt, snarling His horns in the weavings of *tynged*, your brother's arrow looses itself into the chaos and darkness, and he will follow."

"Then what does that make me?" Marion protested.

"An answer. You bear the arrow's gift and put it to string. The Lady measures *tynged's* tangled weaving and plaits it. A rebirth, bringing future from chaos."

Marion laughed suddenly. "Even here, we clean up a man's messes."

Eluned chuckled, then gave a lock of Marion's red hair a tug, sudden and sharp. "Enough of men and boys. You spend enough time on that now as it is."

Marion felt a flush crawl over her cheek, but refused to duck her head. Her mother's hands softened, once more stroked through Marion's curls and put light pressure at her temples. "Yours is the rite of making, changing. Already you counsel your brother in the ways of our path, so what has changed, there? Look into the water, think upon the tangled weft. Surely 'twill unravel before you."

Marion leaned forward, peering into the bowl. Her mother's fingers trailed through her hair and down her back, a soft touch, grounding. The water within the bowl was still, reflecting back only wide-open gray eyes, freckles dusted over fair skin, auburn curls frizzled from the damp still lying upon the ground. Her lips tightened in frustration, echoed in the bowl.

"Breathe upon the water," Eluned murmured, rising, moving away to begin pacing her circle once more. "*Anadlu y tân dy enaid.*"

Marion repeated the words, twisting her tongue about the ancient syllables. A chant. A charm.

Breathe the fire of your soul.

A charm of making, as she breathed across the water's surface and it rippled. Shivered.

It started low, almost beyond true hearing but nevertheless there. The sound pressed behind her ears, escalating, one note leading into another. She frowned, angled her head to one side then the other, but the feeling… sound… did not abate. If anything, it grew in intensity, and when she pulled her hands from about the bowl to press fingers behind her ears, the bowl began to shudder.

The image reflected in the water—gray eyes, crimson hair—bled and ran in rivulets, gray turning to smut-dark, and crimson to bright licks of flame.

Breathe the fire….

Marion angled forward, bending closer. The silver of the bowl was bright, so bright as to burn the backs of her eyes, yet she did not turn away. She merely brought her hands forward once more and held them, fingers splayed, out and over the sudden brilliance. Spoke, no murmur but a command, soft and dangerous.

"*Anadlu y tân dy enaid.*"

And the brilliance opened up beneath her.

Soul-fire, burning bright, hot and deadly-vengeful: the hunter watches— burns—*as his prey walks before him. Helmless, joking with his fellow soldiers, identity no longer a cipher or a question burned long ago into a tiny boy's brain. Walking the waning moonlight untrammeled....*

He should not be free.

Marion heard the thoughts as if they were her own, yet they were ones she had never guessed at, never let herself feel: *I remember. I know who you are. What you did.*

Instead of sleeping in a borrowed bed, a hunt is joined. Solitary. This must be done alone, and the hunter's hand must be the one to mete the justice left undone. His tools are simple but precise: a flying rowan found and witch-wood gathered, a fire kindled, a branch split and carved and spoken over. Then signed with blood and cast in fire, fletched with goose and the cerulean tufts that mark his own, his covenant. The hunter is but a fledgling witch, but the right—the rites—of vengeance give his fingers skill, give his tynged *a final, fateful potency....*

Marion shuddered, tried to close her eyes.

She could not.

The weapon forged, now it is human prey the hunter stalks....

Human? Not likely. Scum. Spawn of a damned and Motherless race that should never have been allowed to step foot on Her green, fecund soil. Bow strung and ready, hunter teases game, pulls it from guard post to forest fingers, sets it to follow him in a merry chase that will lead to but one thing.

*Hunter crouches, sets spell-wood to string, sights. Whispers Death along the shaft, sets peacock tufts a-dance. "*Marwolaeth.*"*

"Death," she echoed, a whimper, a heated breath across contained water, and the scene rippled, danced in silver fire. "Nay, you canna, you *must* not—"

Death. Death finds you now.

The hunter clicks his tongue against his teeth, mocking. Prey halts mid-step, not a pace away as Hunter casts off his shadows, uncloaks his being.

She knows the one who steps from the tree, takes aim with his witched arrow, calls the spell:

*"*Marwolaeth yn canfod chi nawr*!"*

"Will!" Marion's cry shrilled into the morning. "Will, *nay*!"

... as the man who raped and killed his mother falls, an arrow in his throat.

ଔ

"N—!" ROB bolted up from his pallet before he'd fully woken, a hoarse gasp truncating whatever protest he thought to make. He sat there, shuddering with panic and unsure where he was for the longest moments of his life, his own breath thumping deep in his chest, held hostage by whatever it was.

Then the tight band of panic/fear/horror behind his eyes popped, and his breath released, and he fell forward, clutching at a thin woolsey blanket and thick-bedded straw. Dust motes danced up about him and his eyes followed them, up into the early-morning sunlight coming in from the east-most stable entry. The motes rather abruptly staggered, whirling in new dervishes as they collided with a figure leaning on the front partition of the stall where Rob had slept.

And memory returned to him, further displacing any panic, banishing dreams back where they belonged.

Rob blinked, started to thank the stable lad for letting him sleep here, then realized it wasn't the lad standing there. This figure was broader, taller, with a nimbus of ginger-gilt hair.

And there was absolutely no hay in that hair, combed all sleek and smooth.

Unlike Rob, who realized abruptly that he was all over straw, even to a long, thin strand of it caught in the fine line of fur along his breastbone. His tunic was hanging unlaced off one shoulder, it sidled somewhat back in place as he raised a hand to his head and encountered even more straw.

Of course. It figured that His Lordship would show up looking like a well-groomed warhorse when the peasant had been sleeping in that horse's stall and looked like something from the rubbish tip.

And Rob was doubly daft, he was, to start along that line of thought this early in the morning, and before even a chance at breakfast....

"Did you sleep well?" Gamelyn's voice had a strange undercurrent to it, almost hoarse, and he gave a cough, clearing his throat.

Rob considered the question, gave a fond smile as he remembered what had sent him to sleep, indeed well, at that. "I did. And yourself?"

Gamelyn shrugged, backlit shoulders betraying a maroon color to his tunic as they moved. Then he inexplicably ducked down behind the partition. There was a *clank*, then a slow rattle of something metallic, but he didn't rise right away.

With a puzzled shrug, Rob rolled to his feet, gave a shiver and shudder that set the blood moving in sluggish veins, then stretched to set his back a-creaking and scratched at his belly. Setting fingers to his tunic edges, looking for and thankfully finding the lacing hanging there, he started to tie it together, raising his eye to perhaps find where Gamelyn had disappeared.

Only he hadn't. Gamelyn was standing at the little cot's entrance, profile to the bright sun, a tray in his hands. "I... um. I thought you might be hungry."

It wasn't until after Gamelyn had led him out to a small table at the stable's stone frontage that Rob wondered how Gamelyn had known to find him in the stable lad's cot instead of the guardsman's quarters with Adam. But the odd, almost wary looks that Gamelyn kept darting his way were daunting, as was the curl of heat in his gut that would have made the words stutter and tangle on his tongue anyway, had he uttered more than a few of them together.

So he concentrated on eating. And most abjectly did not notice Gamelyn's hands, deft and economical with the knife as he trimmed the rind from the cheese and cut pieces of apple to dole out between them. Or the way his lashes brushed his cheeks, tipped with bronze not unlike the freckles scattered beneath them as he looked down at what he was doing.

Or how Rob found himself thinking of what had been gifted him the previous night, bedding and breath… only it wasn't the stable lad's mouth upon him Rob was imagining as, across the table, Gamelyn sucked an apple slice off his knife like his mouth was *made* for….

Rob bit his tongue. Intentional, and sharp. Because the inseam of his leather breeks was tight enough to geld him by sheer pressure alone. Were he sitting across the table from that stable lad there would be no question what they would do, and merely an exchange of touch or eyes meeting to ask, aye or nay. But this wasn't the stable lad. Or Simon.

He'd already given a wrong look to his "betters" on this trip—two, counting the glare he'd given that bloody-minded sadist of a soldier and the Motherless clot had *deserved* it—but all it had gotten Rob in return was an aching head and a reminder of just how bloody powerless they truly were.

"I…." Gamelyn also seemed to be struggling for words, for some reason. "I wish you could stay."

Nay, you really don't.

"There you are!" Adam came striding over, and the relief in his voice tickled a thin worry in Rob, hearkening back to waking, panicked, from a dream too dread to remember straight away. "I looked for you when they brought breakfast to the guard." He slowed, seeing who was with Rob—and their repast.

"Hullo," Gamelyn said, smiling. "I brought enough for you, as well."

"Hullo, lad," Adam replied, soft. "Thank you kindly, but I've already broken my fast." He turned to Rob, blue eyes strangely muted, dark. "Son. It's time we headed home."

Rob started to question, then saw the set to his father's jaw, the disquiet in his stance, and fell silent. Worry once again began to chew at him, an instinctive reaction that he couldn't halt, or truly define. Without another word he turned, went to saddle the horses.

Midway through, the stable lad came, gave silent assistance. He handed the rein to Adam's horse over to Rob, dark eyes shining and a shy smile on his lips, then touched reverent fingertips to the stag amulet on Rob's chest and started to back away.

Rob held up a hand, dropped the reins to ground-tie the horses. Setting his own fingers to the leather amulet strap, he tugged it over his head. The stable lad's eyes went from shining to apprehensive; he shook his head tightly, backed another step.

"Nay." Rob said softly. "I know it was a gift. But now, I'm gifting it back to you. Please, accept it."

The stable lad smiled, then, and bent his head, allowing Rob to thread the amulet over his brown hair. Rob pulled a bit of chaff from it; the lad nuzzled his hand then reached out and took a bit of straw from Rob's own curls. Eyes meeting Rob's, he let it flutter to the ground. "M'name's John, lord. My people are of Hathersage."

"I'm no lord. I'm of Loxley, not far from there. My name's Rob—"

"I know, lord." And the lad vanished into the stable's shadows.

Bemused, Rob took up the reins again, gave first Arawn then his father's gelding a pat, then looked over to the entry.

Stopped.

Gamelyn was there, his brows furrowed; when he saw Rob turn to him, his eyes flitted aside. There was a flush to his cheek that, had he been one of Rob's own people, would have been telling. As it was, Rob could not even guess at what it told.

Instead, he walked back out into the sun, a horse at each shoulder.

Adam came over, took his horse. "I've already made our thanks to Sir Ian," he said and tipped his chin to Gamelyn. "Good day, young master." It was unaccountably terse.

Rob had to look away. "Will you come to the Chase anon?" he asked of Gamelyn, and immediately wanted to thwack himself upside his own head. Was he just *looking* to suffer?

"As I can." Gamelyn wasn't looking at him, any more than Rob could meet his father's gaze.

"All right, then," Rob said, and swung up on his horse.

☙❧

IT WAS the hardest thing he'd ever had to do, go down to the stable as if nothing had happened. The tray had helped. Having something to do with his hands had helped. Because more than once Gamelyn had wanted to reach out and comb the straw from Rob's black curls—just like that stable lad had done!—and if that wasn't *more* than foolish.

It seemed almost… dangerous. For some reason. Like he should go to confessional—and right this moment—kneel down and let it spill from his lips, be taken from him and absolved….

As if he'd not knelt down enough during the night, begging forgiveness for something he wasn't sure he even understood. He couldn't even take it to the confessional. How could he ask for absolution from something he couldn't even put a name to?

He wasn't sure what was more disturbing: that Rob had let another lad touch him like that, or Gamelyn's own reaction to it, all tangled and unholy and….

"Gamelyn!"

Oh, God in Heaven. One thing he did not at the moment feel up to facing was Johan.

"Gamelyn, the lad said you were here; show yourself! Papa wants you!" Johan rounded the corner, boots thudding on the entry stones of the stable walk, trailed off as he saw Gamelyn bent over the little table, putting mugs and leftover scraps onto the tray.

"Leave that, lad, I'll have someone fetch it. Papa has sent for you." A pause. "What are you doing breaking your fast in the stable, of all things?"

Gamelyn straightened, leaving the tray and turning to his brother. "I brought down some food for R—for the forester's son."

"Which he could have gotten in the guardsman's cot like his father. Are you courting the lass's brother, now?"

"Good *God*, no!" Gamelyn retorted, furious for how his voice canted up, tight and high.

Johan merely blinked. He smirked and made a show of crossing his arms. Gamelyn abruptly wished he could wipe that smirk off in the dung heap. "It just shows that you might have some common sense after all, to make an effort to disarm and charm the brother of the girl you're fucking—"

With a growl, Gamelyn swung. His fist landed, an uppercut to Johan's chin, and sent him flying back, skidding backward over the entry stones.

Neither one of them could, for long moments, believe what had just happened. Green eyes met green, both wide.

Then Johan, inexplicably, laughed. "Well, well, Brother. I guess that's payback for that lovely scratch on your jaw."

Nay, but I guess it might be a fair start. Brother.

"Fair play to you, then." Johan put out a hand. "Help me up."

"Help yourself up," Gamelyn gritted out and, turning on one heel, he quit the stable.

꧁ IX ꧂

"NO QUESTION it was murder. Foul and treasonous. I saw the results myself." Otho gave a small, muttered curse, kneed several of the whining, milling hounds from underfoot and continued shrugging out of his cloak. He gave a smile to his wife, Alais, as she took it from him, tsking over the muddied state. A servant promptly relieved Alais of the cloak; she motioned to another, who rushed over with a bowl of water and a cloth over one arm.

Otho nodded thanks, cupping the water in his big hands and splashing it over his grimed face, his words coming in small bursts. "Who would expect it? One of the king's own foresters! The villein is long gone. We didn't find the dead man until after sunup. Of course I headed home straight away." He finished his ablutions, mopped the proffered cloth over this face and neck.

All the scions of Blyth and their honored visitor were listening, shocked and absorbed. They had just sat down to luncheon as Otho had arrived in the great hall, agitated and still filthy from the road.

"Your haste at returning is warranted, son," Sir Ian approved. "You can tell us more during the meal... Sire! Lass! That's enough!" The hounds so named retreated, one with a yelp—not necessarily at Sir Ian's order, but because Johan threw a cup at them.

It took everything in Gamelyn's control to not leap up and start asking questions. Cheeks burning, he kept his eyes upon the hunk of bread in his hand. At least he was sure of this much: Rob and Adam were well on their way home, and far away from what their companions had seemingly done. It had nothing to do with Rob.

"I do apologize once again for barging in on the meal like this—particularly to you, Reverend Lady," Otho directed to their guest. "But I wanted to catch you before you left with too light an escort."

Abbess Elisabeth was pale—and no wonder. "It was just the one man, you say? None else were killed? The villeins harmed no one else?"

"Well, what they did to the one man was quite enough." Otho sat down to the board, gratefully filled his platter from the tray his wife handed him. The hounds that looked to him in particular settled down for the wait—now that the excitement of greeting was over, they'd get their share in time. "The man was found near the southern tree verge, staked out like a goat left for wolf-bait. They'd mutilated him."

A harsh intake of breath from Alais.

"Good Lord." The Abbess crossed herself.

Gamelyn focused on the bits of sausage baked into the bread, found that he was getting less hungry by the moment.

"Otho." Sir Ian gave low rebuke. As Otho looked down, uncomfortable, Sir Ian continued, "When I asked for details, I did not think you would be heedless amongst our womenfolk."

"Heedless, perhaps, but necessary, Uncle." The Abbess folded her hands on the table, set a level gaze on Otho. "I would know. Was there more?"

Otho did not cease looking uncomfortable. "There was. It was a pagan thing, some sort of ritual. Or so your woman—your seneschal?—confirmed."

"Sister Deirdre." The Abbess nodded. "She knows much of these things. She once belonged to one of the pagan cults, before she saw the evil of her ways and came to the Church for absolution."

"You have one who was a witch in your retinue, Niece?" Sir Ian seemed taken aback.

"If a soul wishes to repent, should I deny them the way to God?" the Abbess pointed out. "She does good work in my service, knows from experience how to interpret the ways of the demon worshippers. Deirdre has even made it possible to bring such as do not repent to justice."

"She turned on her own?" Gamelyn hadn't meant to ask it aloud, was sorry he had as Abbess Elisabeth's gaze turned to him.

"Once she chose to walk in light instead of darkness, they were no longer 'her own', as you say." The Abbess's tone was indulgent, but uncompromising for all that. "Cousin Gamelyn, you speak with kindness in your heart, but it is misguided. When someone is relentless in their pursuit of evil, often there is no hope for them outside Heaven. Or Hell."

Gamelyn put his gaze back to his half-eaten loaf.

"Well," Otho continued, making inroads upon his own meal, "your man was left surrounded by some sort of markings. Runes, your acolyte called them. She would not read them aloud, but said they had to do with betrayal and revenge." He chewed, swallowed, took a quaff of wine then added, "They'd circled him in salt. Even I know what that means."

"What does it mean?" Gamelyn asked and, from the table's end, Johan snorted.

"And you're supposedly the bookish one. Salt is for purification, little prat."

"Johan," Sir Ian rumbled. "We have guests."

Gamelyn glared at Johan, who winked at him and turned back to his plate.

"Well," Otho put in, "Sister Deirdre seemed to think it meant something else as well. Your man," he told the Abbess, "also had an oddly fletched arrow in his throat."

"Oddly fletched?" Sir Ian queried, cutting an apple into quarters. He offered one to Gamelyn.

Otho nodded and took a gulp of wine. "Peacock fletching."

Gamelyn dropped the apple quarter amidst the rushes on the floor. One of the hounds leapt on it, then gave a growl upon discovering it was fruit, not meat.

"Take care, lad," his father said. "Have another."

"I doubt it would fly," Johan put in.

"Oh, they do." Gamelyn spoke before he thought.

"You barely know your way about a crossbow, let alone a peasant's weapon," Johan dismissed.

For once, Gamelyn was glad of that dismissal.

"This was no mere peasant's weapon. It had all sorts of witch-marks on it," Otho said, then shuddered and crossed himself. "An evil thing, and no question."

"Not only murder, but sorcery." The Abbess was grave. "God will punish them."

"I do not think Nottingham's sheriff is one who will rely solely on God." Otho picked at a tooth with the fine point of his knife. "He vowed to find the man—or men, both of them were gone by morning—and see their heads on his gate."

"Sheriff FitzAaron was detailed to greet me and formally assign some of his men to the Abbey," Elisabeth mused. "But I did not expect him so soon. What a cold welcome for him."

"He just arrived this morning. Just in time, at that. FitzAaron is a ruthless one, my lady; he'll see the deed done."

"Cousin, please." The Abbess had a lovely smile, no question. "We're all family here; no need to stand on ceremony."

"Speaking of ceremony…." Johan attempted a drink from his goblet, frowned as it proved empty, and held it up as a servant quickly poured more. "You had that head forester here, Papa. Gave him your hospitality, fed and housed him as well as his scrawny brat and their rounceys. Pity he's not still here. You could have held him to account."

"How is it his fault?" Gamelyn protested.

"Not his fault, certainly." Otho shrugged. "But 'neath his account, since 'twas his man did the deed."

"My responsibilities do not extend to holding one of the king's foresters to account. Nor do yours," Sir Ian pointed out.

"Surely it is the responsibility of any good man to hold an evil one to account," was Abbess Elisabeth's soft rebuke.

"Of course," Sir Ian relented, "you are correct."

"But they did nothing!" Gamelyn insisted. "It was their companions who did evil."

"Are we not our brother's keeper?" Johan misquoted softly, flipping his eating knife through his fingers and looking directly at Gamelyn.

No fear. The voice floated up through Gamelyn's consciousness. *They'll only sense it, and then you're nowt to them....*

"So if your brother does something idiotic," he challenged, "then you should be made to suffer for it for no other reason than he's kin to you?"

"I do," Johan drawled. "All the time."

"Lads!" Sir Ian growled. "How many times must I remind you we have a guest? This is the dinner board, not the armaments practice alcove."

"You're sure of that?" Otho scoffed. "The entire castle's a bloody war zone between these two—"

"Otho!" Alais protested. Then, "You see, honored Cousin, what family ties have landed you into."

Elisabeth laughed. "I have four brothers, Cousin Alais. I've no doubt your husband's siblings *are* minding themselves."

Otho snorted, kept eating. He bit into a piece of meat, grimaced at it, then tossed it over his shoulder. The hounds leapt upon it with delight—and noisy squabbles.

"True enough," Sir Ian concurred. "But for now, Niece, you must allow us to ensure your safety. I know you had planned upon continuing to Worksop today, but I must insist that you delay your trip"—he held up a veined hand as she started to speak—"until at least the morrow."

"The sheriff insists as well," Otho said. "FitzAaron is detailing soldiers to meet us at the Nottinghamshire side of Tickhill; he'd come to Blyth proper if he had Yorkshire in his jurisdiction as well as Derbyshire." A grin. "He and our sheriff don't see eye to eye on much. If that villein disappears east into the Peak instead of south and the Shire Wode, Nottingham will get little help from de Lisle."

Sir Ian started to speak; Gamelyn watched as he caught the Abbess's eye, gave a slight smile.

"I think he might in this case," Elisabeth said, then also smiled, dipped her head to Sir Ian. "You forget, dear cousins, that Yorkshire's sheriff is also family. Brian de Lisle is one of my brothers."

ઌ

PEACOCK fletching.

Peacock fletching.

Gamelyn had fully intended to head straight to the library after the meal. Instead he had come as far as the door out into the courtyard, seen the commotion there—soldiers gathering gear and getting ready for their escort duty on the morrow—and parked his buttocks in the window next to that door to watch.

And cool off. He was still worked up from the exchange with Johan, the unfairness of those assumptions, and….

The peacock-fletched arrow.

A "luck charm," Marion had said, as lightly as if she were discussing the fortune of a hare's foot, or cold iron over the doorsill to keep the fae from entering. But when she'd shot it, the thing had indeed proven remarkably accurate.

It couldn't have been the same arrow. But… for her people, she'd said. Her family? The people of Loxley? The forest people?

Christ's blood, he might as well say Rob was indeed that demon lad he'd first thought him, and that his family was of the fae!

There was no help for it. Gamelyn would have to brave that crowded courtyard and do some reading. Figure this all out. Shinnying from the windowsill, he halted, looked across the courtyard to the stout door leading to the library, and frowned. There had to be a way to ask Brother Dolfin about the arrow without involving Rob and Marion. Dolfin already knew some of it; unavoidable, since he heard Gamelyn's confession, mostly to do with lying to his family about why he went to Loxley.

Gamelyn's cheeks heated. Considering last night, his confession was entirely overdue as it was. Not that he truly wanted to contemplate any of that just now….

"Cousin?"

Gamelyn started, gathered up his vagrant thoughts, and turned. The Abbess was gliding down the hall toward him, the seemingly ubiquitous and silent novice several steps behind, like a gray ghost. "Reverend Lady," he acknowledged, dipping his head.

"Come, Cousin Gamelyn, please. We're all family here. No need to be so formal." There was a smile on her face as she came to stand beside him. "Did I disturb you? You seemed lost in thought."

"I was thinking, but you didn't disturb me."

"Were you, perhaps, going into the courtyard?"

Gamelyn hesitated, then nodded. After all, to reach the library one did have to cross the courtyard.

"Excellent! I find that my digestion improves if I take a walk after mealtime. Would you consent to accompany me, show me around your home while I am waiting for your brother to gather suitable chaperonage for my departure?"

"I…." He was quite used to the presence of important strangers—but this was different. Somehow. "I would be honored, Reverend Lady."

"Cousin, please."

"Cousin."

They walked out into the bustle. There were a few clouds that the previous day's gusts hadn't blown away, but mostly sun warmed the cobbles—a nice change from the dreary past days. As they picked their way around people organizing saddles, weaponry and the kit that accompanied every escort—even one of a half day's ride at the most—Gamelyn pointed out some of the more important points. The well. The weavers and dyers who had set up a thriving business in a remarkably short time. The smith and his very valuable forge. It was a good way to occupy his attention other than with what he might not know until he got another chance to go to Loxley. This time, with more care than ever.

"I must confess, I had an ulterior motive in wanting your company, Gamelyn."

It sent a tiny thrill of apprehension down his spine. Surely it was a guilty and hypersensitive conscience that suggested she knew, somehow, where his thoughts had been circling.

"Your father spoke to me last night about your interests. He was hoping I could aid you."

Interests. Again, the apprehension. Why should he 'ware her questions? Rob and his father were innocents run afoul of a renegade in their ranks. And the enchantment that surrounded the forester's cottage, Eluned's talents and Rob's… oddities… had nothing to do with the sorts of paganism and blasphemy that the renegades had put into practice. Perhaps Rob and his family were… Heathens. But crofters' ignorance did not mean witchcraft. Surely arrows fletched with peacock feathers weren't all spelled to some arcane evil.

And surely there was no way she could know what he had seen last night, or the unseemly interest it had held for him.

Abbess Elisabeth was peering at him with her lovely, too discerning dark eyes. They were merely deep brown, but reminded him, sudden and disturbing, of the canniness in Rob's black ones.

"Wh-what interests?" he asked.

"In a holy vocation?" Her smile broadened and she put caressing fingers to the cross at her breast. "Why, are there others I should know about?"

This time, apprehension ramped itself into result. The remarkable self-control that had done Gamelyn justice in his dealings with Johan clicked into abrupt use, bringing with it a surety that he gathered about him like a fine-spun cloak. "Ah, of course. I'm afraid I was letting my mind wander. Sometime when one woolgathers it's hard to catch back up."

"Indeed. I'm sure you've done this tour more than the once, and you're young enough—intelligent enough—to be easily bored. Let *me* attempt to occupy your thoughts for a bit." Another smile, and charmed, Gamelyn smiled back.

"Your father was right to confide in me, Cousin. If you feel that you have a vocation, I could be of some help to you in your pursuit of a good position. You seem a fine, thoughtful young man. Your father says that you read to him often, and have a fine hand, take his letters for him. You have been a dutiful son, a respectful prop and stay for him in his illness."

Gamelyn couldn't help the pleased smile that quirked at his mouth.

"But it is not wrong to think about the future. Uncle Ian has lived a righteous, full life, and as saddening as it is to those of us he will leave behind, 'all flesh is grass'—"

"'And all the glory thereof as the flower of the held'," Gamelyn finished softly. It put an ache in his throat—he did not want to think of his father dying, not yet. Surely he still had some time.

"Even so," she replied. "You are quite surprising, young sir. Not many lads your age know Isaiah that well."

"Actually I usually prefer the New Testament to the Old," Gamelyn confessed. "But the language in this particular quote is all the finer, I think."

"And he knows the difference!" the Abbess marveled. "Do you know the Latin, then?"

"Of course. '*Vox dicentis clama et dixi quid clamabo omnis caro faenum et omnis gloria eius quasi flos agri'.*"

"'Of course'." The Abbess chuckled. "And not without a little pride, I see."

Gamelyn flushed again, apologized. "Brother Dolfin is always saying my pride will be the death of me—"

"Yet to develop any talent adequately, one must realize one's own worth, otherwise risk squandering such God-given gifts. Great goals must have great aims." She peered at him for a moment. "I'm afraid I must agree with your elder brother in one thing, however."

"Johan?"

"Indeed. He thinks you have not the makings of a soldier." Her gaze slid to him as he stiffened, albeit slightly. "My agreement has a different taste, however. It would be a shame for a brain such as yours to be wasted in battle."

It sent another flush of satisfaction through him. A welcome sensation, that; there were, in truth, very few times he could grasp this sort of pleasure. Often there was a pure and unsullied lifting in his heart when he gave himself to prayer. Reading a beautiful and complex turn of phrase seemed to set soft, powerful music in his heart and mind. Of course, the short, snatched moments he had with Rob and Marion in the green Wode, often in quiet companionship, and....

He halted mid-step, jolted by what had next come to his mind. It was only yesterday, the memory: Rob's prickles and pride turned to a nurturing quiet so rarely displayed, the feel of his callused, slender fingers smoothing against Gamelyn's face, the....

The lovely-wild grace of Rob's throat, bared to the moonlight, submitting to the stable lad's caresses….

Oh, *God*! Gamelyn commanded his thoughts to restraint—unaccountably successful—for the Abbess didn't ken that a new, even more disturbing truth had taken him. Neither was the novice even bothering to heed him; she walked, head down, lost in her own contemplations. Probably prayer, and Gamelyn envied her, sudden and strong and no matter that it was as great a sin as any lust. The novice looked at peace, contented, untrammeled. *Untouched.*

Gamelyn gave a tiny start as the Abbess put a concerned hand on his arm, but she paid no heed, merely continuing her statements.

"Elder siblings are always keen to assert their rights, Gamelyn. Uncle Ian loves you dearly and Johan views that as a threat. I would heed that as a warning, and think not too long upon your future. The Church would welcome a young man such as you." She smiled, gave his arm a pat, and continued on. "And of course, with the financial support your father promises to you, in addition to my sponsorship, you would find your way to a very fair situation.

"Now, would you show me the stables? I like my palfrey overmuch, I fear, and saved some roots from the table for her."

Glad for the distraction, Gamelyn gestured and led the way. He'd taken merely a few steps when he realized the barn was where Rob had… *touched* him.

Gamelyn tucked the sudden tremble of his hands into his tunic sleeves and kept walking. He knew his cheeks were heating again, and for no good reason. This was not pleasure… not exactly… nor was it pain… at least he didn't think it was, though there did seem to be something hurtful in it. It was something else entirely. Something that he couldn't easily classify and didn't understand at all.

Dutiful, he saw the Abbess and her silent companion to the stable, and did not—*did not*—go anywhere near the stable lad's cot. Then he retreated to the silent stacks of the library behind the chapel.

Gamelyn avoided the chapel proper, found himself further relieved—and for no good reason—that Brother Dolfin wasn't in the library, either. The familiar, sane comfort of parchment and leather bindings reestablished some semblance of order to his scattered thoughts.

Unfortunately, there weren't many answers to be found. Gamelyn finally looked up from his examinations to find the day nearly spent, the sounds of the courtyard outside dulled considerably, and a huddled figure waiting just inside the door, peering everywhere but directly at him.

How long had he been there? Gamelyn blinked, straightened. His lower back twinged a protest, quickly disregarded as Gamelyn recognized the soldier.

It was Much, the one whom Johan had assigned to dog his steps—and report on them.

Gamelyn straightened further, eyes narrowing. "What do you want?"

"I… I've been looking for y' every which ways, milord," the young soldier said. "Since I came back. I had tae find y' and let y' know."

"Does my brother want me, then?" Gamelyn gave a longing glance to the books spread on the table, then began to gather them up.

"Nay, milord. 'Tisn't that, and I want you tae be understandin' what is… what I… I ent knowin', y' see? Had I known, I nivver would've…."

He was stammering, Gamelyn realized suddenly, nearly speechless with some sort of dread.

"There's nae help for't, y'see? Lord Johan, he orders us new lads, he does, and I gots to do as he says. Surely you understand, he's yer brother an' you gots tae do as he says, right enou'."

"Why are you here, then?" Gamelyn said, frowning.

"I meant nowt by it. Y' must tell 'em, tell th' Mother that I dint mean tae mess with Her consort, or His own. John tol' me, he did, what I'd done and that I should be sorry… and I am, I nivver wanted to give offence… only John ent understanding, he ent a soldier likes tae me, and I gots no *choice*. Please, milord, please tell 'em, please say you understand why I has to follow y' to Her place."

"Her place?" None of this was making any sense. "Look, I'm not angry with you. It's not your—"

"Please, milord. Say you'll tell 'er. I'll say nowt t' betray you, nor what passes between you and the Hunter—"

The Hunter. Who in Christ's good name was the Hunter?

Wait. Brand had said it, once, with the same, strange reverence. The "Hunter," and his son.

"Brand and his lad think your father's hung the moon."

"Adam?" Gamelyn said suddenly, softly. "When you say the 'Hunter', do you mean Adam? Or Rob?"

The young soldier paled. "I meant no 'arm, that I swear tae y' milord. Her ways are true tae me, and I mean no harm to Her consort. *Please.* Please tell 'er I won't betray 'er own!"

A disturbance in the chapel, the door swinging shut, and bootsteps pausing at the door. In the tiny fraction of a moment Gamelyn's attention was diverted, Much had slipped out the side door and disappeared.

Mystified, Gamelyn sat there for some time, then began to put away the books.

☙ X ❧

"SEE to our horses, boy, then come straight away in. Don't dawdle."

Rob took the rein from his father, watched him march to the cottage. Then, mouth tightening, he went and did as bidden.

It had been a fast ride. They'd pushed both their horses and themselves, and the miles between Blyth and Loxley had been quickly eaten away. In silence. Any time Rob had thought to speak, he'd taken a second look at his father's taut profile and kept his mouth shut.

Something had happened. That much he could ken even without the peculiar senses that seemed to only rear their head when they chose. They sure weren't being a lot of help to him now.

Surely his father would have told him, had it been something wrong with his mam or Marion. Surely he would have *known*....

It was the only surety he had right now, that realization. Anything else could wait while he did right by their sweated mounts. He untacked them, gave them each a bit of swede. And they certainly deserved a good rubdown. Rob took his time, his smile coming easily as he scratched the exact spot on Arawn's withers that would make him stretch his neck and upper lip, quivering.

And found his thoughts going to Gamelyn.

That shouldn't surprise him, should it, when Gamelyn had responded to his touch with no less pleasure than Arawn... only more subtle, as if Gamelyn wouldn't know what to do with such a pleasure unless it reared up and bit his arse.

Arawn's knees were trying to buckle. Rob chuckled, gave him a slap on the rump. "It's quite easy, you see," he told the black. "I want him. It's that simple."

Only, it wasn't. It should be, and it could be, but it wasn't, and the sense of it clanging about in his head, unanswered and complicated, was enough to make Rob want to run into the middle of Loxley Chase, crouch on his haunches and howl like a deranged wolf.

Instead he finished brushing down Arawn then his father's horse, threw woolen blankets over their haunches, and tied them to the manger. They'd have to cool more before he could feed them, and it was time he went in, found out what was going on.

Beside the fact that the little stable lad, John, had possessed a marvelous mouth and Rob wanted—really, *really* wanted—to find out if Gamelyn….

Impossible. Forget it. He probably had a better chance of coaxing Will Scathelock to give it a go.

"Has Scathelock come here, then?"

His father's voice shook with something that felt like rage, yet smelled more of pain and fear than any fury. Rob halted halfway to the cottage.

His mother's voice answered. Rob was too far away to hear what she said, but again, the fear was there. The pain.

Rob started forward, his steps more rushed as it broke over him like a wave. Scathelock. What had happened to Will? George?

"—spelled the arrow?" Adam's words, first unintelligible, raised back into clarity, escaping the windows of their cottage as if it was too small to hold his voice. "You Saw it?"

Marion's voice, soft and dull. "I did. He waited until everyone was asleep, then went and found the rowan. He knew what he had to do from the moment he saw the soldier unhelmed. So he killed him." Sudden and shrill, her voice rose. "And it was deserved! You canna say it wasn't!"

"Deserved or no, he went too far! One brazen act, and it could be t' ruin of us all!"

By the time he reached the cottage, Rob was running.

"And what good is any of it—our powers, our places!—if we have to keep bending our necks?" Marion retorted. "Worse, because when cattle need butchering, they receive our reverence at least! That one; he deserved what he got and *more*!"

"Marion, you don't understand." Eluned sounded nearly in tears.

Rob took the cottage steps two at a time and slid to a halt just inside. Marion's eyes leapt to his, as if in escape. Eluned also peered at him, standing behind Adam. Adam was sitting across from Marion, who had her head in her hands.

Rob said the first thing he could. "It was Will, wasn't it?"

Adam looked up, held Rob's eyes.

"He killed that soldier, aye? 'Twas the one who murdered his mam, waint it? He said…." *Said he knew his voice. That something was… familiar.*

Adam looked away. Eluned wrapped her arms about Adam's shoulders, murmuring to him.

"I… I canna believe it. We were t' meet on th' m-morrow at the ale house, Will an' I," Rob stammered.

"Thinking of drinkin' at a time like this!" Marion yanked her hands from her face, rising from her chair. "Are you—?"

"I ent thinking of ale," Rob protested, stung. "It was just… I… aw, bugger, think what y' like, then!"

He had the satisfaction of seeing Marion's face blanch, and then it leached into anguish as he fully took in that face: white, tear-streaked, full of hope shattered. It was too much to bear, that he had rended his own; Rob whirled and escaped the cottage.

Eluned's voice rose, calling him, but Rob kept going. Running, not with the panic of the hunted, not with the hunger of predation, but horror. *Helplessness.* He had to move, to breathe, to react… do *something*… yet nothing was possible save the running. His feet had eyes in them, as ever, took him careful and cautious into the Wode, where the dark and the green and the mists covered him, soothing as lullabies sung with a honeyed tongue.

He should have known. Should have seen it… should have *Seen* it, known what was coming, because otherwise, what good was any of this… this *tynged*?

As suddenly as anger had lent him speed, it deserted him, leaving him lurching to a halt in a gnarled stand of trees. With sudden ungainliness, Rob lurched sideways, panting, and half fell onto an ancient oak. He clung to it, laid his cheek upon it, breathed it in as if the iron strength of the old tree could somehow morph itself into him.

He wasn't sure how long he hunched there, eyes clenched and teeth bared, wishing he could at least cry but no tears coming, even as a favor. Finally he shuddered and opened his eyes, turned around and put his back to it. And breathed.

There was an odd gap next to him; a hawthorn had been coppiced in the recent past, sending tender shoots that rose up beside him. They caressed his fingers as he reached down and touched them, sunk to his knees. Rob sucked in another deep, slow breath; wood-rot and bruised green filled his senses, steadied and grounded them.

He should have known. Not only that Will was set on vengeance… always had been, just waiting for it to fall, ripe, within his grasp… but that Marion had fancied Will.

It was all lucid and sudden, clear as the night around him, pocked with stars and cool as an early summer's evening could be. Marion had fancied Will Scathelock, and now any hopes had been taken from her before she'd even realized them. All the scorn she'd heaped on Will's flighty ways and uncontrolled urges were signs Rob had been too thick-witted and self-involved to read.

He'd been so convinced she liked Gamelyn.

Self-involved—aye, that and more. Because he'd been convinced that Marion and Gamelyn were infatuated with each other, not looking past his own nose… not looking where his own wanting was leading him. And now that Rob had more than ample evidence—proof of his own passion, evidence of where Marion's heart would fain turn—the way cleared only to become more convoluted.

And why was he thinking on Gamelyn now, of all times? *Will* was his friend. His dearest friend save Marion—and Will was like him, of his own kind—Will had killed one of the sheriff's men. And Rob had never seen it coming.

Sure, and when Will wasn't wooing Calla and Rob wasn't tilting into Simon, they had sat to drinks across the alehouse table. And for every hour Rob and Will had spent getting buzzed and bragging, they'd also spent another getting blind drunk. And while Rob was a morose drunk, Will was an angry one, with where else for that to lead but to the both of them railing against fate, bemoaning the conquered and damning the conquerors. Sotted with drink and unspent fury, Will had diagrammed and detailed the suffering he'd give the man who'd murdered his mother. Rob had listened and agreed and felt utterly powerless, because what good was having such things as sorcery and Sight when you couldn't so much as See your way clear to a place where justice would be done?

Why was he thinking on Gamelyn? Dreaming of him? Rob should bloody well despise him! And instead Rob *wanted* him… and the recognition curdled on his tongue: humiliation instead of joy, resentment instead of release.

Will was his friend. Was his oldest, best friend and might have been Marion's lover. Instead Will would be riven from the Shire Wode, likely outlawed for seeing justice done. While Gamelyn was of the ones who'd ground them into dirt, was merely some noble having a lark in that dirt for reasons Rob still didn't fathom and certainly was unable to fully trust.

So wrapped in his own misery, Rob almost didn't hear the low-pitched voices. The urgency of them alerted him; that and the barely audible drag of a boot not a pike's lob away. Instincts pinning him to the wide, worn shelter of the oak, Rob rose from his crouch, soundless, breath held behind his teeth.

"What must I do?"

The voice was shaky-soft, almost plaintive, threaded all hollow. Rob had never heard such in his father's voice—for several halting breaths he was unsure it *was* his father's voice.

He peered around the tree, saw his father kneeling, a scrim of moonlight tracing his lowered head. A familiar silhouette stood before Adam, sheltered from even the moonlight by a thicket and a stand of overarching trees. Cernun's shape wavered, from fur-wrapped old man to pale, ancient hind, all of it overlaid with the visage of the ebon, horn-crowned shade. Rob gritted his teeth, closed his eyes, and shook his head, ever so slightly. Now was no time for visions or dreams.

Now was reality. What good were dreams?

"They'll send for me. They'll summon me and I'll have no choice but heed, for I'm forester to the king and one of me own has broken the laws I am sworn to uphold… Lady protect me, one of me own… *our* own! Of us, sworn to our covenant—"

"From the moment he spelled the arrow, he was lost to us." Cernun's voice was forbidding.

"But it waint just be 'he', aye? FitzAaron might well declare them both outlaw and set *me* to hunt them. My underforesters. My responsibility."

Adam's voice was breaking, raw. It was… unnerving. Rob gripped tighter to the tree and tilted his head, truly not wanting to listen but unable to do otherwise.

"You must do what the law commands, else lose all."

"He's only a lad—"

"He's a man."

"He's a *boy*," Adam insisted, "who lost his mother to that bastard he killed. The same one who struck my boy down like an animal, and what did I do? *Nothing*."

"What could you have done?"

"I don't know!" It was full of helpless fury. "Had I known who it was, I would have killed him myself."

"You do not," Cernun answered, just as terse, "have the luxury of dealing death."

"Yet I am Lord of Life and Death, the Horned One—"

"The Horned One, aye. Talk of death is obscene from you, life-bearer. You are *not* the Hooded One."

Rob watched his father recoil as if Cernun had struck him, and felt… nothing. It was as if those words—*the Hooded One*—had sucked from him every reasonable response, setting a hum and twitch of *tynged* to fill his senses.

"I know Scathelock." Adam's voice, when it sounded again, was wooden. "He'll not let Will be taken from him, too."

"It is ever a father's prerogative, to shield a son."

Layer upon layer, the words seemed to echo into ten more, tens upon tens of meanings threading out beyond him, possibilities….

Nay. Rob dug his fingers into the bark. *I need to hear*.

"They have broken covenant and it could betray us all. You have told me of the Maiden's visions; what has the Mother Seen?"

For long moments, Adam did not answer. When he did, his voice was wooden. "The Hood comes, bearing the goddess's terrible arrow. But it is the nobleman's son who walks alongside, who would supplant him and bring the battle 'twixt the Lords of Summer and Winter."

"Those of *cruithna* know the ways of the Lady deeper than any horns can pierce. And She knows *all*. *Abred*, *Annwn*, *Gwynfydd*… all worlds are within Her sight."

"Then why does she look into our son's future and See… nothing?"

Nothing. It rang, echoed deep into the Wode. Rob tried to turn away, couldn't, had to clench his eyes shut. His head was fairly throbbing and Rob wished he could just lop it off and be done. It was too much. Too much.

His own future, a cipher even to Mother-kind. The *cruithna*, the People of the Barrow, his mother's kin. The trine of the *Ceugant*: mortal, other, and undying. A Hooded One to deal death where the Horned One could not… like a king's executioner, then? With a nobleman's son to supplant him?

It made… no… sense. Only broken covenants. Fathers shielding sons.

When he finally could look back toward Cernun and Adam, his father was gone, and instead of Cernun there was only the great, ebon visage of the Horned Lord.

Suddenly He turned, fixed gleaming eyes upon Rob. Rob found himself unable to move, rooted in place as if he were the oak beneath his hands.

Then it gusted away, wisped into smoke and darkness, leaving Cernun looking after where Adam must have gone.

"I know you're here, youngling."

Rob froze.

"If now is no time for visions and dreams, then when will it ever be?"

Suddenly Cernun was beside him, hand upon the oak that Rob still leaned upon, and either the old man had moved that fast, or Rob had again lost track of time.

Rob was no longer sure which was more possible. "What… what will happen to Will and his da?"

"They go to face their own *tynged*, as must we all. Young Scathelock accepted that when he spelled the rowan to the fires of death. Everything is taken with a price."

"They paid it first!"

"You have no idea what has been paid and what has not. You are too young to understand the meaning of consequence, of sacrifice."

Stay, and watch the King die. Do you not know the true meaning of sacrifice?

Cernun sucked in a quick breath and his gaze met Rob's. "So. *That* is what you see."

Rob wasn't sure what was more disturbing, the way Cernun was suddenly looking at him, or that the old man had also heard, somehow, the memory of the Horned Lord's words from the Seeking.

"But then, how could I expect otherwise? You have never been the innocent one, have you, Hob-Robyn?"

The very sounding of the name seemed to echo through the Wode, to call him. Rob shook his head, denied it, denied… all of it. "You canna mean that you would have my da turn his back on them. Or betray them."

"What is the meaning of betrayal?" Cernun countered. "Other than it is oft met with more betrayal. It is the way of things. The web is spun, merely to be plucked and torn and spun again. The question is, my son, are you willing to hold fast should it wrap you, or will you tear it to win free?"

"I don't und—"

"Don't you?" Cernun angled forward so abruptly that Rob jerked back, butting up against the oak. The old man's eyes began to gleam, hot as the need-fires on Beltain, and like smoke from those huge fires came the ghost-stag, wavering into being, coalescing between them. Black as night, fire-coal eyes, horns spread wide against the moonlit trees; the rank smell of must and the bitter-soft taste of earth tickling at the back of Rob's throat….

You stand firm, proud. It was Cernun's voice, but… not. *Do not presume upon mere mettle over long, Princeling. You must move, swift and sure. Time is catching us up, twining us fast.*

There was no longer a question of who spoke: god or man. One was human, possessed of mercy and doubt; the other older than the trees, giving quarter to no trace of weakness. The Horned Lord leaned closer, hot breath gusting over Rob's cheeks, purling down against his throat. It chilled, making as if to ice panic into Rob's very bones. Settling his spine against the hard wood, he snarled back.

Good. You show no fear but…. Nostrils flaring, the Horned Lord snuffed a sharp breath. *I can smell it, nevertheless.* A small chuckle. *You think you know fear? You know nothing, boy. Nothing. But you will.*

Rob reached out quite by instinct, felt only the tender, new tendrils of the hawthorn to hand. Instead he dug his fingers into the bark of the oak and closed his eyes. Not that it mattered—he could still See the Horned Lord, limned in gilt against the darkness….

Even now, you reach for innocence, set yourself against the oak and hope he will hold your back. But first must he be woken from an unwary, unwise slumber. For if the coppicing comes before the waking, it is doubtful he can survive.

"New tendrils grow, from a coppice." Rob found his voice. It shook, soft and hoarse, answering on mere instinct, yet his answers made no more sense than the questions. "An oak's roots grow deep."

Aye. They do. And that might yet be your undoing. Do you really think yourself able to cozen him in? Is he prepared to draw back a scratched and bleeding hand? For Oak is ever your rival, is he not?

Silence. Breath held behind his teeth, breath fading from his neck, the Horned Lord's visage wavering as if the air had thinned.

Then He scattered, flits and sparks melding into mist, and….

Darkness.

Rob sucked in a huge breath, opened his eyes. They were smarting.

And Cernun was gone.

☙ ENTR'ACTE ❧

"I'LL not fight you, Adam."

"You know why I've come, George."

Aye, he knew. Just as he'd known why Adam *had* to come. There was no choice, no choice for any of them, really.

Why had he ever believed there might be one?

They had come riding, five of Sheriff de Lisle's soldiers led by the king's forester, over the land George's father had worked, and his before him. George had hoped his son would work it, after him, but he should have known. Will was no likely farmer.

His neighbors had disappeared, were no doubt huddled in their cots, unsure whether disaster might rub off on them as well. He didn't blame them for that. Again, what choice did they have?

The soldiers had dismounted, tied their horses, and waited just inside the wicket gate of his steading as Adam had come to his door. At least they gave Adam that much deference. Of course, Adam had worked hard to gain that respect, to ensure the safety of his people; likely it didn't hurt that the leader of de Lisle's small contingent was the English captain who'd been with them when this entire mess had started. Stutely looked uncomfortable.

Good. It was good to know that an outsider saw the wrong of what was happening.

"Where is he, George?"

There was such misery in Adam's blue eyes, misery to set the world wailing, more than in George's own heart at this moment.

He'd cried all his tears. Said all his good-byes. There was only this one left.

"Gone. You waint find him."

Adam closed those eyes, shook his head. "You know what'll happen. He'll be made wolfshead, outlaw. Anyone can hunt him by rights, from nobleman to serf."

"And he'll be free. Not caged like an animal for killing a beast."

A muscle ticked in Adam's cheek. "Then," he said, very soft, very controlled, "I will have t' take you."

"Aye, you will. As I said, I'll not fight you."

Adam stepped closer, voice low. "If I take you, if you confess the crime… 'twill likely appease them."

"Even so."

Adam closed his eyes, took in a deep breath, then opened them. They gleamed suddenly, with unshed tears. "Then we understand each other."

"In this, we do. In others?" George shook his head. "The time comes when nowt we do will appease them. When we'll have no choice but to hide in shadows and strike as we can. As my boy did. Adam, no child should have to see such a thing done to his mother."

"I know. I know, and I'm sorry."

"I know you are, Adam, else I'd not be standing here with you now. But you dinna understand. Not really."

"And you don't understand why I'll not let these things happen. The time for fighting… 'tisn't now. Too many will die."

"Are we not dying, now?" George's voice rose slightly.

Behind Adam, Stutely leaned forward, frowning. Adam knew it; he turned and shook his head. Stutely nodded, crossed his arms, and set to wait.

"Heed me, George," Adam returned. "To protect our people, we play their game."

"I've heeded you long, master of the Shire Wode. You and the one before, you long held light into a darkening forest. We have known… peace. Contentment. Yet more and more, you uphold laws we've no say in making, see justice that waint apply to us. We're safe, aye. And all the while the Sacrifice is winnowed to a mere blood-letting—a nick here, a slice there, a slow seepage of what dignity and pride we had." George shook his head. "Worse things than death stalk us, Horned One. Have y' forgotten?"

"I would give my life for my people!"

"As I give mine for my son." George watched as Adam's gaze flickered. "You have a son, Adam. What will his future hold? What power can even a god's son hold when he bears the weight of such shackles?"

"*George*—" It shook, then Adam looked down. "You ent Seen what I have," he whispered. "You know nowt of what crux my son is perched upon."

George also took his voice down, a bare murmur. "I've no Sight as you and your woman, master, but still I see where this path of submission, of *pretending*, will lead. They'll see our kind wiped from the face of our own Mother—do we just let it happen without a fight?"

"We've the right to make that choice for ourselves. Not for others. That ent the purpose of the covenant."

"Sometimes there is no choice. Like now." George extended his hand, palm up. In it was a dagger.

The soldiers saw the motion and went abruptly alert. The captain took a step forward.

Adam merely met George's eyes. Then he nodded, reached out, and took the dagger.

George lowered his head. "You'll come across my measure, coiled beneath th' mattress." Cernun had been the one to cut the cord to George's measure and mark it with his blood; his own initiation to the covenant. He'd been not much older than Will. "I'd prefer none else find it."

Adam nodded.

"Give it to th' Mother for the fires, when it's over. If you see my boy…." His voice, abruptly, refused to work.

"I pray I never see him again," Adam said, gently.

ಚ XI ಬ

"GO ON, lad, go with your brothers. A nice long hunt, a chance to test what new skills Roberto has taught you." Sir Ian peered at him, gaze canny. "I know you were fond of the forester and his son. This will be just the thing to get your mind off all this...."

As if that was likely. He'd tried over the past few days, really tried, to find a chance to slip away, head for Loxley. Fate had foiled him every time, and now?

Now Gamelyn was torn between several books he'd found, the snack he'd cadged from the kitchens, and the nearly packed rucksack for the hunting expedition that was due to set out at any moment.

This, when those two books he'd unearthed actually had something of significance in them. One was old, about the runic alphabets—Gamelyn hadn't realized there were such things—and the other was newer, a treatise on ceremonial consecration of weapons by one of the founders of the Knights Templar.

"Christ's wounds, Gamelyn, how long does it take you to pack a day's bag?" This from Otho, striding down the hall and into his chambers. "The horses are ready, Johan and I are ready... my *wife* doesn't take this long at her toilet!" Otho trailed off, exasperated as he spied the opened books on Gamelyn's bed next to his pack. "You aren't taking those."

Well, it had been tempting. "Nay, of course not!" Gamelyn retorted. "I wasn't reading them just now, either. They're from this morning, and—"

Otho rolled his eyes. "Lad. Are you ready?"

Gamelyn grabbed up an apple, tried to grab up his cloak and his pack, finally ended up sticking the apple in his teeth so he could gather the rest. "'M 'eathy nah."

"Then shift yourself. The day's wasting!"

ಚಬ

THEY'D herded the boar into a natural cul-de-sac of tangled brush—or so they thought, for things had gone disappointingly quiet. There were six huntsmen accompanying them—all had been send out in a wide arc as beaters and diversions, to drive their quarry farther in. Gamelyn was trailing his two elder brothers step for step as they approached where the boar should, by all rights, be.

"If you hear anything, shoot," Johan ordered. "If it is a boar you won't stop it with one bolt or even two, but hopefully you'll slow it down a bit until I can get a go with the pike."

They crept forward, weapons poised, ready. Behind and to the side, the huntsmen began to fan out even more into their semicircle, purposeful and noisy.

"I hope it hasn't flanked us," Otho muttered.

The forest was quiet. Too quiet, Gamelyn knew. Everything already knew they were here. Including their quarry. Wherever the boar had gone, it wasn't near.

This was pointless. Rob would have given up the stalk already, be casting for new spoor. Marion would be climbing a tree, stealthy-silent—she had a longer eye than her brother and Gamelyn both, was the better scout.

It was a startling realization, that he seemed to know more forest craft than his brothers. He was so accustomed to being the weaker link of their hunting trine at Loxley.

A rustle in the bushes to his right. Gamelyn slowed, slid his eyes toward it.

Otho and Johan kept going.

Gamelyn gave them a puzzled look, shook his head, and resumed creeping after them. Perhaps he'd imagined....

Again. Louder.

Gamelyn turned, saw something close to the ground, twitching in an odd fashion. Odd, because whatever it was seemed not to realize there were dangers about and kept moving. Gamelyn let his brothers go on, hesitated then, curling his finger steady on his crossbow trigger, took a few steps closer.

And froze as he saw it: creeping silent, black as soot. Golden eyes raised to his, stark and glittering, and white teeth shone beneath a warning snarl.

No fear. They'll sense it.

Muscles quivered and the wolf set back on his haunches, ever so slightly. Gamelyn snarled back and pulled the trigger.

The crossbow bolt loosed just as the wolf leapt. There was a harsh, thick thud, a ki-yi that shrieked harsh into Gamelyn's ears, and the black wolf fell nearly at Gamelyn's boots, the crossbow bolt buried deep between his front legs.

"Gamelyn?"

"Hoy!"

Gamelyn looked up, saw his brothers standing a stone's throw away. They looked stunned.

He was a bit surprised, himself.

Reaching down with his crossbow, he nudged at the wolf, just making sure. It was quite dead. But the strange rustling that had alerted him in the first place was still going on.

Gamelyn stepped over the wolf and took careful steps toward the rustling. It had gotten louder. His brothers were striding back toward him. Otho gave a warning hiss, but as Gamelyn rounded the small tangle of bushes, he saw merely a hare. The wolf had obviously already gotten to it; the hare was on its side, thrashing and bloodied, mortally injured.

He reached down, picked it up. It wasn't even aware of him, still in paroxysms. Brows twisting, Gamelyn cradled warm, soft fur for a moment, then gave a sharp twist of its neck. The rabbit shuddered, then went limp.

"Hoy, *lapin*, it seems you have also slaughtered not only your enemy but your namesake for our fires today!" Johan said, coming over to look at the limp body in Gamelyn's hands. "*Excellente*!"

"Bloody hell, Gamelyn, did you *smell* them coming, or what?" Otho was laughing. "Are you part wolf yourself?"

"Fitting, then, that our little brother will have a wolf pelt to adorn the foot of his bed." Johan grinned, sly. "Unless you'd like the silver pennies."

"Silver pennies?"

"You know. Thruppence for a wolf's head. More if the wolfshead happens to be two-legged, granted." Johan shrugged, toed the dead wolf with his boot. "I'm teasing you; you're no peasant's brat in need of a few pennies. Better to keep the skin for your own use. It is very beautiful."

"And our shepherds will thank you," Otho pointed out.

"You'll have to fetch and carry yourself, I'm afraid." Johan was looking off into the distance. "It looks like the men have found sign."

Indeed, one of their huntsmen was motioning. Johan gave Gamelyn a friendly slap on the back—which, naturally, could have felled a horse—and strode off.

"Nice shot," Otho threw over his shoulder as he began to follow. "I'll try to send a lad back to help you."

Their show of triumph was truly his own: the dawning of respect. Gamelyn put two fingers to his lips, blew a kiss of gratitude in the direction of Loxley and his absent mentors.

Slinging the spent crossbow at his side, Gamelyn took a piece of lanyard from his pouch and tied the rabbit's legs together, hung it at his belt. He bent down beside the wolf and, brows quirking, ran a hand down the black pelt.

It was very beautiful. Again, he felt a pang not unlike he'd felt for the pale stag; actually murmured a tiny prayer and crossed himself before he realized what a total git he was behaving. It was an animal—a dangerous vermin, actually, and he was being foolish. More than foolish. The shepherds lost enough of their sheep to marauding wolves as it was.

And not that he'd had much choice. That wolf would have killed him in a heartbeat and never thought on him again. It was never on to forget whose territory this *truly* was.

Gamelyn smoothed the black fur, gave the body some consideration. It was a big wolf, likely heavy, and the horses were tied a good furlong back. "'Fetch and carry yourself', Gamelyn," he mocked sourly. For someone who spent most of his time saying how ill-grown and soft Gamelyn supposedly was, Johan certainly seemed to think he could do the work of two men in "fetch and carry." He started to give it a small heft, just to test it. Because frankly he'd never hear the end of it if he had to ask for help.

He paused mid-motion, frowned. Considered again, but this time upon why, he felt as if there were eyes upon him. His first thought went to the wolf. It was male, not a rangy yearling or a tattered outlier but a full pack member, well fed and strong. Wolves had kin even as people did, in fact mated for life. It was just possible that those eyes he felt upon him were another wolf's.

He reached up, slowly, for his crossbow. Let his gaze slide back and forth, then up beneath his brows.

It was then he saw the stag. Not even a stone's throw away, coming toward him through the green Wode with steady silence. Its coat was pale ivory, dappled gold and green from the light through the trees.

"They be coming back this way, young marster… glory and faith!" The approaching voice staggered off into a gasp.

Gamelyn shot a glance sideways, saw the young soldier, Much, halt in his tracks then amazingly, slowly, go to his knees.

Even more amazing, the crème-colored stag did not bolt. He didn't even blast an alarm. Instead he halted, raised his wide-racked head and peered at them both with mild, amber eyes.

Some part of Gamelyn's brain finally heard all of what Much had said: *"They be coming back this way…."* And Gamelyn's heart lurched in his chest.

"Go," he suddenly hissed, flinging a hand out. "They can't find you here!"

In some twist of sanity, it seemed an old man was standing there, leaning on an antlered staff, hair hanging down his back and amber eyes fond upon Gamelyn. He held out a hand, gave a low, soft whistle, smiled….

Gamelyn squinched his eyes shut, shook his head. When he looked again, there was no man, only the stag giving a small, odd noise—half bleat and half buzz—and, further beyond comprehension, walking *closer*.

"Blessed stones, but he's callin' tae you, m'lord. You." Much's stammered statement sounded as incredulous as Gamelyn himself felt. "He wants you, He does. Best to not make 'im wait ower long," Much stammered as he made a furtive sign against his chest with his right hand.

He wants you.

It didn't make any sense. Much was mouthing superstitious twaddle—about a *stag*?—and this entire situation was impossible. Gamelyn walked forward, hands held out. "Get out of here!" he ordered. "Go on! If they—"

As if in answer, the stag extended his neck, put its nose against his palms.

The breath snagged in Gamelyn's chest, both pain and delirious, unaccountable bliss. The stag's breath heated his palms then curled about them, the warmth traveling up his arms to meet at his heart; even though such a thing was surely impossible, he still felt it, as if the breath had a meaning, a presence that echoed with the roll of air in the stag's nostrils and the sudden hammer of his heart….

"Gamelyn, what are you *doing*—?"

"Holy Mother of—"

"You'll hit the lad, for Christ's sake—!"

A thunder of feet, running into the small copse, and shouts with an edge of panic.

The stag backed, lowered his head. No longer mild, but wild and undeniably dangerous.

"Shoot it, before it—!"

And crossbows arming. Johan quick-stepped off to one side, raised his crossbow. Without thinking, Gamelyn lunged forward and got between Johan and the stag.

Chaos, suddenly. More shouting, and Johan cursing at him to *Get out of the way for Christ's sake!* and huntsmen taking aim and afraid to shoot so close to their lord's youngest son.

Then a sound of hooves, retreating. Gamelyn turned just in time to see a flash of white rump disappearing into the trees.

Not another breath later, he was careening face-first into the dirt, chased by his brother's boot against his backside.

Quick as a ferret he rolled over and regained his feet—not quick enough, though, as Johan backhanded him right back down.

"Are you out of your bloody sodding mind?" Johan raged. "That stag was ready to charge at you and you were just standing there like some idiot peasant drooling before their horned devil, like… like…!" He was obviously contemplating throwing his crossbow at Gamelyn, instead turned and lobbed it at Much's head. With the quickness of one used to dodging the blows of his betters, Much skittered sideways just in time. Fortunately, the crossbow discharged down into the dirt.

"Johan, he didn't do any—!" Gamelyn's protest was truncated by his brother turning back to him, dragging him up from the ground merely to shove him back down on his backside.

"That's true!" Johan snarled. "You were the one who kept getting in the way of us shooting it!"

"I couldn't let you shoot it. It… he came up to me," Gamelyn stammered, unsure what he could say. Or should.

"It '*came up to you*'?" A flabbergasted Otho repeated. "And you let it?"

"I… it... we..." Gamelyn tried to explain, found he had no words that would make any coherent sense. The others had gathered in a loose, purposefully outlying semicircle, most with uncomfortable looks on their faces. Gamelyn was unsure whether it was because of what was happening, or what he was foolishly saying and doing.

He got to his feet, wary of Johan's proximity. "It was… beautiful. I didn't want you to shoot it."

"Oh, bloody…." Johan rolled his eyes, plainly imploring the heavens to give him patience. "Do you think I'd relish going back to our father to tell him you'd gotten yourself gored by some mad buck?"

Johan's ire was real, no doubt. But the disquiet was, too. Gamelyn looked down, said, "I'm sorry."

Johan kept glaring at him. The silence could have been cut and quartered.

Otho broke it, true to form. "You, and you," he said to Much and another huntsman. "Take the wolf carcass to our mounts."

"I should have them tie *you* to your horse and drag you back to the castle," Johan growled.

"It was foolish," Gamelyn said, quiet. "I am truly sorry."

He meant it, every word. Johan obviously believed him, for he closed his eyes, shook his head.

"We're off!" he suddenly shouted. "We've still not found meat for the larder!"

❧

THEY finally found the boar. A sow, with a litter of piglets that would make good eating for several days at least. It took three pikes and four crossbows to take her down, and Johan had delivered the coup de grace then gave fervent thanks to God for such a worthy opponent.

They cooked a well-earned meal on the tree edge before they headed home: Gamelyn's rabbit plus another that one of the huntsmen had taken, plus two skins of brandywine. Johan had pulled that last from his saddlebags with a distinct air of triumph and shared all around—one for his brothers and one for their assistants. The recipe was, according to Johan, "The newest gift to come from Queen Eleanor's lovely bosom!"

Which followed, of course, that on the way home there would be much drink-inspired talk about exactly what else had come from, or been around, Eleanor's bosom. And though Gamelyn wasn't too sure that the Queen Mother's royal bosom was something to be making dirty jokes over, it was so bloody pleasant to be on good terms with both his brothers at the same time that he kept it to himself and laughed in all the right places.

By the time they rode up to the gatehouse of Blyth, the sun was beginning to descend below the trees and they were all more than a little squiffed. Otho was giving orders for the disposition of the game they'd caught to their assistants, and Johan was wondering where Brand was to the gatehouse guards, who seemed anxious to tell Johan something but too polite to interrupt, and Gamelyn was humming to himself and twirling a hank of Diamant's mane with the same two fingers he'd blown a kiss to Rob and Marion with, and wondering how they would fancy some of that brandywine, because it was truly a thing to be fancied....

"Johan! Otho! Gamelyn! Thank God you've come!"

The shrill tone to Alais's voice brought all of them sober, and the brothers suddenly realized how quiet the courtyard was behind her. Otho turned to her, and Johan leapt off his horse and they both said exactly what Gamelyn's thoughts had flown to.

"It's Papa?"

"What's happened to him?"

ঔ

"WE WERE sitting, just playing chess as we often do, and he just… wilted over." Alais was wringing her hands, her eyes red from weeping. "I got him into bed with the help of Donall and the guard standing at the door. He's resting well enough now—"

"Has the leech been sent for?"

Alais made a face. "I have, for all the good it will do—!" She gasped as Johan closed on her, grabbed her arm.

"Woman, you aren't allowed an opinion on this! Did you send for him right away?"

"I told you I did," she spat at him. "Johan, you're hurting me!"

Gamelyn made an abortive move forward, halted as Otho strode forward and, with remarkable ease, broke Johan's grip and shoved him back. "Enough. I've warned you before about your manners toward my wife, Johan."

"Our father's life—"

"Is precious to all of us, Johan." Otho drew Alais to him. "But you're drunk—"

"We're all drunk!"

Otho put his hands up in surrender. "I know. But that is no reason to doubt Alais's care for our father, brother."

Gamelyn had had enough. "And while the two of you piss on each other's boots, he's waiting for us!" he snapped, shoving past them to take the steps two at a time up to Sir Ian's solar.

Two long flights of stairs were enough to send his heart pumping. Not even bothering to catch his breath, he rushed through the entry and stopped just over the threshold, sobering all too quickly as he saw his father.

It was worse than Gamelyn had yet seen. Sir Ian lay propped up, paler than the linens beneath his head, eyes sunken in his head. The leech was there, packing up his things, as was Donall, Sir Ian's body servant, speaking in low tones to his master as he arranged cushions and coverlets.

"Are they here?" his father was saying, and Donall looked up, jerked his head at Gamelyn.

"Here's your youngest now, milord, and if you can't hear the others coming you've gone deaf as well, then."

Sir Ian chuckled, but it was more a cough, and the grin at Donall's teasing was more a grimace. Sure enough, Johan and Otho's voices, still growling at each other, could be heard coming up the remainder of the stair. It broke Gamelyn's odd paralysis, and he lurched forward.

"Papa?"

"Take his hand, lad," Donall instructed as the others entered the solar. Gamelyn eased one buttock onto the bed. "He's still a wee bit chancy in his senses."

"I am not," Sir Ian protested, and reached out. Gamelyn took his hand—it felt more a cold, thin claw than flesh—and put it to his cheek.

Johan had stopped in the doorway to the solar to quiz the doctor, arms folded across his chest and his brows drawn together. Otho was also listening. Alais left them to it with a grimace and came over to stand next to Gamelyn. She put a hand to his head, riffled at his hair. It surprised him; she was not usually so open with her affections.

Her voice was also threaded with concern, shaky. "See, my lord father, your lads are all here about you again. I'm sure Gamelyn will read to you later, should you want."

"I should… indeed." Sir Ian lay back on the pillows, closed his eyes with a small groan. Gamelyn looked up at Alais, concerned; she gave a sigh and shrugged, once more stroking at his hair. But her words were to Sir Ian.

"Shall we all leave you, then?"

"Nay." It was very shaky, but firm.

"The doctor says you need to rest," Johan said. Behind him, the leech was departing the solar.

"I'll rest anon. Come, son, sit with me." He looked them all over and his brows drew together. "You look a trio of sots!"

Gamelyn had to admit that they did, rather.

"You took the brandywine." It was stern, but there was a hint of a smile curving into Sir Ian's cheek.

"I left plenty for you," Johan assured, and his father fully grinned, this time.

"I should think you had better. Did you manage to get some game for our bare table before the drinking started? Tell me how you all fared. Was it a good hunt?"

Johan took a tentative seat on the bed across from Gamelyn. "It would have been, had your youngest not spoiled my shot."

Gamelyn rolled his eyes. Of course, that would be the first thing Johan brought up. After they'd already agreed to not worry their father with what had happened.

Otho came to Gamelyn's defense; drink seemed to have mellowed his earlier irritation. "Perhaps our little brother had a point, Papa. It truly would have been a crime to shoot that lovely old stag. Perhaps he deserves, after all, to live out his days and make more fawns like him. He was very beautiful. His hide was the color of fresh milk and toffees."

"And would have made a lovely foot rest for our ailing father," Johan pointed out.

"I have plenty of foot rests," Sir Ian chided, putting his hand on Johan's knee.

A twinge of something altogether close to guilt and sorrow passed over Johan's face as he looked down and covered his father's thin hand with his broad, brown one.

"I'm sure you found better game than an old, bleached stag, anyway." Sir Ian winked at Otho and Gamelyn.

"In fact, Johan took a boar," Gamelyn said; it was hard to not feel generous with his father's hand so snug in his—and the memory of Johan's face upon the hand he held.

"And Gamelyn took a bunny," Johan put in, smirking across at Gamelyn.

So much for generosity.

"And?" Otho put in mildly.

Johan grinned wider, impenitent, then relented. "Aye, not just a bunny. He took down a wolf, Papa."

"Did he?"

"A clean kill, one shot," Otho added. "Methinks Gamelyn has been practicing his archery a bit. He's gotten quite deedy with a crossbow."

"Maybe when he grows a bit more he'll be able to stand a pike against a boar." Obviously drink had not mellowed Johan enough. "Until then, he can keep to his arrows and books."

"And I'll wrap them in the wolf skin," Gamelyn retorted.

"Milords," Donall interrupted, curt. "Your lord father was bled and needs his rest. He's in some pain. P'rhaps later you can visit again?"

Johan looked as if he'd protest Donall's cheek, then looked at Sir Ian, who was wilting sideways on the cushions. "Of course. Later, then, Papa?"

Sir Ian gave each of them a look, then peered at Donall's stern gaze and conceded. "Later."

For a man willing to face a mad boar head-on, Johan was unwilling to stay in a sickroom for long. He kissed his father's hand and beat a quick retreat. Otho and Alais began to follow. Gamelyn started to untangle his hand from his father's, paused as Sir Ian's grip tightened and his eyes fluttered.

"Lad?"

In the doorway, Otho and Alais paused.

Gamelyn bent closer. "Yes, Papa? Would you like me to come later, read to you?"

"Yes, son. But… something else."

He settled back against the cushions and paused. Gamelyn looked over at Otho and Alais, then to Donall, started to rise again. Again, his father's grip tightened.

"What else, Papa?" Otho asked, gentle.

Sir Ian nodded and frowned, then opened his eyes. "Gamelyn. The wise woman?"

Gamelyn looked up at Donall, who shrugged. "Wise woman, Father?"

"The forester. His wife." Sir Ian's hand came up, brushed against the healing gash on Gamelyn's face. "The lad with the simples jar. Remember?"

Not that Gamelyn was likely to forget. "You mean Eluned. Rob's mother."

Otho was frowning at Gamelyn, curious. Gamelyn told him, "Loxley, the forester. His wife knows of healing. "

"I want her here."

"Surely the leech—" Otho began.

Sir Ian shook his head. "The forester said she would help, if I asked." His eyes were very clear. His grip tightened in Gamelyn's with some of its former strength. "Go, lad. Ask her for help. Bring her here, if she can come."

"Aye, Papa. I'll go," Gamelyn told him. "I'll go tomorrow at first light and see if she can come to you."

"Good." Sir Ian relaxed back against the cushions, and his hand went lax in Gamelyn's.

"Bring her regardless," Otho said suddenly. "If he wants her, then she must come."

Gamelyn peered at him, saw the worry in his brown eyes, then nodded. Putting an arm about Alais, Otho drew her from the solar.

"You too, young master," Donall directed. "Out. Come back after supper. If he's awake you can read to him then."

Gamelyn rose from the bed, peering down at Sir Ian with worry weighting his chest. But not just worry….

There was also excitement.

"And you need to get a good night's rest yourself, mind, if you're to be traipsing all over the kingdom!" Donall was shooing him out, albeit gently, and fussing the while.

Gamelyn shot another glance over at his father, thin and drawn amidst all the bedclothes, then escaped the room, speeding across to his own chambers and feeling like the lowest of scum.

Because he was.

He shut his door firmly behind him, bolted it, leaned against it.

There was no longer any question in his mind but that he was going to Hell… or at the very least Purgatory, for a long while. Because right below the apprehension for his father was elation. He had a legitimate reason to visit Loxley.

To ask Eluned to help his father.

To ask about the arrow, and the other foresters.

To see if everyone was all right.

To see Rob.

Elation skittered and fled, to be replaced with an odd trepidation.

Fear. It was fear, eclipsing down from that moment, down in the barns, when he had seen Rob pinned up against the stable wall by that lad and had more of… something… coursing through him than he'd ever felt in his life. One that even now put a tilt to his breeks and a slow, shivery hollow in his gut.

He had no right to feel like this. Surely nothing more than his body's temptation, a wicked willingness to look at anything—including two lads groping each other in the dark—with a lecherous wish for pleasure.

It was wrong. He should turn from it. And not in any craven fashion that held as much a sin as the thought.

As the *fantasy*….

Desperate, Gamelyn bit at his lip, sawed teeth against soft flesh. Unfortunately all it did was make him harder, and he barely stopped himself from reaching downward to grip himself tight, ease it. Instead, he shoved away from the door and went to the books lying on his bed. He had plenty of reading to do, and no doubt it was a better way to spend his time than some wanton, mindless humping of his hand or the bedclothes.

There was no better way to prove triumph over weakness than to spurn it.

He opened the book on runes, skimmed, and saw a sigil that looked like stag horns. Stopped. Wondered, suddenly, what had transpired out in the green Wode, at Much's reaction to it, at how he himself had reached out and touched a wild thing as if he were… Rob.

Had Rob ever seen that pale stag?

And what would he say about it, if he had?

"…like some idiot peasant drooling before their horned devil…!"

"He's calling tae you, m'lord."

Surely it was no devil. Something so lovely and wild seemed more a bearer of light than any darkness. A unicorn, not a basilisk.

Yet….

Gamelyn was still there, hunched over his books and attempting to wrestle some meaning from them when Alais came tapping at his door. His father had awakened, and would like some reading time with his youngest. Gamelyn acquiesced, marking his place in the old tome and then shrugging on his cape—the sun had descended while he read, and he was chilled.

As he walked to his father's chambers, Gamelyn decided it was imperative he go to evensong this night. There was no doubt he was going to need some guidance on this journey.

☙ XII ❧

"HOY! A fish!"

A splash in the stream before her, patently caused by the rock that had been thrown from behind and above. A tall, lanky figure dropped to the bank, not an arm's reach away, peering into the clear water, expectant.

Marion glanced over to her brother, held his gaze as his brows quirked. He lasted for a few slow breaths then looked down and away, fool's demeanor fading, cheeks darkening.

Then, "I'm sorry. I didna mean it."

She wasn't very good at holding grudges, and she'd never been good at holding onto her anger with Rob. He was too good at apologizing—mostly because when he did bother to apologize, he truly meant it, and put his entire heart into it, plain in his eyes for everyone to see.

So it was surely inevitable that they'd end up on the bank wrapped as close for comfort as a litter of milk-glutted pups. Only this time Marion was the one with arms wrapped about her, holding tight against anything that would hurt them. This time it was Rob doing the insistence, imparting a strength she just didn't have right now and it was Rob, not Marion, who was trying to make the case that, maybe, hope wasn't so impossible.

He wasn't just her little brother anymore. The arms about her were wiry, but strong enough to huff the breath from her when he squeezed—just that much too much, he wasn't yet aware how strong he was. His voice rumbled beneath her cheek, more a soft baritone burr than the clear, high bell of boyhood.

And more hairy, she chuckled, as he smooshed her nose against his chest.

"What's so funny?"

"I was just considering," she said against his breastbone, "how you've somehow grown a wolf's pelt when I wasna looking."

"Um." Suddenly her baby brother was there again as he loosed her with a look of chagrin on his face. "Sorry."

Marion reached forward, flicked the forelock from his eyes. "Our Hob-Robyn has grown up all tall and fetching; could have any lass he wanted did he crook his finger. Aye, any lad, too," she added as he rolled his eyes at her. "Since you'd rather act a tosser than take a wife."

"I dinna think I'm made for a wife," he said, slow and considering. "P'rhaps better so. Horns sit uneasy in a marriage bed."

"Only if the one you wed ent willing to be your Maiden. Look at Da and Mam."

"I do. Da and Mam are… special, but still. What the Horned Lord and the Lady would have them be sets them against each other sometimes. I mean, even Cernun… when he was Hunter, he never wed any Maiden who came to him upon the Bel-fires. I only hope that when it comes to me, I'll be able…." He trailed off, eyes darting to her uneasily.

"When the blood-rut sets upon you, often it doesn't matter what rises you," she told him. "You've had the agaric for the Seeking, but you've never drained a Blessing cup. Anyway." She shrugged. "Da and Mam aren't old. They may *never* be too old."

Aye, still her baby brother; he wrinkled his nose and shook his head. "Do you *have* to say things like that?"

"I think it's comforting, to know that even if your bits get wrinkly—"

Rob started whistling, tuneless and loud.

"—they still work!" she continued, just as loud and next to his right ear.

He made a face, put a finger in his ear and wriggled it. "Well, you've made it so my ears waint work *now*, let alone when they're wrinkly. You can take that Blessing cup business and welcome. Have yourself some big, muscular fellow with fair hair and a whopping great… bow." He smirked. "Assuming he likes lasses with tempers to match their hair instead of skinny archer lads, and I don't steal him from you."

Marion flicked her finger at his nose this time. Returning his smirk with one of her own as he yipped, she leaned back against him. Rob's arms crept around her, his chin nesting into her hair.

Silence, but not comfortable. There was too much lying underneath it, and she finally had to speak of it, bid it surface.

"Da's at Nottingham by now," she said. "He and George."

Rob gave a sound between a groan and a sigh. "It's got to be killing Da, what he's having to do." His voice went hard. "It's *wrong*."

"What else could he have done?" Marion protested.

"And it's more wrong, that he's so helpless." Still hard, that smooth, new-made baritone could have cut steel. "They've no right."

"They've every right—"

"They don't!" It burst from Rob. "I've lost my friend, you've lost one who might have been a lover, we've lost a man who was as uncle to us." His voice broke, wavered then came back, a little harder, a little older. "We've lost our da. He rode away from us several days ago, and we waint see that man again, you and I. He's our *da*, Mari, and they're hacking bits from him like he's nowt. *He's the Horned One*. But what good has his power, his Sight done him? His *tynged* was there, before him: life-giver, t' hold peace, protect his people… and it's all gone wrong." The arms around her were shaking, fingers clutching at her skirts, and his breath was thick, clotted with unshed tears. "He'll never be the same, and I don't know whether to love him or hate him for it."

Marion wanted to turn, cuddle him close like she had the child who'd had one too many nightmares, or eaten himself into a huge bellyache. But she also didn't want to; she wanted to be the one comforted and hugged close. Nor did Rob *want* comfort, not now—she kenned it as surely as she'd kenned Will's heart in the mirror of the lake water. Rob wanted to stand up, to find strength, somehow, and honor, and a place for those in a world where the only place truly open to him was on his knees, crawling.

"I almost envy Will." Fierce, angry.

Marion jerked around, twisted a finger full of that patch of chest hair, and yanked. Hard.

"*Ow*!"

Glaring at him, she held up her prize—not a scalp's worth, but enough to make her warrior ancestors nod encouragement.

"Bloody *damn*, Marion, what are y—?"

"Don't you *ever* say that again." She shoved her face close into his, saw his pupils, only discernible from ebon iris by a thin inner ring of indigo, contract. "Do you hear me?"

He looked down and to the side, mouth tightening.

"Answer me, by th' Lady, or I'll take my bow and ram it up your fair backside!"

He hunched up slightly, gave a snort that sounded too much like humor for her liking.

"Hob-Robyn, I swear I'll—"

And suddenly another snort from him, and it was laughter, she knew it.

"Ah, Mari," he said, rocking back to lie on his elbows in the grass, giving her full range to wallop him did she so choose—and she might, if he was laughing at her. "Don't you know better than to offer something like that to a boy who does with boys?"

It was absolutely preposterous—and *not funny*—but suddenly Marion was sniggering into his tunic, and Rob was falling back on the bank and chuckling, and then they were both laughing until they cried.

"So you're saying," Marion shoved herself up on her elbows, resting her forearms on Rob's chest, "that you prefer a longbow."

"Better long than short," he quipped, then grimaced and rubbed at his chest. "By damn, woman, I think I'm bleeding."

"Serve you right."

He shrugged, rolled out from under her, and sat up.

"Rob?"

She could see the tendons in his neck twitching.

"Will left a sign in the old place."

"Rob!"

"I know. He took a risk. But he…." He paused. "He needs my help, to know that not *everyone's* abandoned him. He needs to know what's… happening. He knew I'd tell no one. Except you. He probably knew I'd tell you."

"The risk is yours too, Rob, if anyone catches you—"

"They waint. No one knows the Wode like I do—"

"Except Da."

Rob hesitated, then said, "Even more than Da, now."

"Bloody cheek!" Marion reached forward, knotted her fingers in his hair, and tugged. "You're getting too big for your boots, you are!"

When he turned to her, his eyes weren't lit with the normal brazen spark that usually accompanied such a boast. In fact, his face was somber, a bit too pale; he wasn't boasting at all. "Lass," he said, all too soft, "I think the only one who could come close to knowing the Wode as well as I must is you. And I have to beg you to stay home, this time."

"Rob—"

"I mean it. You're in this too deep, Mari, pet, and you know it. You canna think straight. Too much frustration, trouble, and should've/would've lie between you and Charming William."

Any protests she was girding up died a-borning. He was right. He was *right*, and risking entirely too much to have a liability along.

As always, he read her like one of the books she so loved and he so scorned. "Aye, you'd likely trip me up in this. And I've only recently got past tripping over my big feet. In my too-small boots," he added, with a smirk. But it was forced.

She sat back, rather helplessly. "Oh, Rob."

He leaned forward, kissed the top of her head. "I know. But I have to do it."

ꕥ

ROB had everything ready: an old shortbow that was still more than serviceable but that he no longer used, some furs, some victuals in his pack—enough to go on until he found out what Will needed—and a sack of good mead. The last would dull the pain a bit even if it didn't give its normal cheer. He disguised the sorting and cadging beneath a tidy-up of the barn. The first time his mother headed his way, he was busy organizing tack and bedding stalls.

But the second time, he didn't hear her. He merely looked up to see her in the doorway, hat tied to her ebon hair and her simples basket on one arm, watching him silently as he bent, sorting in earnest.

Rob froze in place, a frantic wondering in the back of his mind insisting he could explain, somehow. Maybe.

Eluned came forward and knelt beside him, her basket in her lap. "You'll need this," she said gently, handing him a small tincture bottle. "And this one. And perhaps a bit of this would not go amiss…."

She handed two bottles to Rob after the first, and several sachets and small doeskin bags. Then she reached out and closed his mouth. He hadn't even realized it was hanging open. "You'll catch flies, son. If he can wait until tonight, you can bring him a crock of our supper. In the meantime, I have some things to gather, to make up a few more simples. And you can find out what he needs for his journey. Because you waint know until he tells you."

He sat there, palms full of medicaments, could only say, helplessly, "*Mam.*"

"I hope I needn't tell you to take care." Eluned kissed his cheek, then rose, shook out her kirtles, and strode out the door.

Rob sat there for some time, looking after her and wanting to bawl like a bairn.

Instead he bent back to his task.

The load had to be lightened twice: the first time when he'd decided traveling afoot would be more circumspect than being mounted, the second when he realized that his mother was right: he truly didn't know what Will needed.

This was no lark, no boyhood camping venture. This was literally the line between living and dying.

He would go, anon. Take a few things, find out what Will truly needed and go back under cover of darkness.

Then Gamelyn came riding up just as Rob finished lunch with his sister and was speeding down the front stair.

And every careful plan Rob had made went flying out his ears.

It wasn't just because Gamelyn suddenly looked akin to something out of an ancient tale, more centaur than mere rider upon that great gray stallion, in a cape with the sheen and color of dried blood and fair hair flicking across his face with the wind. It wasn't because this time he had an escort riding at Diamant's tail, a mailed and helmeted soldier that made Rob's mouth go dry with several seconds of honest fear, then his hackles rise in just-as-honest fury. It wasn't just because the likelihood of Rob leaving for any clandestine meeting with a wolfshead was likely swolloped now that a nobleman's son was in residence. Or that Gamelyn was as sure a liability for Rob as Will was for Marion—worse, for more reasons than Rob wanted to count.

It was, somehow, all of those things and none of them, because topping them all was the sense of a warning, a dangerous breath down his neck, time canting sideways and sending itself forward into tens of unknowns.

If he couldn't even trust his own feelings to not turn and gut him, then who could he trust?

Even if he *wanted* to.

"Rob!"

The broad smile made Rob's heart jerk then shudder heat against his breastbone, and all he could think was, *And what evil sprite gave you both that lovely smile and such lovely rotten timing?* Gamelyn dismounted in one graceful, powerful move, took the rein in one gloved hand, and walked forward. One hand on his sword's pommel, there was a proper swordsman's swagger to him that surely, *surely* he'd not had the last time Rob had seen him… had it truly been only a se'nnight ago, that eager pup in the barn?

And how was it, *again*, that Gamelyn should look like every mortal sin his Church could conjure up, while Rob looked like something from the rubbish tip, all sweat, dirt, and dander from mucking out a stable.

And if he had straw in his hair, he'd not even had the mouth job to go with it this time.

The smile on Gamelyn's face slipped, a little, as Rob merely nodded. Rob truly didn't trust his voice. A slight frown quirking his brow, Gamelyn gave Diamant a pat, dug a treat from his purse and spoke the horse's name—ah, so that was how he'd managed to get the nappy bugger's attention.

And that throaty caress of language—directed toward a *horse*!—only made Rob's heart give another lurch and bump.

And he was bloody *pathetic*.

"Sir Gamelyn!"

And why should Marion sound all… *happy*? As if she'd nowt on her mind that a visit from His Lordship wouldn't sweep away like dried-out cobwebs. She came flying down the stairs and pounced on Gamelyn, gave him a great buss on the cheek then a hug that made Diamant cock a wary ear and might've broken a rib or two if Gamelyn hadn't been wearing a chainmail tunic under his surcoat.

Chainmail. Pretentious… *nobleman.*

And Gamelyn's broad, lovely smile returned. He lifted Marion off her feet, gave Rob a glance that surely said, *See, this is what a real greeting looks like, you pillock!* then closed his eyes and returned Marion's hug all the fiercer.

But all Rob could think of was how, did he have the chance, he'd show Sir Gamelyn a greeting, all right, one that would weaken his knees and pop his eyes from his head….

Save him, and he couldn't even ask the Horned Lord for strength. Ask a fertility god with a knob as subtle as a pikestaff to help him deflate?

Aye, *that* was likely.

He's another lad, Rob gave it a game try, nevertheless. *Surely you'd rather I fancied a lass with huge breasts and nice wide hips, to make lots more little fawns to sing your name in the night.*

No answer, but it took care of his inconvenient erection, right enough. Sent it, all nice and pliable, back where it belonged.

"What are you doing here, all…." Marion trailed off as she got a better look at Gamelyn's companion, and Rob could sense the sudden fear in her, felt fury once more lick fire behind his eyes.

"Why is *he* here?" he growled, jerking his head to the soldier.

Oddly enough, the soldier didn't look like the normal bully in mail; his broad shoulders were hunched, his gaze averted to the ground. Hiding something, sure enough.

Marion's gaze flitted to his, warning, even as Gamelyn shrugged, his smile fading once again.

"My father's orders."

Marion pushed back slightly, once more shooting a wary glance in Rob's direction. "Your… father?"

Rob felt the breath stutter in his chest. Casually he pretended to clasp his hands behind his back, one going for the dagger he always kept sheathed above his right buttock.

Gamelyn was smiling. "I'm here on legitimate business, this time."

Rob's fingers touched the dagger's pommel, caressed their way into a grip.

"Off with you, then," Gamelyn told the soldier, turning to him. "Find a place where you'll be comfortable, and you'll have done your duty."

The soldier made a stiff, awkward bow, turned first to Marion then to Rob with somewhat deeper, but hastier bows, then mounted and wheeled his horse. It seemed that he couldn't retreat fast enough.

Again, Marion shot a glance to her brother. "He's… leaving."

Rob had already fingered his dagger halfway to his shoulder blade, nearly free. He paused, uncertain.

Gamelyn was watching the soldier go. "Aye, he wasn't happy about encroaching upon your place this far, believe me. But this way he can satisfy both his orders and his conscience." Gamelyn shrugged, turned back to them. "We've come to an understanding, he and I, seeing as how he seems to be as…." He trailed off, seemed to notice Rob's wary stance. "What?"

"Why are you here?" Rob said, quiet.

"I…." Gamelyn looked confused. "Well, I'm here to make sure you're both all right. And this time, like I told you, my father sent me. He's… well, he's very sick and wants your mother's help; he's insistent that she come and attend to him. It was the perfect way to make sure that you were both all right."

Silence, with only the retreating hoofbeats of the soldier disappearing over the near rise.

Marion smacked Gamelyn upside the head.

"*Ow*! Marion, what the—?"

"You great silly… *git*!" she burst out. "Coming in here all tarted up with a soldier on your tail… after what's happened! Have you lost your bloody mind?"

Gamelyn's mouth dropped. He closed it, put steepled hands to his face. "Oh."

"You'd better do a sodding sight better than 'oh'," she retorted.

"I didn't mean… I'm sorry."

Rob flipped his dagger in the air and caught it, his gaze smacking into Gamelyn's. "I was ready for him, lad. Don't ever do that again."

The green eyes were wide, stricken. "I didn't—"

"Didna think," Rob supplied, and stuck his dagger back in his belt. "Well enough, then. I'm away, Marion."

Marion's slender frame had tensed, again. "Are you sure?"

"I'm sure." he said, and started for the barn.

"Wait… *wait*!" Gamelyn took a few steps after him, halted as Rob turned on him and shot a look that was clearly warning. "But I… I just got here."

Funny, how want could so easily slide into anger and sour, thwarted, in his belly. Rob should sooner reach for the moon than this nobleman's son, and what had just happened was but proof of it. "*Some* of us ent got the say-so," he said, dangerous-quiet, "of pleasing ourselves when and where we want."

"Rob," Marion hissed.

"I have a task," he told her through his teeth, "laid on me. It's a sight more important than any lark, and you know it as well as I."

It was not satisfying to see her pale, but she got the point.

The look on Gamelyn's face seemed, oddly enough, as frustrated and anxious as Rob himself felt. "I'm so desperately *sorry*," he said. "I didn't mean to… you're right, with all that's gone on, I should have known. Christ's blood, Rob, I'm just so glad to see you're both all right! I've had so many questions, I wanted to come as soon as I heard, but I couldn't so much as step foot out of the castle these past days, guards everywhere and—"

"Questions." Rob had found his voice but it was flat, the sour, hollow, *sick* feeling in his belly sinking deeper.

"Well, of course. What would you think in my place? It was an arrow just like the one in Marion's quiver that killed him, and I was worried sick about her—"

"Why? Did you think one of us had done it?"

"*Rob*!" Marion growled.

"Christ, *no*!" Gamelyn burst out. "What do you take me for? My brother said it had peacock fletching, and was used for conjuring, and the soldier dead…." He was stammering, and it was oddly satisfying. "I didn't mean any such—"

"Gamelyn." Marion put a firm hand to his arm. "We know you didna mean to—"

"He never *means to*, does he?" It burst from Rob, all to the sudden, and he couldn't have stopped it, any more than he could have touched the moon and the stars. "But he comes and goes whenever he pleases, and never so much as a 'will you?' our way. Questions, he says, like we have any answer to owt we can give, here and now or ever!"

Marion was staring at him. Gamelyn too was gaping like *Rob* was the crazy one.

"Bloody hell, just *look* at you, wobbling your gob at me like a landed fish… while everything you say… you…." Just as abruptly Rob was stuttering over his words, confused and…. "You mix me up, make me not think straight."

"Rob—"

"You want answers and I don't have them, y' see? All I can see right now, all I *know* is that there's your people, and mine. Your people can order my mam to attend them like she's a horse to be mouthed and paced and bought at market—"

"That's not what I was asking. I wouldn't—"

"But you just did. I heard you, Gamelyn Boundys, how your da is 'insistent' she come to him, and no matter there are people here who need her, or a house she has to leave—"

"You're taking everything and twisting it!"

"—So my da has to come back to an empty house after going to bloody Nottingham so he can turn his best friend over to rot in the sheriff's gaol for killing one of your soldiers what bloody *needed* killing—!"

"Rob!" Marion grabbed his arm, and only then did the torrent stop, with a gasp of breath that sounded altogether too much a sob for Rob's comfort. But it gave him his control back.

"Why do you want to know about the arrow, Sir Gamelyn?" Every bit of soft mockery in Rob's power went into the question.

Gamelyn either didn't notice or was ignoring him. "I told you. Marion had one, in her quiver. I was worried."

"Worried that our people did the pretty to your sweet little rapist of a soldier? Well, they *have*, and well done them!"

"*Sweet* Lady!" Marion burst out. "Rob, you go too far—"

"Stay out of this, Mari—"

"Oh, lad, I'm in it to the hilt." She put a hand to his chest, shoved. Hard. "And if I'm going to watch you two go at it, it had better to be for more reason than *you* looking for a fight!"

It stopped the reply he'd whet on his lips.

"I don't know what's got into you all to the sudden, Rob, but you're acting mad as a buck in rut!"

And that made him swallow the reply whole. It burned like acid in the back of his throat. Rob couldn't hold Marion's eyes. All steel and storms, they were, when he made the attempt and chased away. Gamelyn's weren't any easier; they weakened him with a mix of fury and, humiliatingly, *yearning*.

"He wasn't *my* soldier," Gamelyn ventured, sudden and quiet. "Or even one of my father's. What did he do?"

Rob gave a tiny shake of his head at Marion, but she frowned at him, answered.

"He raped and killed a woman. We knew her. She was wife and mother to the two foresters."

"Merciful Jesus," Gamelyn said, and when Rob peered at him, Gamelyn was white to the lips.

"I can see how merciful *that* one is by the ones who defend his Church."

"Rob, you can't—"

Rob put up his hands, knew it was surrender and didn't, at that moment, care. "I have to go."

"Where are you going?" Gamelyn asked, very quiet.

Striding over to the paddock, Rob merely answered, "Hunting."

"I was hunting just yesterday." It was still very quiet. "With my brothers."

Rob paused, then shook his head and kept going.

"I saw a stag," Gamelyn said after him. "In the forest."

"Fancy that. A stag, in the forest," Rob sneered. Vaulting the small paddock fence, he bent to scoop up his bow and quiver. "Did he have horns, lad, or did you mistake a doe?"

Gamelyn's glare could have easily been behind an arrow at nock. "Pray give me some credit. Else how are you all that different from my brother who thinks I'm a bookish imbecile?"

And that one hurt. Why, Rob figured he knew all too well, but he merely took in a breath, made as if to check the arrows in his quiver. "All right, then. A stag. In the forest."

"He came up to me. He was ivory, with golden eyes."

Rob flicked a glance at Marion. She was slowly curling her hands into fists, bunching up her dark green overkirtle. "A… *white* stag," she said, meeting her brother's eyes.

"Crème-colored, actually," Gamelyn said. "And it was no ordinary stag, particularly since Much was on his knees in front of it, blithering about what grace 'He' was giving me."

"Wait," Rob said. "Much?"

"My guard dog." He jerked his head in the direction the soldier had gone. "Johan set him on me some time ago. But he's been… discreet. No doubt he's going to camp just east of here, since he's more than once talked about not wanting to 'offend' the Hunter."

Marion sucked in a breath.

Gamelyn's eyes narrowed. "I see you recognize the appellation. I'd appreciate it if you'd enlighten me. Eventually. God save me from rushing you."

Rob crossed his arms. "It might be a sight easier if you'd speak plain English 'stead of all your fancy book talk—"

"Spare me!" Gamelyn retorted. "I think you understand me well enough. So. Stag. White."

"Crème-colored," Rob corrected, in his best plummy noble's accent, and Gamelyn flushed.

Ah, so you're not totally in control of yourself, either.

"As I said," Gamelyn gritted, "he came up to me. Stood not as far away as you are. Breathed on me like he… *knew* me." Even as he said it, Gamelyn was looking at them as if they'd string him up for even admitting something so fantastic.

Because your people would string us up, Rob thought. *Would you, then? Because I don't know what I'm going to do, anymore, if you are like* them.

"I keep tellin' you, lad," Rob growled, "I've no time now to—"

"Why do you keep calling me lad?" Gamelyn interrupted.

"Because you're actin' like one, and a poncy noble's son to boot, assuming what you want to know is more important than owt or nowt I might have to do. But, ah, *that's* right. You *are* a poncy noble's son."

And there's *one for Loxley*, Rob thought, satisfied, as Gamelyn's cheeks pinked and he looked down. Rob hefted his knapsack. "I have to go on," he told Marion. "I'll be back tonight."

"I'll go with you," Gamelyn said firmly.

"Nay," Rob said, just as firmly. "You waint."

☙ XIII ❧

THEY watched Rob disappear into the green, and then Marion put a firm hand on Gamelyn's arm and marched him into the house. Obviously she wasn't following Rob, nor was she about to let Gamelyn do so.

A small part of him resented it, wanting to follow, to make Rob see… something other than what he was obviously seeing when he looked at Gamelyn. But another, burgeoning part was relieved that he had an excuse not to, to stay with Marion as she went over to the kettle warming on the fire and gave it a stir.

Marion was… safer.

"Pottage?" she asked, and he nodded.

"Unload yourself from all that gear. 'Tis warm enough without such things." After some rattling and scooping, Marion brought over a bowl filled to the brim, sided by fresh bread.

"Your cooking is just…." Gamelyn reflected his true feelings with a smile and heart-meant sigh. "My brother's wife is terrible in a kitchen."

"Well, pr'haps she's never had to do on her own. Or cook for a perpetual round of harvesters during the gathering seasons." She scooped a portion for herself and put it at the table, then teased, "Should we take a crock of this to your shy guard dog? Or should I be careful—'tis the shy ones that can bite you without a warning."

"Much? He'd not even bare a tooth to you. You'd make his day," he said, truthfully enough. "His fortnight, probably."

"And you want to know why."

He stilled mid-bite and peered at her. "Does that mean you're going to tell me?"

Marion sat down with her own bowl. "I ent sure it's mine *to* tell."

There was a shuffle of running feet hurrying up the stairs just outside and hurried breaths, and Eluned came bursting in the entry with her hat askew and her skirts tucked hastily into her girdle. Halted, panting.

Gamelyn was sure he and Marion looked as startled as Eluned, food halfway to their mouths.

Then Marion said, half rising, "Mam? Is everything all right?"

Eluned's gaze had come to rest on Gamelyn. It narrowed, and then she took in a huge breath and lowered her basket to the ground. "Is that soldier with you, then?"

Gamelyn nodded, eyes wide.

"Great Lord save me." She shook her head. "I saw him, making himself to home on our grazing common, and I…." She trailed off, then, very obviously, made another attempt. "Well. I was worried."

Culpability twinged at Gamelyn. He had unnerved too many people without meaning to this day. Rising, he offered an arm to her basket; she smiled and let him take it, untying her hat. "On the counter, thank you, lad."

Gamelyn did not miss the querying look Eluned threw Marion as he turned away, but pretended he did.

"Do you want some pottage, Mam?" Marion asked.

"Please. We can all sit, you can finish your meal, and I can catch my breath."

"I'm very sorry, Eluned," Gamelyn apologized. "My father insisted that I have a proper escort." He pulled her chair for her, then Marion's.

"Your father knows you're here, lad?" Eluned looked closer, seemed to consider his face. She waited until he'd seated himself once more, then said, quietly, "He's taken worse, then."

The soft, matter-of-fact compassion almost did him in then and there. Gamelyn looked away, aware that his eyes were glinting in the dim, and nodded.

"Well. I've several things to see to this evening. Marion, I'll need you to take my place with Janet. Janet is from Loxley," Eluned explained, turning to Gamelyn. "She's very ill, and we've all been doing turns at nursing her until her daughter arrives from down river."

"How long, Mam?"

"Ilene is supposed to come mid-night to spell me… well, you. You can sleep over or come back."

Gamelyn felt bereft for no good reason. Both Rob and Marion gone, and this strange tension between the three of them… and serve him right, for he shouldn't be here for anything but his father's need….

"I'll come back," Marion said and took a drink from her mug. "Moon's just away from full and it looks to be a clear night. A walk would be nice."

"Take your bow, mind. Wolves were seen passing through the west carr."

"I will, Mam. Shall I be off anon?"

"Eat, first. And take some hand-work to occupy you; the old woman's sleeping, mostly." Eluned returned her gaze to Gamelyn. "The lad and I will get along just fine."

ଔଓ

ELUNED was another who, like Rob, had grown past the boundary of absolutely safe. And, like Rob, what lay past that boundary was a tenuous affinity, a strange… *lure*, and one that he couldn't quite put name to. Despite that, over the past year and a half in particular, she had become more… distant. Gamelyn would catch her sometimes, looking at him, her gaze daunting. As if she was sizing him up and finding a lack. And the more he tried to fill that lack, the more he would find her measuring.

Eluned never forgot who Gamelyn was, even when he himself did.

Now was no different. Marion had left not too long ago, with a knapsack of mending to occupy her vigil and a crock of pottage sure to befuddle Much into not speaking for a se'nnight. From across the table, Eluned asked Gamelyn questions about his father's condition, quite detailed in spots, some that he couldn't answer and others that he could. Once satisfied, she rose with a nod and set herself to her simples, muttering to herself as she sorted, set things to brew over the fire, mixed and measured. Gamelyn tried, more than once, to start a conversation—Eluned either answered in short, preoccupied sentences or, immersed in her task, not at all. Finally Gamelyn settled himself on the floor and began tending his steel with whetstone and oiled cloths.

He'd honed the sword to a bright edge that cut a strand of hair run across it, and started on his quillion dagger next. It had been his first acquisition with his own means; he'd traded a mail cowl and several otter pelts for it. Johan had scoffed, saying Gamelyn had been swoggled by a new bladesmith and the dagger was too fancy to be of any use, but Gamelyn had been adamant, impressed by the art of the man's work. Time had proven the bladesmith's skill and Gamelyn's instincts—the dagger was as deadly as it was delicate, as long as his forearm with a grip of oak-tanned leather and gold filigrees on the pommel and guard.

A shadow moved over him. "That's a pretty thing."

Gamelyn blinked, looked up, realized his legs were tingling and his hands greasy… and he was working in near dark, as the sun was setting behind the trees past Eluned's garden. "Sorry?"

Eluned was wiping her hands on her apron, looking at the dagger. "You'd best not show that to th' Hob-Robyn; he might not let you go home with it. All you lads, mad for pointy things." She began walking about the little cottage, lighting the oil lamps. Warm gold spilled across Gamelyn's lap, setting the well-oiled steel cradled there a-glint.

"I'm guessing that you've come here, escorted and all, to see me to your father's bedside."

It sounded as severe as Rob's earlier accusations, no matter that she didn't cease her motions. Gamelyn took a considering breath, then said, quietly, "I don't mean to… compel anyone. I was merely hoping"—and damn, but his throat was getting all tight again—"that you could help."

She came over, knelt before him, and took his greasy hands in hers, held tight. "Lad, I'll be frank with you. From what you've told me, there's not much help for your father."

He looked away, gritted his teeth against the knot growing in his chest. It was what he had expected, but it was cursed hard to hear it spoken aloud like that, even through the genuine compassion in Eluned's voice.

"I've been mixing up several draughts for him. The one is strong and sovereign, 'twill ease his pain and help him sleep through the night. The second is for strength, so his mind and body waint crumple in on him. That's the worse of it, for a man. He'll want to be a man 'til he goes, as much in his mind and on his feet as possible. Both will work together, give 'im that."

"You're not coming." Surely he shouldn't feel this desolate.

Eluned must have seen it, for she squeezed his hands again. "I will come. I promise you, lad, I'll come, see t' him. But I'll no' be able to leave with you right away. If it was dire, or burning needful, I'd come with you at sunup and never fear. But as it is, I've several in need who're countin' on me for several days hence, and my man's due to return, either on the morrow or the day after, from Nottingham. Do you understand?"

He did, that was the worst of it. No doubt Johan or Otho would cart her off, will-she-nill-she, as if it was their right to break in and disrupt a life because of will or whim, but Gamelyn couldn't. Wouldn't.

If he did, he'd be just what Rob accused him of.

"I'm sorry, lad. For all of it. Please believe me."

Gamelyn nodded, kept looking away, gritting his teeth to keep the lump in his stomach from rising to his throat and choking him. "Adam went to Nottingham with the forester who killed the guard, didn't he?" As subject matter went, perhaps it was chancy, but better than what was bidding him to break down and bawl like a bairn in the middle of his host's cottage. "I'm sorry, too. For what happened. Rob and Marion said he was your friend."

Eluned released his hands and rose, wiping the oil from her hands. "They both were. But they broke the law, and Adam must uphold that law."

"Marion said that the soldier had killed the man's wife. Why did he not seek the law's protection?"

Turning to him, Eluned twisted her brows in an expression so akin to Rob's it gave Gamelyn a tiny, incomprehensible flutter in the pit of his stomach. "Gamelyn," she chided. "Surely you're not so naïve to think the law works same for your people as for mine?"

It stung, but instead of backing down, he rose to his feet. "Law is law."

"Aye, it is. But laws change, and the access to them can be… chancy. Tell me this. Does that lovely stallion of yours have rights? If, say, he killed one of your villeins by accident, would you confine him, or cut his throat?"

"Of course not!"

"But did one of your villeins kill that stallion, even by accident, what would happen to the villein?"

The answer stuck in Gamelyn's throat; it was unfair, the comparison, yet her point could not be denied. "So the forester—"

"He has a name, Gamelyn. George Scathelock. His son is Will, and Will's mother was named Isadora. Names have power," Eluned added. "Which is why we canna forget them."

"Power, you say. The same sort that Scathelock, or his son, used? Magic… *sorcery*… to circle a man in salt and bind his soul with a damned weapon?"

Eluned's eyebrows rose. "I see you've been doing some learning, milord Gamelyn."

"Books don't say enough, Mistress Eluned. They give rites but no reason, results but no methods. No *whys*."

"You want to know why?"

"I want to know what's happened," Gamelyn said, and his voice shook but he no longer cared. "I want to know if my friends are in danger. If your souls are in danger."

Eluned got a very odd look on her face, as if she was trying either to avoid crying or laughing. He wasn't sure he wanted to know which; the sting of blood had started to rise to his cheeks, and he muttered, "You're mocking me."

"Nay." Eluned was, to the sudden, solemn. "I ent, lad, that I swear to you. I understand that the matter is grave to you, very grave. But I'm afraid there is a mockery, one very strange and sad, to all of this. One you've been too sheltered to truly see."

Gamelyn shook his head. "I only wish that were true."

"Do you know owt of the old religion?" Eluned interrupted.

He blinked, thought about it for a moment. "I know… stories. My nurse used to tell them to me when I was a child. And the old women in the kitchens would give me sweetmeats if I'd listen to them." He shrugged as Eluned raised an eyebrow. "I didn't mind listening. I liked the stories, even when they'd prattle on about other things. And then… Marion and I have swapped stories."

"Have you, then?" Eluned didn't seem best pleased, and Gamelyn frowned.

"Why wouldn't we? I'd tell her stories from the court, of knights and ladies and quests; she'd come up with just as improbable things about ghosts and little people, the old Hob that my nurse used to tell me of. Forest spirits…." He swallowed, hunched his shoulders.

Thought of the ivory stag. And dreams.

"Were your stories true?"

It brought him back to reality. "I suppose, perhaps, they might have been at one time. That's usually how things are."

"True enough. You canna get owt from nowt. Even a story." Eluned gestured to the table. "Sit. I've a story for you."

"A what?"

"What if every story was true, Gamelyn Boundys? What if every story—not just the ones your people deem acceptable, but all of them, from the stories of the people who come from desert lands where an undying sun has seared their skins as brown as fecund earth, to the stories of Arthur and the magic that gained him a crown, to the stories of the old religion where magic runs like water… true. Would that be a good place, then?"

Of course it would. It would be a *wonderful* place; how not? But it would also be a world full of infidels, heretics. Other. God would not approve; that much was plain.

Eluned was watching him; she looked… disappointed. "Sweet Lady, why do your people insist on making everything so simple? Good and evil, right or wrong, black and white… 'tis comforting, to be sure, but not real."

"Is this your story?"

"It might be. Listen. The power of opposites is a sacred one, but 'tisn't the whole. My boy and girl have been teaching you the ways of archery. When you shoot an arrow, it will kill, wound, or miss. Everything has three faces, Gamelyn. There's no absolute to owt in life; what story would try and convince us there is? Unless there's a reason for wanting t' keep things simple."

"I—"

"Shh." Eluned folded her hands together, fixed her eyes upon him. "Long ago, so long that none can remember when the beginning was a beginning, there was a Wheel. No cart wheel, no spinning wheel, but a great one that turned stars and sun, moon and earth. This Wheel never stops, never spins about backwards; it just… goes and comes around. Goes and come back around. The Eternal Return."

He knew that phrase, from the dim recesses of memory as well as of late. Marion spoke of it, often, seemingly in passing.

"When the people that would become us looked around, they saw this Wheel. In everything. In the seasons. In their own lives. In the map the stars would make o'nights. In the rising and setting of the sun and moon. In the swelling of their women's bellies with new life, to see birth and grow old even as they did. And they found they couldna stop the Wheel, but they could hinder it. Or help. And they wanted to understand. So." She looked at him, eyebrows raised.

"Stories. Myths."

"Aye. What if they all are true, Gamelyn?"

"All stories can't be true."

"How not? Take winter, and summer. The Winterlord must craft his arrows of Holly, the Summerlord wield his sword of Oak and be born amidst the blood-berries of Winter's reign and return to 't. Both must live, and die, struggle one against the other and hold the honor of their Queen, the Ivy who lives the year long. She loves them both, and can have neither for long."

"A myth to explain the seasons."

"Of course it is. All o' that and more. Stories start with truth. Sometimes, though, the truth gets so twisted in on itself that it becomes a smaller truth."

"Is that what happened to the old religion, then?" Gamelyn sat forward, chin propped in his palms. "It twisted in on itself, became evil."

"You make it sound so… simple." And Rob was not the only one who could make a word into sibilant mockery. "*All* things can twist, lose their way. Everything can become a threat to someone with their mind too small to hold the vastness of all those stories. And then the truth becomes something smaller, meant for only one man. Or a few… chosen ones."

There was a gleam in Eluned's eyes, not unlike the one he'd seen in Rob's when he'd reached the end of a hunt and was running down the quarry. Gamelyn straightened in his chair, no longer so relaxed.

She saw it, gave a tiny half smile. "Here's one for you, then. Long ago—no' so long to be a beginning, but long enough to be seen as a beginning—there were some angry men. They lived in a desert, where life was hard, harder than you and I can imagine. They had a teacher who would tell them their world was beautiful, made by a god for them to care for. They loved him, and followed him, but he had some notions they didna quite fancy. They didna care for the company he kept. They didna like the idea that beauty and bliss could be found about them; they wanted promises of something better. No blame to them, there; they'd come from a beaten people, like my own. They'd been driven into the least productive lands, their families given no more rights than beasts. They'd felt the lash of a conqueror's whip. They had been shown a clean life, a holy path… but they wanted more. They wanted more than the life that had so punished them.

"Their teacher told 'em to heed him; his time was short, he was a god's son, and so his blood belonged to the land. But his lessons were hard, and they were tired. They wanted something easier. So when the god's son was given to the land by one of his own—when the Winterlord was done to death by Summer's hand—

"You mean Jesus," Gamelyn said, very quiet. "And Judas."

She didn't bat an eye. "And you doubt that names have power? That myths hold truth?"

He sat back, drew in a troubled breath.

"These disciples, they fell to fussing over what his death meant and what he'd told them. Some said one thing, some another. Some could write, so they sat and wrote what they believed the god's son had told them. Others went out and told stories. But, being men with voices and experiences of their own, and being angry—for some good reasons, mind—the teachings… changed. Conquered became conquerors. The ideas changed, from a world for all… a 'kingdom that is all around, but unseen by men'… to a plan. A design, for all people like to play at godding. A set of rules for not only a decent life, but a *just* life. A *deserved* life. A life simple, and righteous… and one to make sure they can keep their anger and their place."

Gamelyn crossed his arms, peering at her.

"Aye. You've heard tell of these men. We all have. Men angry enough, threatened enough—*arrogant* enough—to claim themselves the only ones who can know the will of a god… and in the process rive a woman from her rightful power. Their rules—their laws—are ones no loving, breathing person can possibly follow. In fact, they go against everything the gentle teacher who inspired these angry men taught them. And then they've laid a trip-wire, demanding there is only one way to be forgiven of those impossible things—by giving the rulers more of the power when they already have too much. And anyone who would threaten that power? Anyone who might have a power that was not under their control?"

"But… there has to be law." As he spoke, Gamelyn realized that Eluned had brought them back around, full circle.

"What if your mother had been raped and murdered, then? What if every law in the land upheld that your mother's say over who she would choose to give her *own body* to, that that choice was worth less than a man's rights to poke his knob wherever he wanted? And then gave that man free run of a holy place, your Church? Would you not want to see him damned? To see him thrown into the deepest pit of your hell and suffer your god's punishment? Only, your god doesna punish men who rape women; he only cares for females if they're mares or bitches, with no voice to protest when they're harnessed or beaten!"

"That's not what Scripture says!" Gamelyn retorted angrily, rising up from his chair.

"Have you actually *read* the Christian scriptures?" Eluned merely peered up at him. "I have, Gamelyn, and not through th' eyes of a priesthood who says they're the only ones allowed to ken what lies there, written plain. I could recite whole passages for you, but being a clever, god-fearin' lad, surely you know them, even if you don't want to see 'em."

"I could recite, verse and chapter, whatever you would ask of me!" Gamelyn protested.

She chuckled. "Aye, the pride of you, o man."

He flinched, this time. Of course she'd no way of knowing that was the exact sin his confessor was often railing against.

"Tell me of Lot and his daughters. Not where they gave him as good as he deserved with too much wine, but before that, when he betrayed *them*. Where this supposed godly man was given leave by his god to offer up his daughters for a gang-shagging. We dinna know if their mam protested or no—she wasn't deemed important enou' to have a say. Two guests—male, of course—were more important than the rights or chastity of females. Which is saying something, considering the vast weight your Church gives to being untouched."

Had she given him the opportunity, Gamelyn couldn't have taken it. He was staggered.

"And magic? Sorcery? Your Bible's not full of it? Ah, that's right. Only magic that *men* perform is acceptable. Men can scry, can prophesize, can curse their neighbors and lay waste with salt and ash, can even see fit to burn their sons in offering. Yet a man goes to see a woman for advice, and she's a witch, and damned."

Gamelyn tried to come up with something—*anything*!—to counter. He could not. And all the while she sat there, cool and composed, wielding a rapier to every reasonable, careful construct he possessed.

"Funny, ent it? How Moses was perhaps the greatest magician of all time, yet as long as he too poked his staff where his god told him, all was well."

"Why are you saying all this?" It quavered, and he couldn't help it.

She sat forward, still eyeing him. "You sit at my board and eat my food, then tell me my people are wrong for taking what power they can from a world where they're helpless? My people were born in the old religion before your god walked and spoke his truth. We were born with it just as much as you were born with baptism and wealth we'll never touch. But I waint give your people the right to say that they're the only ones who know the will of god, or even the untangling of their own *tynged*."

Gamelyn kept shifting back and forth from foot to foot. Finally he said, very quiet, "Should I sleep in the barn?"

And Eluned laughed. Not just a small giggle, but a deep, cheerful thing that invited him to join in.

But he didn't. Just stood there, shifting back and forth.

"Lad, lad." She gave a sigh. "I'll make a bargain with you. If you can still trust that I'm a wise woman and not 'evil' after what I've told you, then you can sleep in my house with my trust. Aye?"

"Aye," he murmured, thinking. His brain felt full to bursting.

"Enough of this for the now," Eluned said. "I've apple tarts and new milk for you before we go to bed, and I promise, no more harangues."

Yet he'd gotten more from one "harangue" than he'd gleaned from her in the past years, and certainly more than he'd ever gotten from…. "But… Rob? When's he coming back? And shouldn't we wait for Marion?"

"Nay, there's no sense in waiting up for either of them; they're both like to be late returning. Best to have your snack then get some sleep; you've had a long ride today and another one likely tomorrow. I'll make up a nice meal to break our fast, and you can have your time for visiting during and after." She smirked. "Show my lad that nice shiny dagger you've got.

"For now, let me set you up a nice pallet up the loft. It's not what you're used to having, I'm sure, but you'll be comfortable, I'll make sure of that."

Later, after they'd each scoffed up two tarts and Gamelyn had consumed two mugs of creamy milk, he helped her with his bedding, up and down the ladder with light blankets and a withy mat. Across the pallet from him, she flipped the blanket into place then reached across and gripped his chin in one hand, raised his face to hers.

"'Tis what's to be, you being here," she said, then added, somewhat cryptic, "It might not be so comforting for the rest of us, but we'll see your father's last days in comfort, that I promise you."

☙❧

THE only other time Gamelyn had stayed an entire night had been when Diamant had dumped him in the middle of the woodlands. He'd been less than aware, then, of his surroundings. Now, he couldn't put any of it from his mind enough to sleep.

The flooring beneath his withy mat was sturdy, but Gamelyn discovered there were places he could see through, ones where the wood had shrunk and expanded unevenly, leaving gaps. He had no thought of spying, but Rob's empty bed kept claiming his attention. That, and how Eluned kept puttering. When she finally settled down by the hearth coals, Gamelyn realized he was not the only one waiting for Rob's return.

But Gamelyn was tired, and napped on and off, fitful in the strange surroundings. The final time he woke, it was to voices. He nearly bolted upright, halting it just in time, then lay there, trying to reorient himself. It was Rob's voice that had woken him, and Eluned's answers. More than that he didn't know.

Rolling over, ever so slow, Gamelyn peered through the flooring. Eluned was still by the fire—it hadn't burnt down very far, so he'd not slept that long—and Rob's head was in her lap. She kept combing her fingers through Rob's hair. Rob's hands were seized to her kirtle, and his head was bowed, his words muffled.

Eluned spoke, urgent, and tugged at Rob's hair. When he ducked his head lower, she shook her own and put both hands under Rob's chin, lifting his face to meet hers. His eyes glittered in the candlelight, a starless, endless night; his hair was another, inky spider's tangle over those eyes, and there was a look on his face—something Gamelyn had never seen there, something raw and simple and *exposed*—that fisted an enormous knot in Gamelyn's chest.

Then he saw the tears, spilling silk-wet and gleaming, down Rob's face.

A self-conscious heat stole over Gamelyn's cheeks. He closed his eyes, gritted his teeth, and looked away.

The next time he looked up, Rob was gone. Eluned was also nowhere in sight. Sucking in an almost silent breath between his teeth, Gamelyn rose to his hands and knees.

He couldn't do this again. Something was dreadfully wrong, and Gamelyn couldn't just stay behind while Rob went… wherever it was that Rob was going.

The flooring seemed to conspire with him, not even a creak as he rolled to bare feet, nudged into his tunic and breeches, and grabbed up his boots. Tucking the latter under one arm, he began a slow descent of the ladder. At the bottom rung he twisted, stepped down—then halted in his tracks.

Eluned was just outside the doorway, her back to him, arms wound close about her. As he watched, in an agony lest she turn and see him, she went to the edge of the small porch, on the topmost step.

The window nearest him was an adequate exit, and on the opposite side of the front door. Gamelyn headed for it, slung one leg up to crawl through, spared another quick glance to the front door… and froze, one leg still across the sill.

Eluned was in the doorway, watching him, backlit by the moon.

"Come down, Gamelyn Boundys. Use the front door, if you're set on leaving."

He obeyed—not that he had a lot of choice—and walked over to her, eyes anywhere but on that shadowed face. "I'm not… leaving."

"You saw Rob. And now you're going after him."

He hesitated, nodded.

Her shoulders lifted, a shrug but somehow also not, and she moved away from the door. He started to say something, then realized there was nothing he really could say, and she didn't seem inclined to stay him, for whatever reason. So he padded past her, still barefoot.

He made it through the doorway when Eluned spoke again.

"I canna tell you not to follow my son," she said. "'Tis a path you have been upon since you first came here. But I'd rather you didna. Not now. Not with what's happened. For mark me in this: there are more things than you know at play here. If you reach out for this moment, it will reach back. It will change everything. Change you. Change him."

Gamelyn halted, slid a wary gaze to her. "I don't understand."

"I know you don't. So heed my warning. 'Twill be for the worst if you refuse t' open to 't, mind and heart."

The moonlight was clear upon them both, and her face as visible as if in the light of day. But there was no expression there; she might as well have been in shadow.

"I can't explain," he said, realizing it was no less than the truth. "But… I have to."

She nodded. Then, "Put your boots on. It's been warm enough, but you might find the forest chill this night."

☙ XIV ❧

IT WAS chill, and damp. Unwelcoming. It had taken every skill Gamelyn had first to find Rob, and then to follow only close enough to not lose him, yet far enough to not be seen. He'd had a heart-stopping moment when he'd practically walked up behind him; Rob had stopped to retie one of the straps on his boots.

They wound about, using trails so faint Gamelyn almost didn't see them, but Rob obviously saw them, was drawn to them as if they were roads. Yet he didn't seem to notice he was being followed, and his steps were somewhat shaky, as if he wasn't fully paying attention. Several times he stopped, stared off into the distance; one time he actually spoke, as if talking to someone Gamelyn couldn't see.

More and more, Gamelyn was convinced that he'd done the right thing by following. Rob was not himself, somehow.

Finally, they came to a clearing, gleaming pale. Rob stopped beside a massive oak. He put a hand to it, rubbed fingers over the bark as if petting it like a favored dog, then crouched on his haunches. There was water spreading out beside the oak, fed by a fast-rushing stream some distance away: audible, but faint. There were flashes here and there, around and over the mere: fireflies, tiny sparks of gold to offset the pale sheen drifting down through the break in the tree cover. The latter turned the little lake silver as a penny on a dead pagan's eyes, and as impenetrable.

Such beauty always sent a forlorn wistfulness into the pit of Gamelyn's belly. There was exhilaration, no question, but also something vaguely disturbing about how such loveliness could take custody of not only one's eyes, but one's breath and soul. Venturing this far into the forest had its own forbidden lure of abandon and escape, far off any map and into a wildness that took him... *elsewhere*, somehow. As if the old tales could actually come true; as if Eluned's cryptic warning conjured some truth instead of superstitious fancy; as if superstition would take a life of its own within the thick tangles and shadows of the green Wode.

Rob alerted, rose, moved from the oak toward the west. Gamelyn followed, more cautious than ever, and ended up behind the same oak where Rob had been. He stopped as Rob stopped, then saw what Rob had.

A figure, hooded and cloaked, coming into the clearing.

It seemed enough like a figure from the nightmares Gamelyn had endured recently, and more than once, that he almost called out a warning. Instead he hugged closer to the tree, bid himself wait.

Still, his hand went to his sword.

But Rob went forward willingly enough, and met the figure beside the mere. The two embraced, holding each other by the shoulders, exchanging brief, close talk. The newcomer pulled the cowl back from his face, revealing merely another lad, perhaps a bit older than Rob....

Oh, God. Gamelyn leaned hard against the oak, digging his fingernails into the tough wood.

It was the young forester that had come to Blyth with his father. The one accused of killing the Abbess's guardsman.

Slipping the heavy rucksack from his shoulder to the ground, Rob gave his companion another, fiercer embrace; this one held and was returned with a desperation that sent Gamelyn's stomach lurching. Then the renegade forester was hefting the rucksack and melting away in the trees, leaving Rob alone beside the pool.

Rob kept watching for some time, clenching his fists against the silence. To the sudden, it seemed his legs refused to hold him. Rob sank down to his haunches, wobbled slightly then sat, curling tight with arms and knees, head sinking forward, hair spilling over his face and shoulders. Again silence, spinning into long moments. Then Rob flung himself back, arms overhead, supine on the deer-cropped turf. Gamelyn was afraid to so much as breathe for fear he would be heard—indeed, it was passing strange that Rob had not already heard him.

And since Rob had not, it was obvious that Rob was… compromised, and it was even more obvious that Rob would not thank Gamelyn for seeing him like this.

On the other hand, it wasn't exactly safe or wise to leave someone not paying attention alone in a dangerous place. Nor could he hope to avoid discovery if he moved, now.

Gamelyn stayed. Kept watch as Rob lay there, staring up into the treetops as if he found clarification in the spastic lanterns of the fireflies, in the solid, swaying roof of branches and leaves. Whatever that answer was, he also seemed to find some sort of heart in it, for after a time he rose, walked closer to the water's edge.

It was the place for retreat. Instead Gamelyn found himself held—pinned, almost—in place as Rob shrugged from his tunic.

The faint mist of light set him almost ghostlike, all midnight locks and moon-pale skin, whipcord flexing beneath. Even more disturbing were faint, white markings across back and ribs, linear but oddly jagged, reflecting like fine satin in the uncertain light.

Whip marks. Gamelyn sucked in a breath between his teeth—both horror and anger—and realized the mistake the moment he made it. Rob made no outward sign other than a slight stiffening of frame—Gamelyn wouldn't have known what he was witnessing if he'd not seen it before. Rob took a few steps, dropped his tunic on the earth in seeming nonchalance, but the dark eyes flitted over every direction, noted every approach. When Rob turned toward his hiding place, Gamelyn closed his eyes, willed himself breathless, still.

Sweat had begun trickling down the small of his back before Gamelyn dared to open his eyes again—and then it was the sound of water that gave him leave.

Rob was nowhere to be found. Gamelyn almost stepped from his hiding place, baffled and worried. He espied the pile of clothes on the bank at almost the same time Rob erupted from beneath the water. Staying merely long enough to take a gasp of air, Rob dove again, a pale crescent in the inky water, leaving little but a wake of ripples and rising air bubbles. He did it again, and again, as if he were trying to cast something behind in the glittering wake.

Surely it was worry that snagged the breath tight in Gamelyn's chest. He did not know how to swim—nor, in fact, did hardly anyone he'd ever known—but obviously Rob did. Things here never were as they should seem. Gamelyn found himself leaning harder against the oak as Rob finally rose from the dark pool's edge, shaking the wet from his shoulders, flinging then slicking the wet hair back from his face. The water wasn't deep, there, pulling down his chest to circle and lap just beneath his navel.

The fireflies were creeping toward him, dancing over the water's surface in what might have been termed curiosity, had Gamelyn not doubted their tiny forms were capable of such a virtue. They skated ever closer to the stranger in their realm—yet neither was he a stranger. For when Rob reached out, extended his fingertips, beckoning, the fireflies came.

The breath knocked in Gamelyn's chest; still, he couldn't release it, nor could he take any more in. It was not the first time he'd wondered, half illicit fancy and half troubling concern, if Rob was inhabited by some demon or changeling. And this… this was not simply Rob bewitching some animal with his gaze and voice. He seemed kith and kin to some feral forest spirit, summoning fey lights to sip the water he cupped, as offering, in his palms. The fireflies courted him, dipped and danced about him, garlanded him in white-hot gems, glided over his damp, brown arms and pale torso with flits and flickers of gold….

And Rob was… *smiling*. Not the too quick flash of humor, not the mocking, one-sided smirk, but a tender, heart-scalding thing that Gamelyn was sure he'd never seen directed his own way, if at all. It was… unlikely, fantastic… there was in truth no name that Gamelyn could put to the feeling. It was that foreign, flickering through his being with a dart of heat and radiance not unlike those tiny bewitched fireflies.

Gamelyn had grown careless with his absorption. He'd already crept half around the tree to witness whatever it was that was happening; a slight stumble had him flinging out an arm to steady himself.

Tiny lights scattered into darkness. Rob crouched, whipped about. There was a whine and hiss of sculpted air next to Gamelyn's head, then a sting against his bicep and a solid *thunk* as a short, thick dagger pinned his tunic sleeve to the tree.

Breath came to Gamelyn then, rushing out then in like a smith's bellows, sending him even more giddy. He met Rob's gaze, at first found nothing there but shadows in the dark. The air Gamelyn needed so desperately snagged in his lungs again, painful, and an eerie trepidation held it there. What stood before him was no gentle wood sprite, but an untamed demon.

Rob blinked, and his eyes began to warm, from ruthlessness to recognition. Only then did Gamelyn find it possible to breathe, and move, and he made it simple. Reaching around, he made to tug the knife free. Unfortunately, he was at an impossible angle, and it was in deep. He might as well have tried to pull legendary Excalibur from its equally legendary sheath of stone.

Rob began to wade out, slowly. Never once did he take his eyes from Gamelyn; finally, he spoke. "I knew you'd follow me. I knew it, and yet I did nowt. How is that?"

Maybe Gamelyn was just going at it from the wrong angle. He shifted, gave another try at the knife. "If you knew it was me, then why am I standing here with a knife in my tunic?"

No go that way, either.

"If I hadn't known, then mayhap you'd be trying to yank that knife from somewhere more… damaging?"

"I am bleeding, you know."

"But are you damaged, Sir Gamelyn?"

Marion's fond name for him always seemed a curl of insult upon Rob's lips. "*I'm* not the one mad enough to have a swim in the middle of the forest in the middle of the night. Are *you* damaged, in the head?"

"Aye, the questions are rife this night, eh?" Rob had reached the bank, water sliding down his body in a myriad of tiny rivulets as he approached, step by slow step. Gamelyn was rendered weak-kneed by the sight, by the soft, soundless grace, as if a ghost were gliding over the ground toward him.

Forcibly, he framed some sort of speech. "Then here's another question for you. Will you come and get your bloody knife?"

"Ah-ah." A flash of teeth in the faint light. "Language, m'lord."

"Would you stop with the—Sweet Christ, are you *drunk?*"

It didn't show in his gait, not a bit of it, but Rob's gestures were too calculated, his voice slurring faint about the corners. "Drunk. Am I, then? And would it be on t' mead? Or on life? Mayhap, on *time*? If I could make the choice, fair Gamelyn, I'd choose the honey ferment. Its effects are much more pleasant." A low laugh. "I do apologize. For the knife. I figured did y' follow, I'd have heard you comin' for a furlong at least. But I do seem to be a bit less than meself tonight. So. Well done, you."

He was drunk. Must be. There was a lithe wantonness to everything Rob was doing, an… exposure that had little to do with any state of undress. Yet that stealthy grace and the body displaying it were startlingly more in Gamelyn's mind than they should be.

Whispering entreaty to whichever saint would listen, Gamelyn averted his eyes, took refuge into annoyance. "How typical."

"Typical?"

"Typical for you, to pad a faint kiss with a slap."

"Are y' saying you'd prefer just the kiss?"

Gamelyn was not about to even acknowledge that with an answer. *Not*. "I'd prefer you got your knife out of my tunic."

Rob crossed his arms and cocked his head. Grinned again. And all Gamelyn could consider was it was wrong, wrong, *wrong* that he couldn't keep his eyes focused to the ground, to the sky… sweet Jesus, to *anything* but Rob and what he wasn't wearing.

Reason was no help, either. It had fled into mordant disapproval of how, again, Johan was an idiot with no appreciation for elegance. He had called Rob scrawny, and it wasn't so. Gamelyn was staring at the proof of it, as if he were seeing it for the first time. Rob was perhaps just that much beneath his best weight, lean, certainly, tall and lanky obviously… but not scrawny. The water slicking and beading his skin defined every curve of muscle on him—and muscles he definitely had. It was not a fighter's body, not built into bulk from wielding heavy armaments, or carrying chainmail. Yet there was strength and power there; his shoulders, if bony, were broad and muscled from bending the yew, and….

And merciful Mother of *God*!—but Gamelyn could not believe he was standing here, pinned to a tree by his friend's knife! The same friend he was eyeing up like some camp follower.

His *male* friend.

Worse, Rob kept affirming the maleness by not bothering with the meager pile of clothing still lying on the turf. Instead he advanced upon Gamelyn—naked and dripping and unconcerned with either—propped one hand against the tree, and wrapped the other about the knife hilt.

Blinked.

"I do believe I threw that a sight harder than I meant to."

Gamelyn started to reply in kind, found himself rendered mute as Rob, tongue between his teeth, shifted his weight, leaning first his shoulder then his bare haunch against Gamelyn. Muscles bunched in Rob's left shoulder as he pulled. There was gooseflesh rising his skin, dark hairs alternately springing upright in dry chill or slicking in runnels of wet; long, ebon ringlets hung, sticky-wet, against his scalp and shoulders. Gamelyn tried to look away, instead squinched his eyes tight-shut. It merely opened his nostrils—and his companion's smell was a pleasant one, not the sour whiff of sweat left too long stale, but of damp and green, of rainwater on juniper boughs, of the spiced-sweet ferment that was indeed upon Rob's breath as he huffed then spoke.

"You have to move."

Gamelyn opened his eyes, found Rob peering at him. Answered, thickly, "That might prove a bit difficult."

"Just pull your sleeve free and—"

"This is my favorite tunic!"

"Aw, and surely you have more than you need—"

"Is it the drink, then, that makes you sound more and more like your mother?"

Rob blinked again. "Well," he said, "*there's* sure means to put a fellow off."

Inconceivable. "What," Gamelyn gritted out, "in the name of Mary, Jesus and Joseph are you *talking* about?"

Rob's eyebrows did a small, twisty dance, then settled for one up, one down. "*You're* the one as mentioned kissing."

Gamelyn counted ten. For various reasons. Then stammered, "I… I w-will not. Rip up my tunic. Pull. Harder."

The eyebrows were joined by a smirk. "I canna get the leverage. You'll need to move, lad—"

And whom was he calling 'lad', anyway?

"—unless you want me crawlin' atop you."

"*What*?"

"No need to be squeaking like a ten-year-old lass." The smirk had broadened into downright cheek. "P'rhaps y' should unlace your tunic, then?"

Gamelyn started pawing at his tunic laces.

Several moments later, he was still pawing. And swearing under his breath.

"Bloody…." Rob shook his head, left off his knife and bent to Gamelyn's laces.

"I can do it!" And again a paean to Mary, Jesus and Joseph, but he hadn't intended his voice to spike up like that *again*. It was only….

Only….

Rob smacked his hand. "*I'm* the one who ent an absolute hames with his left hand, remember?"

"I also remember that left-handed children are the Devil's brood," Gamelyn sniped back.

"And *I* seem to remember your bloody-minded priests saying red-haired people have no souls. Granted, you're no' so flame-haired as me sister, so p'rhaps you've a bit of a soul. Either way, you've no rights judging me left hand, particularly when it's helping you out of a predicament—"

"A predicament *you* caused—"

"I wasn't the one spying on someone's bath…." Rob trailed off. His fingers spasmed. "How long were you watching me?"

Gamelyn immediately knew what Rob's thoughts had bent toward. His friend. His *outlawed* friend.

"Not long," he said, truthfully enough.

Only long enough to see something I've never seen in you before… something you still refuse to show, even beneath the possibility that I might have *seen….*

Rob gave him a thoughtful look, then resumed his attention fully—almost relentlessly—on the lacings. The tunic was short, but laced all the way down its front. Rob's touch was surprisingly deft and impersonal, avoiding any contact of skin with skin, yet every movement of those nimble fingers seemed to coax Gamelyn's skin to shivers.

It was impossible that Rob didn't notice, and once he pulled the lanyard free from the last grommet, he laced it almost absently in his fingers, held it up for Gamelyn's inspection. Met his eyes and held there.

Silence. Gamelyn swore he could count the beat of his own heart in tandem with the pulse that thickened, *quickened*, beneath the skin of Rob's throat.

This was wrong. Somehow. *Depraved.* He should retreat, should turn away, should… something. But none of those things were remotely possible. It was as if he was charmed by the twitch of Rob's fingertips, tangled in the lanyard, held to that shadowed, unreadable gaze. And all the while, Gamelyn was desperately trying to shrug his free arm from his tunic. Like he could get away.

Like he wanted to get away.

Rob bent closer, set his fingers to Gamelyn's shoulder, and pulled at the sleeve. The lanyard, still wrapped in those fingers, rolled and tugged in the smooth wake of the linen, and Rob's thumb followed, a callused caress. The snag and smooth of that hand down his arm, the sight of fingers trailing, lingering over fabric, sinew and flesh, the feel of the cloth falling free… yet the fingers hesitated, lingered, just a touch. Just a *touch*, and Gamelyn was rising, immediate and hard as any stallion scenting a mare in season.

Rob's nostrils flared; his dark eyes lit as if one of the fireflies he'd beckoned had kindled, smoldering, behind them. His expression tipped, from arrogant to assailable. He brought his leather-tangled hand to Gamelyn's cheek, riffled his fingers through the lock of hair falling across Gamelyn's eyes.

And any shame, any righteous protest choked itself in Gamelyn's throat, charred beneath a sudden conflagration of *need.*

And Rob cupped his hand at Gamelyn's nape, leaned forward, took Gamelyn's mouth with his.

Again, the shock of *touch.* The hand firm at his nape, the roll and bite of leather against neck hair, Rob's mouth upon his—gentle, so *gentle*—but merciless. Gamelyn was still half snared by the knife-pinned tunic, now Rob's mouth and body and hands pinned him, as suddenly fierce and unforgiving as the realization that, somehow, Gamelyn was kissing him *back.*

It was inconceivable that a body could contain this much raw sensation and not combust. No mercy. No *mercy*—and it broke something within Gamelyn, sent him shuddering and whining thinly in his throat. Rob cupped Gamelyn's face in both hands, drank his whimpers like brandywine and laved the dregs with his tongue.

Somehow Gamelyn's swordbelt had kinked crossways, and his knife was working its way between them… nay, that was no blade. It was *Rob.*

Gamelyn reared back, breaking the kiss. The old oak caught him, held him, and Rob kept peering at him. Both of them were heaving air as if they had been running full-out through knee-high overgrowth. Rob bent in again; in a brief flare of panic, Gamelyn ducked his head sideways. He was thoroughly unprepared for how Rob nuzzled at his cheek, breathed in his ear, then ran his tongue along the rim. Was just as sideswiped by how his body quivered, arched and sought Rob's, recognizing the lithe power of it, drawn to the heat of it like… like….

Like fire, bewitched to the gentle, tenacious sway of some mythic forest lord. Like *fireflies….*

"What are you doing to me?" The whimper escaped before Gamelyn could bite it back.

The hands cupping Gamelyn's face shook, stilled. The fleetest of hesitations, then Rob gave that tiny shrug of his, relegating such matters to the realm of plain and unfettered. Instead he ran his tongue over Gamelyn's lower lip, whispered, "What do you think I'm doing?"

"I think…."

"Stop thinking, then." It was a growl.

"I…. We can't…. I…. *Oh.*" This as Rob nipped at his upper lip, gave a slow, fabulous shove of his hips.

"I think we are."

"But I…. We…." This time it was his sword that tugged sideways and dug its pommel into the lower edge of Gamelyn's ribcage. Yet was so… insignificant beneath the pressure of Rob's body, of the hard arc butting against his own, pinned between their bodies and against the tree. "I…. You…. We're…."

"Shut the bloody fuck *up*, Gamelyn." Rob bent closer, nipped Gamelyn's mouth open. Stole the whimper from Gamelyn's throat, answered it with tongue and teeth. Shoved his hand down between them, then with a shift and a wriggle and a twist of his hand….

Oh, God. Oh, *God*....

He was going to die. And then he was going to Hell.

"Bloody damn." Rob gave a sudden murmur against Gamelyn's mouth. "You never have, have you? At all. You really never *have*—"

With a growl of rent fabric, Gamelyn yanked his arm from the dagger's point and cupped both hands against Rob's temples. Snarled his fingers in black curls. Rob's mouth tilted in a smirk, and Gamelyn covered it with his own, shoved his hips forward as Rob's hand claimed him again with a stroke and squeeze.

Again the sword lurched against Gamelyn's hip, some wildly improbable chaperone of virtue. This time it was Rob who winced. With a frustrated growl, he yanked at the swordbelt. He didn't stop kissing Gamelyn, but gave several more growls against Gamelyn's teeth as the belt foiled him. Gamelyn reached down, fumbled at the catch and loosed it; belt and weapons hit the roots of the oak with a dull ring of sheathed metal. But that was insignificant, also, beneath the reality of Rob snaking his hand into first Gamelyn's breeks then his braies beneath, shoving them impatiently down, freeing.

"My, what a fellow you have there," Rob purred, another small quirk tucking into his lip. "Almost as large as that bloody fancy pig-sticker you insist on wearin'. Sir Gamelyn." Again, a slap with the kiss; Gamelyn thought to protest that last, for Rob never, *ever* meant it save in mockery. Instead he found himself hung on Rob's eyes. They were fathomless as the trees tracing the inky sky, glimmering with the firefly flashes as if filled with stars.

Looking at *him*.

Gamelyn was going to die, unshriven and with every sense he owned cupped in the palm of Rob's hand, and he didn't *care*. Rob was shoving him against the tree, *hard*, yet Gamelyn barely felt the bark abrading his bare back. All he knew was the fierce, damp breaths spent into his mouth, the hard, hot line of Rob's body. Gamelyn groped down with his free hand, fumbled and then found what he sought. It lurched against his fingers, butting against his palm, eager.

"Aye, that's it, you know what to do," Rob breathed in his ear. "Or do your sort not know how to have a good wank, either?" This was accompanied by a slide-stroke-*twist* of Rob's fingers that nearly made Gamelyn's eyes bug out of his head.

Maybe "his sort" *didn't* know how to have a good wank.

The silken weight in Gamelyn's palm lurched again as he ran experimental fingertips down the underside. Rob grazed his neck with his teeth, his chest expanded in a quick, delighted sigh, and Gamelyn almost came, then and there, just from the sound of it. The knowledge that he'd caused it.

The reality that he could cause it again.

And Rob kept *looking* at him, from their hands back to Gamelyn's face. Then he smiled, a fleeting, wild thing half of delight and all of deviltry, and knelt.

Get up, you idiot! Gamelyn almost said, because surely this was taking a bad joke entirely too far. Instead he nearly swallowed his tongue as Rob gave an impatient yank of Gamelyn's breeks down to his ankles, took his erection in both hands, and leaned forward.

Searing wet, the caress-nip-tug of fingers, the mind-boggling vision of Rob's tongue curling and lapping, then his mouth widening, taking. Perhaps the sparks flooding the back of Gamelyn's eyes were from knocking his head back against the tree. Perhaps he was no longer going to die but actually *dying,* with Rob's hands and mouth the only things to hold his debauched corpse. Perhaps it was wrong—*had* to be because it felt *so... damned... good*—so then it was *filthy* wrong that all Gamelyn wanted was to arch forward, shudder and shove and welcome death if only Rob's tongue and teeth would accompany him there.

And those eyes, dark-lit as the pool beside them, soft and wanton and still *watching* him. Agile, callused fingers trailing up his belly to tease at his ribs, the lacing to Gamelyn's tunic still twined in them, a bite and chafe as seasoning to the smooth, gentle touch. Rob's eyes gleamed as Gamelyn gave a shivery moan, sent his hand curling around and down to clutch at Gamelyn's haunch, urging. Took him deeper, suckled, *nipped.*

Just like that it was over; no stopping it any more than Gamelyn could stop himself from jerking his hips, twining his fingers into black hair, and thrusting hard into that lovely, all too capable mouth, gasping Rob's name.

Over.

Rob pulled him down, forward; Gamelyn wobbled to his knees, braies and breeks still tangled at his ankles and hands still wound tight into Rob's hair, breath hoarse and huge against the stillness.

And Rob was still *watching* him.

Again, that leather-wrapped hand lifted to push the sweat-damp hair back from Gamelyn's forehead, so gentle as to hardly be believed. Rob leaned forward, nuzzled his cheek, and before Gamelyn could even speak, Rob was pulling him down into the grass and curling up against him, as close as fur to skin.

It swallowed him entire: the touching, the *nearness*. It was twice as intimate and thoroughly as devastating as the sex had been.

"God," Gamelyn whispered. "What… what have you done to me?"

"Are y' talking to your god," Rob murmured against his ear, "or me?"

Gamelyn wasn't altogether sure he knew, and it gave him another deep-set shiver.

"Let's see, then," Rob continued, still that throaty murmur that stole every sense Gamelyn had left. "I've thrown a knife at you, kissed you, wanked and tongued your knees out from under you." His mouth curved against Gamelyn's cheek, a bare hint that merely confirmed the rich satisfaction in Rob's voice. "Aren't you glad I decided to bend the knee, m'lord?"

"Stop… stop calling me that."

"Mm." Rob trailed his hands over Gamelyn's ribcage, sending twin flickers of pure sensation up and down his spine. Too much… it was *too much*, and Gamelyn shuddered, made a slight retreat. Unaccountably, it didn't seem to put Rob off. He seemed to understand, which was impossible because Gamelyn wasn't sure he comprehended anything at the moment. "Aye, well. There's no need rushing you, after all. Not when you've given me such a gift."

"Gift?"

Rob rose slightly, propped on an elbow, chin against his cheek. "'Tis good fortune to share new pleasures." He was smiling again, that lovely, unguarded expression that twisted Gamelyn's head off its axis and left him a-stagger. "All flesh is a gift to the Lady; to find a new delight is doubly blessed."

Gamelyn didn't know what to do with any of it: the words, that smile, the hand that had crept around to tickle the downy ceriphs of gilt hair on Gamelyn's chest, the quite unsated, substantial heat which gave a heavy lurch and quiver against the curve where Gamelyn's thigh and buttock met. And he certainly didn't know what to do with what Rob said next, in a voice soft as the grass that cradled them, "I've looked at you all this time and never *seen* you."

The implied emphasis begged a response. Of its own accord, Gamelyn's hand reached out, stroked the unruly forelock back from Rob's temple.

The hand was trembling.

Rob smiled and cupped it with his own, then kissed it and rolled to a crouch. "How is it someone who knows so many ways to make war knows nowt of how to make love?"

The question sent a small culpable shiver down Gamelyn's very bare tailbone. Love.

Two lads couldn't love, not like this.

The thought drained from his mind as Rob stood and stretched, lithe as a prowling wolf and nigh boneless with grace.

God, but he was… *beautiful.*

"Sweet Lady, but I need a bath." Rob held out his hand. "Come swimming with me."

"I don't—"

"You didna know how to kiss me but a little while ago. You're needing a bath."

Hell suddenly seemed so cold and far away, compared to the light in Rob's eyes.

ꟹ XV ꟸ

THERE was sunlight sending a warm tickle across his cheekbones and a line of heat up and down his front. Something with the sleek-fine texture of flax clung to the damp of his lips and the unshaven scruff of his chin, and in his nostrils lingered the scent of hay and lake water, oak bark and bruised bracken.

Rob opened his eyes upon a lover in his arms, and his heart jerked in his chest as he remembered. Yesterday, and into the night. From fear had sprung fury, then frustration, to the wrench of parting…. *Will*, he thought with a bitter pang… to the cry of his heart into the forest, asking for answers. How the answers had come to him, first with the fireflies gathering, then this.

This. His heart jerked again, lurched up into his throat then gave an almighty thud and slip back down against his breastbone. He nuzzled his lips against the still damp silk of Gamelyn's ruddy-gold hair and breathed in, mapping the scent of him as much as Rob had mapped the length and breadth of him by touch during the night.

This. He'd had lovers, loved most of them after one fashion or another, but….

This.

Of all the things he had Seen, why never had he recognized this other self looking from Gamelyn's green eyes? Never dreamed that they could share a breath to warm his heart and spin out behind his eyes, untangle every knotted skein and weave *tynged* into such possibilities? No longer merely a ghost in the night with a fate no one could feel, no longer a sport, a mystery wrapped in a riddle, unseen beneath the threat/promise/surety of a dark, smothering cowl.

It should have been impossible. Yet here they were.

And *oh*, but Gamelyn undressed all lovely. It must be some cruel order of family or Church that had so far kept him unbroached, for surely he could have already had his pick of partners. He was substantial, as powerful as the warhorse he rode, muscles all layered and sculpted beneath pale skin, well able for that great longsword stuck into the ground beside them. And the freckles on him!—he had those lovely freckles *everywhere*, even misting about the light fox's-pelt leading from the dip of navel down.

Rob smirked. Quite a longbow, there. In fact, he would swear he remembered his tongue mapping more than a few freckles there, too.

And bloody *damn* but it was tempting—more than tempting—to kiss Gamelyn awake, perhaps indulge the sudden tightening in his groin that was already insinuating itself into the cleft of those copper-dusted buttocks.

Rob entertained the sudden fantasy of bending Gamelyn over the roots of their sheltering oak and shagging him until he cried mercy, then smirked as his anatomy lurched eagerly toward just that goal. It was obviously not satisfied with Gamelyn's awkward but eager hands during their swim last night, or with the frotting on the bank after, or even the sleepy hand play as they'd curled up beneath the shadows of the old oak. Aye, that last had been after they'd rolled atop the crossed—and bits-pinching—pile of Gamelyn's sheathed sword and quillion knife. Rob had, in a fit of temper at the bloody things, thrown the knife so that it stuck in the oak next to his own, still imbedded in the bark along with a piece of Gamelyn's favorite tunic. Then Rob had unsheathed the sword and stuck it in the ground. There must be something to what his mam was always teasing about boys and pointy things, because not only had Gamelyn watched him do both with plain lust in his eyes, but they'd both gotten hard as posts, and if it hadn't been for the fact they'd tongued and stroked each other silly several times already, there would have been rutting. Under or over, Rob wasn't picky. Though his knob certainly had a firm preference this morning.

His stomach, however, was talking even louder. He was going to wake the dead with it, let alone one shagged-out lad who was frankly bloody gorgeous as he lay there, sleeping in Rob's arms.

Rob inched out from under Gamelyn, cautious and noiseless. He rose and put on his clothes, still without a sound, took up his bow and two arrows, then left Gamelyn sleeping cradled by the oak.

After all, there wasn't owt couldn't be improved by a good breakfast.

ଔ

WHEN Rob returned, not long after, it was with a brace of coneys hanging from his belt, retrieved arrows stuck into the knotted cache of his hair, his bow carelessly slung over one shoulder and a song of dubious repute on his lips.

The song warbled and went silent as he came across Gamelyn snugging his swordbelt about his hips, fully dressed save for his unlaced tunic and the "bloody fancy pig-sticker" still stuck in the oak behind Gamelyn.

No doubt the tunic was unlaced only because Rob still wore the lanyard, wrapped about his wrist.

They both stopped mid-motion, staring at each other. The copse was quiet around them, broken only by the birds fluttering from branch to branch, the sudden splash of a fish, the burbling of the stream that fed the little mere.

Gamelyn was the first to look away, his fingers resuming their rhythm. "I thought…." Fingers tangling against the leather, he trailed off and flushed. "I wasn't sure you were returning."

"And why shouldn't I?" Rob frowned and held up the two rabbits. "You were sleeping, so I thought I'd be fetching breakfast."

Gamelyn remained silent, resumed buckling his swordbelt. Once finished, he set to tying off the scabbard's thigh rigging.

"'Tis what I do, most times," Rob continued, feeling as if he was forcing the words from his throat. "When Marion goes hunting with me, she starts the fire. She's not one to be out hunting so early."

Still silence. Gamelyn was still finding inordinate interest in arranging his sword on his hip.

"There's nowt, though, like the feel of a forest morning on your skin, the mist in your lungs. Everything's new, somehow. Alive."

Usually it was Gamelyn who babbled, too quick with words and uneasy of silence. But now and here they had switched places, and Rob, unable to contain the spew of words, finally, *finally* understood what it was that made Gamelyn sometimes just not shut up.

It was curling in the pit of his gut right now, a warning as chill as the set of Gamelyn's shoulders.

Or Gamelyn's words, quick and just that much too forced. "I have to go."

Rob considered this, made himself move again, a careful advance. He reached the spot where he'd woken not so long ago, tangled in a lover's arms and, taking the arrows from his hair, stuck them in the ground. Considered that, at this moment, pointy things seemed more to hollow his heart than fill his cod-wrap. "You… have to go," he repeated, quiet.

"I do. You know I can never stay long, and…." A flush began at his neck, rose to his cheeks. "They'll be expecting me. I shouldn't have…." Again, he went silent, and Rob watched him, tried to read him and found it passing difficult, which was odd. Usually Gamelyn was an open book; now he seemed on guard, defensive.

Ah. That was it. "I'm sorry," Rob said. "I didna mean to just leave you here on your own. I should've known better, should've woken you." He smiled, walked closer. "I wanted to, believe me. It was grand, you snugged up all close, and…."

His words trailed off—choked off, more like—dismay curling tight fingers about his throat as Gamelyn retreated, nearly stumbling in his haste.

"D… d… don't!" Gamelyn stammered, and Rob stopped in his tracks as he saw that Gamelyn actually reached for his sword hilt. As if realizing the same thing, Gamelyn looked down at his hand, flexed his fingers. "Stay where you are," he husked out as Rob started forward again. "Don't come near me."

Confusion was not a comfortable emotion for Rob. Neither was the niggling, hollow sense of something faithless and fearful being offered up by every twitch of Gamelyn's being. "What's all this? What are you playing at, Gamelyn?"

"What am *I* playing at? You can really say that, after…." Gamelyn shook his head, not looking at him. "That's rich, coming from you. You're the biggest trickster I know—"

"*Not with this.*"

Gamelyn blinked, peered up at him. Rob wanted to smack the look from his face, insecure in either its innocence or willful ignorance. Instead he clenched his fists, brought one of them to his breast.

"My people," he said, low, "aren't about playing games with their hearts. I thought… thought that when we gave each other pleasure, it was… more than play."

Gamelyn seemed, for a moment, to be searching for words. Finally they came; not what Rob expected, low and curious, almost musing. "Your people."

Rob nodded, leveling his gaze hard against Gamelyn's. Gamelyn didn't drop his regard; again, he seemed to be searching for something.

Whatever it was, he found it. But Gamelyn denied it with a hard shudder, tore his gaze away. For long moments, he was silent. Then, "It isn't a game. Even if it was… I cannot play."

"Canna? Or waint?"

"I don't know what you've done to me, but—"

"What I've *done*. To *you*." A kick in the gut would have been easier to take. "You bloody-minded…. It's all my doing, then, is it? And none of yours?" Rob clenched his teeth over all the things he could have said, would have said had his heart not been up in his throat, choking him. Finally he said, all too soft, "Liar."

The green eyes were shadowed, still cast aside. Gamelyn's face was devoid of any expression. "It doesn't matter." It was dull. "I have to go."

Every sense Rob had was veering from anger to astonishment and back again. "I see."

Only in the end, he had refused sight. Let himself be cozened by a mixing of loneliness, mead, and despair into reaching for the one fire he'd bloody well should've known would torch him. Because from the first moment that he'd touched Gamelyn… touched him and been shaken just enough sideways to reach for what he couldn't let himself trust….

Reach for innocence… the meaning of sacrifice… be your undoing… ever your rival….

But he had trusted. Gotten in too deep and then dove further, let Gamelyn's innocence cozen him, let that lovely body and what Rob had thought was a heart laid open in juniper-green eyes crack open the carapace of his own heart. Just a crack. Just a possibility.

Just wide enough to bleed him out.

"Nay." Rob flung the rabbits at Gamelyn's feet, was gratified to see him jerk, surprised. "I didna see. I should've. I should've known I'd never be nowt but sport for some nobleman, in t' end of it. And I *never* should have trusted that you were any different from *your* people."

Gamelyn was staring at the brace of rabbits. "It's not so—"

"Ent it, then? You're so good with that bloody sword, so good at *making war*"—Gamelyn's cheeks suddenly flamed, and Rob curled his lip—"so why should I be surprised that I'd be nowt but another war game. It's flirting with death you're doing, lying with me. You're gaming me, a fine-dressed fool playing a daft game by lowering himself to root in the dirt with a peasant—"

"Stop it—" Gamelyn snarled.

"But you're not minding if I tongue your knob, are you? On my knees, like a proper villein."

"*Stop* it!"

"But I'm not one of your villeins, Gamelyn Boundys. If I lie with you, it's because I *choose* it. I'm a free man and no one's property, *not even yours*—"

The swing came so fast Rob barely saw it; instinct alone bade him duck. But he wasn't as lucky with the second one, right on the heels of the first—a shove to his chest that propelled him backward and onto his arse in the dirt.

"Do you think I'd risk Hell if you were nothing to me but *property*?" That too burst from Gamelyn, no less catapulted incendiary than Rob's own angry pain. When Rob tossed the hair from his face and peered upward, there was the swollen backwash of unshed tears behind the green eyes. "We're talking plenty of if I value you! What about if you value *me*?"

Anger scrambling into abrupt confusion, Rob scrambled to his feet. "Value you for…? What are y—?"

"I cannot do this, Rob. We cannot do this again. It was an… error in judgment. A mistake."

That *hurt*, with a bewildered pain beyond any manner Rob had yet endured, from whip or gauntleted hand or nobleman's edict. It would have likely been easier had Gamelyn drawn his sword and run him through—certainly more understandable. "A… *mistake*. You cold, misbegotten son of a—"

"I'm *not*—!" Gamelyn audibly gritted his teeth. "And you say *I'm* daft. We're both fools. You were wrong to tempt me and I was wrong to… to *want*… Christ's *blood*! Don't you even see what we've done?"

Surely Gamelyn must be speaking Frank, or some other language he'd learned from his books that sounded like English but wasn't, because Rob couldn't comprehend any of it. "So now you're at least admitting it was we, not just me. So what have *we* done?"

"What we've done"—each of Gamelyn's words fell like stones, crushing—"is sin."

"Sin?" Rob repeated, incredulous; the word even tasted bad on his tongue. "I don't understand how—"

"And that's where *you're* daft, Rob Loxley. You're right. This is no game, not at all. Our Church and Crown call it sodomy, what we've fallen to, and what our families would do to us if they caught us is nothing—nothing, I tell you!—compared to what punishment God will bring down on us!"

Rob said the only thing his mouth could shape. "Sweet Lady, what kind of god do you *have*?"

"He's your God too!"

"Nay. Nay, he ent, and—"

"Stop it!" Gamelyn strode over, gripped his arms. "You can't possibly—"

"*You* canna possibly think evil has owt to do with what we gave each other!"

Gamelyn's face was white as the chalk Cernun used to mark rune-wards upon the entry to the caverns. "And we can't do it again. We'll be damned, if God hasn't already turned His face from us—"

"You keep saying 'us', but this I'll have no part of. This… whatever it is… I'll have nowt to do with any god cruel as yours—"

"Don't *say* that!" Gamelyn's fingers turned into iron, shook Rob like a terrier slaughtering a rat.

"And you say your god is love… while all the day his people spread nowt but hate and horror! What kind of people could let a god's son die for 'em, then betray him by throwing his gifts back in his face?"

"Gifts? More like damnatio—*uh*!"

Rob snatched at Gamelyn's wrists, pressed thumbs into the tendons, swift and brutal. Gamelyn gave way with a sharp gasp, and Rob leaned in, covered that gasp with his mouth. He grabbed Gamelyn's hair when he tried to pull back, pushed him up against the oak and kissed him, hard and thorough.

Gamelyn tried to shove him back, but Rob used every bit of pub-wise trickery and leverage he'd ever learned and refused to give way. He merely pressed closer, ground up against Gamelyn. A strange noise came from Gamelyn's throat; his hands, solid against Rob's chest, quivered then softened, shot upward to tangle in Rob's hair, insurrection and submission both. And Rob courted both with lips and teeth and agile tongue, with breath and pressure accepted them.

They were both shaking when Rob broke the kiss with a huge gasp.

"If that's what your god calls damnation," he breathed against the taut cords of Gamelyn's neck, "then damn me, love, because I'll not turn from it."

"You don't understand." Gamelyn's reply was hoarse, nearly a sob. "You can't. You won't. Do you think this is…. Do you think I *want*…?"

"Then don't leave me." It was a quavering whimper that sounded more like the lowliest wolf in a pack crawling on his belly—*bred to it, you are, nowt but a drudge, a villein, a* slave—showing throat to his betters. It was a plea... *begging...* humiliating, and Rob couldn't halt it. Couldn't stop himself from begging further, a whimper against Gamelyn's temple. "Please. Don't go."

This time, Gamelyn didn't just shove; he twisted, slammed an elbow into Rob's ribcage, then up against his jaw. There was a creak and pop—his ribs, Gamelyn's arm, Rob wasn't sure—but it felled him like a hammered ox. Pain flashing behind his eyes, Rob rolled over, tried to stand, failed.

And by the time he could, Gamelyn was gone.

☙❧

GAMELYN had run halfway back to the foresters' cottage before he realized what he was doing, and then it took every ounce of will and strength he had to force his feet to a more sedate pace, and not let every least sound impel him.

Now that he'd slowed, his breath heaved akin to a smith's bellows, setting off the same sort of inferno in his chest. His face stung from the branches he'd fought through. His unlaced tunic was half off his shoulders, held on merely by his swordbelt, which was all kinked sideways. Every other stride his sword was thwacking his arse. His boots were knotted with slender, greenstick ropes, vines and bracken he'd mown through, not thinking.

He'd panicked.

It was the ultimate humiliation.

So how much more humiliating was it that he fell to his knees then forward onto his hands, clutching at the earth beneath him, beseeching strength. For he had none—that was certain. Not even strength enough to weep.

Get up, he told himself. *Go back,* was his second thought, and it sent a wave of heat and horror commingling through him. It all but set the panic off again, nearly made him lurch to his feet and run. Again.

Instead he forced himself to stay, dug his fingers in harder, lowered his forehead to the earth.

He'd left his knife behind. Stuck in that sodding tree. He was not about to retrieve it. Not now. Perhaps not ever.

Instead he prayed, with every fiber of his being, for release from this... this *thing.*

Damp heat teased at his hair, wafted down his exposed nape, and he sucked in a breath to cry out, lurched up, looked up. The breath hissed out between his teeth, impotent.

The pale stag stood above him, mild, gold eyes regarding him.

And Gamelyn hadn't heard a thing.

The stag extended his neck, massive tines glinting pewter and ivory in the dappled morn, and nuzzled at Gamelyn's hair.

I'd expected better from you, boy.

Gamelyn shuddered as the voice permeated every sense he had. Kneeling there in the dirt, he wondered if he had, finally, lost what reason he still had.

Much better. After all, don't you know who you are?

No, he really didn't. Not anymore.

When you follow an intention, you cannot be surprised if it completes itself. To flee from what you have yourself helped set in motion... once is foolishness. More than that is cowardice. You are seldom a fool, Gamelyn, and perhaps that is part of your problem. Yet you are no coward. You are better than this.

Intention. He hadn't gone out into the forest intending to… to…. He *hadn't*. He'd taken leave of his reason, that was what had happened. Had wandered beyond any pale, had, with every step into the primeval depths of the forest, let some underlying malevolence creep up on him, and take his senses from him….

Give his senses to him, more like, in a wretched and beautiful agony.

"So it's all my doing, then, is it? And none of yours? Liar."

Gamelyn put his palms to his eyes, scrubbed as if to lave away every memory, every sight, every feeling. That was the worst, the knowledge that it *was* a lie, that it couldn't be just Rob. Rob hadn't changed. Something did lie, gnawing at his own heart. Some sort of sickness had sunken soul deep, making him privy… *weak*… to beguilement.

And not just any beguilement.

The stag was a demon. It must be. It had to be. Gamelyn clenched his hands together against his forehead, started to pray aloud.

Will it away. Beseech it begone, cover it in another intention—God's intention, God's wrath…

What exactly *are you praying for, boy? And to whom?*

"Why are you still here?" Gamelyn cried back.

A small chuckle tickled up against his senses, and the stag's head bobbed up and down. *The pride in you! The arrogance! You yourself have opened the door, Gamelyn, and you will not find it so easy to bung me back in.*

Staggering to his feet, Gamelyn shook his head and backed away. The stag merely took another step toward him.

Gamelyn ducked to one side and fled.

But even distance could not stop the stag's voice from following: *Have you not spent enough time denying what you are?*

What you are….

What he was, was weak. Sinful. An arrogant, prideful *sodomite*.

He didn't stop until he'd gotten to the barns, and Diamant's box. Gamelyn forced himself to some calm, took a deep breath, and walked into the box.

Diamant wheeled an eye at him, rolled a snort through his nostrils; Gamelyn patted the thick, ivory neck, tried to utter something soothing, or cajoling.

He wound up collapsed on his arse end, curled up in the straw with knees to chest, head falling back against the stall's wooden partition.

And Diamant didn't play up, or try to step on him. Instead, the stallion bent over him, gave a soft, throaty whicker, then nuzzled his face. Warm breath sifted his forelock, down over his cheeks and breast.

Like the stag….

The tears came, then.

"MOTHER says you forgot these."

Gamelyn turned from where he was saddling up Diamant. Marion stood in the doorway to the little stable, one hand held out. In it were the stoneware flasks with the medicines for his father.

The sight of those two small bottles nearly made him lose control again. He'd meant to be gone before they'd risen, but it had taken some time to regain his composure and by then he'd heard the sounds from the house. Still, he'd *forgotten*. This was what he had come for. This, not….

He was going to Hell. There was no longer any question in his mind.

Marion came in, kirtles tucked up and in one side of her belt, a shawl flung over one arm and curls flickering muted flame from the streamers of sun beginning to creep over the treetops and through the openings on the eastern wall. She was as slender and graceful as a birch, as lovely….

As her brother.

No. Rob was not… *not* lovely, not like *that*. It had been a lapse in judgment—*in sanity*—to go after him and to… to do what they had and… and Gamelyn *would not* allow himself to *do* this.

Gamelyn took the flasks from her, grabbed some straw to pad them, and started tucking them in his saddlebags. "Thank you." It grated, too high, past the sudden tightness of his throat.

This was, he realized, good-bye. He couldn't come back. He'd never see her again.

"And you left this on your bed." What Gamelyn had thought was a shawl over Marion's arm was instead his cloak. She draped it across Diamant's dappled croup, her gray eyes seeking his. They were so transparent, uncomplicated… and all too perceptive. As if she somehow knew everything that had passed in the forest between him and her brother.

No, she couldn't know. Couldn't. And why couldn't he have wanted her instead? It would have made a sordid thing out of one of the clearest lights in his life, yet would it not have been better, had he determined to sully friendship with lust, to…?

No. *No*. Oh, God, what was he *thinking*? He had lost his reason, lost his way.

"Gamelyn?"

He nearly leapt out of his skin as Marion touched his shoulder. Her gaze, thank all the saints he could name and some he couldn't, no longer seemed so knowing, only concerned.

"Gamelyn, are you all right?"

He looked away and took Diamant's rein, shook his head, a tight, useless gesture. "I… don't feel well. But I have to go. Now. My father is waiting."

"I understand. I'm sure the medicine will help him." She smiled, somewhat rueful. "I'm sorry we couldn't spend more time together. Next time, eh?"

Next time. It felt like a sword thrust to the chest—not a heart wound. Nay, this would bleed out for a long, long time. "I… I don't know when I'll be back."

Marion smiled. "You never do."

And why was he hoping that she would try to stay him, beg him to stay?

Rob had begged him. Rob had. *Begged* him. Yet he had run from it like the craven little rabbit Johan was always calling him.

Marion wasn't Rob. She leaned forward and kissed his cheek, then stepped back as he led Diamant outside.

ଔ

ROB came back after luncheon, in a foul mood but with two coneys for the dinner pot. Eluned's pleased comments only prompted several monosyllabic grunts—yet she didn't, as was her wont, query her son as to his whereabouts during the night.

That wasn't like her, surely. Marion gave her mother a puzzled look. Eluned never let them wander o' nights or sleep anywhere but in their beds without some sort of interrogation.

"Willow and the goats need their feet seen to. Also the cow." Eluned took the rabbits over by the wash basin and hung them head-down from a hook over it, inspecting them.

Rob gave a curt nod, threw a leg over the bench, then set himself to making silent inroads on the cold mutton and cheese Marion set before him.

"Ha," Marion said, purposefully light into the silence. "What's *this*, then?" She tapped at Rob's shoulder, then reached down and gave a tug at what had caught her eye.

Gamelyn's quillion knife, stuck in the back of Rob's belt next to his own dagger.

Rob snatched at her wrist, clamped down.

"Ow!" she yipped and swatted at his pate. He looked down at their hands, seemed only then to realize what he'd done, and swiftly loosed her.

"'M sorry," he muttered, turning back to wolfing down his meal—not without twitching the knife back secure into his belt.

There was a bruise starting to blossom along Rob's jaw. Marion started to speak but didn't have the chance.

"I've need of Willow early this afternoon," Eluned said, her back still to them.

Rob's gaze slid to his mother's straight shoulders, held there, then dropped. He shoved his plate away and stood. "I'm no' so hungry, after all. I'll go see to 't now."

This from the lad who'd already wolfed down three-quarters of his plate. Marion watched him go, bewildered.

"Leave it, pet." Eluned was gathering up her basket. That wasn't unusual—this time of year entailed regular gathering expeditions. What was odd was her demeanor.

"Mam…."

"Give your brother breath, Marion." The way Eluned said it was peculiar and twofold; it could have meant "give him time," or "put some life back into him," but Marion wasn't sure which.

Neither did her mother expound any further. Eluned merely finished tying her straw hat about her head—the sun was bright when it peered through the clouded sky—and departed.

Marion strolled over to the door, watched Eluned disappear into the east-most copse, and leaned against the door. Not too long after, Rob led the little jennet from the barn and tied her to the fence. Marion watched him set to work, noticed that he did merely that, spent none of his usual affectionate attention toward Willow, and a frown began to gather between Marion's brows.

Usually she could read her little brother like one of the books Gamelyn brought them. Often it took time, and patience, but she would parse a meaning from it in the end.

She walked over to the fence, climbed up. Sat there, silent, as her brother kept working. Willow put her black nose up to Marion, coaxing a pat that she was plainly miffed Rob hadn't given, and Marion obliged.

Rob's belt was conspicuously absented of Gamelyn's long knife—but then, he'd moved his own dagger to his boot top, common enough practice when trimming hoofs. Likely he'd set it aside, out of the way.

Gamelyn must have forgotten it. He had, after all, nearly forgotten his cloak and the simples. Add that to the bruise on Rob's face and the black mood, and he and Gamelyn had likely had some set-to. Very likely, in fact, since Rob had been ready to pick a fight with Gamelyn just the previous day.

Marion let it go. She had something else on her mind, anyway, now that Eluned had gone. "Rob. Were you with him?"

Rob jerked, swore. A line of blood welled on his hand where the knife had slipped, and Willow started sideways. She hit the end of the rope and promptly threw a pitching fit.

Marion gave a good curse herself and leapt out of the way, off the fence. Rob was holding his wrist and still swearing. Willow was grunting and hauling backward, her substantial haunches gathered under her, sliding and quivering with effort.

"You waint pull *my* knot loose, you bloody daft mare!" Rob shouted at Willow, and Marion trotted down the fence line, hopped it and headed for Rob.

"Give me—" she ordered, snatching at his cut hand. "Give me that!" With a roll of his eyes—toward her or the still plunging mare, Marion wasn't sure—Rob obeyed.

He didn't loose the pressure on his wrist, and a good thing; it was a nasty slice, bleeding gushes but not, thankfully, in spurts. Marion yanked at the rag tying back her hair and used it to wrap his hand, tight.

"Bloody damn, Marion, that *hurts*!"

About the time she'd finished wrapping Rob's hand, Willow gave a great, final heave backward, then lurched forward. As soon as the pressure had left her poll, she stopped fighting, still blowing.

"Daft mare," Rob said, going over and patting her with his uninjured hand. "You'd think you'd learn. And I canna hobble you *and* do your feet, y' git."

"I think you'd best let me stitch that, Rob."

Rob shrugged. "At least it ent my better hand. I was nigh finished, t' boot. But you'd best even her up. I'll hold the silly bitch so she doesn't have to be tied."

They ended up having to take off her head collar and put a rope about Willow's neck—the knot had been twisted too tight on the fence to be easily loosed. A dutiful Rob followed Marion's instructions, holding his injured hand upright while Marion took the hoof rasp and sanded down the uneven edges on the mare's feet.

Marion tried again, when they were inside and she was stitching the finger-long gash closed. "Were you with him, then?"

Rob flinched as the needle went in, audibly gritted his teeth, and stared at his other hand, white-knuckled around the braided ball of rags Eluned kept for just such emergencies. His dagger lay between them, with a charm laid upon it to cut the pain.

"Did you see Will?" Marion persisted, when he didn't answer.

The sloe eyes rose to meet hers, blinked, then closed. Rob gave a huge sigh, shook his head as if to clear it, then murmured, "Aye. I saw him."

Marion's hands trembled; she forced them steady and made another pass with the needle as purposeful and calm as if it were fabric, not flesh. "How was he?"

Rob flinched again, let out a curse that could have scorched the table, then growled, "Did you bother to sharpen that thing, lass?"

"Well, *lad*, if you don't tell me how Will was, I might have to bang it point-first against the table then finish my stitching," Marion growled back.

Rob shrugged apology, his expression turning unpleasant. "How do you think he is? Scared. Alone. He's been… gah, *bugger*! Been declared outlaw and his father's rotting in gaol. It was all I could do to convince him not to go after his da and break him from the Nottingham gaol—"

"Oh, he canna!"

"I know. But it took…." Breath hissed out his teeth as Marion took another stitch. "Took every bit of persuasion I had to make him see… that. I told him Da was doing everything he could for him… bloody *fuck*!" Rob jerked, threw the rag ball across the room, hard, and so quick her eye could scarce follow, he snatched up his knife and jammed it point-first into the table.

Marion started, but managed to keep her hands steady. "One more stitch. Then y' can be throwing and stabbing things all you want. I might join you."

"T' knife charm wasn't working worth a good toss anyway," he muttered and fell silent, jaw clenching, as Marion finished up. She tied off the gut thread, bent and sawed the ends off with her teeth, then packed the wound with Eluned's powders and set to bandaging.

"Not that owt Da could do'll matter," Rob snarled, and his profile was hard, set as stone. "He's a forester, Marion. A free man, a yeoman appointed guardian to the Royal Wode by king's warrant. Yet because he's English, not a bloody Frank, his word's worthless. His oaths mean nowt. *He's* worthless, to likes of *them*."

His voice was shaking with such emotion it made Marion's own heart thud, hard, in her ears. "Rob—"

"Will canna even come here, to this house where we love him, where he should be given sanctuary by right—"

"Cernun forbids outlaws in the covenant." Even as Marion said it, the defense seemed hollow. But she had believed it, once. Understood the reasons for it, the contracts given—and taken—by those of the Shire Wode, the rules and cautions enforced to ensure the safety of not only the covenant, but the common people who looked to them. She had no real right to put aside a belief merely because she had a personal disagreement with it.

Rob reached out, yanked his knife free of the tabletop, and flipped it through his fingers, considering it. "So how does it feel, sister-mine, to moon after something you canna have? What they'd all warn you off?"

The wanton cruelty of that sent Marion stumbling to her feet, gaping down at Rob.

"But then, *you* never warned me off Gamelyn," he said, and palmed the knife, looking down. His eyes glittered, red-rimmed. "'Twould have been better if y' had."

Gamelyn? It threw her sideways against her own perceptions, shook them and made her reconsider her brother's mood—and the one meaning amongst many.

Gamelyn this morning, in as foul and flummoxed a mood as she'd ever seen him. Marion truly thought he'd simply gotten up earlier than herself, had been somewhat baffled by her mother's insistence upon taking the cordial *to* him, and the cape. Had been somewhat flummoxed herself to find Gamelyn instead making to depart, and that after he'd made so much last night of waiting… *worrying*… until Rob returned.

It clicked into place, a meaning as hard-hitting, no doubt, as Rob's realization of Marion's own feelings for Will.

"I canna stay in here," Rob muttered, shoving away from the table and lurching to his feet. "I think I'll *smother*."

Marion watched him stumble out the door, was following before she could even think.

He hadn't gone far—just to where the trees began to thicken. He was wandering in the curtained branches of the old willow where they had played as children. They had braided the willow's branches, hung from his limbs, climbed as far upward as they could… always, always aware that, even in the willow's embrace, there was only so high they could ascend.

She approached, held her palms up to the willow's caress, watched her brother jitter and writhe within his own being. Finally she couldn't stand it any longer. "Rob. Tell me. What *happened*?"

He shrugged, but it was more a reflex than a response. "Happened. Something's… happening, aye. Trying to happen. I thought it was me. But I ent sure, anymore. He's… it's… turning me inside out. It's like I'm walking without my skin but then… after… it didna stop. Even sleeping, it's there. Just… there, waiting. Not quiet. Like a beating heart, or breathing in the dark."

"It wasn't just Will you met in the Green last night." Marion reached out, brushed the curls back from his cheek, let the touch linger in hope of gentling him. "Was it?"

The cheek beneath her fingers was warm, the pulse point below it lurching and jumping. "We'd shared the mead skin, Will and I. I wasn't sure"—his gaze slid to meet hers, apologetic—"when I'd see him again. I told him… what you'd asked me to. Then I told him he had to stay alive. For his father. For *you*."

She sucked her breath in between her teeth.

"Aye, it wasn't fair. But it made him listen." He took the hand she had laid against his cheek, pulled her against him, settled back against the willow's thick trunk. "He'll wait, now. He'll go south into the Shire Wode where none'll find him. Lie low until it's all passed. And it will, Marion. They'll forget. Sheriffs change, and they'll get their worth out of George's hide."

Again, she took in a sudden, shocked breath.

"It's what George wanted." Rob's growl buzzed against her shoulder. "It ent likely I'll ever sire a child I can lay claim to, but I can understand that much. Fathers should protect their sons."

There was a bitterness, dug deep, that Marion couldn't understand. She angled her head so that her cheek was up against his. "Did Gamelyn come after you, then?" She tensed. "Did he… did he see Will?"

"I don't think so. But I wasn't thinking very straight, what with the mead and… well, everything. He… Gamelyn… he turns me inside out even sober, and the forest was so *alive*, last night." He sounded… lost. "I didna know he was there. It was so easy to just… lose myself."

Trepidation laid an icy trickle down her spine. "Rob—"

"I don't think he saw owt. The fireflies, maybe, when I spoke to 'em—"

"*Spoke* to 'em? You knew he was there, but—"

"I'm not as daft as that!" he snapped, pulling back. "I know that Mam and Da both have forbidden us to show him th' magic, but I didna know anyone was around and…." He shrugged, and when he spoke again, his voice was flat. "I think I can say that, had he seen me draw down the moonlight, he never would've let me near him."

"So you did get near." *Finally*, was all she could think, *since you've been pining after him longer than you even know.*

He nodded.

"Did you lie with him?"

"It's not always that way, lads with lads," Rob said, gaze sliding away and his cheek darkening. "It's not *always* just the mounting."

"Well, little brother, it's not always that way, lasses with lads, either." Marion couldn't help the smile in her voice. "Was it nice?"

A small groan escaped him. "It was… until it wasn't."

She frowned, remembering Gamelyn as he'd left. Furtive, evasive… unhappy.

"I need him, Marion. I *need* him, like growing things need rain and sun. When we were lying together, I could See *tynged* untangling before me, like the wool twirling, long and sleek and fine, on Mam's spindle. Then…."

Marion waited.

"He *turned* on me, Mari, saying we'd… we'd made some *mistake*. Like we'd picked the wrong arrow, or made an ill shot. He kept saying how what we had done was wrong… evil… like something so… so lovely had to be all twisted up into a judgment or game called foul."

The Church made overmuch grief about "sins of the body," Marion knew; they were too concerned, really, to assign "evil" to anything that they hadn't thought up themselves. The only "evil" Marion had witnessed so far was the way the Church's minions would twist every nature—body, spirit, even the earth about them—from blessed into profane.

She looked at her brother's hunched-in misery, and for long moments she wasn't sure whose innocence she mourned more: Rob's, for thinking Gamelyn would come to him in joy instead of fear, or Gamelyn, for thinking there was no more to pleasure *than* fear.

"He kept talking about being… damned, just for touching me. About how his god saw nowt but evil in such things. A simple blessing of body and heart, and he thinks it's wrong. Some of it's because he's noble-bred and I'm nowt. That's no hard guess." Rob gave a shrug as if the notion wasn't cutting into him as keenly as the hoof-knife had earlier, as if the words weren't choked with tears he refused to let rise. "But it's the touching, the loving… I don't understand. I *don't*. He thinks I'm nowt but… damnation for him. Likely I am. It's sure he's nowt but misery for me."

"Surely that's not true," she whispered. That ashen-faced, unhappy lad who had escaped—aye, now she knew it for the escape it had truly been—Gamelyn would have sauntered away whistling if what happened had been as unimportant as Rob thought.

"He thinks it is. He said so. And whatever that means?" Rob flung the forelock from his eyes, finally betraying the glimmer and spill down his cheeks. "I don't think it means what he thinks it does. I think damnation is what the world was like in that moment he had that look in his eyes—when he wanted… *needed*… but still turned and walked away."

"He'll come back. Surely he has to come to his senses, to realize—"

"I don't think he'll come back, Marion."

"Oh, Rob."

"Mam will be delighted. She's never trusted him."

"She never trusted where he came from." Marion was gentle. "It's not the same thing."

"But it means the same in the end, doesn't it?" Rob's voice had also turned strangely gentle. "Only now it's on both of us."

☙ XVI ❧

HE RODE hard those first miles, a heedless and wonderfully mindless gallop with which a game Much did his best to keep pace. Face hot, eyes bright, teeth bared—and the tears kept coming as if daring the wind to dry them—Gamelyn pushed. And pushed. Diamant showed his mettle by leaning into the pace, leaping over obstacles in their path and lunging around others, surging forward as if his rider's fury and longing fed into him like heat lightning.

When they did slow, winded and a-sweat, the silence pounded in Gamelyn's ears, punctuated by the steady clop of iron-shod hoofs on the hard road.

Much kept silence the entire way to Blyth, and took Diamant to the stables with his own rouncey as Gamelyn dismounted.

It was in him to run for the chapel, to unburden himself so his father and brothers wouldn't see the wickedness surely scrawled—a brand, a mark of retribution—upon his face. Further evil, surely, to bring further weakness into the chamber of an already sick man....

Gah!—that was superstitious nonsense, no more sense to it than to Rob's blasphemous questions. If the medicine in his bags would help his father, he had no business tending to his own needs before that, anyway.

Nevertheless, he was very glad that the only people he saw were ones who would give him no undue attention unless he asked it of them. Like the servants, sliding through the corridors with lowered gazes and purposefully soft gait.

"But you're not minding if I tongue your knob, are you? On my knees, like a proper villein..."

"Get out of my head," he gritted.

"...not one of your villeins, Gamelyn Boundys. Not your property, and if I lie with you it's because I choose*...."*

"Shut up!" he snarled, then clapped a hand over his mouth as it rang down the hall. He looked up just in time to see one of those villeins—*his serfs, his property, his father's property*—duck his head lower and shoo another into an alcove and out of the way of their obviously ill-tempered lord.

"...that I bent the knee, 'm'lord'...."

He fled into his father's chambers as if a demon were after him.

No, no demons. A demon lad, who'd grown tall and lithe and lovely.

"Gamelyn, lad. I was just thinking on you."

Sir Ian was on the far end, seated in his favorite chair next to his book table. The massive stone fireplace was dark—the spring had been uncommonly warm, after all—but next to that and the upsweep of gabled stone arch, Sir Ian looked small. Frail. He was swathed in furs and woolens despite the heavy draperies pulled over the windows. The room was warm, too close.

The book table was piled with books, but also had a chessboard set up, crowned here and there with the ornate wooden pieces that Sir Ian had himself carved for the mother of his sons. He had played it, many a time, with first Johan then with Gamelyn—Otho had never cared for it—and now he was playing with Alais, who turned to Gamelyn with a slight smile.

"Your papa was talking of you, as well, little brother. Did your trip go well?"

Gamelyn nodded. He wasn't sure he trusted himself to speak just yet.

"I think he was hoping you would read to him." Alais rose, still smiling. She was obviously feeling the heat of the room, clad simply in a sleeveless linen overdress over thin crème muslin. The household keys jangled at her girdle as she approached Gamelyn and laid a dimpled, white hand on his arm. Her next words were for his ears alone. "He's having a bad day and was worrying after you. I'm glad you came straight up from the stables...." She trailed off in sudden puzzlement, brushed her fingers through his hair, and held up a crumpled leaf. "Did you have an argument with a tree?"

I might have, at that. At least this time the thought—albeit hysterical—was his own. Not... memory.

"You do look a bit wild, though—are you too tired to sit with him?"

Gamelyn shook his head, finally felt he could trust his voice. "I'm all right."

"Is the wise woman with you? Do I need to make a welcome for her?"

"She could not come with me, but she assured me she will, anon. And I have medicine she made special for him."

"Well, then." She gave his cheek a pat then raised her own voice for Sir Ian's benefit. "I'm going to the kitchens, see about a bite for this wandering son of yours. If that's all right, Papa?"

"I wouldn't mind leaving off this game." Sir Ian gave his daughter-in-law a mock frown then, aside to Gamelyn, "Alais is trouting me as roundly as she ever does. Never play chess with a woman, son. They defy logic and play on instinct. Women would take the Holy Land, did more of them take up a sword."

Alais chuckled and went to him, laid a kiss to his head. "No swords for me. I'm a danger to my own thumbs when I put a knife to the roast."

Sir Ian snorted.

She raised her eyebrows at Gamelyn, her concern obvious.

Did he look *that* wild-eyed?

"I'm fine," he said again, quite firm, and she smiled.

"Then I shall leave you and Papa to it." With a susurrus of blue linen and a waft of clove pomade, she exited.

"Come sit, boy. Take off your cloak and belts… here." In the faint light, his eyes seemed sunken into his head, clad in shadows of gray as they focused upon Gamelyn. Sir Ian's smile, genuinely given, nevertheless stretched too thin.

It hardly seemed possible that his father had changed so much in a day and night. Of course, Gamelyn himself had changed….

He would *not* think upon that, not now.

"I'll have someone see to your boots," Sir Ian continued. "They're filthy. *You're* filthy. You've ridden too hard, I wager."

"Diamant was eager to go; I let him."

"I hope you did not put the wortwife to a pace she could not take…." Sir Ian trailed off, his eyes flickering as Gamelyn started to speak—was it disappointment? "She would not come."

"She will. She could not right away leave, that is true, but she promised," he emphasized, "to come before the se'nnight's ending, and I believe her. She sent medicine in the meantime."

A smile. "That was quite thoughtful. Here, son, take these old slippers of mine." Sir Ian toed his own sheepskin-lined slippers toward Gamelyn. "Donall is resting, but call the paxman outside my doors and have someone see to those boots."

"Nay, Papa, please don't worry anyone. I'm fine for now." With every step Gamelyn felt himself relaxing, enough to unbuckle his swordbelt and lay it carefully aside, to shuck both cloak and overcoat and realize how tired he truly was.

"Whatever did you do to yourself, boy?"

"Eh? Wha—?"

"Your arm. Did you have trouble on the road? I keep telling you that the roads can be dangerous, yet we had to set someone after you since so many times you insist on riding alone. What happened, son?"

Gamelyn realized what his father was concerned about at the same time it came to him that he wasn't tired enough. Not if the mere sight of that blood-spotted, torn sleeve could raise a tent in his breeks and send his breath tight in the mere space of three heartbeats.

"I do apologize. For the knife. I figured did you follow, I'd have heard you comin' for a furlong at least…."

"It's nothing. I was clumsy in the barns, nothing more," Gamelyn blurted, moving to his saddlebags. "Here, let me show you what Mistress Eluned made for you even as I watched." He pulled both bottles from the protective swath of straw he'd packed around them, held up first one then the other. "She said the best thing to do for you now would be to manage your pain. So you're to have a measure of this as you need and another of this one before you retire at night, to help you sleep. Where's your cup, and I'll pour—"

"In a moment, boy. Come, sit beside me."

Gamelyn obeyed, setting the fired-clay bottles on the table next to the chessboard. He knelt next to his father's chair, took the bony hands in his own. Sir Ian's fingers were warm in Gamelyn's, the skin like overused parchment, dry and too smooth.

"Manage my pain, eh? No doubt she told you there was not much else to do for me but make me comfortable, eh?"

Gamelyn stiffened.

"Never you mind, lad; I know how it is. Whatever time is left will be God's blessing. I've lived a good life, done my duty by Church and Crown, and as a result I'll leave my boys with the means to make their own lives. It's enough."

The frank acceptance of it hit Gamelyn, hard.

Don't go. Don't leave, not yet.

To be covered with another voice, napped with velvet and pain: *Don't leave me. Please, don't go....*

For mad seconds he wished he could lay his head upon his father's lap and sob out his troubles like a child.

Acceptance? Nay, his father would never accept *this*.

"I won't say nay to any ease, of late," his father was musing. "Though pain is good for the soul. No doubt our dear cousin the Abbess would corroborate that."

The statement was threaded through with weakness and admittance of guilt. But instead of nodding compliance, irritation niggled at Gamelyn. He leaned forward, gripped tighter to his father's hands.

"Then she would be mistaken. You have been a righteous man all your life and now is your time to rest."

"Dear lad." Sir Ian smiled. "She is a very holy woman, and no doubt she has a point... nay," he soothed as Gamelyn stiffened, "you did not make the journey for naught. I will take the wortwife's potion, and look hopefully for her visit. I should rather have the strength to end my days on earth upright, rather than in this chair. God will judge my failings, in the end, and that is well enough."

"Only a cruel God would deny ease to one of His best!"

"I'll have nowt to do with any god as cruel as yours...."

Silent memory came upon the heels of protest and struck Gamelyn behind the eyes so swiftly that he gasped. He dropped his head into his father's lap to hide the sudden sting of tears.

"There, lad. You seem so sad." The open concern in his father's voice was more brine in an already raw laceration. The thin fingers faltered, nevertheless had the strength in them to pull Gamelyn's face up to meet his.

"It's only...," Gamelyn tried, faltered, then tried again. "I don't want you to leave me. Not yet. I... I feel like I have only begun to *know* you."

He had never before spoken the words aloud. Never before realized how true they were.

Sir Ian sighed, nodded. "I feel the same way. Here you are, nearly a man. I would like nothing better than to see you wived and giving me grandchildren. Or"—one eyebrow arched, a return to imperiousness—"knowing you, giving yourself to a higher calling. None of my sons save you have the will or the inclination for the priesthood. You seem to have the necessary—aloofness?—of temperament."

Gamelyn barely controlled a wince. Before, he'd always prided himself on his detachment, his ability to be cool and considering….

"You cold, *misbegotten son of a—"*

"I'm not*—!"*

His eyes were stinging; Gamelyn looked down, away.

"I spoke with Abbess Elisabeth before she left for Worksop. She is quite interested in you, Gamelyn. She believes you have a gifted intellect, that with the proper sponsorship you would go far in the Church." Sir Ian kept patting his hand. "I'm proud of you, son. It would be a worthy choice for your situation. If it is what you truly want, you should have that path."

What was wrong with him? The Abbess had obviously not been telling pretty lies, had gone so far as to speak not only to him, but to his father. In fact, it had only been a few days ago that Gamelyn had spoken to Brother Dolfin about it. Only a few days ago, he would have leapt at the chance. Would have left tomorrow, did his father give the word.

Only a few days ago.

Before a demon lad had spun him widdershins in a spiral of want.

Before he had known what it was he longed for, and that had little to do with sterile comforts and safe boundaries, had everything to do with a fae wind that whistled untamed through the green Wode….

"Gamelyn?"

He wasn't sure he trusted himself to speak, merely laid his head once more against his father's knees and held tight to the thin, strong hands.

"Son. Don't worry. I'll see to your future. I have no intention that you, of all my boys, should have to go begging to anyone."

Gamelyn shook his head, finally made himself peer up at his father, give that much comfort. Wicked at the very least, damned at the very best, Gamelyn should repent not only of what he had given into last night, but for sitting beside his dying father and mourning not merely that father, but something gone within himself.

Gone, with something else taking its place, strong and merciless and indecent.

I am not the son you meant to raise, Papa, he thought but hadn't the courage to say. Instead he smiled, said, "I know you will," and was both heartened and guilt-ridden as his father leaned forward and kissed the top of his head.

"We will see it done, then."

"Well. Our little *gadelyng* returns."

The scorn in Johan's voice rose irate answer in Gamelyn; he tried to lurch upward from his father's embrace. Sir Ian didn't let him, held Gamelyn's hands in his lap with remarkable strength.

"I will not tell you again, Johan," Sir Ian rebuked. "It is not fitting, to call your brother such a thing."

Johan was set in a purposeful lounge against the door, all innocence. One would never suspect that he'd just called his brother an itinerant boor—or, in its underpinnings, a gipsy's bastard. "It's merely play on his name, Papa. Gamelyn, *gadelyng*." He shrugged, smiled. "I meant his wanderings, nothing more."

The last time Johan had called his younger brother thus in their father's hearing, Sir Ian had soundly thrashed him. But such punishment was no longer possible, and Johan was growing bold in that lack...

Sir Ian let it go, all too easily. "Well. Now I have two of my three best accomplishments in life at my side. Where is Otho?"

"It looks like you were doing well enough with Gamelyn's company," Johan said, his gaze strafing Gamelyn. "Otho is overseeing some ridiculous market-stall haggle. Three vendors claiming the rights to one space… bloody peasants! Too stupid to control their own fancy, let alone govern themselves in anything."

"... flirting with death you're doing, lying with me... lowering himself to root in the dirt with a peasant..."

Gamelyn winced. Johan's eyes moved to him, cool and gauging.

"I see your cup." Gamelyn rose, giving Sir Ian's hands a quick squeeze and release. "I'll fetch it, pour you a drought."

"So the old witch had a potion for you?"

"Don't call her that!" Gamelyn retorted.

"Forgive me." Johan's eyes belied the apology and glinted, dangerous. "Perhaps, little brother, you can tell me why did you not bring her as your lord father asked?"

"She had other duties—"

"More pressing than tending to the mesne lord of her village?"

"Johan, with your name-calling and doubts you blight the name of a good woman who has offered to help your father in his need," Sir Ian warned. "She has promised to come by se'nnight's end."

"She'd better," Johan murmured as Gamelyn passed him. Then, louder, "Forgive me, Papa. I doubt she's all that old, at that. The forester was in his prime, and I've heard rumor tell his wise-woman is as lovely…." Alais came in through the doorway, and he added, "… as our own trothed sister, here."

Alais cocked an eyebrow at him and didn't stop her forward progress. She held a large tray laden with roast chicken, early lettuces, and fresh bread. "Make yourself useful for more than buttering the bread of your brother's wife, Johan, and clear the table. I brought enough for us all."

Instead, Johan pulled another, larger table close to Sir Ian. "Too many bloody books to bother moving."

"You're as fond of that word as…." Gamelyn hesitated just before he said, *Rob*.

"And who would that be, little brother?" Johan queried, quick as a ferret.

"It doesn't matter, does it? Save he's right," Sir Ian countered. "You are overfamiliar with that word."

Alais settled the tray, watched Gamelyn pour a small dose from the stoneware bottle into Sir Ian's cup. "Is that brew from the wortwife, then?"

Gamelyn nodded and handed it to his father.

"Good. No more of this nonsense from the leech. He'd have you racked with pain, he would, and bleed you to death in the meantime."

"He's a good man," Sir Ian protested, with a grimace at the potion. "Why do these things never taste good?"

"I doubt not he's virtuous; it's his healing skills I question," Alais quipped. "As to the brew, consider the sharp taste penance. I hope it works. We've missed you in the hall."

Gamelyn saw her glance at Johan as she said it. She took Johan's slights and attempts at intimidation, rolled them into a hard ball, and lobbed them back in his face. Gamelyn wished he had her nerve.

Of course, Otho was a lot bigger than Johan, and had basted his head several times when Johan had gotten too overbearing.

She's Otho's wife, after all. His... property.

Oh, *God*! Gamelyn nearly dropped the bottle, tightened his grip just in time. Aye, he'd had such thoughts before, in scattered snippets, but why now? So many, so close together, so aggressive.

He knew why.

If he ever saw Rob Loxley again, he'd baste *his* head.

"Maybe Gamelyn's new paramour has a dirty mouth to go with the dirty feet."

Gamelyn whipped his head around to stare at Johan, who crossed his arms and smirked.

"Well, *lapin*?"

"Paramour?" Alais blinked, then smiled. "Ah, is *that* why you've been gone so often, Gamelyn? Could it be our little brother's absentmindedness has a good reason?"

"I… I don't know what you mean," Gamelyn retorted.

"Oh, come. Confession is good!" Johan came over and slapped Gamelyn on one shoulder. The blow looked conspiratorial, but could have in truth felled an ox. Gamelyn didn't stagger, refused to give so much as a glare.

"Paramour?" Sir Ian grumped. "What is this?"

In reward for such self-control, Johan merely laid an arm on Gamelyn's shoulders. "Tell them, brother. Don't be shy."

"Perhaps our lad has finally found love." Alais was quartering the chicken, preparing a plate for him, but her smile toward Gamelyn was fond, the tease gentle.

"He's in love, all right," Johan said, "Love that counts. The forester's daughter holds his cod-wrap in her hands, sure enough."

The uttered "her" gave Gamelyn leave to once again breathe. Unfortunately, relief became anger which, as usual, had no place to go but deep in his belly, burning.

"Johan," Alais warned, "one day you'll go too far."

She was ignored.

"How lucky for our little brother that he had dear Papa's blessing to visit this last time?"

"And here we were, just talking of your future in the Church. I pray that you have not taken undue advantage of Mistress Eluned's hospitality." Sir Ian's expression was severe.

Gamelyn was beginning to feel like a rabbit indeed—one in a trap. "I have not!" he protested. "They have treated me courteously, and I would not betray…." His voice choked in on itself.

"I canna tell you not to follow my son…."

"Gamelyn?" Sir Ian's voice had not softened. "Have you taken liberties with the forester's daughter?"

Gamelyn raised his chin and said with complete conviction, "No, my lord. I have not."

Sir Ian peered at him, then nodded, satisfied. "It would have surprised me, surely. You have been such a good, chaste lad."

Gamelyn wished the floor would swallow him up, found himself perversely grateful for Johan's tight hold.

"And a bit of a fool, it seems," Johan murmured.

"You're gaming me, a fine-dressed fool playing a daft game…."

Shut. Up.

"I do not intend to return," Gamelyn said. It was quiet. Beaten. "Until you have need of more medicine, of course."

Sir Ian nodded. "I think that would be for the best, considering. And if there is need for your return there, son, your behavior must be exemplary. It would be ill done to return Mistress Eluned's courtesy with a lack of self-control. It is… difficult to be your age, my boy, but you are no animal. Granted, peasants can be wanton, heedless as any brute beast. Their scope is limited, like small children. It is ever your responsibility to see that you do not mistreat them, even regarding their indiscretions."

So it was his fault… but in the end not?

Was Gamelyn the only one who could make no sense out of what his father had just said? He looked around at his family and suddenly wondered how this had happened, where he had come from, how he had come to be related to these people, how he had been denied the dubious grace of *being like them.*

There was no answer to be had here. The internal maelstrom had only ramped itself tighter, more furious. He should have gone to the chapel. Confession would help. Prayer would give him solace, guidance.

Absolution.

Alais was serving their father, and Sir Ian was tucking in; Gamelyn didn't realize Johan had drawn him slightly away until it was too late.

"Hearken what a fine game you play," Johan said against his ear.

Game? What game?

And why did he only hear Rob's voice, a furied echo of the contained threat in Johan's voice: *"Don't play with me, Gamelyn...."*

Shut up... shut up shut up*!*

"And it won't work, do you hear?" Johan's grip on his nape, deceptively friendly, nipped hard and flowered pain up into the base of Gamelyn's skull. Leaning closer, Johan whispered, "You may be the old man's favorite, but you're an afterthought. An aging man's last attempt to prove his virility. Why he loves you so much despite the fact that birthing you killed *our mother?*" It was not the first time the accusation had been flung his way, but Gamelyn had never heard it spat with such venom. "*I'm* the eldest, *petit lapin*. Never forget that. When Papa is buried, it is I who will own your destiny. I who will say what shall be yours and what shall not."

"I'm unlikely to forget," Gamelyn snarled back, low. "For you never give me the chance."

"Even so." Johan loosed him. "Then we understand each other."

"Boys!" Sir Ian ordered. "Come eat."

Gamelyn slid his gaze to meet Johan's. Johan smiled, then shrugged and walked over to their father.

ଔ

IT WAS a magnificent dagger. One could think it too delicate, with the wide, filigreed quillion and the long, slender blade. But it was serviceable as well as lovely.

Like its owner.

For that was the most important thing, that it had been Gamelyn's.

The moon was setting over Mam Tor, a waning sickle beyond the stark gray stones surrounding him, descending into the black shadows of the forest's treetops. Rob was kneeling amidst the ring stones. With a touch of the pommel to his lips, he passed the dagger, hilt to tip then tip to hilt, through the fire he had lit upon the center stone.

His father would not approve. His mother would fork an evil eye at him—likely right before she boxed his ears. And Rob was frankly positive that Cernun, did he discover his protégé preparing a dubious blood rite on a hallowed doorstep of the Barrow-lines, would kick his arse and starve him in the caverns for a month. But Cernun was nowhere to be found, and Rob had to know what none would tell.

He laid the knife edge upon his unbandaged left palm. Better to hear Marion's fussing than to lame his good hand as well as the other, but for this he had no choice. Any left-hand path was a chancy one, but it was, after all, Rob's stronger hand....

Suddenly there was a shadow on the stone, nigh eclipsing the fire, and rage in a low voice. "What do you think you're *doing*, boy?"

A boot kicking the fire, smoke and ash scattering across the altar, and a wiry hand grabbing his tunic and shoving him back. Rob went sprawling, as much from shock as the strength of the shove, and rolled to his hands and knees before Cernun.

"You canna—uh!"

With uncanny speed and strength, the old man lurched forward, grabbed Rob's tunic front, and yanked him close. "Are you now thinking to tell *me*, boy, what I can and cannot do?"

Before the rage in those clear eyes, Rob had no answer.

"Did you really think you could do this, on my doorstep, and I would not know?" Cernun growled, and shoved Rob back. "You are powerful, young stag, but not that powerful. Do you think there is anything—*anything*!—that happens in my forest of which I am unaware?"

"Then where were you two nights ago?" Rob shot back, stumbling to his feet. "Where were you when Will needed you? When I...." He choked off.

"Will is no longer of our covenant."

"He—"

"And what happened between you and the young lordling 'twas what brought me here!"

Rob fell silent, trembling all over, gripping tight the hilt of Gamelyn's dagger.

"What were you *thinking*?" Cernun gave a snort. "Now that I ponder it, you *weren't* thinking, two nights ago *or* now. Unless what's in your cod-wrap now does your thinking for you! You would call a blood rite... *you*? A stripling barely come to his power would think to hold the Wheel still or even turn it back!" He leaned forward, roared, "*Why*?"

"I want answers!" Rob snarled back. "You speak in riddles, my father waint speak of this to me, my mother canna even *See* my future...!" Rob's voice cracked, uncertain.

Cernun crossed his arms, gave Rob somber regard. "What would you ask of Him, then?"

"He speaks to me. More and more. And Gamelyn has seen the king stag, an ivory one. He saw what you See."

"Nay, lad." Softer. "What the nobleman's son sees is very different."

"But no one Sees him as I do. Do they?" Rob shot back. "*Why*?"

"None ever sees the Horned Lord the same."

"That's no answer and you know it!" Three quick steps, and he was standing a hand's width from Cernun. He was so much taller than the old man—he didn't remember that before, and it both gratified and disturbed him. "Tell me, then. Can you See what lies ahead for me?"

"The future is never easily kenned, young stag. To have the uncertainty of a rent in Time's fabric is not unknown. Particularly when things have so recently come adrift—"

"But she couldn't See before, either. Come adrift? Because of Gamelyn…?" He trailed off, then said, "And why would it be because of him?"

"I think you know the answer to that," Cernun said, almost gentle. "Or you would not be here now."

Rob closed his eyes, brought the heels of his hands up as if he could scrub away both sight and Seeing. "I… *know* him. I… touched him, and I never meant it for owt. It was just a lark, just a possibility… but then it lit somethin' beneath my skin and in my veins, cold fire… sweet Lady, I've never known the like!"

"Did you think the winter does not love the summer? And the summer the winter? They are a part of each other; how could it be otherwise?"

Rob snorted; he couldn't help it. It sounded so suddenly and inexplicably *mad*. If there was such a thing as mad in a world of magic, of gods that walked the earth like strange half-beasts. "You talk like I'm part of some story. Like what me mam used to tell me for bed."

"Your father did you no service by only giving you truth in careful and chewed mouthfuls." Cernun opened his hands as if to hold the weight of air and earth upon them. "We *are* the story, young stag. You know the spirits live amongst us; they also live through us. It is all one."

"*Not to him*. I know what his people are," Rob persisted. "Cernun, I never meant for it to be like… this. I didna want this. I know what stands behind him, what I should run from, never think to touch… but that's not all of it. I know it. I know *him*." Rob clenched his fists, slid them down to his breast, thumped. "It's here, *in me*. I canna get away from it. I can still feel him, breathe the breath of him, close my eyes and See it, swirling, in my Sight. He's in my *blood*."

"The both of you are edges on a spinning triskele, flung apart yet held together. You are not the first, nor the last, not even the only in this story, this time. All of us have this knowledge, deep within us, like a seed. Few of us see it sprout, much less bear fruit. But those of us in which it does?" Cernun shrugged. "It is never easy, and there are not always easy answers."

More riddles. Rob hunched his shoulders, took a few half steps toward the altar, looked down at it. Ash and grit and a few embers, dying. "Easy or no, I have to know. I have to know what this *is*, and I know the Horned Lord knows. He's… watching me. Waiting. I have to know what I must do. I have to know why."

"You can't help but understand the attraction of it, the knowledge that one doesn't exist without the other… but *you*." Cernun shook his head. "You are a mystery, wrapped in a riddle, and there's not a one of us who can pace you, find you before you act. And now you would scorn a Maiden's touch, would spin the Wheel widdershins, take your rival as your lover. Rob, you *cannot*."

"It seems," Rob said, wavering, "I already have."

"And so you have given him the means to betray you. To betray us all."

"I *will not* believe that."

"He is of the ones who'd see us dead. 'Tis time for waking, aye, and you have set it spinning wild as any storm. You have waked the Oak, tangled and twined him in Holly, but neither of you, in the end, can deny what you are. *He is your rival*. It is what he was born to be and there is nothing you can do about it."

"Are these your words?" Rob asked. "Or the Horned Lord's?"

"Are we not the same?"

"Not always," Rob whispered, and the moment he spoke, he knew it for truth. "Not anymore."

Cernun was staring at him, almost puzzled, and he seemed… vulnerable, for the first time since Rob could remember. He was an old man, growing worn, growing hag-ridden with the unchancy nature of his god's power.

"There may be truth in what you say," Rob persisted. "But you canna answer with His truth. Not without Him."

"He comes, possession or visitation, when and if He chooses. One does not bid the Horned Lord to heel like a hound."

"He shall answer *me*." Rob brought up the knife, put the edge to his palm.

"Rob—"

"*Datgelu'r eich hun*," Rob growled—

Reveal yourself—

Sliced.

And all the sound went away. Time filled, then spilled out from behind his eyes, timing itself to the beat of his heart, then slowing it to a slow thrum and thud. The blood welled through his fist; Rob turned it, squeezed. Watched it drip down, dance and steam on the altar stone as if it were an iron pan over roasting coals. Leaned forward to place the blooded knife upon the stone. His hand, extending, was slowed to a quarter of normal. Pressure laid itself upon his skin, popped his ears, pressed behind his eyes. As if he were swimming deep underwater….

Underwater, with echoes and ripples and the ever-present echo and hum of sensing, and space.

The knife tried to slip from his fingers; he held to it, forced control, set it lightly as a feather on the stone. The stone gave, wove and wobbled, shimmering like threads in a loom, floating.

A blood rite sinister, eh? You want this badly, youngling.

Rob looked up. Across the altar stone, the trees had gone black, and there were no stars. A shape, both beast and man. It dropped before him, swift as arrow flight, to crouch on the south edge of the altar, a hooded, faceless figure with ivory horns and eyes that glimmered hot.

You have courage. That has never been in doubt. But did your rival steal what sense you were born with? The black fingered itself toward him, *tynged* silk-weave turned deathly web.

"He's not my rival," Rob husked. "You canna make me fight him."

A glint of eyes within the hood, and a mocking chuckle. *And there speaks your ignorance, Princeling.*

"If I know nowt, 'tis because you've not told me!"

And why should I tell you anything?

Rob opened his hand, laid it, bloodied palm down, upon the knife blade.

Said again, "*Datgelu'r eich hun.*"

Watched with dry eyes as the Horned Lord shuddered, gleaming eyes drawn to the altar.

"I will know," Rob said. "No more riddles. No more half-truths. You say he is my rival, but you will tell me why."

I think you already know that, little pwca. *The new religion would crush the old, and how fitting is it that the two born into this breath of the Wheel would be on opposite spokes? Yet you.* A chuckle, grim, then almost sung. *You would scorn a Maiden's touch, would spin the Wheel widdershins, take your rival as your lover... The Old One has it right, you are Fool, indeed!* Again, the mocking singsong: *A mystery, wrapped in a riddle, and there's not one of us who can pace you...* The Horned Lord bent closer. *I will pace you. I will ride you until you drop.*

"How am I the fool?" It was pure bravado, no more, but it served to shatter the fear icing Rob's veins. "I'm what I've *always* been. 'Twas you made the choice of me, slicked the magic over my birth-caul. Who, then, is daft as a ha'penny?"

The Horned Lord bared the white canines of a predator, snarled, *What you are, child, is heir to an ungentle and ruthless Kingship. What you will be is the one to wear the cowl of death, to contest for the right of life, to dance the eternal return. Such things are not won with stolen kisses and empty scabbards.*

This was no gentle, loving Summer of warm days and velvet nights, but the gales of Winter, the frost and flood and famine. Rob cowered down despite himself, snared too hot and close for bearing. The golden eyes blazed; the horns upon His brow were hung with tattered velvet. The Horned Lord smelled of green and damp, blood and sex, heat and fury.

Then He gave a sudden, deep laugh, the undercurrent pressing deep against Rob's ears. *Ah! I see! You would make the pact: wed yourself soul and heart's blood to our sweet green Wode, defend the virtue of our Lady, give our body to our challenge. But you, arrogant little* pwca, *think you can twist my tail. You would play the game by your rules, not mine, and throw a gauntlet at my feet, dare me to stop you. You would see yourself the Maiden's twin, not Her husband, and have your rival struggling in your arms after another fashion, send a thousand little deaths toward the one Sacrifice.* The laugh sobered into silence, heavy and heady. Then:

You intrigue me. It is not… unthinkable.

Rob tried to voice a reply, could not. He was panting, sweating, shuddering with the nearness of the god, with His intemperate fury and passion.

Aye, now you *begin to see.* A hot breath against Rob's forehead. *I will have you both, one way or another. Your rival Sees what is before him, feels the calling. He no longer has the choice. The question remains: Will he submit or will he fight? Your little rabbit has gone to ground in cold stone walls, into that bleak hole of doubt and betrayal into which the priests of the White Christ have corrupted those teachings. Do you really think yourself so skilled—or him so ignorant—that you could cozen him once more into the holly? He has already drawn back a scratched and bleeding hand.*

"I…." Rob staggered. He could feel his body, somewhat, pinned to the altar. Blood and tears, spittle and sweat; all binding him there. Holding him.

Here is your quandary: if you submit, or die, or fail, *then you will be the last of your kind. Summer will reign and twist the world into light that never dies, that burns itself into destruction. Or.* A pause. *If you bid him submit to you, Winter's reign will steady itself in the darkness. We have had peace, yet it has become stagnation, and the flames of insurrection have been left unfanned too long.*

Eyes rolling up in his head, blood steaming on the stone, shuddering…. Rob had left his body unkept too long, yet he could not wrest free, not return.

Do it! Give yourself to the Wode, young stag. Take the horns, reach forward into what is yours and break your father's tines. When the Son is born, so dies the Sire, and Son grows to Sire… let us be done with this nothingness and slavery, call Hunt upon the trine of all worlds and bring the Ceugant *into being, here and now!*

For you could, you know. You could.

"Hear me, Hob-Robyn." It came, whispering and wavering through the black; first a tug, then a command, curling and lifting in the language of the Barrows. "Hear me. *Breathe me.*"

The Horned Lord straightened up, scented the air. Rob found that spirit mimicked body; he was laid out on the slab, shuddering in uncontrolled waves. The Horned Lord crouched over him. Both of them held Gamelyn's knife. Yet as they watched, another hand joined theirs, running down the blade, blood dripping warm down the fuller with the scent of hot smoke, burnt reeds and sandalwood. And the summons, again.

Cernun was there, white hair unbound, free hand reaching out, touching the Horned Lord's tines. He opened blue eyes filled with gold, whispered a name. Ebon rippled, streaked with ivory where he touched, and the Horned Lord's head dipped, as if gentled.

The Horned Lord took the dagger, laid it, with Rob still holding it, gently across Rob's stomach. Then He bared his canines once again, gave a bow.

Wisped away.

"*Anadlu*!" Cernun held him closer. "Breathe, Rob. Breathe! Lady, find Your son… answer me, Rob!"

With a huge gasp and hoarse cough, Rob fell back into his body. Felt his heart speed, his lungs burn, his body flatten with the press of Time itself, the dagger still cradled in his blooded hands like a child, and Cernun's arms still fast about him. There were tears in Cernun's blue eyes. It startled Rob; he'd never thought the old man cared for him all that much. "He will take you, lad, if you let Him," Cernun said. "You must not let Him."

"'Twasn't… easy," Rob husked, and Cernun chuckled despite himself.

"Fool."

"He called me that."

"And He was right. Get up," Cernun said. "You're too big for me to be carrying you anymore. I'll give you a hot drink, though I think I should more boot you all the way home."

❧

HE HAD been in Blyth's cavernous chapel for over an hour, waiting.

Gamelyn had not spent it idly; he had been on his knees for much of that time. The rest he had spent in lighting candles for his mother. Beneath the reminder that Johan had thrown at him, Gamelyn was particularly mindful of her.

I'm sorry, Mama. I didn't mean to… I swear I didn't.

Was she even now looking down upon him, disappointed in everything that he had done, and become?

Usually the quiet, and the welcome darkness lit only by wall sconces, and the wisps of flame on the altar before him, were all he needed to cleanse his heart, to rededicate his soul to his world and his God.

Today, it wasn't helping.

Today, everything that he had ever done, from the birth that had killed his mother to what had happened yesterday, was flensing him like tiny, keen knives.

Gamelyn had begun his devotions with a prayer to the Virgin—then had thought that rather inappropriate, considering. Instead, he had bent his thoughts toward her Son. Jesus had broken bread with whores and misfits. Surely Jesus would have it within his great heart to listen to one poor, confused sodomite….

Then it came to him that Jesus's most beloved had betrayed him, with a kiss.

And his brain started whirling with everything Eluned had told him. Stories. Myths.

Truths.

What is truth? Pilate had asked, and washed his hands.

Pressing his head upon his clasped hands, Gamelyn wished he could do the same.

It would do him no good, any of this, until he'd made his confession. Some matters were too grave. He'd no right to seek comprehension from the pure of heart with his own so sullied.

Steps sounded from the outer hall and Gamelyn leapt to his feet. Grimaced as blood-starved limbs began tingling—he'd been kneeling too long.

Served him right.

The tingles were beginning to become stabs as Brother Dolfin rounded the corner. Almost hidden behind a large armload of rolled parchments, there was no hiding that his tonsure was somewhat shaggy and two goose quills were stuck behind one ear. Broad and tall, the bulk of muscle gone slightly to fat, it was Dolfin's habit to tuck one edge of his cassock into his woven belt—he didn't much like the confinement of the long garment. His muscular legs and long, brown bare feet made quick progress over the flagging stones and his sandals dangled at his belt, as they often did, opposite of where he'd tucked his robe.

"Gamelyn! Have y' come for the library? I'm sorry, I've started locking it if I'm away on errands; we've had some folk not taking proper care unless supervised…." His thick brows twisted together, seeming to ken Gamelyn was in distress.

"Not the library, not now," Gamelyn said, quiet. "Can you hear my confession?"

Dolfin blinked. "Straight away?"

"*Please*."

Whatever pending matters the monk might have had, Gamelyn's desperate tone seemed to decide him. "Of course. Let me shift these to the library, I'll be right out—"

"In private. Please."

Again the furrowed brow, then Brother Dolfin nodded. "Then we'll both go in. You know there's no way to hear anything there, 'less you're hanging from the upper stacks. But," He gave an apologetic grin. "The keys are hanging from the back of my belt, if you'd be so kind?"

Gamelyn unlocked the door and let them both in.

The library was small, mostly shelves and cubbies, but boasted a long table, several stools, and an old, padded horsehair chair. Dolfin unloaded his parchments on a spare stretch of the table then motioned for Gamelyn to close the door. He had a moment of hesitation as Gamelyn went straight to the chair and knelt before it, but recovered quickly and came over, sat.

"*Ignosce mihi, Pater, quia peccavi,*" Gamelyn began, leaning his forearms on the chair, closing his eyes gratefully as he began. The ritual of the Latin was its own magic, taking Gamelyn elsewhere as it always did. Brother Dolfin's responses were soothing, and finally… *finally* the words came to his tongue as if they also had been pent up too long, were just waiting for the comfort of the familiar, formal expression to spill over, transform writhing, horrified silence into speech.

Anger. Pride. *Lust.*

Brother Dolfin sat for some time in silence after Gamelyn had finished the formalities. It did not worry Gamelyn; Dolfin usually took his time, made sure he was speaking with God's consent and not just his own. "Ah, Gamelyn. Young men are quick to anger. Pride is ever a struggle for you. But lust? I m'self must confess to you this much. I'd wondered how one with such a warm heart could be so cold to the body's desires. Your confession relieves me; you are human, after all."

He was tired of hearing it. *Tired.*

Conversely, it soothed him. If he was so cold, then surely this heat would die, leave him once again untrammeled in his own skin, untouched.

"Did some lovely peasant girl give her young lord a temptation past all reason, then?"

Temptation. It lurked even here, within the confessional—the temptation to just nod, go along. His chin even ducked down farther, bodily response trying to take him along the easiest path.

Of course, *that* was most of the problem, wasn't it?

Trying to make his voice work was more than difficult, but Gamelyn forced it outward, hoarse and unsure. "It was a peasant, but not a girl. It was a… lad."

You're the one as mentioned kissing….

Demon indeed. *Get out*, Gamelyn told Rob—or his avatar, or his ghost—*of my confession.*

"Ah," Dolfin said.

Then, silence. Gamelyn didn't want to look up, to see the revulsion that would surely be on Dolfin's face, the affront. And as the silence dragged, Gamelyn became possessed with the need to fill it with something. *Anything.* "I… it… it just happened. Somehow. I don't know how, I'd never even thought of him… not like *that*…."

Liar.

His own voice, this time, remembering how it had felt when he'd seen Rob with the stable lad. Or watching as Rob glided naked from the mere, water caressing him as Gamelyn dared not.

How Rob had ripped that dare from Gamelyn, pinned him against the oak tree, and dared him back. How Gamelyn couldn't resist….

What I've done. To you. This time, it was Rob. *It's all my doing, then, is it?*

Shut up. Oh, God, shut up*!*

A large, long-fingered hand descended gently atop his head. "It would seem," Dolfin continued, very soft, "that you are not altogether contrite."

Shame burnt Gamelyn's cheeks. To hear it spoken aloud, to have another ken, just by looking at him, this *weakness* of spirit that even guilt could not tear away.

"I am," he breathed into his clasped hands. "I *am*! But I cannot stop… stop thinking about it. About *him*."

"I am correct in the assumption that this was your first experience, aye?"

Gamelyn nodded, eager, into his hands.

"One's first sexual experience is either disaster or ecstasy." Dolfin's voice almost seemed musing. "It seems you were fortunate enough to enjoy the latter—"

"Fortunate!" Gamelyn couldn't help but choke out; he almost looked up but at the last moment checked himself, kept his eyes respectfully his own. "It wasn't just… it was sodomy!"

"I know what it was, Gamelyn. But you weren't some thirteen-year-old virgin trembling in a marriage bed awaiting a groom who'd already outlasted three other brides. You weren't some crofter's wife taken against her will by some mercenary brute—"

He raped and killed a woman… wife and mother to the two foresters….

"It sounds as if the peasant lad was good and gentle to you, and while you pray for your own soul, you must pray for his, and give thanks to God that you were not unkindly used."

"I… I don't…. How does a holy brother know such things?"

"Mother of God, you're so young." Dolfin's voice, so quiet-sure before, seemed to tighten. "Did you really think that amongst a society of men such things would be unheard of?"

This did made Gamelyn look up. Dolfin's face did not hold the loathing or scorn that Gamelyn had feared. Only an odd kind of… sadness?

"We are," Dolfin said, "only human, after all."

The blue eyes were *kind*. It was almost… disappointing. Which made no sense to Gamelyn. Had he wanted to be ridiculed? Excoriated?

Perhaps he had. Then it would be done, over with. Penance, pain, punishment… all had their own release. Simple, meaningful, light at the end of a tunnel of darkness and confusion. The road to true strength.

"Listen to me, Gamelyn. Often the urges of the body are so strong as to take over a young man. Don't mistake my meaning; lust is sin. But man will be sinful."

If that's what your god calls damnation, then damn me, love, because I'll not turn from it....

"Is it not our duty to rise above sin?" Gamelyn protested. "To not succumb?"

"Ah!—there speaks your pride, Gamelyn. Pride is the most… egregious of sins, and one that will be the death of you, even more than lust."

Gamelyn dropped his gaze back to his hands, clenched his teeth. All he'd wanted was to root the wickedness from his heart. All he'd wanted was absolution. *I just want this… this feeling—this* thing*—taken from me.* "I'm… trying. To understand."

"Try harder. This lad, is he one of our people here?"

Gamelyn shook his head. "He lives to the west."

"So he is not… convenient. That is just as well. Unless." A pause. "Have you wanted others? Other lads?"

"I've never… never wanted *anyone* like this. It was… unexpected. He… he was…." *Beautiful*, Gamelyn wanted to say and could not. It was too intimate. His voice dropped down, nearly a whisper. "He seemed so comfortable. In his own skin. As if we weren't doing any wrong."

"If he is of the old religion…. Many of his kind still are, the old gods are not as dead as many would like to believe. As long as one wee mouse drums his hind feet in a burrow, as long as one blade of grass bends over a stream, waving in the wind, they are with us." Dolfin shook his head. "Our peril, to forget such things. If this peasant who woos you is a Heathen, he surely would heed such matters very differently."

Heathen? Old gods?

Of course, he'd had it thrown in his face rather violently of late that Rob and his family… *his people*… were not exactly Christian… but again, to hear it spoken aloud, so matter-of-fact?

"He's your God too!"

"Nay. Nay, he ent."

Confusion coalesced, hard and eager, into probable cause. "Do you think…. Have I been bewitched?"

Dolfin frowned. "What do you think?"

"I… don't… *know*." It was as if he could scarcely get the words out, that they betrayed something deep within himself.

"I don't know, either, Gamelyn." Dolfin was quite grave. "But I do know this. There is precious little magic left in our world, and most of what would be called 'enchantment' is practiced more by those who claim they've fallen victim to it."

Gamelyn blinked. "That makes no sense. If—"

"Listen, lad. People love to cry their own innocence, even if they're guilty as murder. Devil, enchantment, call it what you fancy, it's so much easier to claim someone—or something—made you do something than it is to take responsibility for your own acts." Dolfin twisted his mouth sideways, sighed. "If only it were so simple."

Sweet Lady, why do your people insist on making everything so simple? This was not Rob, but Eluned. *When you shoot an arrow, it will kill, wound, or miss. Everything has three faces, lad....*

"The first step to your redemption, however, *is* simple. You would do yourself—and the lad—a kindness to never see him again."

This was expected.

Then why did it feel as if he were being rent into pieces?

Dolfin was still speaking, somewhat thoughtful. "My Bishop would say that a pagan does not know any better, that we must take the higher ground, pray for pagans and sinners that they not remain damned in ignorance. But His Holiness the Bishop is also human. Prey to the same follies as us all."

Of all the things Gamelyn had expected to hear, that was not amongst them. Brother Dolfin sensed his confusion, cocked his head and smiled, just a little.

"I lived amongst Heathen folk, fought with them, even prayed with them. They are not any more or any less than we. Their gifts and curses come to them even as ours do us. Perhaps they are more willing to accept… oddities."

"Curses. Gifts," Gamelyn murmured. "But they're not the same."

"That would depend upon who you ask. I saw some strange things before I came to God." The monk shrugged. "And things no Christian soul should have to witness, then and since. But this is not my confession, my son," Brother Dolfin said, returning to the careful, neutral compassion he always displayed in the confessional. "It is yours. Pray for mercy, for yourself and this lad you are so conflicted over. There are many kinds of love, and not all need the huddlings of sex. Remember your love and duty to your father, and heed him carefully. He is too ill to be worrying over you. You *must* take care."

Then he laid both hands on Gamelyn's bowed head, began the soft singsong of prayer. "*Passio Domini nostri Jesu Christi, merita beatæ Mariæ...*"

Surely it wasn't wrong to imagine it like to a soft, warm breeze rustling through green trees....

"… *Et præmium vitæ æternæ.* Amen."

"Amen," Gamelyn whispered.

ENTR'ACTE

RALPH FITZAARON, High Sheriff of Nottingham, was neither young nor obliging. He was but the latest play in a crooked game; worse, he knew it and tended to heed his laws more by letter than intent. Crooked game, sure enough, but it was easy to spot the way of him even before the bones were thrown and knuckled. Adam walked a tightrope as it was—it depended on the day which shire Loxley village was considered owed to.

But Scathelock had done the crime in FitzAaron's shire, and for once Sheriff de Lisle had agreed to let a Yorkshire yeoman come to justice in Nottingham.

Worksop's new abbess was, it seemed, de Lisle's sister.

"Loxley." FitzAaron's face pinched more sour. "I wish you could keep your litter of scruffy dogs at heel. First your son, brawling with my soldiers over some tavern wench, and now this. Murder, no less." He leaned forward on the huge table in the even larger main hall of Nottingham Castle and barked at his steward, "Well? Is the villein in custody?"

"Aye, my lord," the steward answered. "He's in the hole now. I took possession of him at the main gate and escorted him there m'self."

Indeed the steward had. He and two guards had kicked George's feet out from under him three times before they'd dragged him away. Adam had felt every blow, but kept it locked beneath a set face and clenched teeth. They'd not dare touch him—his sinecure protected him, even as it had once protected George—and they resented it.

"I have done my duty to the Crown," Adam stressed. "If I might now have your leave, milord, I shall return to—"

"You'll stay, Loxley."

"Milord Sheriff, surely—"

"You'll stay until the Abbess of Worksop arrives and I can see to the fate of this murderer. Then you will carry a copy of my interrogation to Sheriff de Lisle."

"An interrogation, milord?" Adam was careful.

"Of course. The man is charged with sorcery and witchcraft. Abbess Elisabeth demands that he be questioned as to his accomplices."

"He had none."

"You sound so sure. But a witch always has a coven, Loxley. You live amongst pagans; surely you know that much."

Adam crossed his arms, lifted his chin. "Then, milord, I'll need to send a message to my household. I'm expected to some duties in Barnsdale anon. The Earl de Warenne has asked for a tally on his lands." Let the rheumy old clot chew on that for a moment, and perhaps decide that, after all, he didn't need to detain Loxley from doing an earl's bidding.

"Send your message, then. Surely someone can take your place. Or," FitzAaron said, pettish, "are the rest of your men in gaol as well?"

Adam met FitzAaron's eyes and wished him to his hell. "Nay, milord."

☙ XVII ❧

"WOLVES don't hunt you because they're cruel; it's their nature. If you're weak, they attack. Aye?"

Rob nodded, finding inordinate interest in a bit of branch caught in Arawn's black mane. Both twig and horsehair clung to his fingers with the damp. It was a fine, soft day; more commonplace and welcome than the wet hanging over as of late, sultry and refusing to fall. *A poor woman's face cream*, his mam had opined for as long as he could remember.

Unfortunately, she was determined to slather a few more opinions onto the road this day. Even Arawn's mien seemed more of sullen endurance as they rode eastward.

Or he could just be sulking because their pace had been more walk and trot because Willow's short legs couldn't keep up with him at the canter.

"Well, that lad is one of the conquerors, son, born and bred 'neath Frankish rule. He's not of us. Not so special to shrug away all of it because of the light in your eyes."

Rob was feeling decidedly sulky himself. "Are you going to lecture me the *entire* way, Mam?"

Eluned shifted in her saddle and fiddled with Willow's rein. "I wasn't aware that I was giving a lecture."

Rob slid his gaze to meet hers, brow furrowed.

"Aye, well, then. You've not had to live with your temper the past se'nnight—"

Oh, aye, he had. And the doubt, regrets, and misery that had lived beside it. And the dreams....

Cernun had warned that he'd opened a proper puzzle box. Rob peered at the healing scar on his left palm, knew that he'd none to blame but himself for it.

"And I could have found someone to accompany me to Blyth. One of your father's other underforesters. Then you'd not have to—"

"Mam."

Eluned fell silent, looked off into the distance. They'd long since left the thick woods of the Common behind and were now riding through lowlands. The smell of earth-rot and mold was heavy in the air; early summer was doing a full day's work plus overtime in the bogs and fens.

"The Earl de Warenne needs the tally," he finally said. "I agreed to take tally in Da's place, since he sent word he's not to be back from Nottingham for another se'nnight. The tally is to be done on the game and fish in Barnsdale between Conisbrough and…?" He raised his eyebrows, waiting.

"Blyth," she supplied. Then added, "Don't be giving me your lip, boy. I know perfectly well what your excuse is for escorting me. I also well know it's just that. An excuse."

"The work had to be done—"

"And had the work to be done in the Chase? Or Wakefield? Would you have leapt so eager-like, then?"

Rob rolled his eyes and his mother snorted.

"I'm on to you, lad. What I *don't* understand is why you're set on *him*. There's plenty in Loxley that would see to your needs. That nice boy—the fletcher's son?—for one."

Bloody buggering damn, did *everyone* know about Simon?

"And more than a few lasses who would gladly be handfast to the young Hunter—"

"Mam!"

"You're old enough to start wanting a wife, now. A wife would see to you proper. You and Marion both, mooning after what you canna have, and I only hope that time'll heal your sister's heart, but *you*… oh, Hob-Robyn, you're butting yourself up against traditions older than time. And you'll pay for it."

He'd heard *this* one before. "*Mam*."

"I know, I know. 'Tis the way of things that males will sometimes tup each other, dominance or play or inclination, but the Hunter doesn't lie with his rivals, he defeats them. Like the king stag, he proves his prowess then takes the Lady to make the marriage and the quickening."

"More little fawns to sing the Horned Lord's name," Rob murmured, somewhat sourly. Heard it. Heard it, *heard* it!

"Well, and you aren't a fawn anymore, to be butting your head to play with such things. This is no game, son."

"Neither am I nowt but fodder for a Lord's reaping—be he nobleman's scythe or the God's horns!" Rob burst out. "Would you have me heartless, then? Have an act that should be meaning something be instead forced and dead? Aye, *there's* a myth to set th' Wode to blight worse even than the Christian god! *That* one would say the entire world is nowt but corruption to be mastered and laid waste, but are th' Lord and Lady any better, if we offer them up nowt but a soulless hand-fuck? Which of us are scorning flesh and blood and passion th' more *then*?"

Eluned was peering at him, stricken. Rob hadn't meant to say such a thing to his mother, but it was done and said and no turning away from it even though the silence dragged out between them, punctuated only by the sound of hoofs on the soggy road and Willow snoring deep in her chest like she always did on a lengthy journey.

"You ask hard questions." Eluned finally said with a sigh, and she looked off down the valley. There was a village coming into view over the horizon—fields plowed and planted, and people out in the wet to work them. "That's the answer, ent it?" She gestured. "There. The sowing of seed, the harrowing and reaping, the seasons wheeling about us in their eternal return. What are we *but* fodder beneath it?"

"Then what's the point?" He couldn't stop asking it, even with the Horned Lord breathing hot down his spine and His hounds nipping at his heels. "What is the reason t' any of it?"

"Reason?" She shrugged. "Is there reason to a lone tree? To a starlit night? Is there even truly any purpose to putting arrow to string? Or is it enough just to take aim?" She met his eyes with a quizzical half smile that seemed somehow familiar; he realized the expression was his own. "Perhaps we've all after a fashion lost our way, mired in what must be rather than what is. One thing remains: we give reverence to what sustains us. If we don't, then we *are* dead. Dead, existing only to feed."

"Is that what you think I'm doing?"

"No!" she retorted fiercely. Then, softer, "Nay, son. Sometimes our hearts are contrary things, and they'll go where they will, not as we'd tell 'em. If I seem… well, frustrated? It's only that I'm your mam and I worry after you. It's not only that the lad's a lad, it's that he's not our kind and I canna see this path you're on ending in owt but the same sort of unhappiness you've been rolling in the past se'nnight. And," Eluned shrugged, a tiny smile tucking into her cheek, eyes glimmering, "maybe I want grandchildren."

"Oh, Mam." The anger broke in him, and he let out his breath in something between a sigh and a chuckle.

"The worst of it," she furthered, very soft, "is what potential that lad has. Squandered."

Squandered potential, innocence lost, lies clung to even if they scorned and scored… and she didn't know the half of it. Didn't see it, perhaps even refused to see it. The possibilities, fevered and brackish, that Rob had himself glimpsed. Not for the first time, Rob wanted to ask his mother what she had Seen in the runes and the fires. And, not for the first time, he fell silent, confused.

"He's not of us."

He is. He's of me, *canna y' see?*

No. She couldn't.

Eluned shook the damp from her hood and pulled it closer to her forehead. The rain was growing more steady. "I just wish you didna have to go to the castle."

"I ent staying."

Eluned slid a glance to him, curious.

"I'll see you to the gate, right enough. Make sure of your welcome. You said Sir Ian would extend every courtesy, but if he doesn't have someone to escort you home, then?" He shrugged. "I'll be near."

Eluned's eyes narrowed. "What are you up to?"

"Waiting." Rob looked at the village, beginning to fade behind them in the rain and mists. On the edge of it, a dark, mist-shrouded figure watched them, seeming to suck all the light as he moved forward. Only tines gleamed, lit with gray and rain.

Rob took in a shallow breath, blinked.

It was still there. Still following.

Did you think I have less stake in this than you, little lovelorn son?

I'm not... lovelorn.

Lust, then.

It's not that simple.

Make up your mind. Fight him or fuck him, but I will see it through with you.

"Rob?" The sharpness of Eluned's query suggested it was not the first time she'd spoken.

"I'm sorry," he said, quickly turning to her. "What?"

"I was wondering," she ventured, slowly. "What if that lad wants to know why you didna come along?"

"But I did come along, Mam," he said and smiled. "Just not inside the castle."

His mother was frowning. "And if he asks after you?"

"He waint." *Because that would be admitting something, wouldn't it, Sir Gamelyn? But did you ever think that to say nowt is admitting all the more?*

Hot breath, singing against his ears as if the Horned Lord rode beside instead of behind him, and the memory of challenge ever present: *It is not... unthinkable.* The ebon spirit was still there, creeping over the horizon. *The question remains: Will he submit or will he fight?*

Why did his mother not seem to sense the Horned Lord's presence?

She cannot See your future. And that is me.

Her own son was a great rent of nothingness... Gamelyn was a distant threat. The spiral dance of *tynged* spun out around him, spokes of scattered fates and futures, and sometimes he could scarcely see what was around him for what he Saw before him. Was it a kindness for her? Torture for him? Both?

They rode a long while in silence. Rob was the one who broke it, purposefully. "Mam?"

"Aye, pet?"

"Talk to Marion about the grandchildren. She'll be more… receptive."

Eluned smiled, then bent over in her saddle and laid a kiss on his cheek. "Mayhap I'll mix a little potion for young Gamelyn while I'm there."

"Mam."

"Or give him a kick in the arse."

Rob grinned. "*That* I'd pay good marks to see."

☙

"E NOMINE patris, et filii, et spiritu sancti…."

It was a woman's voice Gamelyn heard as he approached his father's solar, fresh from sparring practice with Roberto. Then a soft "Amen," as his father's answer, with the female voice… not Alais. And no maidservant would be praying with her lord.

Gamelyn hesitated, peeked in.

Abbess Elisabeth was leaning at Sir Ian's bedside, listening. It looked too much like the end of a last confession for Gamelyn's comfort. He supposed he shouldn't be surprised the Abbess had come, nor that he'd been so preoccupied with his own… whatever-they-weres… to heed that they'd received an important visitor.

He'd spent the last se'nnight either riding out on business for his brothers, working out his frustrations in the armory, or praying in the chapel. His knees perpetually ached. And only occasionally did it sublimate… other things. Which ached even more. And while swordplay oft wore him out and took the edge off his aggression, the sheer physicality of it also had the unfortunate possibility of fueling it.

Otho and Johan were mildly surprised at his efficiency, Roberto was best pleased with his practice, Brother Dolfin was understanding and didn't shoo him out as he well could have….

"Gamelyn!" It wafted from downstairs at the end of their hall; also feminine, but recognizable. Alais. "Gamelyn, are you up there?"

He quickly backed from his father's entrance and padded down the hall, bare feet sticking, sweaty, to the paving stones. "I'm here!" he called down the stairwell.

Alais met him halfway up, skirts tucked in one hand. "There you are! She's here, asking for you or Papa."

Gamelyn frowned. "What? Who?"

"Your wise woman from Loxley." Alais smiled. "She's come to see Papa."

He stood there, frozen on the stair for several slow, jerky heartbeats. Before any thoughts, warning or otherwise, could form, Gamelyn lurched forward, down the steps two at a time.

Alais tangled her fingers in his hair, and he gave a yip.

"For the love of Christ, Gamelyn, at least go and put on a tunic and boots! You look like you've been beating up the straw men in the armory. And losing!"

☙❧

A QUICK toweling off and Gamelyn still wasn't thinking clearly. He got down the stair before he realized his tunic was wrong-ways out, nearly tripped on the bottom step with his head enfolded in fabric, and then spent more time untangling it since it was sticking to his still sweated torso. Once he could see again, he kept going.

He ran across the bailey and came within easy sight of the gatehouse before he realized that his alacrity had just laid waste every intention, every vow he'd made standing, seated, and *kneeling*, of never seeing them again… never seeing *Rob*.

He should turn around, right now. Not go anywhere near this. He was repentant. He did not want to sin again.

"Surely you did not come all this way alone," Johan was saying. "The forest is no place for a woman to be wandering alone."

"But then I was not wandering, milord. Do not forget that my husband"—a slight emphasis, which, judging by Johan's manner as he leaned up against the gatehouse stones, was well reminded—"is head forester to Barnsdale and the Peak. I well know this area. Neither," she smiled and tipped her head, "did I come alone. My son gave me escort to your gatehouse."

Something like longing but altogether close to terror rose up in Gamelyn's throat, choked him, then slid down to hit with a great, hollow thud in his belly.

He was here? Oh, God, Rob was *here*?

"Your son wants manners, then, to drop his lovely mother off at the gatehouse and just leave her there."

"Well, you know how young men are." The chide was inclusive of Johan; he either ignored it or was oblivious. Suspicion was high with the latter.

Gamelyn didn't see Rob. Rob had left his mother at the gatehouse.

Eluned turned and saw Gamelyn's hesitant approach. "Gamelyn!" A lovely smile, then she walked over, gave him a quick embrace.

It surprised him. Eluned had never been all that demonstrative before. Yet there was some advantage; he could cover his own confusion by hugging her back, and…. Was it all that wicked to give an inward snicker at the thwarted surprise in Johan's face? Obviously Johan was under the mistaken apprehension that his baby brother had just stolen this lovely peasant woman out from beneath his nose. And Gamelyn wasn't too keen on correcting him.

Neither, from the sly look upon Eluned's face, was she.

"And here I thought it was the daughter you were after, *petit lapin*." Johan made a stinging bid to reassert his own superiority. "I must say my brother's slovenly manner of dress does not match his unerring eye for a lovely woman," he told Eluned. "I hope to speak with you later, of course, but for now, let my little brother take you up to our father." His gaze strafed Gamelyn. "Don't keep him waiting long."

Gamelyn was ripped in twain by conflicting impulses: one to plant a boot in Johan's buttocks as he strode away, the other to look past him to see if Rob had even come past the gatehouse….

If he had, it was no concern of Gamelyn's. It couldn't be.

But his eyes were not his own. And they quickly found what they sought. A horse and rider waited just inside the gatehouse, hugging close to the stones, biding in the shadows as people came back and forth. The horse was tall, long-limbed, black. The rider was wearing a hood; not a hint of light touched his face.

Dreams. There was a hooded figure in his dreams.

The hood dipped in a tiny bow. Acknowledgement? Challenge?

Was it even Rob?

Gamelyn knew. He could feel the familiar gaze all but burning his skin.

"Can you help me with these, please?"

He started and turned to see Eluned removing her pannier baskets from Willow. Gamelyn's heart gave an absurd lift as he saw the little jennet, then plummeted as he saw who had sneaked up, quiet and eyes downcast, to take Willow's bridle.

It was the wiry little stable lad who'd pinned Rob to the stable wall and given him the same as Rob had given Gamelyn against a tree in the green Wode shadows….

Oh, *God!*—was it always going to be like this? Was Gamelyn going to have a lean, dark-haired ghost haunting him in every corner?

The stable lad was obviously not at all affected by Gamelyn's predicament; he didn't so much as raise his eyes, merely led Willow away once Eluned finished offloading. Against all sense or sanity, Gamelyn found himself looking over to the gatehouse.

The horse and rider were no longer there.

"Surely I've not been paying attention," Eluned said, looking up at him from where she'd knelt beside the baskets. "It's been barely a se'nnight, yet I think you've grown up while I wasn't looking." Her eyes—*Rob's eyes*—skirted over him, made due note of sweat-wet hair, quickly donned tunic, and the sword still athwart his left hip, and… was that disparagement he saw?

Courtesy, and the ritual of welcome, was an abrupt save for his sanity. "I must apologize at greeting you in such a state. I'm fresh from sword practice and was on my way to change." Gamelyn bent down and took two of the three baskets—she had already taken one—and offered her his arm. Bemused, she took it.

"Surely you could've kept me waiting, milord. Your brother is quite the charmer." A tiny smile tucked into her lip, she looked over her shoulder to where Johan had turned to watch after them and murmured, "Or so he thinks himself."

Gamelyn couldn't help but smirk.

"I'm sorry it has taken me so long to journey here. We've had our share of worries. But I'm sure you know that." Eluned's expression was unreadable but not exactly affable. "Even had you given the medicine in overlarge doses, though, you should have been well enough. Has it been helping?"

"Aye, it has. He's been sleeping better."

"But not over much?" She nodded as he affirmed her guess. "Good. 'Tis always tricky, the dosage, when you've not seen or smelt the one who needs it. Take me to him."

⁂

THE Abbess was still there, but confessional was over and Alais was also there, with Donall, tidying and readying Sir Ian. As usual, he was growling at all the fuss, but his face brightened as he saw Gamelyn, and he didn't wait for introductions.

"Gamelyn. This lovely woman must be the maker of that remarkable ointment, and the mother of the lad who tended it upon you."

Ingrained manners and courtesies came in quite useful, disguising all sorts of uncomfortable moments. "Aye, Papa. This is indeed Mistress Eluned of Loxley," Gamelyn said, handing her in. "Mistress Eluned, my father: Sir Ian Boundys, Lord of Blyth and the Boundary lands, noble vassal to Huntingdon and King Richard."

"It is an honor to serve, milord."

"An honor to accept your service, Mistress Eluned. Gamelyn, if you please?" He waved a thin hand at the others, and Gamelyn nodded, continued his introductions.

"My sister by marriage, the Lady Alais. This is Donall, my father's body servant. And our honored cousin and guest, the Most Holy and Reverend Abbess, Elisabeth of Worksop." Gamelyn tipped a bow to the Abbess, who gave him a brief smile then continued to examine Eluned with the same gaze she'd give a body insect. Eluned returned the favor, but gave the same polite dip of head and knee she had tendered the others.

"With your permission, milord," Eluned said, "I will prepare."

"And I will be happy to assist you, if you will allow," Alais offered.

"You are most welcome, milady." Eluned's words were to Alais, but her attention seemed absolute upon her patient. "'Tis possible that I will need to venture from the castle whilst I'm here—with your permission, of course, milord."

It was odd, seeing Eluned so deferential. There was still a calm, quiet pride to her, but it was leavened with lowered eyes and careful speech, with a *wariness,* and one that Gamelyn had never before witnessed.

"Your people can order me mam to attend them like she's a horse to be mouthed and paced and bought at market…."

Another proof that Gamelyn had not managed to purge Rob's presence so successfully.

"You will have whatever you need, Mistress," Sir Ian said quietly. "And my youngest will, of course, escort you wherever you need to go."

"So don't go wandering, mind," Alais teased Gamelyn, relieving him of the baskets.

Sir Ian gave a snort.

A hand, quite firm, touched Gamelyn's elbow. He slid his gaze to see the Abbess had moved to stand beside him. "It would seem," she said, soft, "that we are extraneous at present."

Nay, Gamelyn had merely thought that Eluned was unaware of him. Bent over her baskets and speaking softly to Alais, Eluned's gaze slid first to Gamelyn, then the Abbess. Then she frowned, turned away.

A frown on his face to match, Gamelyn allowed the Abbess to lead him from the solar.

ଓଷ

"YOU have been wandering?"

At first Gamelyn was unsure what the Abbess was referring to. He'd accompanied her in polite, if silent, escort thus far to the chambers she had been given.

Not that it had been utterly necessary, since the gray-clad acolyte had met them, as if magically summoned, just outside Sir Ian's solar. But it was the polite thing to do. His father would have expected it of him.

"I beg your pardon?" Wandering… his *thoughts* were certainly wandering, as impossible to gather together as the litter of lively kittens that the stables' prolific queen tabby had recently deposited in Diamant's manger.

"Alais mentioned it." The Abbess was giving him the same penetrative stare she'd given Eluned.

"Ah. Well, I do, on occasion, ride into the forest." He shrugged. "You know that my situation here is sometimes… problematic."

"Of course," she soothed as she gave a quick smile. "I sometimes wonder that the trial of living with elder siblings was not part of the reason I easily considered convent life. Of course," she added, with a small genuflection upon her breast, "it was not the most important one."

The novice followed suit, and Gamelyn as well, if a little belated. "I understand."

"I think you do," the Abbess concurred. "I have been making inquiries as to options for you. If you prefer to… wander, many of our holy brothers travel in their duties. Is that how you came to know the wortwife?"

The abrupt shift back to the original tack was mildly unsettling. It didn't help that it was getting altogether close to things he was in no disposition to discuss with an abbess. But not answering would be even more incriminating.

And surely it was merely his guilty conscience that deemed her attitude akin to questioning a criminal.

"It was," he answered, purposefully light. "When I was younger, I was thrown from my horse in the woodland at Loxley Chase. Her son found me there with a split head, took me to his home where she cared for me."

"Does the woman have a husband?"

He nodded. "He is head forester of Barnsdale." He walked a few steps before realizing the Abbess—and her acolyte, of course—had stopped. Then he realized what he had said, and what connection it held to the Abbess.

"The same forester who has surely, by now, delivered that sorcerous murderer to Nottingham, I presume?"

Of course, she would have found out from asking anyone. So why did Gamelyn feel chancy, as though he were backing a half-broken and hot-blooded colt?

"It would seem so," he answered.

"And is she a baptized Christian, this woman you have brought to your father's bedside?"

Again, it seemed an accusation. His gaze went to the Abbess's, puzzled, and he gave the best answer he knew. "I don't know."

"You should know, lad." It was chiding. "Ill can linger in the fairest form. We are all susceptible to it, but a handsome young man such as yourself?" She shrugged. "You have a particular susceptibility."

Fair… handsome… susceptible…. For a smattering of insanely panicked seconds, Gamelyn thought, somehow, that she *knew*.

The Abbess continued, and Gamelyn realized with a sick sense of not quite relief that she was speaking, not of Rob, but Rob's mother. "Someone as ailing as your father is doubly vulnerable to such ill. We must assure that his vulnerabilities are protected, not taken advantage of."

"Mistress Eluned means him nothing but good. She did not have to come—"

"She is a peasant upon your father's lands. Of course she must tend him if asked. And I do not say a word against her, not now. Only that we must take care. Your defense of her is from a pure heart, and it does you credit, but you must take care that naïveté does not lead you astray."

Gamelyn stiffened, was absurdly pleased to note that he topped her by half a head. He was getting bloody tired of everyone telling him how young he was, how trusting and naïve… how *stupid*. "You underestimate me, Reverend Lady."

"Cousin, I assure you I do not."

"I assure *you*, I would not bring anyone to my father's bedside to do him harm."

"I did not say that you would do so knowingly," she replied, folding her hands into her sleeves. The novice did the same, but it was in a manner that suggested she was not truly present save for bodily reactions.

For the first time, he felt not envy but discomfort. "I have known Mistress Eluned for some time. She is a good woman, respected in her croft. My father heard of her skills and requested she attend him. Her medicine has done him more good than what the doctor has prescribed. How is this a problem?"

"We do not know anything, at present. That is all I say. But you must take care of your father, Cousin. Such women can be… dangerous. They do not keep themselves to a woman's place, or often even to God's plan. Any healer can be cozened with their power, but a woman who knows the secrets of healing is often privy to other, more insidious secrets."

Gamelyn started to protest further, but memory stole into his righteousness, pulled a slipknot over it and choked it close.

"... In the right, even more, to heed some caution. Not every castle's keeper would hear of a woman brewing potions and think 'healer' instead of 'witch'...."

His father, not so long ago in the stables, affirming Adam's cautions.

Gamelyn closed his mouth and inclined his head, all courtesy. "I understand, Reverend Lady. I will take your words to heart."

Her hand came beneath his chin, raised it so his gaze met hers. He'd seen its like—Rob, glowering down an arrow at nock. "That is all I can ask, Cousin." Her hand then strayed to his shoulder; not for the first time, Gamelyn considered that her physical manner was overfamiliar for a woman wived so powerfully to God.

And Christ's blood, but his own conscience was creating apparitions! He was her kin, a possible compatriot in Christ's worship—need there be any other reason for such familiarity?

"Can I ask of you to let the stables know I will be departing on the morrow? I will, of course, see your father before I leave. And naturally, come back as often as he requires to see to his spiritual comfort." A charming smile. "Brother Dolfin is a good and kind man, but he tends toward lenience. Your father understands more than most that a soul nearing Heaven needs firm guidance and powerful prayer."

ƈ380

FIRE was a powerful thing, magical, a summoning scraped from rock and air, fed by tree and dried leaf. Cheering with a flip side of deadly, a bastion against darkness and predators. Surely his ancestors who had crouched in their deep, dark burrows had felt the same way.

It was also capricious. Rob hunched beneath the overhang of rock and tree root, hood still pulled over his head, and contemplated the pile of as-yet-unlit deadfall he'd gathered. He well knew how to find burnable wood even during a hard rain, and the kindling and char-cloth were dry from his own bags. He eyed the dagger and flint in his hands; perhaps the flint wasn't sharp enough. Then he shrugged, narrowed his eyes, and held the tools out over the wood.

"*Llosgwch*," he whispered, naming the burning then willing it, with another strike of his knife against flint.

A blue spark was the only clue that any magical assist had been called into being, and the fire burst into hungry life. Soon he had tended it into a steady and nearly smokeless warmth, cheery and drying his damp toes.

Rob pitched a bit of dried meat onto the flames. He'd brought it with him—it was never wise to go recklessly hunting outside one's own territory, even when invited. His gaze followed the flames as they flared, devouring the meat; Rob kept a keen eye on the smoke until it abated. It was also never wise to make unnecessary announcements of one's presence. Yet it was greatly unwise to skimp on an offering of thanks. His mother was right, there—anyone who thought to use a power without giving due to what sustained it would forfeit more than the whisper of soul-breath it took to call such magics.

He wasn't so sure he wanted to agree with her on other points, though.

One of the nearby trees started to shimmy and sway; Rob alerted, but only for the few seconds it took to peer around the caverns. Arawn had managed to creep in his hobbles over to a large and likely tree and was scratching his arse against it. Rob smirked. He'd cut plenty of fodder; just before sunset he'd unhobble Arawn and picket him closer to the fire—safest in case wolves were sneaking close by.

He leaned back against his saddle and wondered how things were going in the castle. He'd watched them welcome his mother at the gates, made sure she nodded to him before turning his horse and heading upland, to wait.

Had seen Gamelyn, tousled and sweated and looking altogether shaggable.

It wasn't fair.

"You've got plenty, you tightfisted old trout," he told Gamelyn's god. "Leave this one to me."

Like that one would listen to the likes of him, anyway.

But then, Gamelyn had seen him, as well. Gotten all fumble-fingered and stammery, helping Rob's mam unpack her simples. A smile touched Rob's mouth. He took off his boots, spread clammy toes against the heat of the flames. His smile sobered.

Aye, Gamelyn had looked. Only the once, and not again after.

You could bring him to you. It would be so simple.

Rob didn't have to look to know He was there. He'd been aware of Him even at the castle gatehouse. Felt, all along, the tingle of dread and exhilaration commingling in his belly and tightening his breath.

It would be as easily done as the fire-making. Maybe three breaths given, four… he would come.

Rob wasn't so sure. "I thought you said he had his own power."

The Horned Lord gave a snort: challenge and dismissal. *Denial is not power.*

Again, Rob wasn't so sure. Gamelyn's denial was certainly bludgeoning into him with all the force of a well-plied quarterstaff.

You hold part of his tynged *within you. You saw it winding about you, recognized it, drew it close as you coupled. Being what you are, such magic is more powerful than any herbs or mommets.*

Rob was even less sure of that. He took another bite of venison, stared into the fire. It still had flecks of white-blue, tracings of the magic still inhabiting it. Rob grimaced; he still didn't quite have the habit of control, yet. He would have to sprinkle the ashes with salt. It was dangerous to leave such things lying about, careless. "He's seen you, hasn't he?"

Not this form. You are the only one for…. A rumble of breath, considering. *It has indeed been overlong since I have roamed the woods with these eyes, and for that I thank you, Hob-Robyn. But yes. The sapling Oak has seen me, not only dream but flesh.*

"A white stag, he said. Crème-colored," Rob corrected, with a curl of lip that was both snarl and smile.

He was ripe for the touching when first I met him in these very woods. I gave him my breath upon his hands as a promise; not long after, he followed your steps. You took my breath from him, gave your own promise of it. Another snort, but this with muzzle/face lifted, testing the air. *He dreams. Every night.*

"Of me?" The thought gave him a not-unpleasant shiver. Conversely, it warmed the cool and wary attentiveness that the Horned Lord's manifestation laced within him, taut as a bowstring.

A manifestation which seemed lately to appear all the more.

Of us. Make him come to us, young Hunter. Breathe the spells and bind them... bind him. *It is time.*

The weight of the demand was thick, coursing through him, blood and breath and bone. Unrelenting. Rob gritted his teeth, said, "And would he ever forgive me if I did such a thing?"

He already thinks you have bewitched him, Hob-Robyn.

"But I have not. That truth will win out—"

Will it?

"I have to believe it will. I have to believe... in *him.*" Perhaps it was as simple as that, after all. "I don't want him to... to hate me. I can wait."

Child, child. The great head shook, slowly. *Struggle or surrender, it is all one in the end. One young as you has no concept of waiting. I have waited centuries.*

"Then another fortnight should make no difference to y—"

A rustle, from off to his right. In one swift, silent motion, Rob rolled to his feet and snatched up his bow. Stringing it with a soft grunt, he put arrow to nock and stepped in front of the fire, concealing his face from the light and letting his eyes adjust to the dim.

A young peasant came padding gingerly from a thick stand of bushes. A lass of no more than ten or twelve, she had a basket on her arm and a loose braid of pale hair that gleamed in the dying light. She knelt at one spot, grubbed about for a moment or two, then rose, brushing her fingers on her skirts and shoving the hair from her face. Rob frowned—daft girl-child, to be out this close to nightfall!—and started to lower his bow, speak. Then she turned, saw him. With a not altogether welcome incursion of senses, Rob saw through her eyes—Saw what she did, and *had*....

At first, nothing special: a lean young man muttering to himself for no good reason, a fire that did not smoke, and shadows in the small cavern. He did not look up, so she had kept up her mushroom gathering. Then alarm started licking at the back of her throat, and her feet had grown clumsy. The man had risen, drawn his bow and looked right at her, hooded and backlit by the fire, with shadows forming behind him into a black shade with pale horns and glittering embers for eyes....

The basket dropped to the ground. The girl let out a small, breathless wail, then turned tail and fled.

Rob watched her go. So much for hiding.

"Bloody *sodding* damn," he growled, and lowered his bow.

The basket, at least, had a goodly pick of mushrooms.

☙ XVIII ❧

HUNTING.

No beaters, no tat of hunting horns or clap of wooden staves to drive the game: Gamelyn is alone with his quarry.

And a merry chase it leads him, over wooded hills, through bogs that squeak and burble with covert threat. Yet he never catches up, never catches more than a glimpse of ivory hide.

Yet this time the forest clears, opens in front of him. The stag is there, pale hide gleaming copper from the low-lying blood moon, golden eyes blinking. Waiting.

As Gamelyn watches, it begins to change... to fade then swirl then drift like smoke into darkness... darkness that would suck all the light from the world and from his heart.

The stag has vanished. In its place stands a tall, ebon shade—a hooded man-shape, but not merely that, for it has ivory horns a-tangle with holly and ivy. They branch from a brow Gamelyn cannot see and beast eyes shine, dim jewels, from a face the hood obscures.

It is... terrifying and lovely, young and vibrant yet older than the oldest thing of man.

It must be... has to be... evil.

And as if the thought has changed the shape of his existence, Gamelyn no longer holds a staff in his hands, but a crossbow. While part of him screams in horror, another part of him screams for blood, and he raises the weapon to his shoulder. Whispers words—alien, twisting on his tongue—he does not know them, yet cannot help but utter them:

"Anadhlu. Marwolaeth at eich… tynged."

They echo, as if the forest itself twists them back into his own tongue: Breathe. Death be yours...

And he shoots.

A scream, shrill, and wind roars through the clearing, buffeting him. An ivory stag leaps into the air, stumbles... and as it stumbles it is once again a hooded figure, falling forward, limp, with a crossbow bolt through his chest.

Gamelyn lurches toward it, but as he advances his steps become smaller, more hesitant.

Horrified, he falls to his knees beside it. Beside him.

Black hair spills out from the hood, glinting red beneath the blood-moon. There is blood gushing from Rob's mouth, and blood soaking Rob's tunic where the bolt has gone in. Ebon eyes take Gamelyn in... surely it cannot be with... satisfaction?

"I've been waiting," Rob whispers, coughs, shudders. "But I never thought t'would end like this...."

Gamelyn shot up with a hoarse shout, rocked into a crouch before he realized where he was, and what it had been.

Another dream. Only another thrice-damned and unholy dream.

Only *this* one….

"No." It was a groan from some deep, shattered place he'd barely known he had. Gamelyn put his hands over his face and hunched there, quivering.

Presently he became aware of the clouded, starless night just outside his window, and the faint breeze that came in from it and swirled just inside, as if it dared go no farther into the stagnant air of the castle. Gamelyn had several nights ago kicked his coverlets to the bed-foot, but the bottom linens of the feather tick clung to his buttocks and the back of his thighs, sucked him down.

He rolled from the bed with another hoarse groan and staggered over to the window.

Relief. It wasn't much of a breeze, but it tickled cool across his skin, lifted lank, sweat-damp hair from his cheeks and nape, breathed fresh into his lungs.

Then he dragged on tunic and braies, made his escape. Such as it was.

The night watch atop the gatehouse had become used to Gamelyn's presence over the past fortnight. They had at first watched him warily, but now ignored him save with a quick tip of their helmeted heads and a polite, "Good evening, m'lord," to their master's youngest son.

Gamelyn would usually not incur on their watch too long; he would walk the parapets just long enough to clear his head and breathe the winds—both mild and fierce—that would come down the valley from the River Don. Gamelyn had, ever since they'd first come to Blyth, loved this walk in daylight—he had come to realize it had its own magic at night, as well.

Tonight one of the guards was well recognizable. Much's blue eyes lowered as he dipped his head, kept to his steady, back-and-forth march along the narrow, gray-stone lane of the parapet.

Gamelyn propped his hands on the outermost wall, shoulders rising up almost to the back of the skull as he leaned out into the breeze. Closed his eyes. Breathed it in.

Anadlu….

Jerked, eyes popping open, breath hitching in his chest, and saw it, just this side of the forest.

The ivory stag.

"D'you see it, m'lord?"

Gamelyn started at the hiss just behind him, turned to find Much leaning on the parapet, gaze fixed on the tree line not a furlong away.

Gamelyn couldn't speak.

"Aye, he's there. Believe that, m'lord." Much leaned slightly closer. He seemed more intent upon getting his message across than hesitant of Gamelyn. And why should Much be hesitant? Gamelyn was nothing, a lord's late-gotten son, *gadelyng,* a wretched sinner who had gotten sodomy all woefully tangled with affection.

More, Much was looking at him. Curious. Concerned, even. "You'll have t' go t' him, m'lord. Iffen you don't… he'll not let you rest."

Yet… if I do go after him…. Gamelyn had never followed the dream so far. Had never shot the stag… never *wanted* to shoot the stag. And *Rob….*

He looked down at his hands, surprised that he didn't see blood smearing them. It made him want to bay at the moon like a lonely mad wolf. Would that moon, if not hidden by clouds, betray itself as a gibbous blood moon?

"I can't," Gamelyn whispered. "It brings evil…."

"Nay, m'lord," Much protested. "Th' only evil in Him is what *you* bring."

"What… I bring."

"The Great Stag is nowt of evil, or of good. That I swear to you, m'lord." Much fell silent, dipping his head as a brace of soldiers passed by. Intent on their own conversation, they passed without so much as a glance at their lord's son and his guard.

"He's a demon."

"Nay. We're the demons." Much met his eyes, sudden and entreating. "Lookit what we've done tae our selves, tae our world. I'm not smart as the likes of you, m'lord, but I know that much. *We're* the demons, and the things we do make Him cry."

Like Jesus, weeping on the cross for the sins of the world.

"Ask the *si* woman," Much said, suddenly. "She knows."

"Eluned," Gamelyn said woodenly.

"You brought her here. You're of Her, en't you?"

"Am I, then?" he murmured.

"Surely she'll give you what you need."

ঔ

THE dream.

He'd not slept well after, and bloody *damn* but his shoulder hurt as if it truly had been nailed by a crossbow bolt. It had been so *real.*

The cross dangling over his head, and he can't breathe around the bolt stabbing fire into his chest... helpless... and the cross melds into the black as the Abbess comes forward, picks him up, and strokes the hair back from his face. Motions to the hooded bowman—the one who shot him!—to come forward, tells him:

"See? So easy. This is how a demon dies."

And the bowman steps forward, shrugs the hood back from fine, ruddy-flax hair, and Gamelyn's green eyes are so concerned... curious, almost, as if he'd caught a rare-marked rabbit in a forgotten trap....

The cross. The Abbess. The one image that stayed constant, no matter the trappings, and refused to go away though he kept trying to forget it.

Rob gave a shudder, deep down from toes to nape, and threaded his pack strap over his head. Ensuring it lay, snug and comfortable, off the sore shoulder and against his ribs, he took up his bow and hung his quiver beside the pack. He had a ways to traverse, today, a duty to perform.

Looking about the little cavern overhang where he'd sheltered last night, he decided any traces were well-hidden, secure. Rob had spent some debate into the wisdom of staying—he'd been seen, after all—but it was likely the girl would tell a tale that would more keep others away than draw them. This was a good place, comfortable enough. Convenient to the territory he had to scout and tally, convenient to the broad, flat rock nigh to a stand of rowan where he and his mother had agreed to leave any communications.

Convenient to the lad.

The breath stole through the cavern, caressed his nape. Try as he might, Rob couldn't deny the whisper's statement. Nay, Gamelyn possessed all the denial, enough for five.

I told you, my son. He dreams.

Had it been so thick of him, Rob wondered, to hope that Gamelyn's dreams were of kisses, of gasps against sweat-slicked skin—not betrayal, an executioner's rite of blood and death?

One leads to the other, and back again. Summer melts Winter's ice to streams and rivers, and Winter covers Summer in chill and quiet, holds him sleeping for the Lady to wake. For aeons has the struggle been joined. Sacrifice, final or in little gasps and moans, is what you must do. I care not which you choose. Or which of you will wear the Hood.

"I chose." His growl, Rob realized, was altogether close to being a hysterical sob. He regained control—had to, as he picked up his saddle and bridle and headed over to Arawn. Terror could still swamp him in the Horned Lord's presence. But, as always, Rob's terror would so easily turn to the one thing that sustained him, kept him from quailing beneath that inhuman gaze....

Fury. *How dare you play me like this? Demand of me like this? Invade me like this?*

And the triumph: that not every thought Rob possessed was in turn possessed by an immortal presence. The Horned Lord did not respond to his anger, merely stated, *You think you have chosen. Whilst your rival flails in a mire of indecision.* The horn glinted as the great head shook. *Dismal. Most unsatisfying.*

"Then go haunt *him* for a while!"

I am, believe me. Until one of you acts, I have no choice.

Rob hesitated, then clenched his teeth, shook his head, and threw the saddle over Arawn's broad, black withers.

"AND the Holly King, Green Lord, Green Hob, found a young Lord sleeping beneath the leaves of the Oak, and waked him by tugging at his ear."

"Was he beautiful?"

Gamelyn heard them before he saw them: voices coming from the bailey, clear as bells on the morning air. He recognized Eluned right away, the lilt of the Welsh Border Marches unmistakable. The other voices were high, mingled with giggles. Children.

He had attended Matins, felt rejuvenated—cleansed—from the rites. The Abbess had directed prayer, and in the cadences and stops of the Latin, her voice truly was akin to an angel's.

But the little ones' voices... it was the type of magic that angels would surely sing for. And Eluned was weaving it as surely as she wove her story. Gamelyn espied the little group all gathered on the front stoop of the weaver's cot: a mother with an entire bevy of acquired children—and more than a few adults, as well.

Children. A family. One more thing Gamelyn would leave outside Church doors. It gave him a strange, displaced pang. He had never thought upon it before, never contemplated upon what he would not have, only what he would escape.

"Lads aren't beautiful!" One of the youngest lads protested, and an older lass tapped him on the head with her fingers. "Well, they aren't!" he insisted.

"Aye, but this one was," Eluned said. "Fair and golden as a summer afternoon, lovely as to break the heart of many a comely maiden."

Another child spoke up. "And he did, aye?"

"Who's tellin' this?" an older woman chided. "Your smart mouth, or th' Mother?"

"'M sorry."

Eluned laughed. "You're right, lass, he did. But it wasn't the Maiden's heart he broke, it was the Hob's."

"Tell us of Hob!"

"Well, Hob. Everyone knows Hob; he can be young or old, handsome or plain, your faintest, fondest dream or a harrowing nightmare. He's tricky, and clever with his hands, a thief and a rogue. A *pwca*, one of the fae who'll lure you into the green Wode and wrap you in his spiderweb, keep you there all young and fresh whilst everything in the real world goes on without you.

"Hob. He was the Maiden's consort, y'see. He blew the ice onto the leaves, and wrote her name in the frost. He wore the horn-crown and she would twine it with ivy and holly. He made ice for Her to slide on, and snow's fall to nestle in Her curls—"

"He shouldna woken that fair young man!"

"Well, some things are meant to be. Sweet Green Hob knew the price of waking the Oak King, knew he'd have to chase after his own *tynged*."

"That's a funny word," a young one said, and Gamelyn had to agree, surreptitiously creeping forward. He'd heard it, not only waking but sleeping, and perhaps Eluned would say what it truly was.

"Mm. No more than any other word, and it means many things. Destiny, path, dreaming… all of it and more. If you can catch even a glimpse of *tynged* threading out before you, then you're a fortunate one."

"What of Hob and the Maiden?" a lass asked. "And the young Oak?"

"They belong together, all of them; they love each other with a passion to fill the world. Summer and Winter will die for their Lady, and each for the other, aye?—but they canna live side by side. They are rivals, and one always must die at the other's hand, one must give his blood to the land." Eluned's eyes flickered around, seemed to spark upon Gamelyn, then went behind him, turning flat.

Gamelyn frowned, shifted, and peered over his shoulder. There, in the recesses, was the Abbess' seneschal. Sister Deirdre was watching—not Gamelyn, but Eluned—with piercing eyes and set lips. It was… unnerving.

A young boy's skepticism regained Gamelyn's attention. "Is all that true?"

Eluned's gaze left the nun, slid to meet Gamelyn's, and held as she continued. "If they were, what a world that would be, aye? Wild, chancy. Who could trust such a world?"

"I would!" another child stated.

"Nay, you canna trust chaos, canna shape order out of the wild. Love it? Aye. Trust it? Maybe temporarily, like this castle."

"Blyth has been here a long time," Gamelyn found himself saying, and the group around Eluned, nearly as one, started and began to murmur uncomfortably amongst themselves.

"Not that long, milord," Eluned replied. "But what I mean is, what would stay, did every person vanish? Not this castle. Not any castle. The forest would take it, lay it waste, wear it down to a pile of stone. Nowt we make stays, not even us." And she smiled, reached forward and tousled the hair of a girl who had crept close. "But while we are here, we can tell stories. And hold to each other. Aye?"

There was a smattering of agreement, many of the gatherers hesitant now that they knew of the presence of their lord's son. They started to disperse, and Gamelyn sighed, shrugged at Eluned, then turned to head back the way he had come.

The alcove behind him was empty. Sister Deirdre was no longer there.

❧

"MUCH seems to think you might turn him into a toad."

Eluned gave a little "Ha!" beneath her breath; it sounded triumphant. Gamelyn wasn't sure if she was answering him or not, discovered the latter as she dropped to her knees.

"Another month and this would be harder to find," she said, gesturing to a plant that, to Gamelyn's eyes, looked little different from the others near it. "Fresh is always better for this case. 'Twill not give your father more time, but I can give him ease and his wits about him."

Harder to find? They'd already spent most of the time between breakfast and lunch looking. Gamelyn would hate to see what Eluned defined as "harder."

Not to mention, he was staggering from lack of sleep and his stomach was beginning to feel as if he'd drawn his sword and cut his throat. Some lookout he was proving. If a barbarian horde appeared on the horizon right now, the most Gamelyn could do was yawn at them.

As if to belabor the point, his stomach growled. Loudly.

"I told you to bring a bite, lad," Eluned said, taking a dibble from her basket and beginning to poke around the plant's base. "A toad, eh? I think that just might be beyond my abilities."

"He seems convinced. He steps carefully about all of you." There. He'd said it but hadn't actually *said* it.

Eluned set to digging up the plant with sure, capable motions, cut it in two, then put half into her basket and re-earthed the remainder. Only then did she look up at him. "It's a bit far from the river, lad."

Gamelyn blinked.

"If it's fishing you are indeed doing," she clarified. "Are you hoping to land me, or my son?"

Think fast, Gamelyn. Fast. "I was wondering what you were going to do for an escort, when you leave for Loxley."

"Rob will come for me, should I need him. I think he was hoping your father could see to an escort for me."

Gamelyn looked away

How will he know? Is he watching?

Waiting?

He was not going to ask. *Not.*

"Y'see, the master of Conisbrough asked my husband to do some tallies on the game and fish between here and his keep." Eluned straightened up and gave a stretch, pressing one hand to her lower back. "My, but the ground gets further away every year. Truly a predicament for one as short as I." She smiled at Gamelyn, who was puzzling over the seeming change of subject. "Adam would not return from Nottingham in time, so Rob is doing those tallies in his stead. But your father was aware of the tally and has kindly agreed to have several guards escort me home so Rob's duties will not be interrupted."

He was still here, then. Somewhere.

"Your paxman, Much, I do believe, is one of them, as Sir Ian mentioned he has a guard who has traveled to our croft before. Your father apologized," she added, "for not sending you. But he seems to think that you are infatuated with my daughter, and does not want to have you tempted more than necessary."

Gamelyn felt his cheeks heat. "My father worries over nothing. It was only that Johan misconstrued my reasons for coming to Loxley. It's not true, that I swear to you."

"No need for any swearing. I know it's not true." Eluned started walking. "Though I will admit there was a time when I thought otherwise, it's quite obvious you have no more interest in Marion than she in you. Nay, lad, it's my son who fascinates you, not my daughter."

Gamelyn froze in his tracks.

"I told you." Eluned kept walking, scanning the ground. "I told you what would happen, but still you followed him."

"I never… I don't…." *You didn't tell me that!* Gamelyn almost babbled, but at the last moment gritted his teeth so hard that sparks of light flared behind his eyes. Tried again. "Eluned. *Please*."

She stopped, peered over her shoulder at him. "Please what?"

Ask the si *woman*, Much had said. He'd thought to ask her yester's even, after she'd told the story….

You know that story, don't you? You've never heard it before, but you know it, deep in your heart….

"What I said, about the toad. I was just…. It's only that, well, Much calls you the *si* woman. He's not the only one. The peasants here seem to… know you. Like yesterday in the bailey. Even the Abbess, she thinks you're—"

"A witch?" Eluned said, very quiet.

"No! And if she does, she's *wrong*!"

"You say that as though it might be the most horrible thing you can imagine. Even," Eluned crossed her arms and peered at him, "more than your 'sins of the flesh'."

"She's gone," Gamelyn said. "Left this morning, so it doesn't matter what she thinks. You... he... your family does not see things in the same way I was raised to see them. But I don't think... *can't* think... that what gifts you have make you into something wicked. The Abbess doesn't know you like I do."

"Maybe she knows more than you think. I surely know her and her kind." She shrugged, and the odd acceptance of it unnerved him.

"I don't understand, Eluned."

"I realize that, lad. But I think you also don't want to understand." A slight frown was twitching at her brow, but otherwise Eluned's face was expressionless.

"That's not.... Please. I'm trying to understand. You were the one who once told me that things were not as simple as I would have them. That—"

"Enough, Gamelyn." She shook her head. "I've told you what I can and more than I should. I am very sorry you've no mother to rely upon, but do not look for one in me. You are not of my people, and you are not my son. You're the one's breaking *my* son's heart."

For all its quiet, the reprimand lashed like a whip. Gamelyn shut his mouth and did not open it again.

ଓଃଃ

ROB had spent a long, hot and exhausting day, both a-horse and afoot. He was more than ready to strip down and stretch out in the cool little cavern for a good night's sleep. It was so sticky-hot that food didn't even sound pleasant—much less the effort to catch and prepare it.

He picketed Arawn to a spot with scarce forage but where Rob had a clear shot should any predator think to venture close. He was too tired to bother with a fire, and the gelding had gleaned plenty of opportunity to graze on their outing and take a good long drink from the river. Approaching his little cavern shelter, Rob yawned, grateful and eager for his pile of furs....

Stopped. In sheer instinct, his hand went to his knife. It quivered upon the cord-wrapped hilt, relaxed.

Flowers were the first thing he saw—a riot of colors laid upon a bed of ferns.

The entry had been swept clean and the fire pit tidied, and a tiny cauldron nestled in rocks and rags to keep it reasonably warm. When he lifted the lid, the smell that wafted upward made his mouth water: a rich man's helping of meat, stewed with roots and sharp, new greens.

And there was a sizeable mound of fresh-mown grass just to the side of the little cave.

The little girl had indeed told her tale, and it had indeed had results—though not ones he had ever imagined. Not without some anxiety, Rob contemplated the pottage. Even given the standard of living that Blyth's peasants seemed to enjoy, several families had no doubt stinted themselves to make this offering. What had he done to deserve it other than camp in their croft and frighten a child?

He tensed, half expecting the Horned Lord's presence to occupy his senses. But the ruthless tension did not come, his own instincts telling him more than any fae manifestation of *tynged* would.

Perhaps he didn't feel altogether worthy of or able for it, but he was what he was, and the peasants of Blyth were acknowledging that: the presence that lived in him, the magic that manifested through him. Marion had it right—this was love, leavened with a dollop of fear that made Rob realize anew the weight of both.

It also made it clear to him that to not accept such a weight would blunt the arrow tip of their courtesy. It would profane their offering, mock their belief.

It would be… cowardly.

Arawn greeted the fodder with a nicker that suggested he was skin and bones instead of a nice layer of fat between sleek hide and muscle. The horse certainly had no foolish and overcontemplated uncertainties such as his master, accepted what came to him and the moment in which it came.

Rob smiled, and went to do likewise.

*

"HAVE you seen it?"

"I have."

"*Where*?"

"Aye, where?"

Gamelyn was waiting for Ricardo in the armory, stripped down to muslin braies and limbering up his shoulders by swinging his arms back and forth. It was still abominably hot, particularly at this time of day, and every opening that could be opened was, to catch the lightest breeze from the still, thick air.

So the voices, coming from just outside the armory's flung-open sally-port, were easily discerned.

"Rose saw't wanderin' the woods as she was gatherin' the pigs. And I saw't meself, in the north pastures whilst I brought in the sheep."

"It's an omen, I tell you."

"Aye, but what kind, I'm asking?"

"What could such a thing mean but for th' good?"

"It's no' just a *thing*. Maisie actually saw 'im close, din't you, Maisie?"

"Maisie *ran* from 'im!" A young voice, teasing.

"He... scared me." Another, even younger voice.

"No doubt he scared you, young miss, because you were out later'n you should've been. Maybe next time you'll gather your mushrooms before dusk settles."

"But she saw't, mind you, saw the Great Stag!"

The Great Stag? Eyes narrowing, Gamelyn crept over to the sally-port, listening.

"He was so tall, and dark," the young voice—Maisie, it seemed—returned. "He had his bow drawn, and th' fire beneath him—"

"Behind him, y' mean."

"Nay, I'd swear he stood over it. And he was... awash in black, he was. He kept changing, from beast t' man."

"And hooded, you said!"

This brought shocked whispers and murmurs. It also brought a harsh intake of breath from Gamelyn as he leaned against the sweating stones of the wall, strained to hear.

"The Hunter showing hisself w' the cowl... that's an omen."

"We could ask the *si* woman."

Good luck with that, was Gamelyn's disgruntled thought.

"There'll be no bothering Herself with such a simple thing. I've already gone, yesterday, and left an offering to placate Him for our trespass."

Murmurs of satisfaction all around.

"Better we keep up such gifts. Then He'll smile upon us. Harvest's still to come. This weather might be gey uncomfortable for people, but 'tis good for our crops."

"And no harm to tickle the Hunter's fancy."

More chuckles. "Maybe next time he'll show himself as a handsome man to woo a maiden. *That* would be an honor!"

Maiden. Hunter. Stag.

"Summer and Winter will die for their Lady, and each for the other, aye?"

Escape, no longer the arcades and arches of chill stone walls and the smooth wood of altars, but sunlight through trees, wind-creak and green.

Dreams.

"He's tricky. Your faintest, fondest dream or a harrowing nightmare...."

That was an understatement.

"You aren't my son... you're the one's breaking my son's heart...."

"No." It was a whimper, shameful and shamed. Upon the heels of that came the thought, unbidden: *Could I have broken his heart? Do I have that much power?*

Is he still out there, waiting?

"I've been waiting...."

Blood on his hands. Rob's blood. "No," he growled. "I won't let that happen."

Is he waiting? Would he? Does he care as much as...

Gamelyn bit his lip, took a deep breath, finished it because... because it wouldn't go away. It was never going to go away.

As much as I do?

He was tired of being unwanted. Untouched. *Cold.* This was desolation. This was loneliness.

Was there a point to avoiding Hell, if one was already there?

ന്ദ

HIS mother met him where they'd agreed, on the second day after their arrival, and she was dressed for travel.

She left her escort down by the great road connecting Nottingham to York, with either side of it planted fields and villeins bent working, the shadow of the castle looming over them.

It looked not so imposing up on the hillside, where Rob squatted on a great slab of rock half buried in the rich earth, letting Arawn graze and watching the approach of a petite, plump figure that said to him in so many ways: *Mother.*

She sat down next to him with a huff of breath and toed off her boots to let her heels rub the fresh grass. "Well. I've done what I can for the lord. He's dying and he knows it; got a lump in his belly that I can all but feel growing. But I've made some good simples for him and told him if he wants to be aware, he has to stop being bled. The second son and his wife, thank the Lady, are both reasonable and see that the leech is of no use. The eldest son thinks he knows the right of everything, though, so we'll see."

"And... Gamelyn?"

"That one is confused as a hare in the blossoming time. I'd almost feel sorry for him. But I don't." She reached out, touched Rob's cheek. "Not when he's playing such a game with you."

Confused. Rob wanted to ask more, but realized it would do him no good. Eluned had made up her mind; he couldn't blame her for it, but there it was.

"So. Are y' ready to come home?"

Rob shook his head. "I waint leave, not yet. I've more yet to see to, several days riding at the least, and still the south to cover."

"Then cover the south on our way," Eluned reasoned. "Come on home with me, son. I can send the earnest soldier back... or, now I think on it, he'll insist on seeing us home. He's a soldier by necessity, not by choice. A nice, respectful lad of the heath who still follows the old ways. More our kind than...."

"Than Gamelyn," Rob finished for her.

"Rob, you're chasing after sommat'll just break your heart... that's *already* breaking your heart. You don't have to stay here to finish your tallies. And your father will likely be home by now. He needs us—all of us—about him now."

He needs you, not me. He... looks at me and sees... something he doesn't like. I don't understand. Everything's changed, Mam, and I don't understand any of it.

It's like the Horned Lord is... walking through him. As if my da's become more spirit than the Lord Himself, growing less instead of more, and I don't know what to do about that, I don't know how to change it!

But this... this moment, this place, this possibility? This I do know. I have to reach for it. Have to try.

"Da would want me," Rob said, hoarse, "to finish what I started."

Eluned peered at him, then looked down the hillside, toward Blyth. "I never thought we'd be this involved in noblemen's games." Rob started to speak; she shook her head, continued, "You'll need to take care, son. There's a woman, there, one who had nowt but the blackest looks for what I was doing for Gamelyn's poor father. She's gone the now, left yesterday, but she'll be back. She's kin to them, and the old man is keen she be his confessor." Eluned gave a shudder. "All I saw when I looked at her was a raven, all that black, and her picking at the bones of dying men...."

"The Abbess."

Her gaze slid to Rob's, beneath a frown. "She is an abbess, aye."

"Wearing a great sodding cross, all jeweled and glittering?" He still couldn't think on it without a stabbing ache in his breast.

"I'm not sure I'd use the 'sodding'," Eluned retorted, her gaze never leaving him. "But, aye."

"She's the one whose soldier Will sent to hell." *She's the one who'll see me there, too, for what I canna guess.*

"Rob," his mother said, "what d'you See in this woman?"

Eluned had always been too canny. But he wasn't going to tell her this. No parent should have to see their child's death, even a hint of it.

"*Rob*."

He shook his head. "'Tis no matter. I'll be careful, Mam. I promise."

"Rob, please. Come away with me, now. There's nowt but danger and heartbreak here for you. Already the castle's beginning to stir with tales."

"Because you're there."

"Aye, and I'm leaving, but what power is stirring the woodlands about Blyth remains." She reached out, put a firm hand to his knee, shook it. "You, Rob. They'll take notice."

Rob was silent for a moment, then took her hand. He rose to his haunches, with both hands turned hers palm up, and breathed across it.

Her brows drew together, and she put her hand to his face. “Rob. Son.”

“They’ll take notice, aye,” he answered. “They’ll have to. And they’ll have to because the dance has begun again. Can you no’ feel it?”

“*Rob.*”

“You canna See my future, what *tynged* spins out from the spiraling in, but I can. *I can*, and I have to follow it, Mam.”

She paled as he said aloud what she had never told him, and her fingers twitched against his face.

Then she nodded and, leaning forward, kissed the cheek warmed from her hand. “Take care, son.”

And he watched, still crouched on his haunches, as she pulled her boots back on, rose and walked, head high, down the hillside toward the soldier who’d see her back safe to Loxley.

Rob watched them ride away until they were two tiny specks past the gray carapace of Blyth Castle. Then he put his head in his hands, whispering to himself, feeling the whispers and the breath of them swirling about in his chest like smoke and mist, then like a spun lattice of leaves caught in a whirlwind.

Then he opened his eyes, extended his hands, palms up, from his breast. Released the magic; breathed across his palms only this time with words, and a power that spun, a dervish whipping leaves and dirt, ebbing and flowing down the hillside and over the gray stones of the castle:

“*Anadlu eich tynged.*”

Breathe your destiny, nobleman’s son. Swallow or choke on it, ’tis time to choose.

❧

“DO YOU need escort, m’lord?”

There were times that Much’s attentiveness was downright daunting. Gamelyn paused from where he’d just given a shift to Diamant’s saddle. “Do you have some kind of trip wire stretched across the door to my chambers, Much?”

“Milord?”

Gamelyn took up Diamant’s girth another notch. Diamant, of course, greeted this with pinned ears and a switch of his tail.

At Diamant’s head, the stable lad—John—gave a murmur and shot Much a quelling look. Gamelyn saw it, because his attention was entirely too focused on this particular stable lad and what experience he and Gamelyn had vicariously shared. Not to mention, Gamelyn had already had an intense and one-sided discussion this morning with the lad about how he really did want to saddle his own horse this morning, thank you.

Gamelyn slipped a hand into his pocket and offered Diamant a bit of swede; the stallion took it greedily and consented to have his girth taken up the rest of the way without letting loose a grouchy and half-aimed cow-kick.

A grin tugged at his lips as he asked, "Much, do you also know when I go to the garderobe?"

"Of course, milord. 'Tis my duty, to be available should you need me."

Gamelyn snorted back a laugh—tried to, anyway. It was a failed effort; he leaned against Diamant's neck and gave in to laughter. If it had a slightly hysterical tinge… ah, well.

Much and John were trying not to smile; they had that look on their faces that all serfs seemed to when they were trying to conceal that they thought their masters absolutely mad.

Gamelyn gave Diamant another slice of swede: apology for piling into him. "Don't follow me this time."

"Milord, your brother—"

"You are my paxman, or so my brother ordered. Yes?"

"Aye, milord."

"Then as my paxman, *I* order you not to follow me, Much. Just this time, I want to ride out alone. Alone," he reiterated as Much started to protest. Once again there was an odd exchange of glances between Much and John.

"I trust that's the end to it, then."

"Aye, milord." Much stood, looking somewhat at a loss.

"On your mount, then," Gamelyn said, bright. "Go ride patrol with the hunters."

"Aye, milord." Still looking befuddled, Much retreated.

Gamelyn finished seeing to Diamant in silence. Of course, that was mostly how it was around the little stable lad. Gamelyn had always thought him mute, until….

He clenched his teeth. The feelings that swamped him every time he thought of anything to do with Rob were… complicated.

Gamelyn wasn't even sure why, but then, he wasn't sure what he thought he was doing. Wasn't sure it would end other than in a frustrating ride in the forest chasing his own tail, and that was probably all he deserved.

He took Diamant's bridle, started forward only to find that the stable lad wasn't budging. Gamelyn frowned, started forward again.

John was still there, patient and unmoving. Then he let loose of Diamant's bridle—with a stroke to the black nose—and brought his hands to his own head, ducked low.

Gamelyn watched him in absolute bewilderment, blinked as John straightened, hands outstretched. In those hands was the leather cord he'd worn about his neck. At the end of it was a wood-and-ceramic carving. Gamelyn's memory jogged itself.

It looked to be a stag's head.

It looked to be the same stag's head that Rob had, some se'nnights previous, put about this lad's neck.

And John was making it plain that he wanted to place it about Gamelyn's neck.

Gamelyn shook his head. "No. Thank you. It's yours, I know. He… gave it to you…." The very fact he'd noticed such a thing was a confession in itself.

John frowned, shook his head, and held the necklet up once more. Since there seemed to be no help for it, Gamelyn allowed him to thread it over his head and tuck it beneath his tunic. It was warm from the lad's own body heat, tingling against Gamelyn's breastbone. John stepped back, put his hands to his face, and blew a breath across them. The breath quivered against Gamelyn's hair and, though it seemed impossible, the stag head ornament seemed also to vibrate.

Then John spoke. "'Twill protect you, lord. And help you find him."

Inconceivable. Gamelyn said, hoarse, "I'm not looking for anyone."

"Yes, lord." The stable lad bowed a retreat and vanished into the barn's shadows.

ENTR'ACTE

"ARE you sure, Deirdre?"

"I would stake my life on it, Reverend Lady."

Worksop Abbey was silent, dark. Its main solar was lit only by the spastic flicker of several fat candles against the inner wall. Their voices did not even carry to the outer room, where several attendants slept, and Abbess Elisabeth's tread, back and forth, was nigh silent. In privacy, and beneath the humid press of night, she had shed wimple and gorget as well as the voluminous cuculla she wore when her official capacity was called upon. She wore a plain nightdress, sleeveless, and her wheat-colored hair, cropped close, was lank with sweat.

Deirdre was clad in much the same fashion. Normally she would sleep in the outer room, with the others, but her Abbess had required her presence and Deirdre always complied.

It was useful, Elisabeth considered, to have one so devoted, and so mindful of their own redemption. Deirdre was a constant reminder that even those imagined eternally lost could be saved, with God's help.

"It has been a long time, and then I was merely another poor sinner in a gathering of pagan idolaters. But I remember *her*. My family and I, we had come from Alfreton—a long way, but we considered it well worth it, then. The Maiden was of the old blood, it was rumored; not just from the Welsh Marches, but deeper still, an unbroken line to the fae folk. And to see Hunter taking Maiden to wife not just in ritual, but in troth… it was considered fair luck to witness."

Not that it was any true marriage, consecrated not by a priest in God's sight, but by doing obeisance before some unholy forest demon. By Deirdre's knowledge, Elisabeth had come to know more than she truly wanted about the pagan ways. Fae tales, false demon gods, brazen fools riding naked in the night with wolves as hounds in some wild hunt toward damnation.

Know thine enemy.

But Elisabeth couldn't help but feel sullied by such knowledge.

"She's older, of course, but there's no doubt in my mind, Reverend Lady. This Eluned of Loxley is a leader of one of the most powerful and insidious covens in all England."

"And she's tending to my uncle, for the love of Christ!" Elisabeth gritted out. "Feeding him lies and false cures!"

"There is no doubt that she is indeed a skilled healer, Lady." Deirdre's words were meant to soothe, Elisabeth knew. But they did the opposite.

"Yet since her healing arts come from the Devil, how can she tend anything but the Devil's wares? Who knows what subtle poison lies in such cures?"

"I saw Sir Ian's body servant test the mixture himself."

"That is not the kind of poison I fear. If she was that stupid, that obvious, the woman would have been dealt with long ago. Nay, she is subtle, and that is the fear. Already she begins her foul work. Sir Ian will hear no word against her, even the smallest. And she has beguiled the boy. You heard him when he escorted me from his father's solar. He was insolent."

"Aye, Lady, but you must remember that a lad his age is fairly made of insolence."

Elisabeth smiled. "That much is true. But it is the direction of his insolence that disturbs me. He defends her like a knight his lady. Or a lover. From what you have told me, seduction would not be unheard of with these people."

Deirdre shrugged then went over to the counter and took up the pitcher, poured wine into a goblet. "And that would not be an uncommon path for a lad his age, either. If I might ask, Lady, why this concern over a lord's late-gotten issue?"

"That 'lord's late-gotten issue' is indeed of interest, Deirdre." Elisabeth took the cup from her, dipped her head in thanks. "He is an uncommon young man. You mention the vices of those his age. Yet I've rarely seen one with such fierce devotion to God. He spends much of his time reading or at his devotions." She sipped the cup gladly—Deirdre was quite gifted with herbs, herself, and her dandelion wine was worth savoring. "There is something altogether untainted about him. He has a unique purity that we all strive for, and seldom achieve. Yet it is there, in him."

"You have been watching him closely, then."

"From the moment his father mentioned a possible vocation for him. Uncle Ian said he would well-dower the boy despite his birth order—and he means it, he is very fond of Gamelyn—but that is not the only boon, Deirdre. Uncle Ian has only ever shown kindness to me. He took my side when my father would have seen me auctioned on the marriage market, talked my mother into siding with me when I would have chosen God's love over any pimply, pretentious suitor. I owe my uncle much; the least I can do is see that his beloved youngest is safely installed in the Church." Elisabeth pursed her lips."I think the boy has averted temptation so far. He has not the sinful and unspoken language about him that can be seen when a man is near his lover's side. But I will keep an especial eye upon him, nevertheless.

"As to the witch." Elisabeth tapped her fingers against the cup, took a last drink. "Tomorrow we leave for Nottingham, to see to another of the pagan filth. I'd warrant this murdering forester is of her coven. And her husband should still be there." Her eyes gleamed. "You did not recognize him when we crossed paths before—"

"I did not think to look, Reverend Lady. I beg your forgiveness."

"There is nothing to forgive. There was no reason, then, to even suspect of the evil he represents. He seemed merely a kind man burdened with an insolent and wayward son. It is a good reminder of the wickedness that can bide beneath a fair face. As I told young Gamelyn.

"But no matter. These people might have infiltrated the shire, they might have a powerful coven at their beckon, but neither am I without resources." She handed the drained cup to Deirdre. "I will see this wortwife burnt or hanged, and her coven with her."

ღ XIX ღ

IT WAS close to evening when he heard it, echoing through the trees: the steady, rhythmic sound of a walking horse. The hoofbeats approached, then abruptly slowed, stopped with a shift back and forth, then began again.

Looking for something.

Bloody damn. Rob rose from where he'd been giving his saddle a good oiling and took several slow, silent steps forward. He'd hoped to not attract attention… well, not the kind that would come looking for him a-horse, anyway. His role as visiting benefactor had no doubt sent Blyth's peasantry abuzz. The small blessing-gifts that had been left here at his cavern had been transferred, as if by magic, to a place outside the tree line to the north. Rob had left a gift there as reciprocity for their giving, and they had adopted it. In fact, he had a gift of fish to deliver before he retired for the night. Despite tying them in the cool stream nearby, it was warm enough they'd not keep forever.

But surely none of those people would turn him in.

Rob frowned at his hands and forearms—they were all over the fat he'd been laving on his saddle—then wiped the palm of his left hand on the leather of his breeks and fingered the dagger from his belt. Likely he was being overcautious. Even if someone had been indiscreet, he was on legitimate business here, and had the documentation to prove it, with Conisbrough's seal.

Then he saw a glint of ivory through the trees, and his heart leapt into his throat then plummeted down into his belly.

Nay, he was being daft. It could be any gray horse. In fact, his eyes could be playing wishful tricks upon him that the rider was there at all… but Arawn was looking too, ears pricked, head and tail lifted. He gave a strident whinny.

The gray answered, a stallion's high-pitched whistle of query and challenge. Arawn nickered, more subdued but also welcoming, as the other horse turned, made his way toward the copse. It was Diamant who answered, picking his way almost daintily through the ground cover. Diamant's rider halted him as they reached the edge of the little clearing, and for long moments they stood there, not moving.

Had they come looking, intent and intending? Or had they come across the clearing only by chance? Tens of tangled and insecure scenarios played their way through Rob's scattered thoughts, were strangled by one focus:

Get off your horse, you tosser. Get off your horse and walk over here, or I swear I'll come over there and knock you off.

Another few heartbeats, so tense and demoralizing that Rob almost started forward to make good on his silent threat. Then Gamelyn threw Diamant the rein and dismounted. Stood there again, green eyes scanning first Arawn, then the clearing, then the little cave, then—finally—Rob.

Rob once again had the peculiar sensation of time stretching around him but without the dreaming or the cutting: his heartbeat was normal, he breathed in the same spans, but the surround seemed slower, stilled and hushed about him. Just as before, he was almost afraid to move, unwilling to step back into the moment lest the loom of *tynged* go spinning wildly past and he loose his grasp upon it, just as he loosed his knife and it rang with impact then skittered on the rocks and dirt.

But then Gamelyn started walking toward him, and the moment grounded itself into Rob's chest, the loom clacking back and forth, the shuttle rhythm his heart and breath.

Gamelyn seemed not so much like the young man who had followed Rob to the mere and then run from him, but the boy who had so inexplicably and determinedly made his way to Loxley. Worn, secondhand riding clothes of linen and leather settled snug about his frame. Shafts of sun caught fire-gold in his hair as he passed through them, betrayed a sunburnt nose and flushed cheeks.

But he walked like the young man, a swordsman's cant. Gamelyn had one hand resting on his sword hilt, the scabbard rocking against his thigh. As he came closer, however, that hand left the sword and hovered at his hip, as if unsure of what to do.

He was... *beautiful.*

Not an arm's length from Rob, Gamelyn hesitated then halted, looking both confused and determined, more akin to someone walking to his own beating than meeting his lover in the forest.

A tiny sound came from Gamelyn—a question, an answer, Rob wasn't sure which, but it didn't matter. Suddenly they were lunging forward, wrapping around each other, *kissing* each other with a pent-up violence that made Rob see stars and fire and not much else. Heat and strong arms, gasping breaths and grasping, desperate hands; fine hair sliding through Rob's fat-slick fingers to gleam like cinnamon-gilt silk; and Gamelyn's hands knotting in his tunic, bruising the small of his back.

And the bloody sword was *still* in the way.

This time it was Gamelyn who broke away just long enough to unbuckle it and fling it aside—not without a flinch as steel rang, pained, against rock—but then Rob was pulling him close again, leaving tiny shimmers to map streaks upon that fair, freckled skin everywhere he touched.

"I've been waiting," Rob murmured against one of those slicks, tracing down Gamelyn's chest, and when Gamelyn gave a strange shudder, hesitated, Rob pulled him beneath the overhang. Pushed him down onto his furs.

"Rob?" It was shaky, hoarse; Rob covered it with his mouth, desperately trying to unlace his breeches with oily hands. Gamelyn finally did that as well, first Rob's then his own, his hands reaching… begging… and he hissed in a sharp breath between his teeth as Rob fisted him. Gamelyn kept staring at Rob as if he could scarcely believe what was happening, and when the breath left him, it sounded like Rob's name, then a few more words, unintelligible.

And aye, but Rob knew what would shut him up, something his slippery hands were good enough for….

Rob wasn't sure what was more satisfying, the sharp stab then the dull pressure that stretched him almost past bearing but sent shivers and sparks up and down his spine… or the way Gamelyn's eyes widened with *no, what are you* doing*—no*! as Rob first straddled and slicked him, then the *yes oh God* yes *please*, as Rob guided him, took him in. The way those green eyes closed as Rob hunched over him, panting, and how Gamelyn flung his head back against the furs, the cords of his neck straining. Rob leaned forward, loosed his held breath to skim gooseflesh over that arched throat, felt the tension runnel from him and the throb of discomfort give way to the throb of Gamelyn deep-sunk inside him. Started to rock, back and forth.

And Gamelyn was *groaning* beneath him, fisting his hands in Rob's tunic, shoving then pulling then shoving again, a mindless, chaotic tangle of *come here* and *go away*. Instead Rob grabbed those hands, yanked them above Gamelyn's head, and rode him until there was nothing left—no future, no past, only this now and this moment—but Gamelyn's body against his, and nothing left in this world—no doubt, no questions—only *just fuck me until I canna think or speak or even* breathe *my name*….

ঔৣ

"DON'T run from me again."

"I didn't—"

"You did."

"But…. You don't understand."

"Aye, you have me there. This is one thing I don't understand."

"This is… it's all *wrong*."

"Then why are you here?

"I don't know… I *don't know*!"

Rob propped up on one elbow and tilted one eyebrow up into his forelock. "Sure of that, are you?"

Gamelyn groaned and put his palms over his eyes. Other than that he didn't move, was still lying on his back trying to get his breath back, still half in and out of his clothes—they'd been more direct than thorough. Rob himself still had his tunic on, though his breeches had been flung aside with that bloody interfering sword.

Gamelyn's breeks were also flung aside; his thin braies, on the other hand, were still clinging stubbornly to one pale, freckled leg.

Fancy that.

Rob reached forward, pulled Gamelyn's hands away from his face. "Enough."

"Rob—"

He didn't answer in words. Instead he leaned forward and took Gamelyn's upper lip between tongue and teeth, let his hand slide down to press Gamelyn's sated erection between his fingers and Gamelyn's belly.

Not so sated, after all; there was a slow but undeniable quiver against his palm. The quiver ran up, hung in Gamelyn's throat, then escaped in a hoarse groan. Rob caught it with his tongue, gave one back against parted lips.

"Rob, I…."

It wavered as Rob gave a roll of his hips. Rob indulged in a slight smile, ran his tongue over Gamelyn's cheek and down to the hollow where his neck and shoulder joined. The waver choked into a shudder, the quiver against Rob's palm into a full-on lurch and stiffen.

"*Rob.*"

"*Gamelyn,*" he whispered back. "Shut the bloody fuck *up.*"

❧

"IS IT so horrible, then? Loving me?" There was a quaver in Rob's voice, vulnerable telltale.

It pulled an answering quaver, deep down, from Gamelyn where he was sitting and staring past the small fire that Rob had kindled. It lit the little cavern in spastic starts and flashes, glinted over sweat-wet skin and reflected out into the night. It even reached for Arawn and Diamant, standing comfortably head to tail just outside, a black shade limned by a white ghost.

"If only it was." Gamelyn reached out, seeking Rob's hand. Rob gave it to him. "Then everything would be so easy. It's just…." The hand clenched. "God, what have we *done*?"

Rob rose from the furs and onto his knees, spooned close behind Gamelyn, his tanned forearms limned against moon-pale chest. All the grease was gone, rubbed into each other several times over, now. "Not half of what I'm planning for the rest of the night."

"Rob—"

"Gamelyn, bloody *damn*! You're strong enough to tie me in a knot and you know it. You want me to stop, then kick my arse and *make* me. Otherwise—"

"I know, I know. Shut the bloody fuck up," Gamelyn finished for him, and suddenly turned, yanked him close.

ღ

"WHERE did you get this?" Rob fingered the amulet resting against Gamelyn's breastbone. It had rolled into the hollow of his throat as he'd flung himself onto his back, still panting.

"The stable lad gave it to me," Gamelyn mused, curling his arms over the top of his head. "He had it about his neck and insisted I take it."

Rob smiled. John, then.

"He said it would help me find you."

"And have you, then? Found me?"

Green eyes rose to his, all but bursting with both doubt and wonder, and Gamelyn reached out, pushed a lock of black hair behind Rob's ear. "I have, haven't I?"

"Mm." Rob sighed. "My toes think so. They're still knotted fair tight."

That impossible, soft-sweet smile appeared, turning into a chuckle as the tucked-back black curl made stubborn recoil into Rob's eyes. Gamelyn's expression went somber as he trailed slow fingers down to the small crescent of horn and silver that pierced Rob's right nipple. "This is one, isn't it?"

Rob nodded. "I don't like things about my neck, so this is how I carry it with me. You really didna know what it was?"

Gamelyn shrugged, somewhat self-conscious. "I just thought you enjoyed pain."

Rob smirked. "This from you?"

"I don't *enjoy* pain."

"Mm. Keep telling yourself that. I hear the sounds you make what I rake my teeth across your—"

"Rob—"

"Or how you squirm when I do *this*." Rob leaned forward, ran his fingertips across Gamelyn's chest and gave a sharp pinch to one nipple.

"*Fine*." Gamelyn's brows were drawn together in a fierce glower, but the effect was spoiled by the smile trying to quiver in one cheek. And the squirm. Definitely the squirm.

"Ah… stop. I can't…." Gamelyn shivered, rose up on one elbow. "Why did he give it to me, then?"

"You canna feel it?"

Gamelyn frowned. "Feel what?"

"He's woven a protection about it." Rob traced light fingertips over it, and Gamelyn gave a shiver. "See?"

From the look in the green eyes, Gamelyn did see. And wasn't sure he liked what he saw. "He said that. I didn't…. So. It's… sorcery."

"Not so contrived as that. This is a more… *natural* working of breath and skill. It led you to me because I wore it for a time." Another smile, Rob remembering that time, indeed short and sweet and full of magic.

"I know," Gamelyn said, half into the furs. His hand had crept up, fingertips rolling at the charm.

Rob's brows drew together. "You… saw?"

"I… I didn't mean to. It was an accident, and…." Bloody damn, but Gamelyn was not only babbling but *blushing*, sitting up and looking anywhere but Rob's face. "The next morning, you put it over his head."

Rob sat up behind Gamelyn and nuzzled at his neck. "Did you watch us?" he purred.

"I'm afraid I did, a little." It was hesitant.

"Only a little?"

"I didn't understand." Gamelyn began a shrug, instead sucked in a breath and arched his neck as Rob tongued his nape. "I'm still not sure I understand."

"Me and John?"

"No," Gamelyn whispered, "*me*. It's… overwhelming."

"O-vuh…?"

"Almost too much to bear." Gamelyn gave a shiver as Rob began to trace his tongue along that lovely pad of muscle arching between neck and shoulder, arched his neck and gave a bit of a purr himself.

"Overwhelming," Rob murmured it against the little constellation of darker freckles at the point of Gamelyn's shoulder. "I like the sound of that."

ଓଃ

"THEY say you're of the fae." Gamelyn had one leg curled around Rob where he was sprawled, half atop Gamelyn. His cheek and nose were buried in black curls, his eyes closed as he breathed in the scent of him: mint and light sweat, grass and horse.

"Who?"

"The villeins of Blyth. They call you the Hunter."

"Mm," Rob said against his chest.

"They say you're a forest spir… uhn…." This as Rob began to trace his tongue along Gamelyn's breastbone.

"Does it matter?"

Rob worked his way—and his tongue—down to Gamelyn's belly, teasing at the fuzz below his navel. Gamelyn's eyes crossed and his brain went blissfully dormant.

And the Holly King, Green Lord, Green Hob, found a young Lord sleeping beneath the leaves of the Oak, and waked him by tugging at his… ear.

Dormancy fled with a jolt. The words were, almost verbatim, what Gamelyn had heard from Eluned, telling her tale in the bailey. Except this was no female's voice: it was deep, and held some strange amusement. Full of power, indisputably male. It wasn't—not quite—Rob's voice; granted, Rob's mouth had been too busy skating across Gamelyn's belly to have spoken. Yet Rob had gone still against Gamelyn, eyes clouded and… vacant, somehow, as if Rob's soul had somehow left his body. The notion was abruptly terrifying

He had heard. Gamelyn would have staked his life on it.

"What *was* that?" Gamelyn breathed.

The black eyes slid to meet Gamelyn's, now with a tiny, blue-white spark dancing deep in them.

Probably only the fire.

But… it stayed as Rob bent, kissed Gamelyn's belly once more then lurched forward, propping a hand to each side of Gamelyn's torso. Peering at him, so piercing and steadfast that it made Gamelyn squirm, though he could not look away.

Instead, he pushed at Rob, rolled him onto his back so that Gamelyn was the one with hands propped to either side of Rob's body. "You heard it, too," Gamelyn said. "Didn't you?"

"What," Rob answered, quiet, "did you hear?"

"A voice. I heard a voice. It sounded a little like you, but… deeper. And it said… it was the words of a story your mother told—"

"My mother?"

"She was telling a story to the children in the bailey. I'd just come from Matins." He trailed off, unwilling to think of that.

"I had a dream, the night before," Gamelyn began again, then just as quickly trailed off, again. If he wasn't keen to put himself back in the cold, sterile church light, neither was he keen to revisit the darkness of that dream, let alone retell it to the one he'd….

"I've been waiting…."

And here Rob was, lying beneath him, in his arms, and Gamelyn had a sudden, horrific wonder if, did he raise his hands, he'd find blood on them. He shoved back, looked at his palms, felt himself shudder with relief when they were pale and unmarked.

Hold fast, young sapling. Blood is also the life… is that not what they teach you in those cold, stone walls? Truth can be found everywhere, you see.

Rob was sitting up, concern twisting his brows, forelock falling into his face. "Gamelyn, what—?"

He hadn't heard it. Hadn't heard the voice.

Blood is the life….

No. *No.* He put his hands over his ears, as if he could shut it out. To imagine a world in which he would hunt down Rob and take him down like an animal was to despair.

To despair was to turn one's back on God.

Yet had he not, already, done just that?

"Gamelyn." It was so soft, his name murmuring against the cavern walls. Rob's hands had reached out, pulling his hands away, cupping his face with a touch as gentle as Rob's voice, as Rob's breath wafting across Gamelyn's cheeks.

"How long have the dreams been coming?" was Rob's next query. Still soft, still matter-of-fact, as if it were nothing unusual.

Nothing damned.

The hands upon his face were insistent; Gamelyn gave in, found his gaze seeking Rob's, his hands rising to grip tight to the tensile strength of those brown wrists. The only other time he'd seen a look so frighteningly open on Rob's face had been on the mere, surrounded by fireflies.

Or this night, Rob holding him down, while Gamelyn took him and all the while felt as if he was the one being taken….

"Pull on your breeks and come with me," Rob whispered. "I've something to show you."

❧

FALSE dawn was giving a faint light across cleared fields as they broke from the tree cover, wary and watchful as a brace of deer. They didn't go far from the trees, a mere stone's throw down to a huge, flat rock jutting from the slope.

Gamelyn remembered this rock, how his father had thought to plow it up from the earth. Several draft harnesses had been broken in consequence, then some digging tools; only when the rock was found to be five times again larger below ground than above did they leave it alone.

Now the rock was… decorated. Set like a banquet table, it had been garlanded with flowers, laced with ivy and braided withies. There was a basket of apples there, several leather- and cloth-wrapped parcels, pewter mugs and wooden bowls. A small and spare feast, but feast nonetheless.

"Maybe next time He'll show himself as a handsome man to woo a maiden. That would be an honor!"

"'Tis only right we honor His visit."

This was what they'd meant.

Only the "handsome man" wasn't wooing any *maidens*.

And Gamelyn wasn't feeling guilty, only smug and satisfied. *Mine*, he told them. *Mine.*

"They came to my cave, the first time," Rob explained, almost shy. "Then, they came here."

Just above the rock, Gamelyn squatted on his haunches and looked to the south. Blyth could be clearly seen, though it looked more a gray stack of aggies with several scattered hither and yon, waiting for play. "You were who they meant. The Hunter."

"Aye." Rob hunkered down next to him.

"But… he's not real. He's a spirit." *A demon*, a tiny righteous doubt gave prompt from behind his eyes.

Not here, he told it. *Not* here.

"Aren't spirits real, then?" Rob's voice was, yet again, so reasonable.

Gamelyn frowned.

"Don't spirits live in us?"

Possession. Doubt was insidious. *Sorcery.*

"And sometimes, when we don't listen, things *make* us listen. Make us… take part. Ent it what every decent person does? Try to live a fine life, bring what blessings and magic they have into being?"

Doubt sniveled, shriveled. "That's why you brought the fish. They bring you gifts and you give them food in return."

"The *eternal* return." Rob hunkered down next to him. "Y' don't get something for nowt in this world. Nature doesn't work that way. Planting has to be done if we expect crops. The fields must lie fallow to rest, and we scatter rot and compost to give 'em back their strength…."

"'To everything there is a season'," Gamelyn quoted.

"Aye, that's about right."

"That's from the Bible, you know."

Rob shrugged. "I've heard there's truth to be found in every book, if y' look. I don't read well enough to look, 'm afraid." Rob lurched up, rested his forearms on his knees. "People need something to believe in. You should know that, you follow the Christ."

"And what do you follow?" It was a dangerous question; Gamelyn was almost afraid to hear the answer.

To hear spoken what he knew had to be true….

Rob gave Gamelyn a look, precocious and patient.

"*They* believe in you, somehow." Gamelyn persisted. "But what do *you* believe in?"

"They believe in what lives in me. They believe in the old gods," Rob said, slowly. "The powers that come, not from someplace far away, but from here." He laid his hand flat against the earth. "It's here, all of it."

"The old gods aren't dead...."

"And you believe in what's... here."

"I don't just believe." Rob turned to him, and it seemed the sunlight had sucked itself up and backlit his eyes with embers. "If you reach out to something, and it reaches back... if you're filled with something greater than yourself, then is it belief? Or what *is*?"

"It sounds like...." Gamelyn frowned, looked down. "What I feel when I pray." He snuck a sideways look, expecting ridicule. Instead he found Rob, chin on hands, listening.

"Does your god answer you back?"

"I... think so. Sometimes. I guess that's where belief comes in. Faith."

"It sounds... peaceful. Trusting."

"It always has been." *Until you... and then nothing would give me peace but you.*

So," Gamelyn ventured, slow, "this, um, *season*. Is it yours?"

Rob gave him a thoughtful look, then stood, approached the rock. He did it as gravely, as reverently as Gamelyn himself approaching the chapel altar; it thrilled the same tickle of energy—of potential—through Gamelyn, the same lift of hair at his nape and arms.

So many things that Gamelyn had thus far seen in Rob, but this raw veneration was a frank surprise. Rob seemed so... wayward.

"The first time, some of the animals took a lot of it before I could get here." Rob shrugged, and just like that, the spell was broken. "Well enough; it feeds what needs it."

"Won't something take the fish, then?"

"Nay, I've warned 'em away."

"Warned them." Again, the tiny thrill at Gamelyn's nape.

Rob bent down, took up a long spray of green and purple, separated a small sprig from the larger and strode over to Gamelyn. Surely he wasn't going to do what Gamelyn imagined he was....

Christ's blood, but he *was*. "Are you actually putting *flowers* in my hair, Rob Loxley?"

"Actually," Rob was grinning, "I am. See, there are some pleasures to be had by having a forest spirit as your lover."

Gamelyn snorted.

"Just don't eat it. It's foxglove. 'Twill stop your heart."

And wasn't *that* beyond apropos.

Rob smirked, then knotted the hair at his nape and shoved a purple sprig in for himself. Gamelyn found himself contemplating how lovely the purple looked, tucked in amongst black tangles, then decided he should just go throw himself from Blyth's highest turret. He was beyond pathetic.

Rob, meanwhile, had left off flowers for a small drawstring pouch. "If this is what I think…."

It was like watching a child unwrap a coveted Christmas gift. Gamelyn had to smile as Rob let out a yip of pleasure. "Aye, these! These are brilliant! I'd never had them before I came here… d'you want some?"

In the parcel were nuts, spiced and honeyed, and since Gamelyn not only knew of them, but had semi-regular access to them, he wasn't about to deprive Rob.

Definitely Christmas. Rob scoffed down the nuts like he was starving, then proceeded to lick the sweet spice from his fingers, one by one. Gamelyn didn't even realize how riveted he was by the sight until Rob peered at him, still sucking his fingers, then sidled up to him and kissed him, spiced sweet still laced upon his tongue.

Gamelyn suddenly remembered that they were on open ground, where anyone could see. He pulled away, cheeks heating. Rob's eyes clouded for an instant—and it hurt, made an empty hollow deep in the pit of Gamelyn's belly—but just as quickly Rob's eyes cleared and he turned back to the altar.

That's what it was, Gamelyn realized. An altar.

It gave him another shiver, this one of apprehension.

He watched, silent, as Rob tucked the goodies away in his rucksack, replacing them with tidbits from his own stash, leaving the fish in a shaded spot.

Neither of them spoke until they'd returned to the cavern, and, with mutual and silent consent, started grooming their horses. Rob was eating again, this time an apple. Not that he'd gotten more than a few mouthfuls—both Arawn and Diamant were making greedy faces and he kept giving them bites.

Each of them knew the day had to start. Neither of them wanted it to.

"Next time, you'd best walk in. Diamant's not exactly a crofter's nag."

"Neither is Arawn."

"He's a sight easier to hide in the dark than auld Testicles." Rob gave the stallion a fond slap on the rump. "Or than you, towhead. Put a bloody hat on."

"And a wig and a squint?"

"If you have to." Rob met his eyes. "You know they canna find us out."

Gamelyn looked down and nodded. Wondered, if in this place, in this little Eden that had somehow been made, there was no sin….

"'Ware the Hob, the Green Man; he'll take you into his kingdom and you'll never come out again...."

And would it be so horrible, after all?

No sin. No guilt. No death or grief or sickness... or if they existed, it was somewhere outside of him—*away*—so it couldn't touch him. Inviolate, touched only by spirit. By a forest spirit that resembled more a dark angel; one with no mercy and all of passion.

"Are you, then?" Gamelyn said into the next silence.

"Am I what?"

"A fae."

Rob stilled mid-chew and slid his gaze toward Gamelyn, unreadable. "Are you making fun of me?"

"I'm *not*. I'm just—"

"Trying to make light of something you waint understand." Rob's voice was flat. Almost disappointed, and that hurt almost as much as that look in his eyes when Gamelyn had backed away. "As if, in doing that, y' can make it less powerful. Less threatening." Rob divided the apple core between the two horses then walked over to Gamelyn, not stopping until he was merely a hand's breadth away. "Are your people so scared, then? Is your god so scared that he would bid his people hunt us, hang us, burn us?" Rob leaned against Diamant's ivory croup, murmured, "Are you like your people, then? Was last night just another tumble... an 'error in judgment'?" Gamelyn's own words, slapping him in the face, and it was intimidating, actually, how well Rob could ape a noble's accent. "Will y' spend this next fortnight praying it never happened? Did I wait for nowt?"

I waited for you....

"No." It was a whimper.

"My mother thinks you are. My father thinks everyone is, at their heart, good. But neither of them think I have the sense of an in-season heifer, trusting you. Neither of them think we can break free of what chains us."

"And what do you think?"

Rob had opened his mouth for another biting response; he shut his mouth, blinked.

"What do *you* think?" Gamelyn said again, very soft.

Rob seemed puzzled. Uncertain. "You know, no one's ever asked me that. Not even Marion, not like that. And now a nobleman's son wants to know what I think. Not *if* I think. Not *if* I feel." Those eyes once again considered Gamelyn, deep and dark and almost cold. "What I think. Right. I think our biggest mistake is just... giving in. Clutching our own chains and bending our necks while they load us up with more. My mam and da? I love them, they've given me so much that's good, and honest... but they're... afraid of what they are. Both of them, as afraid as *your* people. Your churches and priests, clutching at the light because they think darkness is filled with some sort of evil. So they clutch harder to their power. My people are starved, killed, beaten." A strange little twist of a smile. "And yours have all the spiced nuts."

It was so absurd that a snort of laughter escaped Gamelyn. Rob tipped his head, the strange little smile still on his face, and started to turn away.

Gamelyn reached out, unaware of what he was doing until he had grabbed at the back of Rob's tunic and pulled. Unlaced, it fell down Rob's back, and when he started to turn back around, Gamelyn put a hand to his nape, held him there. Slow, considering, Gamelyn raised his free hand to the scars crisscrossing Rob's back. Lean-roped muscle quivered as Gamelyn traced his fingers across the satiny, puckered tissue, like Diamant shuddering at a fly, and ribs separated, arched outward as Rob sucked in a quick, deep breath.

"I felt these, last night. I saw them, by the mere, the first time we…." Gamelyn trailed off as his voice caught, tried again. "Who… who did this to you?"

"I was gormless enough to stop one of Nottingham's drunken soldiers from slapping around a lass at Loxley's tavern."

"Christ. How—?"

Rob shrugged. "I clocked him with m' staff. Pretty hard. I'm not as good with one as Will, but better than any soldier. For all the good it did me. There were ten of 'em, all told. But it took five to drag me out into the dirt and hold me down while one whipped the skin from my back."

Gamelyn's hand trembled against Rob's back, but he refused to draw away. "Did no one… help?"

Another shrug. "Who would? The girl and her sister? Their old da? A bunch of old farmers?"

Someone would have been better than nothing, Gamelyn thought, miserable.

"At least the girl got away. Me da told me I was lucky they'd not decided I was pretty enough to substitute for the girl I'd let escape."

And the thought of *that* made Gamelyn grit his teeth.

"He was right, but it was wrong to just… let them have her. Dogs, they were. Da did travel all the way to Nottingham to complain to the sheriff about what had happened. The sheriff told him I was lucky the soldiers hadn't taken me for some mangy wolfshead and that my lesson had been cheap enough." Rob spat on the ground. "Wolves ent likely to torture somethin' that shows throat. I might have been stroppy enough to get knocked around, but by the time that whip cut me a few times, I was cryin' for 'em to stop. Never felt pain like that my whole life. But they kept going on. And on."

It made Gamelyn so sick with anger that he wondered if he was going to hurl his guts, then and there. Forcibly he reswallowed his gorge, leaned his head against Rob's back. He couldn't stop running his fingers over the scars, as if he could by magic or will erase them. "I'm… sorry." It seemed so painfully inadequate.

"Dogs," Rob muttered. "Are you a dog, then? Does the smell of blood just make you want more? Nine out of ten of your guardsmen would see these lash marks on my back and think it made them free to give me more."

"Are you a wolf, then?" Gamelyn asked, just as soft. "Like your friend you met by the mere?"

Rob tilted his head to peer at Gamelyn. He didn't seem surprised that Gamelyn knew—or he hid it well. "A wild wolf'll kill a dog any chance he gets. Unless, somehow, that dog smells of his own kind."

Gamelyn nuzzled against the black locks curling down between Rob's shoulder blades, breathed him in. "Then I'd have to bathe in forest lakes, roll in green grass and juniper boughs, rub mint into my hair so I'll smell like you."

"You've made a good start, then." Rob turned, pointedly untangled the foxglove from Gamelyn's temple, peered at it. Then he raised his eyes once again to Gamelyn. "Best to be careful. You're already in danger of going back to the dogs smelling of a he-wolf."

And it was either break down and bawl like a bairn, or kiss Rob until he couldn't think straight anymore.

"Don't go," Rob whispered against his mouth. "Please. Stay a bit longer."

The decision wasn't so difficult, after all.

☙ XX ❧

NO MORE time for sleeping, girl.

The voice pulled her from the lovely pale of slumber, not beckoning but bidding. Marion groaned into the lightweight linsey-woolsey that made up their bedding in warmer weather, and dug in all the deeper. Surely it wasn't dawn yet; it felt like she'd just *got* to sleep.

Up with you now, lazy girl. You've slept too long, all of you.

All of who? The utter nonsense of it made Marion roll over with another groan. "Mam, have a heart! I…."

She trailed off as nothing but darkness met her eyes.

Slowly, her eyes adjusted. Moonlight was coming through the window next to Rob's empty bed. Her mother was across the room in her own bed, one plump arm flung sideways, resting in the hollow beside where her husband usually slept.

She had been dreaming.

With a disgusted huff—'twas sure morning would come all too early as it was, without waking for no reason—Marion lay back down, started to draw the light coverlet over her, then realized she was sweating and kicked it back down.

I suppose you are dreaming, but that is no reason to lie about. Get up, *girl.*

Marion sat up.

Better. Dawn comes quickly. We do not have much time, you and I.

Unsure even as she did it, but trusting the security of instinct, Marion rose. She didn't bother with boots or slippers, but slid a tunic over her head and tied loose braies at her hipbones. Starting to tiptoe out, she hesitated, shook her head at herself and crept back to her bed, found the sheathed dagger in its place beneath her mattress and hung it from its lanyard about her neck. As daft to go out in the forest at night unarmed as naked.

Her mother snored lightly, deep asleep as Marion exited and closed the door gently behind. She had to go to the mere. She didn't know how, or why, only that she must.

Sheltered from the wind, dear Maiden daughter, came the answer. *Better to bathe in the moon and draw her down.*

It was inside her head, somehow. Marion had never heard Her like this before. Was this how Rob heard the Horned Lord?

Of course. And if you have never heard Me, it is because you have never listened, before, save in dreams.

The forest took her in, wrapped her close. Rob loved the early hours best, the stirrings of predawn; Marion loved the nights, velvet and deep-quiet. She had missed them, lately; with the menfolk both gone, the chores were all the more numerous, tiring and tedious. Both Marion and Eluned had lately been gladder of sleep and its rest than any thought of wandering.

The night was still, only the treetops shivering and whispering with the lightest of wind. It was still remarkably warm for a late-spring night; by the time Marion had reached the mere a few ells away, she had a light skim of sweat. It was no chore to strip down to nothing but her knife and bathe in the cool, dark water.

The fifth time Marion surfaced from a lovely, deep dive, slicking the ringlets back from her face, she saw it. A flicker in the water's surface, no mere ripple from her passing. She put fingertips to her knife, flipped the rope catch that held it in its scabbard.

Nay, Maiden, no dragon bides in these waters, no kelpie to drag you under. Only spirits, to show you what you must See. For many things have been, here, and will be. You must look at them, and remember.

Many things. They flickered about her, lights dancing upon ripples, images rocking on the calm patches. Marion drew herself still, even held her breath for fear of disturbing the mirror of the surface

It had been a tangled, untouched thicket for so long, trod only by deer and bears and an occasional wildcat, then….

It had been a source of water for a small, dark people painted with indigo and woad, flitting through the forest without a sound, hardly seen, drinking from the stream feed yet giving the mere a berth, recognizing the holy mirror of it by instinct rather than lore.

They are your mother's people, your people. They fled north when the conquerors came.

It was where the conquerors had indeed come: a tall and fair people who hunted and enslaved the dark, painted ones, yet they had garnered geld in doing so, were also brought to heel. These conquerors brought horses and dogs to better hunt the forests… but they too avoided the mirrored mere as if it held a sickness. The surroundings grew more tangled. A magical place, that none dared touch.

Until your mother's people began to return.

It had been Cernun's Maiden who had drawn the moon down upon the water for the first time, sung the magic back into being and called the spirits to life.

It had been a small, dark family, blood and bone of the Barrow-lines, who had bought themselves free from their Saxon captors and stayed in Saxon land. They had come here, asked the mere spirits for permission to settle, and since there was a tiny Maiden in their midst who could sing to them in the old tongues, the spirits were pleased to listen, to be gentled and let her swim their waters.

It had been where her mother and father had been handfast, where Marion herself had been born, a child's wail into a still, cold night, soaked in by the mere's memory.

It was where Rob had whispered the mere's name in the mornings, had called a Summering lover to his side.

It was where Rob had last seen Will….

She reached out to this last, but as her fingers touched the water, ripples obscured and sent it sinking.

You long for what eludes your touch. You and your brother both.

"Shall I…." Her throat was dry despite the wet. "Shall I see him again, Lady?"

It is not to be, now. Perhaps it is never meant to be, but such things are never constant. Look at what your brother has shaped. Was it her imagination, or did the Lady seem… amused? *My Consort is not one to have his tail tweaked lightly. But then... he does enjoy the game. Moreso if Chance also plays.*

"Game? Chance?"

The Lady shrugged. *He is, after all, male.*

Her flesh, where it was uncovered by the water, was drawing up, drying and quivering from her pubic bone up. "And all of this," Marion murmured, skimming her fingers back and forth where the moon pictures had played.

Is your birthright. Maiden is often merely a title, a given honor for a moment in time, a crown made of withies and ivy that lasts for but a night or a season's blooding. With you, as with she who bore you, it is what you are.

"So my mother—"

Knows this. It is woman's to keep and remember this sacred story. And it is time to tell it to your brother, so he may sing the spirits gentle by right and not mere instinct.

"He is… not here."

I know. You must go to him.

Marion shivered, began to wade from the mere. She didn't really want to… and it seemed the water pulled at her, bidding her to stay for just a while longer. "Rob is—"

Courting a lover. Yes.

"Well, aye, and I'm not sure he'd welcome me now—"

He needs you more than you know. They both do.

"Both?"

You are part of the balance, Maiden. You are not the arrow's bloody point, but one of the foundation edges which hold it in the quarry, which set it to the shaft and allow it to fly.

"*One* of the edges." Marion knelt upon the bank, peered into the water. The moon's face drifted past her, and she trailed her fingertips along one side; moonlight spread out from her touch.

Heed what the waters have told you. Do you think they would have allowed their Hunter to call the magic with anyone but one whose spirit they recognized?

"Gamelyn." Marion breathed, then shook her head. "That's hardly possible."

You seem so certain.

"He's… Christian. A noble's son." Even as she spoke the words, she realized they were mere echoes of her mother's doubts, her father's worries.

Even so. I told you, the Lady chided, *that my Consort enjoys a good game with Chance.*

Marion had to chuckle. Her knees and shins were sinking into the soft bank, her fingertips still skimming the water, teasing strands of moonsilver into the goddess' hair.

Heed your heart, not the fear in others'. You know the truth. You are the Hunter's sister-twin, the Huntress owned by no man. Your brother would seek to take his rival's heart instead of his blood. The Hooded One is the Horned Lord's weapon but he is also mine: my Son, my Consort. It is only right that your brother's soul would seek a balance. Enough blood will be spilled in his reign.

Chilled, Marion brought her fingers from the water, felt a thick shiver course up her spine.

We have long known peace, but the price has been high. The pendulum must now swing another direction. It is the way of things.

Marion thought of all the things gone so horribly wrong, wrapped her arms about herself, closed her eyes.

Nay, the wrongs have not yet begun, my bravest of daughters. It will be a brutal time and you must stand fast. The Ceugant is in gravest danger, from within and without. The Hooded One will be blooded upon the night of sacrifice, his heart broken by the seeds of betrayal. Brother will turn against brother amidst the crypt, one will seek to sell the other as slave, burn a fiery cross into his breast to placate a king. And a raven of the White Christ would seek to scatter you to the farthest winds, would cloak with black wings My power, try to claim it, tame it. The links must be forged now, the trust must be made and held to, no matter what. As long as you are together, Holly, Oak, and Ivy, back to back and heart to heart, nothing can stand against you.

The voice faded as the moon crept from the water, setting behind the trees. Marion knelt there for some time. Dawn was beginning to streak the sky when she finally moved, got dressed, and headed for home.

ƆᴣƐ

"SWEET Christ, Rob, you really *are* hopeless at this."

"It's like holding a shunt of firewood that's too long to put in a pit," Rob complained. "Too long, heavy as hell, and p'rhaps on fire in the bargain, because that edge would sear a nice gash in you, no question, and… *bloody* damn!" This as Gamelyn, for the sixth time in quick succession, gave a twist with his own sword and sent Rob's blade flying across the clearing.

And the ginger-haired sod was *grinning*. "It's about time you looked a proper pillock while doing something," Gamelyn called after, as Rob trudged over to retrieve the sword. Again.

He'd found it tethered to Gamelyn's pack; no more than an emergency spare, really, like Rob's own short bow that he always carried but usually scorned in favor of the Welsh-made, rune-incised longbow he'd only last year grown strong enough to pull. The sword was a shorter, uglier thing than the fine blade Gamelyn wielded with such finesse, and definitely had a mad on at being wielded by a ham-fisted peasant. Rob was fairly sorry he'd ever made the suggestion that Gamelyn teach him how to use it.

"That's it, then." Rob feinted left, then stepped back, dived sideways and down into the sun-scattered grass, coming up from the roll with staff in hand. "*This* is a man's weapon." He tossed the hair from his face, eyed Gamelyn.

Gamelyn rolled his eyes, gave a negligent twirl of his sword. Raised his free hand, held up the first and second fingers. The meaning was unmistakable.

"That's just plain rude, then," Rob protested.

With a smirk and a shake of his head, Gamelyn gestured again, the two fingers twitching, the meaning still unmistakable:

Bring it.

Bloody arrogant prat. Rob shifted an eyebrow upward, pinned the staff between arm and ribs, then reached down to tug at his boots.

"Sun'll go down anon," Gamelyn said, lazy, then gave a yip and ducked sideways as Rob lunged forward, the staff plunging toward Gamelyn's head.

"Cheeky sod," Rob told him. A flurry of blows, and Gamelyn was driven back nearly to the cavern mouth. "Ha. Watch what you're doin' and quit faffing that cute arse so close to our fire."

Gamelyn feinted, then ducked straight down and rolled past Rob. And fetched him a tap on the arse as he went.

"Who's faffing what?" Gamelyn accused. "But I agree, you are much better with a piece of wood than a sword, after all."

"Aye, well, I just prefer to stroke my wood two-handed."

Gamelyn stared at him, then laughed. "You *sod*…!" And yipped again as Rob flew forward. "All right, then. We're done."

"Are we, then?" Rob pitched his staff into the air, caught it, then fetched out with several more lightning-quick blows.

Gamelyn countered them, then swung his sword, not unlike a battle-axe, right between Rob's hands. Two separate pieces went flying, and the sword tip left a streak of blood welling across Rob's breastbone.

"We are," Gamelyn told him. "Done."

"You'd rather *chop* wood with that great sword, then?" Rob blustered, swiping at the trickle of blood with his thumb and licking it off.

Gamelyn merely smiled, cocked his head, and brought the sword tip up from Rob's chest to lie flat against his neck.

Rob considered it for a moment, then shrugged, stuck his tongue out, and ran it up and down the flat of the blade.

"So." Gamelyn snorted. "You'll… tongue your opponent into submission?"

Rob merely cut black eyes his way. "Works with *you*."

∞

IT ENDED up where almost all their sparring matches ended up—another struggle, only horizontal and naked instead of vertical and minimally clothed.

And then they headed for the nearby lake. The early heat had but intensified over the time Rob had been there—or so he said—and it was nigh unbearable in the small cavern about midday.

Gamelyn was, under Rob's tutelage, learning to swim. Or to at least not sink like a stone. Keeping his head above water wasn't as hard as Gamelyn had thought it would be. And he had the most incredible sensation of… *freedom*… when he went leaping off the rock that seemed to be Rob's favorite perch.

Rob had needed to fish him out only the once….

Was this what love felt like?

Was this what love was?

All Gamelyn could think about was Rob: the lithe, almost unreal *grace* of him, swimming or running or riding… the deadly economy he displayed in the forest, watching him find a trail from nothing, or watching the lithe muscles push/pull against the long Welsh bow as if it were featherlight, and not so heavy a draw that it made Gamelyn's sword-hardened arms quiver… the way those black eyes would light on him, light *up*… the way his laugh would break into a snort when he'd laughed so hard he'd run out of air… and Gamelyn loved, *loved* to make him laugh.

Loved watching him. Loved talking to him, touching him. Loved sparring with him, lying beside him, kissing him… kissing *all* of him… loved tupping him so hard he would shudder and whimper and stuff the heel of his hand into that lovely, full-lipped mouth so he didn't cry out loud enough to wake Blyth all those furlongs away.

Loved making him cry out.

Could two lads… love each other? So impossible—*sin… damnation… Hellfire… lost*—in the world outside the green Wode. But here, it seemed possible. Inevitable. It was Eden.

Eden.

And just as inevitable that it couldn't possibly last. For surely they were eating of every fruit in the Garden….

"You keep saying that." Rob smirked. "And you keep not going."

"I don't want to go. They won't miss me, I know, but if I'm gone more than a few days all together, they might notice. Start to look. Find our garden, here." The thought of it chilled him.

What will you give me, princeling? What will you sacrifice for your… garden?

The voice was never far away of late. The one, honey-tongued serpent.

"Mm. The Wode's no garden, believe me. Winter's no cozy lord's fête. But from what you've told me, that garden sounds right boring." Rob smirked and rolled atop Gamelyn, licked his nose. "No sex, after all."

Gamelyn chuckled.

"Ah-ah… see? You wouldn't like a place with no sex." An eyebrow disappeared into the black forelock. "Would you?"

Was it wrong to be ecstatic that Rob sounded… worried? "It's… it doesn't have to be exact. It's more… the idea. A place where evil cannot touch."

"What would be the point of such a place?" Rob flattened his hands upon Gamelyn's breastbone, rested his chin atop them. "If you don't know what evil is, then how can you appreciate the decent things? Nowt to compare it with. No struggle to *be* decent." He shrugged. "Not only boring, but pointless."

Having theological discussions with Rob was *not* one of the things Gamelyn loved. They made his brain hurt.

He tried again. "But to be in God's grace. To walk with Him, in the cool of the evening, by your side—"

"Walking with gods?" Rob gave a tiny shove, flipped onto his back. "That's not all it's cracked up to be, some days."

"I mean God. The presence of all creation, the true source, Father, Son and Spirit—"

"The end and the beginning and all between." Rob nodded. "But that's here, Gamelyn. If that's your god's grace, it's all about us, in every tree, every river, every star in the sky. We see it, feel it, taste it, hear it. *Breathe* it." He murmured something Gamelyn didn't understand—another language, surely, that sent tingles and shivers along his skin. "*Tynged* is here, in th' green Wode. In your… garden."

Tynged. That was one that Gamelyn knew by now, and some deep place within him recognized it even further, hugged it close. The simple surety with which Rob talked of such things spun him dizzy. If he were Christian, he'd be some holy man, lit from within, walking a sacred path….

But he wasn't. Rob was Heathen, a pagan. Had never seen the face of God, never prayed for Christ's mercy….

So quick to judge, to name and tag and declare what you don't understand. So sure, little princeling, when you've never truly lived.

The voice was deep, and powerful, and undeniable.

Gamelyn buried his head in his arms, clutched fingers in his hair.

Even your priest admits to us. The voice stretched thin, then wavered into an echo of Brother Dolfin: *The old gods aren't dead… we forget that at our peril….*

This, then, *was* Eden, where gods spoke in velvet voices and possessed lads with eyes mild and wild as a summer storm? Where gods walked amongst them, shades and whispers in the cool and green?

Where a god's son whispered love words into his hair, stroked bow-hardened fingers down his naked back and made him believe… *believe*… in magic?

"… love you. Let me. I want to. You like *this*." And Rob's fingertips slid down into the cleft of his buttocks, slick from oil or spit or… it didn't matter… as Rob gave a push-*twist* with his fingers, flaring a simultaneous pop of sensation behind Gamelyn's eyes and out his toes. "It's even better. You've seen it with me… you like doing it to me. It's lovely, and I want to make you feel it."

Just this last thing, this one thing…. Surely it wasn't so much. And he wanted it. He *wanted* it. Wanted to feel what Rob felt as he arched back with Gamelyn deep inside him, wanted Rob to shove his face down into the furs, hold him down, fuck him breathless….

Yet just like the last time Rob had broached this, every nerve ending on his body froze with negation. It *was* the last thing. The last step off a cliff that he was somehow terrified of making… and he pulled away, curling up into a seated ball with his arms wrapped about his bent knees.

"I can't. Don't you understand, *I can't*."

Rob was still on his knees, peering at him, bewilderment backlit with darkness. "I don't mean to make you do what you don't want to… but I don't understand. It's just another way."

Another way. Another step off the cliff….

Gamelyn tried to explain, could only recite, in a dead voice, "'If any one lie with a man as with a woman, both have committed abomination—'"

Rob's breath sucked in sharp, as if Gamelyn had punched him. "So when you… when you tup me, what does that make of me, then? A woman? An… abahmin?"

"Abomination," Gamelyn repeated dully.

"That means evil, aye? What you keep callin' 'sin'." Rob shook his head, curls falling into his face, yet they couldn't mask the revulsion in his voice. "I'm not a woman, nor you… begging the Lady's pardon, but I don't want to be a woman, so how could we do owt a woman would?"

Gamelyn tried to answer, found that he had none. It made too much… sense.

"Worse, it sounds like you're saying that something a woman does is evil, and that… that I *really* canna work out." Again, a head shake; Rob rocked back on his haunches, busied himself with wiping his fingers on the rushes padding the furs. "Gamelyn, all we're doing is loving each other. And it's like… like sometimes you're set to rend yourself into little pieces over it. It makes me sick to m' stomach to see you like this, so miserable with this… this sodding weight you canna seem to put away… and all because of what some money-grubbing priest tells you from a *book*?"

"Not all priests are like that, Rob. And it's not just any book—"

"I'll say, because it sounds more evil than owt I've even heard tell of—"

"*Rob*—"

"A book that says love is wrong. That says women are… abomination. *That's* an evil, that very thought. My mother's evil? Marion's evil? Th' Lady Herself, evil?"

"Rob—"

"But what else to expect from people who've come in, taken our lands as their own and put chains on us—uh!" This as Gamelyn reached out, grasped his wrists, shook him.

"I'm sorry. I'm *sorry*." Gamelyn trailed off as Rob ducked his head aside.

Gamelyn swore he'd seen the glimmer of tears.

"Never liked reading," Rob growled against his wrist. "Too many thoughts gathered all ripe in one place, too many scrawls and marks t' make anyone's head full to bursting. You and Marion can have it, and welcome. Anyway." He peered up at Gamelyn and perhaps there were tears glimmering about the edges of his eyes. He didn't have a chance to look further, for Rob put his hands about Gamelyn's face and kissed him, hard. Then pushed him back into the furs and straddled him again. Said, in one of the changes of mood that seemed as quicksilver in Gamelyn's hands, runnelling here and there, changing from one thing to the next so rapid it was oft hard to keep up: "I like it when you fuck me. And I don't want you unwilling to owt."

And by damn, but he could have Gamelyn's eyes crossing in bliss and his knob akin to stone in the time it took him to breathe twice. "That's funny, coming from one who's coerced me into more than—"

"Have I, then?" The smile was back on Rob's lips, but hadn't quite reached his eyes.

"I didn't mean it like—"

Rob leaned forward, sliding his pelvis back and forth against Gamelyn's, sliding his lips along Gamelyn's cheek. "I know," Rob whispered. "Half the time you don't know how to say owt you mean. You think I don't know the difference between 'full stop' and 'don't stop'? Like this." He ran his hand down between them, gripping, then sliding and twisting.

Gamelyn reached for him, pulled him close.

"Mm. More? How about…." A shift, a slide, and they were both bare, nestled and twinned in Rob's hand. "*This*."

"Oh… *God*."

"And *that's* 'don't stop' if I've ever heard it, aye?"

IT SEEMED so strange, as if the past nights hadn't happened or the morning broken. Horses saddled. A black-haired young peasant, shrugging bow and quiver onto his back and securing saddlebags to his black rouncey. A ginger-haired young nobleman, mounting his gray courser with a practiced ease that belied the swordsmith's hardware he carried.

Rob knew he could never mount like that with a piece of iron strapped to his leg, it just wasn't on.

He was betting, however, that Gamelyn couldn't shoot a pheasant's eye from horseback. And smirked. Aye, well then, Gamelyn couldn't do that standing *still*….

Rob walked over, Arawn following, and looked up, met the green gaze with his own. Held out his hand, palm up. From his first two fingers dangled the quillion dagger.

Gamelyn's eyes widened and his brows knit together. Then he smiled, shrugged. "Keep it for me," he said, light. "Until next time."

Rob peered at him for a long moment, then nodded. Closing his fingers about the knife's leather-wrapped hilt, he stuck it in his belt. Then he reached up and grabbed Gamelyn by the breast of his tunic, pulled him down into a kiss. "Don't make me come for you," he murmured against Gamelyn's ear. "I will, if I have to. And I don't want to embarrass you in front of all those brothers who think you're poking my sister instead of me."

And felt satisfaction curl, heated and smug in his gut as Gamelyn leaned closer, whispered against his cheek, "Shut the bloody fuck up, Hob-Robyn."

ઉઝઙ

SHE'D not yet spoken to her mother. She wasn't sure she wanted to, that it was proper to bring such things into the light of day.

And over the next few days, Marion came to realize that there were some things she could no longer lay before her mother, like a little girl blurting out secrets at bedtime or a winsome request for approval. This was… beyond any of that. It wasn't a lack of trust, or love… it simply *was*.

And they were busy, not only with the householding chores, but the plant gathering and storing and drying. The last days of spring were always busy for a wortwife; only so many days to gather a season's bounty needed for the year's use. Not only that, but Beltain was approaching, and there were deeper concerns to address.

Cernun left the sign at their door as he did upon the moon-dark heralding every season's fête. This time it was a mommet from last year's wheat, braided all about with a spray of foxglove and peacock's feathers, in honor of the goddess's eyes upon her suitor. Beltain was the time of the Great Marriage, after all, the time when the Lady took Her Consort to Her bed of earth.

Only Marion found it, and some predator had killed a fox right upon their doorstep, leaving the fox's hind end slung across the mommet, with blood all over it and the step. Eluned was horror-stricken, and took it to the mere to cleanse it, and when she returned, Marion almost told her mother everything. The omen was too dire, too apropos.

It will be a brutal time. You must hold together. You must forge the links now, make the trust and hold to it no matter what….

Eluned's face, white as any ghost and wearied, gave her pause.

It never seemed to be the right time. The work was staggering, never-ending; the evenings they would eat, too tired to bear more than perfunctory conversation. Even the nightly ritual where they brushed and braided up each other's hair for bed—one honored from the time Marion could manage a braid with a pudgy child's fingers—had become a still point of silent relaxation between dinner and sleep.

And then, the evening Adam rode in, Marion realized that her brother had called it all too closely.

Their father was not the same man, and never would be.

"Da!" Marion ran to Adam as he dismounted, and he scooped her up as if she were a bairn again. But the arms that held her seemed thinner, less hale, and his face older, as if they had stepped into fae and he had remained in the real world, felt those few se'nnights as years.

"Oh, lass, how good it is to be back in my own place." He kissed her cheek, put her down.

"I'll take the horse, see to him," Marion said, reaching for the rein with one arm still around her father. "You go on up to th' house—you look as though you could use a meal or two."

"Or three or six," he replied, and for an instant the father she knew was there, with his sly teasing. "The food's terrible in Nottingham. They've not your mother's way with a roast, and I've not found a pottage to match yours. How does your ma and brother?"

"Ma's at the cottage. Rob's...." She trailed off, not certain of the impact of that news.

"*Adam*!" Eluned came running down the steps, and Adam leapt like a horse at the starter's shout, ran toward her. It was a lovely sight any child should be lucky enough to see, the open affection of two parents too long kept separate. But there was a desperation in it that made Marion more wistful than pleased, and she turned away. Murmuring to her father's gelding, she led him toward the stable, determined that she'd take her time brushing him down, give her parents some time to themselves.

And—*coward*! Marion accused herself—let her mother be the one to break the news to her father about Rob's preoccupation Blyth-ward.

⟨ XXI ⟩

GAMELYN made it back to Blyth as stars were beginning to appear and the chapel bell was tolling the end of Evensong. He snuck up the stable stair and vanished into his chambers—surely tomorrow was time enough to face the consequences. If anyone had, in fact, missed him.

The next morning he was up before dawn, unable to sleep, dressed in fresh tunic and breeks, and down in the kitchens for an early snack. There was a reckless melody playing along every nerve he had, twisting any discretion into pieces and blowing it widdershins; by the time Gamelyn had eaten a good portion of cheese, sausage-stuffed bread, and washed it down with good ale, he had all but decided he would just creep back up to his chambers, grab his rucksack, and head out again before anyone could stop him.

Still gnawing on hard cheese, he took the stairs two at a time, humming beneath his breath, and almost laid out Alais coming down. Gamelyn grabbed hold of her just in time, steadied the tray she was bearing.

"My word, lad!" Alais chuckled. "Where have you been? And to return singing!"

Gamelyn paused, then leaned forward and kissed her cheek. It surely was a sin to feel this much joy and not share it, somehow.

"Faith!—but you are in a sunny mood!" Alais smiled, reached out and straightened the lay of his tunic, then hesitated. "What's this?" Her fingers flicked at the lanyard and charm. "That's a pretty… and what have you done to yourself here, lad?" She pulled the neck of his tunic aside, probed a spot that briefly stung.

Gamelyn remembered, suddenly, the mouth that had given him that spot—the teeth that had latched on, *hard*, and how he'd been so close… *so close* that it had sent him over the edge, then and there….

"Well, well," Alais said, and she was smiling as if they were both in on some joke. Ever since she had heard that Gamelyn had a crush on the wortwife's daughter, Alais had been intent on seeing romance in every light step he took.

Well, she wasn't far wrong this time.

"A bit of a wild one, eh?"

Bit of a wild one… that was, perhaps, the biggest understatement Gamelyn had heard lately. He touched the bruise on his neck, and it throbbed, as visceral as the sudden stiffen and throb against his breeks. Another thrill of memory coursed through him: Rob, kissing the blossoming bruise as they lay gasping their breath back, but it had not been apologetic and Gamelyn hadn't wanted an apology, or even needed one.

"Well, curb that ardor," Alais continued, her voice lower. "Johan has been looking for you, high and low. Something about an errand to Worksop and the Abbess requesting you specifically. He's in a mood, I'll warn you. Had the cheek to accuse me of trying to get in your father's graces! As if I do this"—she jerked her head to the tray, tears suddenly swimming behind her blue eyes—"for anything other than your father's a good man and I love him…. Grasping sod. He thinks everyone's like *him*."

If the thought of Johan on the rampage didn't cool Gamelyn's ardor, the sudden and guilt-ridden realization—that he had spared few thoughts for his father the entire time he'd been in the Wode—certainly did. "Is Papa well?"

"He's fine, Gamelyn." She gave a sniff, shook her head, shrugged with a little smile. "It is what it is, your papa's circumstance. But he's no worse. I've kept that bloody-thirsty leech from him, so between that and the wortwife's potions, I'd say he's doing a sight better. He did miss you these past several evenings, but he understands that young men have other things to occupy them than their aging Papa."

The needles of guilt ramped up into a sword thrust of shame. "I'll go to him. Right now. I didn't—"

"*Gamelyn*! There you are—by *God*, where have you been?" Johan's voice rang down the hall, furious.

Alais gave a little "I did warn you" twitch of eyebrow and made a hasty retreat.

ꕥ

THE "audience" with his brother was a tactile, bristling affair that left Gamelyn seething, but seething with very explicit instructions. First, he had better quit mooning about and wandering off—if he had to dip his wick he was to not spend several days' worth at it. Second, while it would suit Johan just fine if Gamelyn spent less time playing up to their father, their father did want Gamelyn, for some unfathomable reason, and Gamelyn was to indulge him in it at least once a day, and quick was, of course, preferable. Third, that the Abbess's visit to see to their father's soul was due four days hence, and as it was their duty to escort her, and she had specifically asked for Gamelyn to perform that duty….

"Don't muck it up," was Johan's parting shot. "You're not to go anywhere—*anywhere*, mind you—until you've seen her safely here. You'll report to me when you leave. You'll take not just your tame paxman but two others as well. And you're not to make any detours toward your grubby forester friends on this trip; I'd like my guards to come back alive."

That was just nasty. Gamelyn sent a gesture his “forester friends” had taught him after Johan’s retreating back. Then went to see his father.

Sir Ian was sleeping, but lightly, and spent some time in fairly lucid conversation with him, mostly about the wandering troubador whose troupe was still here—and that Gamelyn should take time and see them as he could. The troubador had come and entertained Sir Ian in his solar the previous night, caught him up on the court gossip, and shared a meal with him by the fire.

“So you didn’t miss me,” Gamelyn said, somewhat relieved as he knelt by the bed—as if at prayer and just as penitent.

“Of course I missed you,” Sir Ian said stoutly, then yawned. “But not horribly. He was a good storyteller. He’ll be here tonight, so I hope you can join us.”

There was a pathos in his father’s voice that Gamelyn had never heard before. Donall was glaring at him, also; not cheeky enough to say anything out loud, but certainly letting it be known that he disapproved of anything that would take Gamelyn from his father’s side. Where he belonged.

Both together were a lash that whipped him like a disobedient hound. Gamelyn bent his neck and took his father’s hand between his. “I’ll be here. I promise.”

Instead of cheering Gamelyn as it normally did, Sir Ian’s rare smile took the butt of the whip to his conscience. “Perhaps I can even talk you into a walk ’round the bailey with me in the morning? I’m doing quite well with Mistress Eluned’s medicine.” The smile turned crafty, and Sir Ian leaned into Gamelyn. “Between you and me, the leech is simply furious. Swears she’s poisoning me. I heard him say it overloud, so I had him put in the stocks. Far too many people took pleasure in throwing horse shit at him.”

Gamelyn didn’t have to fake his laughter; it bubbled up, impossibly genuine.

“Ah, lad, it’s good to hear you laugh. You seem in such a good mood today. You’ve been moping too much. Alais swears you have a lady friend. I do hope it isn’t Mistress Eluned’s daughter.”

“I swear to you, Papa, she is but a friend.”

“Good. Perhaps I am old-fashioned. Johan says it’s well past time you were salted—but Johan’s inclinations are not something you want to adopt. You should treat a lady with honor, not basely. He thinks I don’t know what he gets up to with the serving girls, but I do. He thinks confession wipes the slate so he can sin again, but you and I know it isn’t quite that simple, eh, my boy?”

Gamelyn did not flinch. Miraculously.

“Perhaps he’s right, and if you’re old enough to go to war, you’re old enough to indulge in a few sins. Our king is looking for soldiers. Again. And money. Always. I can ill afford either, but another tax is being poured into his coffers. He’s no Henry… ah, there was a man. Lionheart will beggar us yet. He’s borrowed more from the Templars, I've heard. They already hold notes on half of England."

Indulge in a few sins. Sir Ian's arrows might have been flung quite without intent, but they hit their marks no less successfully. And such talk about the king… usually Sir Ian was not so free with any criticisms of his betters. Gamelyn peered over at Donall, but Donall was not heeding his master's remarks. He was still quite occupied with scowling at Gamelyn.

"Well, if you're not indulging, I'm sure you're contemplating it."

If his father's thoughts had to be all over the map, why did they keep returning to this particular thing?

"Just make sure you take confession with Brother Dolfin regularly. I would not tell Abbess Elisabeth, though. I know the confessional is sacrosanct, but she is a woman and would most certainly not understand. As she's in the midst of looking for a good placement for you, there is no sense prejudicing her favor. I understand you're to bring her here for me."

"I am." Gamelyn squeezed his father's hand gently and gave a wary eye to Donall, still hovering on the edges. "I'll leave you to rest, for now."

"You'll come later, then?"

"I promise you, Papa. I will be here."

Gamelyn made it out of the solar before the tears betrayed him, sudden and startling, to spill and run over his cheeks. He leaned against the wall until he had some control, eyed the corridor leading to his chambers.

Eyed past it, to the stair that would lead down and outward. To the chapel.

Prayer. Peace. Forgiveness.

For what? The lies? The horrible culpability that he was spending time with his lover instead of his ill father?

For Rob?

Once the confession started, he would have to tell it all, and he wasn't sure he was ready for that. Ready for the penance, yes. Ready to swear to never do it again?

He ended up retreating to his chambers.

ര

IT WAS a perfect day for a ride.

The heat had finally broken, and a bank of clouds had rolled up the valley of the river Don, bringing the less-than-rain/more-than-mist that dampened everything and could, midwinter, be misery for days on end. Now, with Beltain's approach, it was a welcome kiss upon Rob's cheeks, filling his lungs with lovely moisture, coating his outer clothing and his curls with a slick that looked more like fuzz than damp.

It *was* close to Beltain, Rob realized with a jolt.

Perhaps he could convince Gamelyn to come. It would show him what they were about more than any tangled discussions where Gamelyn listened, his eyes wheeling wide like a horse looking to spook, and where Rob tried to explain things that really couldn't bear explaining.

Perhaps Rob had offended Gamelyn more than he'd thought, and that was why he'd not returned yet….

Nay, he was *not* going to mope about like that.

The cool had perked Arawn up as well, black hoofs dancing as Rob had saddled him. They still had the northwest edge of de Warenne's land to cover, along the Don; Rob had to set some nets and weirs to make an estimate of fish numbers. He was sure to catch himself some fancy fish for his supper, and perhaps some for the people of Blyth as well.

Gamelyn had promised to show; had genuinely seemed to want to come along. It constantly amazed Rob how little Gamelyn knew about how such things were done. Perhaps as a third son—and that sadistic git Johan constantly reminding him of it, so it seemed—there was no need for him to know the smaller details of being "lord of the manor."

Not that Gamelyn talked that much about life in the castle. Not that Rob wanted a constant reminder of it.

There were some subjects that were off-limits, and that was fine.

But he wanted Gamelyn here, riding beside him. Lying beside him at night. Not sleeping that entire night and during the day, too. Swapping compliments disguised as insults. Even learning how to wield that bloody great sword that seemed to deny ever becoming a part of Rob—a constant clumsiness, unlike like his bow or staff.

Gamelyn was pure grace and power, handling that sword. Rob smirked. Gamelyn was also getting to be fairly powerful with his other sword, and Rob had no objections to that, none at all. Rob missed the reciprocation, though.

He missed *Gamelyn*. It was a strange feeling, a yearning he'd never before been so taken by. A need, really, one just this side of uncomfortable and carrying as its baggage more than a little worry.

What if that Motherless chapel's siren song of unfathomable guilt and put-upon misery had won out again?

What if Gamelyn had decided he just didn't want to come, after all? That he was done with the game?

Only it wasn't a game, and Rob was not going to start in on *that* again….

଄ଈ

"...WANT you going back there, Eluned. It's too dangerous. This bloody crow of the White Christ has set Nottingham to slaver on our heels. He's just waiting for the excuse."

Crow of the White Christ? It sounded familiar, but as Marion climbed the steps to their cottage Adam's voice continued, scattering that thought into many more.

"Blyth's lord is kin to her, and when she takes her suspicions to him, 'tis likely he'll listen."

"You said George didna tell her—"

"He gave her things she wanted to hear, things cheap enough at the price about the making of th' arrow, and the ways of using it. He made up things that set a gleam in Nottingham's eye... the pious fraud! But nay, he gave nowt of value."

Marion stopped at the door and went no further. Her father was stalking the floor, hot-eyed and hunched, as if some sword had run him through. Eluned sat at the table, watching him helplessly, tears streaming over her cheeks.

"The magic held on him and I made sure of it." Adam's voice cracked. "'Twas the longest night of my life... the only thing that held me strong was that *he* needed me."

"Is he...," Marion started, and her own voice failed. But she had to know. "George is dead, ent he?"

Adam turned to peer at her, then slowly nodded.

Marion leaned against the door lintel, tears stinging her eyes.

"She asked George where to find the covenant," Eluned murmured, slow. "Surely she could not accuse *you*?"

"She could not. But she'd like to. Worse, th' bitch is connected to everyone in power. Thankfully the sheriff I report to is no' so pious. De Lisle has authority over me, not FitzAaron in Nottingham, and I know he's already refused to heed his sister's fire-eyed warnings about 'pagans overrunning the shire'. He told me as much when he gave the orders to give George to Nottingham." Adam's voice gained strength. "We'll take more care. Move the Fête deeper into the Shire Wode, to the stones of Mam Tor. There's none as dares goes that far, and few outside the covenant who knows the place."

Marion shoved back against the lintel edge until her spine scraped at the wood even through fabric.

The Hooded One will be blooded upon the night of sacrifice....

"I saw the Lady. In the mere."

This was met with a spectacular silence. Eluned, in particular, had paled, her mouth dropping open.

"In the... mere?" she said, very slow.

"She showed me the story," Marion said. "Of what had come before. And…." Still, she was loath to speak of it, as if it was supposed to remain, burning, in her heart until she got to the place of telling… wherever that was. Instead, she settled for the basic upshot of it. "She told me that I had to go to Rob."

"Well, *that* will be done for you," her father said. "Rob is coming home. I'll have a good night's sleep and a meal and go drag his arse back here where it belongs."

The ire in her father's voice boded no good for his son; usually Marion was not thick enough to put herself in the middle of it.

Usually. "She told me I was to go *to* him."

Eluned was watching her, frowning. Adam shook his head. "Nay. You'll not go. It's bad enough that Rob's there."

"He's courting Gamelyn."

"I well know whose tunic he's wanting to lift, and it's bloody nonsense."

"What if I told you it wasn't nonsense?"

Eluned was still peering at her, frown deepening into contemplation.

"What if I told you that Gamelyn could very well be part of the Lady's plan?"

"What if I told *you*, Mistress Sauce, you've no opinion on this?" her father retorted. "You'd let your baby brother roger the bloody *king* if he took the notion!"

"That's not—"

"Marion." It was tight. "I've had the worst fortnight of me life, and no mistake. I am not going to argue with you over some noble's brat that your brother has taken some mad turn over."

"The Lady is—"

"The Lady is no doubt ready to roast your brother over slow coals for not paying proper attention to a lass. He's the *Hunter*."

"Are we no more to you than prize fawns for the Horned One's use?"

"Marion!" Her mother. "That's enough!"

"I Saw Her, and She warned me, Da. Warned of the danger comin', and the blood and fire and th' changing."

"Do you think we've not Seen the changing happening?"

"Happening, or going to happen?"

Eluned shook her head. "Marion, you canna scry the future with any certainty."

"So you know what She says and I canna."

"Marion. That's not what your ma is sayin'. You have to realize—"

She knew her father wasn't thinking straight, that he was wearied beyond words, sickened by what had happened. It didn't help. "Did you See what would happen with George?"

"Mari—"

"I did. Even Rob didna See… and you *always* take Rob's Sight seriously."

"Sweet Lady," Adam beseeched into his palms. "Mari, pet—"

"Don't 'pet' me. I should have all the respect for my Sight that Rob does, p'rhaps more, because while he might well end up more powerful than I, I'm the eldest!"

"Marion, it's no place for a young lass—"

"I'm old enough to be wed and bedded and have my own bairns, so I'm old enough to know my own mind. And I think you've been listening to your Churchgoing underforesters a wee bit much if you're goin' t' refuse me *because* I'm a woman!"

Adam threw a look at Eluned. Eluned had sat back in her chair during Marion's outburst, arms crossed.

"Is that why, then?" Eluned queried, all too calm. "Because you'll get no help from me on that front, and you know it."

"Bloody *damn*," Adam said, and flung himself down into the nearest chair, glaring at the scarred wood of the board.

Eluned reached across, took her husband's hand. "Perhaps you should let her go, Adam." She tried a smile that didn't quite work. "If nowt else, to make sure you and Rob don't kill each other."

Adam stared at her for a long moment, then gave a short laugh. There was no more humor in it than in Eluned's smile. Then he shook his head. "Aye, well. Can a man get any supper?"

"Supper and a decent bed, love," Eluned said. But she didn't stop looking at Marion.

❧

TWO sunsets, two sunrises. Endless errands about the castle for his brothers, daily work with Roberto in the armaments gallery, walking with his father about the bailey. The first passed the time, at least; the second tired his body and made him recall Rob's clumsy attempts with the practice sword; the latter gave Gamelyn honest joy, for while Sir Ian's gait was more considered, he was walking without pain and with some semblance of his old strength.

Yet Gamelyn still felt trapped. As if he would jump out of his own skin.

You are not meant to wear a hood, my last-born son. You are meant to wear the sun and spread your wings across the Summering.

The voice spoke to him in the dark hours, and when he slept, he dreamt of quiet green and a lover's touch….

It was as if he were bewitched, as if the charm about his neck had stoked fire into his soul, possession instead of protection. He even took it off several times, but the dreams started, then. Nightmares: fire and screams and a loneliness that made him wake choking, desolate, lost.

Protection, the stable lad had said, and Rob's touch upon it, light as a breath upon his skin, and when Gamelyn put it back at his throat, the nightmares stopped. But the loneliness lingered.

On the evening of the third day, he finally took refuge in the only place he knew.

He had never spent this many days without respite in the chapel. Gamelyn's knees ached against the wooden rail, where he had spent the past half hour in front of the altar, stuck in some kind of horrific limbo where no prayers would come. He was unfit to pray, that was it, must be it; he had spent the past days in a hollow, pinioned Purgatory and the days before that in a strange, alternate lifetime of something that he still could not describe as anything but filled with stunning, darkling beauty.

But Gamelyn was stubborn and desperate, finally dissolving into alternate fits of misery and contrition expressed by either tears, or holding his breath until the tears stopped. The latter, however, made him queasy and faint; finally he just let the tears come and hoped that, at this time of day, no one would come into the chapel.

Finally, the prayers came, even if he was presently unsuited to pray them. He was left trembling, exhausted….

Empty.

And it was his own fault. He knew it was, yet still he could not tear those halcyon days from him.

It would be… sacrilege.

He looked up at the cross, the twisted and beatific agony in Christ's face, and wanted to weep again.

"There is no sin that he has not known, you know. None that he would not understand."

Gamelyn started; his elbows went sideways and he narrowly missed racking his chin on the altar. He fell to hands and knees, peered upward to see Brother Dolfin striding over, worry plain in his expression.

"Oh, dear. Forgive me." Brother Dolfin squatted beside him. "I truly thought you knew I was here; I was cleaning the ledges when you came in and I could have sworn you heard my greeting…. Here." Broad hands gripped Gamelyn's arms, helped him rise, and made sure he was steady before they released him. Not for the first time, Gamelyn considered the strength beneath that plain woolen, and that Brother Dolfin must have been one hellacious battlefield adversary in his former life. As Rob was so fond of teasing, Gamelyn was no skinny archer lad.

Rob. *Rob….*

"I haven't seen you here in a while, Gamelyn."

Gamelyn shrugged, backed out from under Brother Dolfin's grip. "I've been… occupied. With some exploring. And my reading. You gave me a lot to think upon, and I've been—"

"It's that forester lad, isn't it?"

Gamelyn froze. Slid his gaze sideways to take in Brother Dolfin. "That forester lad's" other fondest statement—*for someone who's so good at closing his face into a stone cairn, there's times you're no great shakes as a liar*—had come home to roost. Brother Dolfin's eyes were narrowed upon him, canny.

"Mm. I should have seen it. But I also have been preoccupied with your father's health, and some research my Abbot has me doing for him, and… Well."

Gamelyn looked down, away. "I… I should go. I have to venture from Blyth first thing tomorrow and have yet to see to the arrangements; the Abbess has asked for me to be escort for her trip here to my father, and…."

"I see." It sounded… disappointed?

Get in the queue, Gamelyn mused; it was tinged with gloom but also with some anger.

Brother Dolfin's hand rested on his sleeve again, startlingly gentle.

"I think you'd better make the time for confession. To me, here and now."

Gamelyn frowned, looked at Brother Dolfin.

"Better me than the Abbess," the monk insisted and there was a shrewdness to him—calm, but with a knife's keen edge. "Please, Gamelyn. I think we know each other well enough for this trust. Heed me, and let me hear your confession."

ଔ

FOR once, Brother Dolfin's penance had been strangely lacking in strictures, pridewise. Instead, he had focused on other things: the importance of faith, the mercy of Jesus and His humanity, the importance of knowledge to fight the threat of despair and anger.

"Ira—*Anger—is the well-paved road to sin. In the grip of anger, we can do horrible, horrible things. And* Accedia... *it is called Sloth, but in truth it is Despair. To despair and lose all hope?—that is to turn your back on God. Do not assume any knows the totality of God's plan for us. And none of us are beyond God's love and salvation, Gamelyn.* None *of us."*

Confession, and a good night's sleep, and Gamelyn felt like he could draw breath freely in the dim light of false dawn, no longer pinned down by the weight that had threatened to sink him since he had returned to Blyth with too many precarious secrets.

If he was not exactly untainted, he was at least cleansed.

But he would rather be traveling into Eden instead of Worksop.

❧

ROB waited.

And waited.

The first days he had spent engrossed with the river counts, tallying up the numbers in his head. Marion preferred to write such things down, but he had a better memory behind his eyes than skill with nib and paper. The days had been too busy to think overmuch on a missing lover, but the nights were different. Rob had eaten himself sick on fresh fish and wallowed in the furs that still smelt of Gamelyn, altogether miserable.

The fourth day he spent in the cavern, cleaning his saddle, which had gotten wet one too many times in the river—and smelt of fish—and had finally thrown it across the room because the fat he used to oil it had him hard as stone and *wanting*.

The fifth and sixth days were more tallies, cramming more numbers in his head and hoping—unsuccessfully—they would crowd Gamelyn out, and on the evening of the sixth day, Rob realized he had finished his obligation.

He had nothing more to block out the misery, no reason to stay here, plenty of reason to go.

He hadn't heard the Horned Lord's voice in over a se'nnight, but that night Rob *felt* him, crawling under his skin and through his dreams. Nightmares.

It had been pent up too long, all the frustration and fury, all the hurt and longing and possibility of betrayal….

Flirting with death.

Nothing but a game.

Rivalry or rutting, the Horned Lord whispered and ran fingers of flame and smoke through his hair, *I care not which. He is yours and you must take him.*

"How can I if he's not here?" he cried back.

The seventh day dawned, and he totally lost it.

Arawn put up with the noise and the banging coming from the cavern, but when the furs came flying out like enormous hairy bats… well, that was it. He spooked, hauled at his picket until it snapped, and thundered off.

Rob ran after him, throwing every vile curse he knew and, finally, as Arawn's black rump disappeared into the forest, he hurled a dirt clod after him and screamed abuse.

"That's just fine!—fine, then, you lazy sodding brute! Why don't you just leave me too? Why don't you just… just…."

Fury seeped from him, wretchedness took its place, and Rob fled back into his cavern, eyes hot and spilling.

Fell to his knees and sobbed like a child.

Doesn't want you, never did... nowt but a peasant, no more than a slave to bend your back... you're bugger-all to the likes of him. Nothing.

He'd never felt like this, so inadequate and miserable and... *helpless*. Never known such pain since the time those soldiers had yanked his limbs to the four points, ground his face in the dirt and held him down for the lash... never felt like he would die from pain alone since then....

Until now.

Rob wept until his eyes burned, his brain throbbed thick in his skull, and his nose clogged so tight he couldn't breathe save in rasping, openmouthed pants, his thoughts zigzagging from pain to comfort, whispering them as if to fill the sudden, empty silence.

"Sweet *Lady*, Marion, I wish you were here. I miss you. I miss your smile, the way you whack me upside m' head when I'm actin' addled, that clever brain of yours...." Rob curled up in a ball on the chill, hard floor amidst the wreckage of his haven—of his *life*—put his head in his hands, and started to laugh. It was bitter, and ragged, but he had to, because there was surely no crying left in him. "Those last two would be most help right about now, pet, because 'tis sure your brother's thinking with t' smaller brain in his cod-wrap and needs a good swift clout about now...."

A shadow fell over the cave entrance. Rob froze, hand going to his knife... only he didn't have it. It was still sticking in the tree where he'd thrown it.

Slowly, every nerve in his body primed—fight or flight—he raised his smeary, clotted-up eyes to the intruder. There was a knife drawn in one hand and, oddly, the coiled-up, broken picket line in the other, and behind, nosing at a broad, well-clad shoulder stood Arawn, covered with mud and blowing, looking as abashed as Rob himself abruptly felt.

"Um," said Gamelyn, looking around the cavern. Rob abruptly saw it all through startled green eyes: the furs and coverlets lumped and trailing at Gamelyn's feet, the bedding boughs kicked hither and yon, blackened coals scattered out the entry, tack and rucksacks heaved up against one wall with contents spilled and scattered. "Are you... all right?"

Diamant sauntered into view, pinned his ears, and snaked his head at Arawn. Arawn gave a squeal and lashed out with his hind feet.

Suddenly Gamelyn had his hands full of two sparring horses. He sidled just as Diamant's front hoof flashed where he'd been. Arawn decided he'd taken enough from the stallion—this was his pasture, after all—and the fight was on in earnest.

"Bloody sods!" Gamelyn burst out, yanking at reins, and Rob lurched up, launched himself into the fray.

It was rather a relief.

Squeals and grunts, shouts, ivory and ebony hides colliding and hoofs flying. Gamelyn cursed as a hoof smacked him in the thigh. Rob snatched at Arawn's rein, missed. The second time, he snatched it, and between the two of them they pulled and smacked the two horses apart.

Everyone was heaving, staring each at the other, wary and anxious. Gamelyn shook his head and closed his eyes. "They've been acting tossers since I found Arawn—"

"I told you not t' bring the horse, y' poncy git—hoy, Testicles!" Rob suddenly shouted as Diamant puffed up and reared. "He's not a mare to be bred, put your rod back in th' pouch, you flaming daft tunic lifter of a horse—!"

Gamelyn started laughing, then. Hard. And before he knew it, Rob was laughing with him.

"I cannot believe you actually called him a—"

"Aye, that's right daft comin' from *me*, eh?"

"You've got to be—"

"A fine rider makes a fine horse—"

They didn't stop giggling like proper idiots until they'd gotten the horses tethered—across the clearing from each other—and started back to the cavern. It was Gamelyn who sobered first, grabbed Rob by the sleeve.

"Rob?"

Rob looked away, shook his head.

"Rob." This time Gamelyn pulled him close, peering at him. There was so much behind his eyes, suddenly; too many tangled worries and suspicions raking claws against Rob's nerves.

In answer, Rob lurched against him. Kissed Gamelyn until his knees weakened, and then pulled him down on the forest floor where they tangled in some bizarre shadow box of the battle they'd just broken up, with just as much desire but toward the opposite of destruction.

Or… perhaps not.

There was something in Gamelyn that Rob suddenly recognized—the fear, the thrill of adrenaline… the fight… flight… how close to the edge they both were running.

He'd learned how to unbuckle the swordbelt, learned how to tug and unravel the hitch-knot at Gamelyn's thigh, lobbed it aside, and started working on Gamelyn's breeks. "Where were you?" he growled out.

Gamelyn already had Rob's tunic off, was ghosting his mouth down Rob's breastbone. "They wouldn't let me go."

"I waited for you—"

"I tried. I kept trying and—"

"I thought your god had taken you back. I wasn't sure—"

He stilled, hands knotted in Gamelyn's hair, both of them crouched before the other like two wrestlers at a midsummer fairing, and Gamelyn also went still, clutching Rob's tunic where he'd pulled it half down his shoulders.

Finished it.

"Wasn't sure if you'd come back to me."

For fear was not an alternative and struggle was what they were meant to do… or so the Horned Lord said….

Then he saw his own fear, reflected in Gamelyn's eyes.

Then he saw nothing but a blur, because Gamelyn was kissing him again, only it wasn't tender, wasn't sweet or hesitant, but keen. Ruthless.

Hard enough, merciless enough, brutal enough to slay even fear.

Fingers sliding, snarling, mouths seeking, suckling, biting. A roll, a shove—again seeming as much a wrestling match as any lover's tangle—only Gamelyn was not holding back and Rob was getting pinned at every opportunity. A lucky twist gave him the upper hand, and he took it, grabbed Gamelyn's arm and flipped him over. Held him there, shoving Gamelyn's forearm up between his shoulder blades, curled hard against his back and pushed his hips against Gamelyn's buttocks. Gamelyn tried to pull forward, twist around, but Rob wrapped both arms about him, snugged him closer before he could free the one arm, then slid one hand down to curl about his erection and the other up across his chest.

Pushed again. Pumped his hand.

Gamelyn shuddered, his head falling back on Rob's neck.

"So," Rob breathed against his ear. "Is it 'stop'?"—he pushed against Gamelyn's haunches one more time—"Or 'don't stop'?"

A harsh intake of breath and an arch, ever-so-slight, of Gamelyn's back. "No fear," Gamelyn whispered suddenly, Rob's own words back to him. "If you show fear, they'll have you."

"Are you afraid, then?" Rob breathed. Because he was. *He was.*

"Afraid enough," was the hoarse reply, "to let you have me."

Rob held him there, both of them trembling, then let him down.

The first push made Gamelyn tense all the more, knock his head into his hands and clutch at his hair.

"Easy," Rob whispered against his spine. "Easy. I'll go slow—"

"I… it won't—"

In answer Rob pushed again, and Gamelyn cried out, a harsh grunt wobbling into a hiss and a bone-deep shudder as Rob thrust even deeper. Then again.

By the fourth slow thrust, Gamelyn was hoving up beneath him. *Begging.*

Rob worked him, hand and hip and voice. And Gamelyn kept moaning beneath him, sharp breaths into whimpers into growls, and beneath all of it the demand:

More. More…. Harder.

Rob didn't know what had changed… why… but it sung sweet in his ears, this admission—submission—of soul. It was fear, aye. It was relinquishment of fear. It was throbbing ache into searing pain into fierce, rippling of pleasure… dark and relentless and absolutely, unmistakably devastating.

ଔ

"I COULDN'T get away. My brother has been at me and at me. Papa wanted me with him, and I couldn't just…." Another type of confession, just as needful, and almost as raw against his throat. Gamelyn knew his voice was usually soft and unassuming—unthreatening, which was a constant blessing *and* curse—but now it had an edge to it, felt gritty. And no wonder. The sounds that Rob had driven from him, the hoarse cries that had literally echoed into the forest's silence. And every time Gamelyn thought of it….

No fear. Fear vanquished, and not only desire but love was sitting atop the carcass, waving victory with a blood-spattered sword. Gamelyn had looked damnation in the eye, spat in it, and begged it to take him. And the only remorse he felt at this moment was that he had been so foolish about something that had been so… bloody amazing. Not only for himself, but Rob.

"I couldn't just leave him."

"I understand."

He pulled Rob closer, buried his face in damp, black locks. They'd retreated back into the caverns, made hasty repairs to the bedding, and settled in to recover. The rushes hadn't packed quite the same, however, and they would have to find more before night came. For now, Rob was using him as his part of the pallet.

Rob *understood*.

"And then I had to go and escort Abbess Elisabeth to Blyth. That was another day's work." Rob stiffened slightly, and Gamelyn quickly explained, "She's as bad as Johan, watching me like a hawk. I kept trying, but couldn't get free. I didn't know how to let you know what was happening… it was bloody miserable. I'm sorry."

"So how did you get away, then? What with your brother and that abbess watching you."

"Papa said he wanted a report on the tallies you're doing. So Johan sent me to 'find the forester who was doing the earl's tallies, even if he'd already gone to Conisbrough'." Gamelyn smiled, bit at his lower lip. "So. Have I found him, yet?"

"It might take you a while to find this forester." Rob played along, twining his fingers into Gamelyn's then cupping their hands against Gamelyn's chest. "Mayhap the entire night, I'm thinking."

"Mm. Hard work, looking for the man. Vagrant that he is."

"What," Rob said slowly, "does that abbess want with you?"

"Not so much what she wants with me, but that Papa has asked her to find a good place for me. I'm only a third son, after all, and I've no prospects outside the monastery."

"You *want* to be a monk?" Rob still didn't raise his head, but he gave a tiny, almost imperceptible shudder. Gamelyn realized, suddenly, that they'd never spoken of any future. Ever. They'd shared a few dreams, and wishes and wants....

And Gamelyn wasn't so sure what he wanted anymore. Outside of this time and this place.

"The monasteries aren't so horrible. It's not just about being a monk. I can further my education more there than anywhere else. You talk of tales and stories? There are countless stories contained in the books of the monasteries. So much to read, and learn."

"Sounds a place Marion might like." Rob snorted suddenly. "Exceptin' the males-only rule and the no sex."

It was meant in jest, but the reality of it was a blow. "Rob," Gamelyn whispered. "What are we to do?"

"I don't know."

They lay quiet, holding tight for long moments, then Rob propped himself up, peered at Gamelyn. "You talk of being damned. Of damnation," Rob said, ever so soft, and Gamelyn tensed. He'd never been the one to bring it up. Never the one to speak the word save in thrown-aside curses.

"I told Marion once that damnation wasn't what you claimed. I had me own thoughts upon it, but now I know. It's what my heart feels every time I have to watch you walk away and know you might not ever be comin' back."

Gamelyn closed his eyes. "I've one for you. All the while I was at the castle without you, knowing that you were here, so close to me... but you might as well have been in another existence... that was Hell."

"You asked me once what I believed in. I believe in *this*." Rob raised their hands, laced together like an embroidered bodice. "I believe in this." First a kiss to their hands, then a kiss to Gamelyn's pale, freckled shoulder, then one against his cheek. Gamelyn turned his head, tried to catch Rob's mouth with his own, but Rob ducked his head, one side of his mouth tucking and turning up.

"Trickster," Gamelyn said against his ear. "Tease."

"Is a thing worth believing in if you can catch it too easily?" Rob murmured. He nearly slipped from Gamelyn's grasp, instead gave a yip as Gamelyn tangled hard fingers in his black hair and held on.

Then Rob turned to him, kissed him dizzy, then pushed him back and said, hoarsely, "I believe in *you*."

From fear into love. It was enough to be here, be with Rob, think of him and deny Hell... no, *embrace* Hell.

Because if Rob *was* going to Hell, Gamelyn wasn't going to let him go alone.

☙ XXII ❧

"ARE you trying to have yourself shagged so hard that riding might be painful?"

"Mm," Rob said, only this time it was a purr as he wrapped his arms around Gamelyn's neck and licked at Gamelyn's lower lip.

Of course, Gamelyn was already unsure he was going to have the most comfortable ride himself. And if Rob had his way.... "We are expected to arrive no later than today, if you remember."

"An' that 'lord and master' voice waint work on me. You expectin' me to bow? Or beg?" A snort. "I'll make *you* beg, I will."

"And you honestly think I don't know that by now?" Gamelyn decided they could just leave the horses saddled. It was not even afternoon yet. They had time. "You'd better get on with it, then. We really do have to arrive there sometime today—"

Rob abruptly shoved away from him; any protest Gamelyn thought to make died aborning as he saw the wary light in Rob's eyes, and the hand that dropped, instinctive, to his knife. Gamelyn put a hand to his sword, then heard it. Far away, a rhythmic pace that could only be hoofs approaching.

Gamelyn started to speak; Rob put a hand to Gamelyn's lips, head cocking sideways. He frowned, shook his head, held up one finger. Gamelyn reached down, pulled his sword from its sheath as Rob slid silently to Arawn's off side and unlaced his bow from his pack.

They couldn't hide, with horses all saddled and packed.

So they waited, Gamelyn with his sword and Rob with an arrow to string and a few stuck, as he often did, close to hand in a hasty knot of hair at his nape. The unseen horse was advancing unerringly toward their camp; Diamant challenged it.

"Should've tied a bloody stone to his tail," Rob muttered, half drawing his bow.

The other horse answered, and Arawn nickered distinct welcome as the arrival came jogging into the clearing. Rob sucked in a surprised breath, then muttered a curse and relaxed his push on the bow. Gamelyn also recognized the riders: the burly, brown-haired man and the flame-haired young woman seated pillion behind him.

Marion swung her leg over and slid to the ground. She had a smile for Gamelyn and a pat of her hand to his cheek as she passed him and gave Rob a hard hug. Rob was smiling, that lovely wide-open expression that so seldom graced his features, and he swung her about, hugging her tight.

Adam had not yet dismounted. His blue eyes swiftly took in Gamelyn and just as swiftly dismissed him, then strafed the camp, noting the tied and tacked-up horses, the cavern and clearing that showed signs of a lengthy habitation. Then they settled on Rob as he let his sister down and stepped forward, still holding Marion's hand but the smile sliding from his face.

"'Tis good you're nearly ready to travel," Adam said. Gamelyn had forgotten how deep his voice was. "We've come to take you home."

଼

"I'M SURPRISED you didna bring Mam as well. We'll be havin' a fairing here in the Wode anon!" Rob sniped. "Why don't we just set up a few cottages and a forge whilst we're at it?"

"Perhaps," Adam said, "because we're not t' be staying here?"

"Likely you're not," Rob agreed. "But I'm not finished with the job I was given—"

"I gave you the work, son. Now I'm saying you are finished with it."

Marion watched Gamelyn rock, foot to foot, on the edge of the clearing as he watched Rob and Adam face off within the cavern like two angry bulls. Their voices carried, clear enough, and more than once he angled forward, obvious in his wish to say something, anything.

Marion decided she'd better intervene when Gamelyn actually took a few steps forward, and grabbed his sleeve.

"I wouldna, were I you." As he turned to her, puzzlement and alarm both in his features, she gave a tiny shrug and resumed the chore she'd started when Adam and Rob had begun arguing—brushing her father's chestnut gelding. "It's been brewing, this."

"You're here to take him back, too?" It sounded… desolate. Strangely enough, the very fact heartened her.

It meant that boy in the barn, riding away from her brother, had been just as heartbroken. He was here, with Rob. Despite any odds including, it would seem, her father's ire.

Back to back, none can stand against you….

"I'm here for several reasons. Probably the main one is me mam's orders: make sure they don't kill each other. As to takin' Rob anywhere he doesn't want to go?" She shrugged. "Wish me da luck with that one."

Gamelyn watched, shoulders slumping even more as Rob came to a stop in the entrance to the little cave, arms crossed and feet planted. All Rob lacked was a toss of that mane of hair… and he did. Adam wasn't saying a word, glowering first at Rob, then past him to Gamelyn. The glower only increased.

Gamelyn obviously didn't have the same pigheaded arrogance with authority figures that Rob had. He dropped his gaze, turned away. Several times he started to speak to Marion, but hesitated. Finally, he murmured, "Are you against me, too?"

"What do you think?" Marion snapped, then she relented. "I'm not 'against' anyone, Gamelyn. And if I'm 'for' owt, it's that my brother's happy. Is he?"

Gamelyn met her gaze. "I… I think so."

"And you?" He blinked, and she shrugged. "If you're happy, then you can make him happy. If you're not, you're better to ride away and never come back. Because you'll break his heart but good, and then, mark my words, I *will* be against you."

He was silent, still peering at her.

"Gamelyn?"

"I… I *can't*. Just ride away. And I don't want to. When I'm here… this is where I want to be. Not only that, but he *wants* me here, and that's…." He shrugged, gave her a tiny smile. "It's like some dream. I mean, how did we get here? How in the name of Heaven did we all come to this place? But that's the problem too, isn't it? Here isn't… isn't *real*, is it? And the worst? I'm not sure I care anymore."

"Then maybe it's more real than you think," she said softly.

"Maybe," he repeated, very soft. "But the world has a way of crashing in anyway."

He seemed so abruptly miserable that she wanted to hug him, and she did. He was tense for a moment, then softened in her grasp, slung an arm about her, and gave a fierce hug in return.

"And how long ago was it I told you to stay away from my sister?" Rob's voice was a growl, but she heard the tease beneath it. Gamelyn must have also, for he didn't release her as they turned to see Rob striding over to them. Adam was still in the cavern, back to them.

"You're just worried that you might have some competition for this great fair-haired hero," Marion quipped back. "Tell me, how's his longbow?"

Rob gave a sound that was half laugh and nearly all snort, then came the rest of the way and put his arms around both of them.

"Your father…." Gamelyn started to pull away, but Rob held firm.

"I don't care. This is nowt t' do with him. This is mine. My place. You." Moving his hand from Gamelyn's nape to his chin, Rob's fingers rubbed back and forth, a soft caress that made Marion's heart ache gladly to watch. "And while you're here, my lord, you're mine. So have a care."

"I do," Gamelyn murmured, his gaze taking in Marion, then Rob. "Every moment I'm with you."

Rob hesitated, grimaced. "I think you'd best go on without me."

Gamelyn's eyes flickered from mere concern to apprehension.

"Me da's not about to give over easily. And you've been out long enough to have your guard dogs thinking on you. You go, and I'll come before nightfall. Aye?"

There was still a raw apprehension in Gamelyn's eyes, and that told Marion more than any words could.

Rob obviously saw it, too. "I'll come," he said, and leaned forward, gave Gamelyn a kiss. The open affection was obviously just as discomfiting as possible separation; Gamelyn almost backed out of it, but Rob curled fingers about his nape, pulled him, gentled him in. Marion leaned her head on Rob's arm then stepped back, let them have the moment, fleeting as it would have to be.

And when Gamelyn had bridled his horse and stepped up, he was the one who reached down and took Rob's hand.

"No more running, now," Rob said. "I'll come find you."

"You would, wouldn't you?"

"Wherever you go. I ent givin' up easy, if the quarry's worth the catch."

"Am I, then? Worth the catch," Gamelyn added, hoarse.

Rob merely slid sloe eyes to him, quirked a half-smile. "What do you think?" Then, to Marion's surprise, he pulled Gamelyn's long, fine dagger from the back of his belt, touched his lips to the blade, then held it up, hilt first.

Gamelyn watched him, then gave his own small smile. Shook his head. "Keep it for me, 'til next time."

Rob seemed to consider both the words and the dagger, then nodded and replaced it in his belt as Gamelyn turned and rode off.

"No fear," Rob murmured, and there was no little desperation in it. "But I'm always afraid now. Afraid I'll not see him again."

"There's that," she acknowledged, her own bitterness lacing the words. "It's a chancy world. But it won't be by his choice, if it did come to that."

He was still looking after, as if by some means he could still see Gamelyn. Perhaps he could, amidst the tangled, dim-lit recesses of the magic lying deep within him. "D'you think so?" It was still uneasy, and forlorn.

"I do. His heart is often torn, but it is true." She laid her head on his shoulder. "Have you never seen the way he looks at you?"

"Sometimes, I'm afraid to open my eyes." Rob snugged her close, kissed her temple. "Thank you."

"For what?"

"For… looking." He kissed her temple again, took in a deep breath and held it, then let it out in a long sigh. "I'd best go have this out for good. Face the old lion in my den."

*

"HE'LL betray you."

"How do you know? Just tell me that. How do you *know*? You refuse to See owt but what's of your own making, and so it's left you."

"Cernun Saw it, long ago. Sweet Lady, son, do you have any idea of what Gamelyn represents?"

"D'you really think I *dinna* know?" Rob snapped back. "I'm ent that daft or blind. D'you think I've not Seen *tynged* spreading out before me, heard the Horned Lord whispering what I am, what Gamelyn is… what *Marion* is?"

Adam slid his gaze over to Marion, who was leaning against the far wall, studiously avoiding both their gazes.

"I don't underestimate you, son, nor what you hold. But for all your power, you wield it more like an axe than any fine knife. You're powerful, but you're still awkward. And mark me, you must 'ware this much: your season will reap what you sow."

"You keep telling me things I already know, Da—" *Things you should've told me before. Things I needed to* know *before….*

Before it all twined so tightly I couldn't possibly step aside did I want to.

"Rob, you aren't listening."

"I'm listening. I canna help but listen, don't you understand? Have you forgotten that, too? I mean, how long has it been since you've heard Him?"

Adam shook his head. "I've never 'heard' Him."

Rob blinked. Then frowned. "Do you think I'm… lying about it all?"

"I know you're not." It was soft. "I know you canna. Not about this."

"Is that why?" All of it, a cart headed for the edge of a cliff. "Is that why you've turned away?"

"Rob, I haven't done any such—"

"You waint even *look* at me anymore, Da! And when I catch you looking, it's more like you're afraid. Is it because I do See what's happening—not like I have a choice anymore, you've left it to unravel, and if I See more'n you, is it because I can, or because you *waint*? Even Mam canna See my future, so how can *you* come here, try to drag me back, tell me what is right or wrong?"

"What we can See," Adam said, "your ma and me, is the end of all we've worked for, and our children hung amidst of it! We found peace, and now anarchy looms—"

"Maybe it has to!" Rob retorted. "Maybe 'tis time!"

"That's all too obvious, even for my Sight. The Horned Lord rides again, now t' *your* will, and as you will, so will He be. As He wills, so must your *tynged* be spun, and this time He's spinning it with blood, fed with fury and passion… even this!" Adam gestured to the cavern; it took in everything, including Gamelyn's presence still vital and there. "I've not much of Sight about me, I was carrier, not wielder, but Cernun Saw what that nobleman's son was, from the moment he stepped into the forest. He's your *rival*, son, the Summering's lord, your betrayal and danger and death and 'tis no game, here, no mummer's play that Cernun and I have acted out, over 'n' over, mimicry of the Great Dance, this is real! The play has come t' life, the parts cast in this world as well as the others, and you… you lie with it, you flirt with your own destruction!"

"If the Horned Lord wants me," Rob said, "and He wants Gamelyn, then it'll be on our terms."

Adam snorted, shook his head. "If you think to match wits with the Horned Lord, He'll eat you and spit out the bones!"

"How would you know? You've never even seen that aspect of Hi—!" The blow knocked him back several paces, so fast that Rob barely even saw it coming.

"I thought you'd more the stomach for watching *others* knock me about!" Rob spat, and he raised his face in anticipation of the next blow.

"Stop it!" Marion lurched in between them. "No more. Please, no more. It's all been said, and done, and it's done no good, any of it." Her eyes were full of tears.

Adam still had his hand raised, but the will to deliver it had deserted him. He looked at his hand, lowered it, looked down. He seemed… beaten. "I only ever wanted to protect you. Both of you."

Rob backed away, shaking his head. Looked down.

Silence.

"Rob. I want you to come home with me. Your *mother* wants you home."

Still, silence.

"It's not that I've no liking for the lad. It's what he is—"

"You dinna *know*," it burst from Rob, shaking, "what he is."

"Rob, I just—"

"You know what he represents, aye. But you ent knowin' what he *is*. You canna know his… his heart."

A heavy sigh. "I only hope you do, son. Both of you."

This did make Rob look up. Marion had moved from where she'd stood between them, had crept to his shoulder, literally at his back.

"There's more than you know, here," Adam said, desperate. "Even if you take your own way about the lad, you have to hear me on this much."

It was Marion's hand, moving to his arm and gripping there, hard, that made Rob peer first at her then, captious, to his father.

Adam caught his eye, held it. "You think you know, son. But not enough. Remember that. We never know enough, even when we think we do."

"Da—"

"Belt up and listen t' me, for this long and to honor George's memory if nowt else—"

It felt as if someone had punched him. Rob had figured George would be locked up for the rest of his life, but never did he think….

Nay, better then. Better dead than rotting away in some gaol.

"I'm sorry," he whispered, and meant it. No wonder his father seemed so… diminished.

Adam shrugged, a pained and fleeting gesture. "He dint die for nowt. His son is free, and what he gave when they questioned him was what they wanted to hear, not important. But Nottingham is all bent on looking for our people, now. He and the Abbess of Worksop."

Rob gave a jerk and stared at his father, eyes wide.

"Aye," Adam whispered. "none other than the woman who is cousin to your young Oak. You Saw her cross, no' so long ago, shadowing your steps, and oh, son, I fear you Saw it all too true."

"She's here," Rob said, wooden. "At Blyth."

Adam stepped forward, putting a hand on first Marion's, then Rob's arm. "D'you know why?"

Rob shook his head, tried to shake off the sense of sudden alarm. "She comes regular, Gamelyn says, t' hear his da's confession since he's so ill."

"You must take care, son. She will be the ruin of us, if she can find the way. You should come home."

"I will, Da. But not now."

"It's nigh to Beltain. Would you forsake that too, all for a lad?"

Rob shook his head. "And if I promise to be back? For Beltain? I canna just leave him, not now—"

"What else do you possibly think you can do?" Adam protested. "Bring him to the croft t' live? Live here on the edges of everything, amidst this half life you've cobbled together? 'Tisn't *real*, Rob."

"In a world where gods walk and give us th' magic, where babies die of hunger and people are whipped for doing justice, how can any of us say what's real?" Marion said, low.

And none of them knew how to answer.

"So." Adam shrugged. "I came for nowt."

"Nay, Da." Marion went over to him and snaked an arm about his ribcage. "You brought me. I'm supposed to be here. I'll bring 'em home."

His father didn't catch the "them," but Rob did, and he met Marion's eyes, pondering.

ଓଃ

"DID you not hear a word Da said?"

"Marion, don't start wi—"

"I'm starting, and I'll finish it."

Rob rolled his eyes and went back to putting the bridle on Arawn.

Take care, daughter. Your brother's god will send him reckless, hot on the blood-trail. Surely by now you know better than to butt heads so blindly, doe against stag's rack.

How did Rob stand it? Marion wasn't sure she'd ever get used to that little voice, like an itch behind her eyes that she could never scratch. "Look. I know you told Gamelyn you'd come. I know you have to bring the tallies. Just do it in a sensible fashion. With that Abbess bein' there, surely you can just deliver them to th' gate. Surely you don't have to go before the mesne lord himself—!"

"Gamelyn says his da has nowt but good to say of our mam and her potions. And Sir Ian made a firm request to see the forester who made the tallies so he could thank him." Rob reached out, cupped a hand at her nape, and inclined his forehead to rest against hers. "Look. If I don't go, it might be suspicious. And if I do go before him, I'll look innocent as a bairn. I'll be careful. I waint do anything daft—"

"Aye, an' that's likely—"

"I promise, Mari. I'll bend the knee, be all obedient and proper, like, and once I've done th' pretty, I'll snag Gamelyn back here to us."

And the certainty of that last made the roiling of her stomach smooth easier. She'd told Rob what she had Seen at the mere, and it set him all the more determined to find some way to inveigle Gamelyn from the castle for good.

"Just…." She leaned closer, kissed his cheek. "Be *more* than careful, little brother."

ଓଃ

THE castle was as bloody damned huge inside as it was outside. Banners hung along the balustrades, a huge table at the end on a dais; Rob half expected, when he was escorted into the great hall by a pair of mailed soldiers, to find the lord and his family up on that dais like he'd heard kings would do.

And he sure didn't like having those soldiers at his back.

It was a wee bit disappointing to find Sir Ian waiting by the great fire, seated with his feet propped beneath a fur, all casual and comfortable. His family was about him—sort of, anyway, only the one brother, as swart as Gamelyn was fair, stood on the fire side of their father's high-backed chair.

Gamelyn was leaning against the opposite arm of the chair. He was trying to be casual, as well, but Rob saw the slight draw up and tension as the guards escorted him over to Sir Ian.

And Sweet Lady, but Gamelyn was *beautiful*. All tarted up and scrubbed so clean his freckles even shone, and Rob was sure he'd never seen him in blue. Surely the sun had chosen that window to shine through just to gild him all in copper and gold....

And now Rob was sure he was out of his sodding mind. Copper and gold?—gah!

A shadow moved on the far side of the fire. The Abbess came across, holding a cup, which she offered to Sir Ian. Her eyes were intent upon Rob's approach, however. There was a pleasant expression on that face, but those lovely eyes gave the lie, and his own Sight supplied the rest:

I will be the death of you.

He didn't acknowledge it, threat or reply—he had learned that lesson well enough, thank you—and steeled himself to keep his eyes away from her even though he could feel her gaze burning dire upon him. Instead he focused on Gamelyn, let his gaze touch the angle of that jaw and the line of his neck. Thought it was surely a shame they were in this castle, and all, because he wanted nothing more to throw Gamelyn down on the rugs before that great fireplace and shag him until he screamed.

It became more than obvious that Gamelyn felt not only the touch of Rob's gaze but read the drift of his thoughts. He rose from the wide chair arm as Rob came nearer, and there was a softness in his face, a tension in his frame and—aye, bloody lovely!—a distinct tilt to his tunic, was one looking.

Rob had to stop himself from looking. Instead he put his mind to why he was there, approached his mesne lord with a lowered head, and lowered himself to one knee.

"My lord of Blyth," Rob said, soft and respectful. "I am Rob of Loxley, underforester to Barnsdale and the Peak. Your son informed me that you wanted a report of the tallies I have made and delivered to my lord the Earl of Conisbrough. I was bidden bring them to you, and so I have done."

"I remember you, lad." Sir Ian smiled. "For once it is fortuitous my middle son isn't here—he normally takes reports and passes them onto me—but then we would not have had the chance to speak again. My, but you've changed since last I saw you. As much grown into a man as my own youngest, here. How is your mother? Your father?"

"They're well, milord, and me mother asks after you."

"Please give her my thanks, and tell her I am quite well, thanks to her aid. I have had a bit of a downturn," he shrugged, "but no more than expected, in my condition. A se'nnight ago, I was walking the parapets of an evening with my sons. This is my eldest, Johan." Sir Ian gestured to the swart man, who advanced upon Rob, stiffening like a fighting cock and in the doing merely emphasizing how strapping he was. If Gamelyn could likely tie Rob in a knot, this one could tie him in three, no question. "And Gamelyn you already know, and you might remember my cousin, the Holy Abbess of Worksop."

Rob dipped his head to each of them, kept his eyes respectfully downcast—hidden—to the Abbess, in particular.

"Bring some food! This man has news for me; the least we can do is share a meal with him." Sir Ian was proving as oddly likeable as he had before—a mix of hard-headed and genial decorum. The Abbess wasn't best pleased, that was plain. Neither was the elder brother, but then his like didn't take kindly to sitting to sup with peasants, nothing surprising there. "Find our guest a seat, Gamelyn, and pour him some wine."

It was not so easy to keep his eyes to himself when Gamelyn offered him the chair and bent next to him, holding out a pewter goblet full of a wine that smelled of flowers. Or maybe it was Gamelyn. Probably foxglove; it was surely stopping *his* heart.

Rob had really not counted on getting wine. Or on Gamelyn's presence setting his head even more widdershins.

Marion was right. He'd best be more than careful.

❧

"SWEET Christ, but you clean up rather nicely," Gamelyn murmured. "'Tis truly amazing what a comb can do."

They were on their way to the stables. Rob had given his report, charmed Gamelyn's father and several serving lasses—the latter unintentionally, Gamelyn was sure—and even had Johan asking a few questions about the game stocks. The Abbess alone had remained silent—but then, she didn't usually speak during meals anyway.

And it had truly been an act of pure will and strength for Gamelyn not to tackle Rob as he walked—stalked, crept, *glided*!—up to them in the hall and bent his knee, graceful as any dancer. There was none of the scruffy, unkempt vagabond about him today: his hair was indeed combed and tied back, with only a few delicious, unruly strands refusing to stay in place, his tunic was laced up properly instead of its normal—and again by Gamelyn's lights, deliciously—half-masted place of nearer his navel than his collarbones. He was also dressed in suitable layers, overtunic brushed clean and his hood centered for once instead of dragging his tunic sideways. Marion had obviously given him a shave.

He was… gorgeous. Not that he wasn't gorgeous anyway, but….

Gamelyn gave a happy sigh and kept looking.

The black eyes slid sideways, met his. A smirk teased at the full lips. "So. T' have you begging to be had, all I'm needing is to have a shave and wear m' best?"

He trailed off as two serving lasses approached, each with laden baskets. They eyed Rob and Gamelyn up then giggled as they passed.

"Gettin' a bit warm in here." Rob pulled at the lacings to his tunic. "And here I thought you liked me *out* of 'em—"

Gamelyn hissed, "No fair."

"Lack of fairness, my lord," Rob said in his very best noble's accent, "is when you don't get what you want." He was grinning, the *sod*. "Methinks that, should you follow me, we'll *both* get that." He gave a tiny stagger, snorted. "Wup! That wine was more'n I'm used to, no question. Can we leave now, m'lord?"

"Gamelyn?"

They both stopped. Rob gave Gamelyn a wary glance, did not turn around. Gamelyn did, dipping his head to the Abbess where she stood behind them in the corridor.

Gamelyn paused. How long had she been there? And Rob not hearing her?—that was odd.

"If you can part yourself from your… friend," she said, "I'd like a word."

Gamelyn shot a glance to Rob, who still did not look up. "Rob?" he murmured.

"I'll meet you in t' stables," was Rob's terse murmur, and he escaped as the Abbess walked over to them.

And it was unquestionably an escape, Gamelyn realized.

"He seems in a hurry." The Abbess looked after Rob. "One would think he'd something to hide."

It gave Gamelyn a sudden chill. With long-practiced effort, he shrugged it off and raised a poised, cool expression to the Abbess.

"Or," she said, still watching Rob stride off—albeit less gracefully than before, "he's like most villeins and decent wine is overmuch for him. A shame. Were you helping him to his horse, then?"

It seemed an accusation. Gamelyn lifted his chin. "I was merely seeing him to the gate. After all, we've known each other since we were, oh, about ten? Is there something you need?"

"You forgot this." The Abbess held out his eating knife, pommel first. "You should never go anywhere without a good knife."

"I have a…." He trailed off, realizing that Rob had his other knife, the quillion dagger sheathed at his right hip.

It was a very recognizable blade. Not a good mistake to make.

The Abbess gave Gamelyn a steady look, then lowered her gaze, and walked back the way she had come.

ଓଃ

"WHAT took you so long?" Rob was in Arawn's stall, fussing with the saddle. John was there, brushing the black's neck; he exchanged a glance first with Rob, then smiled at Gamelyn and gave him the brush with a dip of his head as he exited the box.

Gamelyn watched curiously as his slender figure seemed to meld soundlessly into the stable gloom and vanish, with barely the tread of bare feet to betray him. "The Abbess wanted a word with me."

Rob seemed in a sudden temper, and his words betrayed it. "I wish you could just stay away from her."

"It might prove difficult." Gamelyn ran the horse brush playfully against Rob's back.

It was shrugged off. "My da was right; that one'd be glad of an excuse to have me clapped in irons. She'd as soon see me whipped as look at me."

"I wish you wouldn't say that." Gamelyn sidled between Rob and his attention to Arawn.

"Gamelyn, if we aren't—"

"Rob." Gamelyn sidled closer. "Let's talk of other things, eh?"

And when Rob started to speak again, Gamelyn shoved him up against the stall boards, bent, and kissed him. He tasted of wine, mulled with spices, and suddenly gave a whimper and kissed Gamelyn back, with a ferocity that curled his toes and set his ears humming.

"Mm," Rob said when they broke the kiss. "That's not talking."

"Says enough, though."

A smirk. "P'rhaps it's the sort of talking you were doing when I was standing before your da. Undressing me with your eyes, you were."

"I couldn't help it. I've never seen you so… polished and proper. My father was very impressed with how you've turned out."

"And it gave you a proper rod in your pouch, then… aye, there it is." Rob's hand was down between his legs, cupping and stroking. "Still hard enough to make the stones weep in jealousy." Rob began nibbling a heated line down his neck.

A rustle and creak made them both freeze. A rusty "mrr-ow" answered their wide-eyed search as one of the barn cats peered down at them from a rafter, moon eyes blinking.

"Perhaps we shouldn't be doing this *here*." His voice scaled up into a whimper as Rob began stroking him again.

"Wine makes a powerful argument," Rob whispered against his ear. "How many times have you told me none comes this way 'cept you. Are y' coming back to the caverns with me?"

"I probably should stay… *God*!"

Rob had slid his hand under the waist cord of Gamelyn's braies.

"Shh." A hand over Gamelyn's mouth. "So you're here to just tease me? Or, are you going to take some convincing? Marion's got pottage waiting. And we've the whole forest to shag ourselves silly in. Or would you just prefer that I bend the knee again, right here and now, before we go anywhere?"

"I would prefer us to be quiet."

"Good luck with that," Rob snorted.

Gamelyn started to protest again, found it dying into dormancy as Rob made no more promises, knelt down, and put those promises into actions.

☙❧

GAMELYN put on a peasant's cap and overtunic he found in the stables and walked out with Rob in full sight of the guards. They rode double on Arawn once they got past the outer gates, made a circuitous route back to the little cavern, and got there just as the sun was beginning to set.

Marion was waiting for them—Gamelyn could smell the pottage she had cooking, and it made him so fumble-fingered that Rob shooed him away from where they were seeing to Arawn.

"Go on, then! You'll rust my brasses, slavering so. Sweet Lady, it's just pottage!"

"Your sister's pottage," Gamelyn swore, "is fit for kings."

Rob snorted, waved him on yet again. Gamelyn didn't wait for a third dismissal.

The fire dried his damp toes, and the pottage—made with the smoke pork left at the altar, plenty of greens, and the roots Marion had found—warmed his belly.

He found, however, that he hadn't considered the full consequences of having a third member to their party when he and Rob crawled beneath the furs and Marion piled in beside them.

"You're…." Gamelyn tried to voice it more than once, finally forced it outward. "You're sleeping *with* us?"

Marion arched an eyebrow upward, and Rob sat up, frowning. "Of course she's sleeping with us."

"But… she's…."

"Aye?" Marion asked, crossing her arms. She was kneeling at the pallet's foot, clad in her thin undertunic.

"Your sister," Gamelyn finished, knowing how stupid it sounded even as it did sound. "I can't sleep with your sister."

"Why not? You sleep with *me*."

"That's different. You and I… well… we…."

Marion looked like she was trying not to laugh. Gamelyn swore—*swore*—that he saw a distinct quirk in her lip.

Rob, on the other hand, was not amused. "Bloody damn, Gamelyn! 'Twill be cool tonight. We've only room for the one pallet. Rutting and sleeping are two different things, y'know."

"I know that, but—"

"Do you still have a thing for my sister, then?"

"*No*!"

"No need t' sound like a ten-year-old girl. She doesn't bite. Not as hard as me, leastways." Rob shared a look with Marion, complete with twisty brows and the beginnings of a smirk, then turned back to Gamelyn. "Have you honestly never shared a bed in your life?"

"Well…." Gamelyn was beginning to feel distinctively defensive, and in more than the one way.

"Sounds bloody cold in winter," Marion put in, actively smirking now.

"Bloody *damn*," Rob said again, "but you nobles have things all t' sixes and sevens."

"I'll sleep on Rob's side, Sir Gamelyn. 'Less you want me to sleep over there by you."

Gamelyn threw a beseeching look at Rob, who cut a glare at Marion.

"You," he said to her, then pointed at the pallet next to him. "Here. And you?" He reached out, pulled Gamelyn down on the opposite side. "Here."

Marion was snickering, now. "Evil wench," Gamelyn heard Rob mutter, but it didn't stop Marion from continuing to snicker as she snuggled down into the crook of Rob's arm. "Never seen such nonsense in all me days."

Then he brushed a kiss along Gamelyn's cheek and settled down between them.

Gamelyn was sure he'd likely not sleep a wink, contemplating what all was in bed with him, but when he woke the next morning, warm and snug, all of them curled together like littermates in a den, it filled his heart with such comfort that he could hardly breathe around it.

ଔଷ

HE DIDN'T leave that next morning. He stayed the next night and through the next, feeling as if he'd come into the fae lands, or Avalon.

Eden.

They spent the days lounging and hunting; they spent the nights counting stars or wishing they could count them and retiring into the cavern with the sounds of rain pattering against the green. They'd sit by the fire and tell stories, or argue—carefully—theology, or do any of the little chores that seemed to need doing, from mending a ripped cape to oiling leathers.

Marion was very good about taking solitary walks—once she realized that her presence rather put Gamelyn off the notion of sexing her brother—and it was only then that Gamelyn remembered the foresters' cottage at Loxley had only the one room. Perhaps privacy was something he'd quite taken for granted.

Rob liked it better out-of-doors, anyway.

And they were making plans. Some of them had Rob wide-eyed, as if watching an archery contest from archer to butt to archer again, back and forth from Gamelyn to Marion as they plotted.

"King Richard is looking for soldiers for the Holy Land," Gamelyn opined. "I've my horse and my blood, a good sword and lance and mail. You could be my squires—"

"I am not spending my days with a bunch of unwashed men," Marion nixed that. "Even dressed as some boy."

"I'm not leaving the Wode," Rob protested. "I canna. I *waint*."

"You could go on to the monastery," Marion countered. "Lots of books, learning and good meals, regular-like."

"No sex," Rob pointed out.

"Depends on the monastery," Gamelyn had to admit. "At least, according to Brother Dolfin. And if I was an… oblate, say?"

"A what?"

"Someone who hasn't taken the vows, but is learning."

"Find a place near the forest, and I'm for it." Rob nodded.

They had options, at least. Perhaps Eden wasn't so impossible after all....

"Come with us to the Fête," Marion said. "Rob and I have to go back, we promised... if you come with us, you'll know, then, what you need to do."

Gamelyn frowned. "Fête?"

"Beltain. Mayday, surely you know that?"

He did. But....

"It's important," Rob said. "It would answer your questions. Every one of my people that can travel, young and old, will be there. It's to celebrate the coming of summer, to make the planting. The Marriage is made, Hunter and Maiden, seed and womb. A child born from that union is doubly blessed, full of t' magic. Marion was conceived on Beltain. So was I."

"Hunter? But you're the Hunter." Another frown.

"Not while me da is alive." Rob leaned over, kissed him. "You and I could make some magic, though. We can take our partners as we please on Mayday in particular."

"So it's a ritual, then," Gamelyn said, hesitant.

"And a blessing no less to us than your mass is for you," was Rob's answer. "Marion's right—if you come with us, you'll *know*."

A Christian nobleman at a Heathen festival... a year ago it would have seemed impossible. But then, a year ago none of them would have even entertained the possibility of leaving Yorkshire.

The third night came, and Gamelyn lay awake.

He had to go back. He had to start things in some sort of motion, see how his father was, settle some things.

Otherwise, they would be hiding forever.

ENTR'ACTE

"MY BROTHER. With *that*."

"I realize it is difficult to fathom, my lord—"

"Difficult to… fathom?" Johan growled, very slow. "And you… saw him with this peasant. With this peasant… *lad*."

"I watched them in the great hall, as I told you. Their language was… too intimate for mere friends. So I followed them to the stable. I wasn't quite expecting to see as much as I did… they were disgustingly brazen." She grimaced. "I blame the peasant. They have the morals of minks. But there was no doubt what they were doing. After, I followed them to the gatehouse and watched them ride off into the forest together."

"It's enough to make a man want to—"

A knock sounded at the door to the spacious chamber.

"Come!" Johan said, and his voice was not steady.

One of his guard captains came in, bowed first to him, then the Abbess. "My lord. Reverend Lady."

"Well?" Johan demanded.

"I looked myself, my lord. There is no one in your brother's chambers. None of my men have seen him."

Johan peered at the Abbess, his expression growing darker. "Look for him."

"My lord?"

"Look for my brother, man! Search the castle! I want him found if he is here, and if he is not…." He trailed off and lurched to his feet, stalked over to the window.

The captain waited.

"Be discreet," Johan said without turning around. "I do not want my father disturbed with this. Not yet."

"Aye, my lord." The guard bowed out.

"I think your caution is very wise, Cousin Johan."

Johan whirled on the Abbess, a look of such choler on his face that she feared she had been unwise. Visibly, however, he took hold of himself. "What do you mean?"

"I do not tell you these things just to put you or young Gamelyn into an awkward position—"

"He's damned well put himself there! I will see him punished for this. But I must have more proof before I go to our father."

"There is more at stake here, Cousin." Elisabeth called upon every bit of her skills at negotiation. They were considerable, she knew, more than a match for this oaf with a temper—if she could get past the temper, that was. "For one thing, your father's love for the boy."

His eyes gleamed, and she knew she had him.

"Listen." She strode forward, settled her hands into her sleeves. "You need proof; I surely have it. Enough things are tied together. I believe this all started with the murder of my guardsman—perpetrated, as you recall, by one of these foresters from Loxley Chase."

Johan crossed his arms, leaned his hip against the table. "Go on."

"I have been trying to uncover the particulars of this for some time. The sheriff of Nottingham has become a staunch ally in this quest, but we have been groping in the dark for proof, for answers."

"And what of your brother?" Johan asked. "His jurisdiction over Yorkshire—"

"Loxley village is part of Nottinghamshire at present."

Johan frowned, went over to his table, and leaned against the chair behind it. "I fail to imagine how my brother's disgusting… choice of a…." He seemed to remember he was speaking to a nun, fell silent as he amended his words.

The Abbess didn't wait. "Gamelyn's unfortunate… infatuation… is but the latest maneuver in a sinister plot. And perhaps, if we take care, Gamelyn can be the method by which we finally drag it into the light and see it destroyed for good.

"I don't think Gamelyn had a choice. I think he was enchanted by this peasant boy. And I think your father's very soul is in danger from the mother of this boy and her witchcraft."

☙ XXIII ❧

IF GAMELYN was going to stage any siege against Blyth, the dusky murk of predawn would be the time to do it. The guards were changing, the gates open in preparation for the normal traffic of the day, and the stables all but deserted. Even the stable lad, John, was snoring and curled up in his cot by the narrow back stair.

Of course, they'd enjoyed no revolts or uprisings since they'd been here, so perhaps the laxity was understandable.

It certainly worked for him. He'd been longer in the forest than he should have, but it had been so hard to leave. Gamelyn crept up to the family wing, worked the door to his chamber open, and closed it behind him.

He halted, frowning in the dark. His chamber felt… odd. Even more strange, the curtain was drawn across his window. Perhaps some servant had been overzealous in their tidying up. There was movement there; Gamelyn tensed until he realized it was merely the wind lifting the heavy fabric.

By feel Gamelyn went to the table to the left of the door, found the flints, the chaff bowl, and the fat candle he always had there. His eyes were growing accustomed to the tomblike dark, and by the time he'd rasped the flint across his dagger several times, his aim had improved. First the chaff, then Gamelyn used it to set alight several candles, spilling their cheer into the room. He nodded and turned….

Halted.

Johan was there, sitting on Gamelyn's bed, arms crossed over his broad chest and feet propped almost negligently on the press beside it. At the bed's foot were standing two of their largest guardsmen.

"Well, *gadelyng.* It's about time you've returned," Johan said, then jerked his head to the two guardsmen. "Take him."

Gamelyn was so stunned he didn't so much as try to evade them, and their grip made it impossible for him to shake them off.

He certainly tried.

"Oh, my," Johan tsked, walking over to him. "Have you heard nothing of what I've taught you? Never go down without a fight." He turned away slightly, then, without warning, kicked out.

His boot hit the outside of Gamelyn's thigh, knocked Gamelyn's feet out from beneath him, and sent splinters of agony up into his hip. Gamelyn hit the ground hard—the guards released him a-purpose, or so it seemed—but mere seconds after he'd sprawled on the stones, clutching at his thigh, the guards grabbed him again, hauled him up.

"Johan, what are you *doing*?" Gamelyn snarled.

"Just a reminder before we go, *gadelyng*... ah-ah." The warning came as Gamelyn lurched forward at the insult; an upraised finger and a nod to the guardsmen resulted in them clutching so brutally tight to Gamelyn's arms that he nearly went down again. "I know where you've been, brother. I know what you've been doing and, more, who you've been doing it to."

Muscles preparing for battle quivered, betraying him. Gamelyn stared at Johan, his heart and lungs vying for position in the back of his throat.

"Thank your stars our father and the Abbess are both concerned for you. I myself am not so willing to spend my cares on someone so intent on spoiling himself with filth."

"H... how?" was all Gamelyn could stammer.

"You can ask them yourself," was Johan's cryptic answer, then he jerked his head at the guards. "Take him to my father's solar."

And if Gamelyn had any fight left, that order robbed him of it.

☙❧

SIR IAN was there, sitting up. He seemed... diminished, somehow, and the enormous chair merely made it worse. Surely only a few days ago he had been better, chatting with Rob. Not as well as he'd been the previous se'nnight, surely, walking the balustrade with Gamelyn, still slow, still ill, certainly—but *lively*.

The voice rose, sudden and deep from memory. *What will you give me, princeling? What will you sacrifice?*

Not this, Gamelyn argued, silent. *I never agreed to* this. *You cannot.*

"What do you mean, marching him in here like some villein?" Sir Ian ordered the two guardsmen, who still had heavy hands upon Gamelyn's arms. "Release your lord, *immediately*."

They did so, backing slightly, looking at Johan uneasily.

"But it is as you were told, Papa," Johan countered. "He arrived mere moments ago, back from sneaking out to the forest to dally with that *merdaille* forester's brat!"

To hear Rob so casually called "scum" made Gamelyn whirl, clench his fists to wipe the sneer from Johan's face. The two guardsmen tensed, made as if to move forward.

"That's enough, Johan!" Sir Ian said, then gestured to the guardsmen. "Get out, both of you."

"Papa—" Johan started to protest, and the two hesitated, peering at Johan.

"This is still my solar and my manor!" Sir Ian flung a hand at the guardsmen. "*Do as I say*!"

This time he was quickly obeyed.

"This is a family matter, Johan," Sir Ian growled as the door shut. "I told you to ensure he came to my solar once he returned, not to bring him like…." Sir Ian took in a sharp breath, closed his eyes, and seemed to wilt in the chair.

"Papa?" Gamelyn whispered, stepped forward.

"Not one more step, *lapin*," Johan hissed, grabbing his arm. "Have you not done enough?"

"Where is Otho?" Sir Ian asked.

"He and Alais have not returned from York, Papa," Johan answered. "They will likely be back tomorrow."

Gamelyn frowned. Surely his father would remember such a thing, now that he was taking the medicine. "Papa, have you not had your dose—?"

"Gamelyn." Johan's hand bit into his arm. "*Shut up*."

"Gamelyn," Sir Ian said, heavy and slow. Disappointed. "Where have you been, son?"

"You know where he's been!" Johan protested. "Surely the matter is—"

"Be silent, Johan," Sir Ian said. "If you do not, you will leave. *Comprenez-vous?*"

Johan flushed darker, and he scowled at Gamelyn before looking down.

"Tell me, Gamelyn," Sir Ian persisted, still slow. "Where have you been? I know you and your brother are not as close as I would have you. I could scarce believe this when he came to me with it—"

"What has he told you?" None of this made any sense. Johan never paid that much attention to him. Perhaps he'd not been as careful as he could have been, but he'd never even imagined….

"Gamelyn." His father shook his head. "Don't play games with me—"

"I'm not playing at anything!" Gamelyn protested, panic starting to crawl along his nerve endings. "Johan would do anything to turn you against me, he—"

"You lying little—!"

"Johan," Sir Ian said, level, then turned that level look upon Gamelyn. "He is your brother, lad."

"And he hates me!" Gamelyn protested. "You *know* he hates me—"

"Gamelyn, that is not what—"

"If he's accusing me of something, I want to hear it from his own lips!"

"I'm accusing you of nothing, I'm merely corroborating what Abbess Elisabeth told me—"

Johan's retort snuck behind Gamelyn's defenses like a poisoned dagger; somehow, he managed not to actively flinch. "And what has she told you?"

"Something I can scarce believe you have done," Sir Ian admitted, and this time Gamelyn did flinch as he continued. "I never imagined you, of all my boys to sink to something like this."

"Please. It isn't what you think," and he trailed off as, this time, Sir Ian was the one to flinch.

"Listen to him, my lord. I truly don't believe he's in his right mind." This soft protest came from the shadows behind Sir Ian, and black draperies whispered as the Abbess came forward. She seemed to materialize from thin air, and Gamelyn wondered how it was he hadn't seen her until this moment.

And realized that he hadn't paid attention for far too long.

You know they canna find out about us. Rob had said it, and now it seemed that they had, and Gamelyn felt as if everything he had ever held dear lay before him on an altar with the knife poised above its heart. The clues had been there, all along: Sister Deirdre, watching Eluned with wary eyes—and Elisabeth herself, making soft threats against the possibility of witchcraft. Brother Dolfin, warning him—obliquely, but nonetheless a warning—*"You must take care"*—and later, a caution not to attempt to face Worksop's abbess without the clean heart of confession shielding him like mail and leather. And the Abbess herself, curious about the charm that still lay about his neck.

Even now, as the Abbess glided over to him, Gamelyn could feel her eyes riveting to the small amulet beneath his tunic. It was… warm, somehow, as if warning him. Johan's scowl had become uneasy, and even Sir Ian was eyeing Gamelyn with some caution, as if he more trusted the Abbess's words than his own son's. And why not? His son had done nothing these past se'nnights but lie to him.

And his father's words, leaden with worry. "I fear you're correct, niece. He has been acting so… wayward and strange of late."

Elisabeth's dark eyes pinned Gamelyn in place, yet not so much that he didn't retreat as she raised her hand to him.

"Gamelyn!" Sir Ian said, shocked.

"There's no need for fear, lad." Her voice was quiet, altogether reasonable as she put her hand on his shoulder, held him still. "Your brother's methods leave a bit to be desired, but I warned you of that, did I not?"

"What have you done?" he whispered.

"Only what I had to do to help you." Elisabeth murmured back, then raised her voice, directed it to Sir Ian. "It is as I told you. It's all been a lie, and your son an unwilling pawn in an evil game."

Pawn… game… *evil*? "What has she told you?" Gamelyn peered at her, disbelieving, before his gaze fled to meet his father's.

Sir Ian looked… beaten. "She saw you, Gamelyn. Saw you leave with the forester's son. Two days, you were gone."

Gamelyn realized his teeth were chattering, small and silent; he was literally chilled with dread.

"That... *peasant*... he came here and seduced you on my very step!"

"Papa, it wasn't—"

"And I let these people into my home! Took their poison!" Sir Ian passed a hand over his face, shaking his head.

"No." Gamelyn lurched forward; first the Abbess's hand gripped, then Johan's, halting him. "Please. She only meant to help you. Please tell me you won't stop taking the medicines Eluned brought you—"

"Do not speak that woman's name in this house!" Sir Ian thundered. "Help me? While she helps herself to everything I hold dear? She flattered all of us—even Johan says she flirted with him. My niece even warned me that the woman might be after you, my youngest… I scoffed. I *scoffed*, and look what my trust has gained me. That woman sets her brat on you, sets a spell about you… he was here only two days ago, setting his spell about all of us—"

"No. You don't understand," Gamelyn said, shaking his head. "It wasn't *like* that. It—"

"None of us here wants to know what it was like, *lapin*," Johan growled, and loosed Gamelyn like he was diseased. "You are either mad or our cousin is right: you *are* bewitched."

Bewitched. A deeper chill fetched itself through Gamelyn. Sodomy was enough to condemn him… but witchcraft would condemn everyone else.

"Rob didn't bewitch me. That much I swear to you. I was… weak, that I will confess, but there was no witchcraft. He is a good person, Papa, I would swear to it—"

"Good? How can seducing a chaste, God-fearing lad into vile acts be considered 'good'? How can you just *stand* there and say such things!" Sir Ian paled, leaned back in his chair.

You did this. Gamelyn could feel Johan's glare strafing him. *You brought him to this.*

Worse, he couldn't disagree. He had, hadn't he?

The Abbess's hand, still upon his shoulder, slid down to his nape. Before he could stop it, she had threaded her fingers through the leather thong about his neck, and pulled the stag amulet from beneath his tunic.

"This, Sir Ian. This is part of the answer." She clutched it, pulled Gamelyn by it, closer to his father. "I told you I'd seen this about his neck on our journey back from Worksop."

"It is nothing!" Gamelyn protested. "It was a gift, nothing more."

"A gift from whom?" Sir Ian had gone even paler, staring at the thing.

"Sister Deirdre knows of such things," the Abbess answered, and turned to Gamelyn. "Do you even know what it is, lad?"

Gamelyn shook his head, said again, “It is nothing.”

Her grip tightened, and he found himself propping back, the leather biting into his neck, sending the chill into further ice. “Hardly nothing. It is called a ‘charm of making’. Its purpose is to set someone’s will to something. To make something happen.”

“I… don’t think so.” Only Gamelyn knew. He *knew*….

He said it would help me find you.

And have you, then? Found me?

“To make you fall in love, perhaps?” She leaned closer; Gamelyn found himself propping back harder.

“Did that pagan give it to you?” Sir Ian demanded.

“Papa, no!” At least it was the truth. “Rob has never—”

The Abbess gave a swift jerk of the cord; it bit into Gamelyn’s neck then gave, making him stagger. “The lad has enchanted you!” she hissed, holding the charm before his face. “With this. He is a witch, from a family of witches. They are from one of the most powerful covens in six shires!”

She flung the necklet onto the stones, then stepped on it, crushing it.

“If that peasant shows his face here again, I want him arrested!” Sir Ian ordered. “Or better yet, shot.”

“*Papa*!” Gamelyn lurched forward, fell to his knees beside the chair. “No. I beg you. You don’t understand.”

Sir Ian reached out, touched his face. “Oh, son. You’re the one who doesn’t understand.” It was so reasonable, so gentle that Gamelyn found himself doubting his own senses. The hand shook, and Gamelyn raised a hand, cupped it against his cheek.

Just as abruptly, it turned hard. “You will go to your chambers, Gamelyn. Now.”

Gamelyn blinked, looked up. Sir Ian’s eyes were as hard as the hand within his own.

“And as I cannot trust you, Johan will make sure you do, and lock you in.”

“Papa, please. Listen to me. Don’t—”

“There will be guards posted, Gamelyn, and the servants will see to your needs. You will stay there until I decide what must be done.”

❧

THE bed was cold when Marion woke, and Rob was gone.

Perhaps he’d gone hunting. But Arawn was missing—though his saddle and bridle were still upended in their corner. It was still dark, but there were signs, small and perceptible, that dawn approached. Perhaps he'd taken Arawn to graze early. Perhaps….

Well, there was no telling, with Rob.

So Marion busied herself. She tidied their bed, built the fire back up from banked coals. She got water from the stream beyond the hillock, hung it to warm but not boil dry. When she ran out of things to do, she went to find him.

Dawn had finally begun fingering the trees. Rob's passing was fresh in the morning damp, easy to follow. Marion saw him as the trees thinned before her, became the pasture overlooking Blyth. The sun was breaking through clouds here and there, rays of gold across green. Just to one side of the flower-strewn altar, Rob was perched on a small promontory of rock and, sure enough, Arawn was picketed nearby, greedily tearing at the damp grass.

She walked down the hill, enjoying the sight as much as he obviously was. The Wode was beautiful, but there wasn't this type of vista to be had in its depths. "When do they usually come to the altar?"

"After morning chores. It's early yet, but we'll need to keep a watch. I try to not be visible. Makes 'em nervous." He was holding Gamelyn's quillion dagger in his hands, playing the new sunlight up and down the blade.

Marion clambered up on the rock next to him. "Canna sleep?"

"Nay. 'M all prickles and nightmares. It's silly, this. I know he's well able to take care of himself."

"He is a fine strong lad, no question there," Marion agreed, wry, then reached out and touched the dagger's hilt. "He'll be back for it. He promised."

"I know. It's daft of me to worry. To… miss him."

"I miss him, too." She leaned her head on his shoulder, and he wrapped that arm about her shoulders. "I'm afraid he has *you* whipped all south at bed-warming, little brother. I think Gamelyn could out-heat a damp pile of compost."

Rob chuckled. "Tell him that, then. I want to see his face." He reached out, tugged at her hair. "Nay, this is why it's so warm. Between the two of you, there's freckles, red hair, and temper enough to heat the whole bloody cavern."

"Aye, you're outnumbered, no question. Best watch yourself."

They fell silent, watching Arawn graze.

"Something… doesn't feel right," Rob finally said. "Like I'm backing an ill-tempered horse. Lady and Horned Lord, both with us, but I canna help thinking the god in particular is bound and determined to throw some storms at us."

"'Tis what He does. You might as well as cry at the rain for fallin'. It's all about the testing, the survival."

"Tell me again, what She said t' you."

Marion had no protest to that; the words were a comfort. "To forge the links and hold to 'em. That as long as the three of us are back to back, 'tis sure nowt can touch us."

"And here we are. Separated. I shouldna have let him go."

"What else was there to do?" Marion sighed. "What side d'you suppose Gamelyn's god is on?"

"Gamelyn's god wants him back. That one doesn't know how to share."

"Not what his people think his god is, what he *is*," Marion specified.

"Is there a difference?" Rob asked. "Really? In what we think they are and what they are? The Horned Lord told me…." He shuddered, couldn't help it, even the memory of that power could send him to shivers. "Told me He'd not roamed the woods with such a form in ages. That I'd set Him free. *Me*."

"Then perhaps Gamelyn needs to free his god." Marion's voice was stout.

Robin snorted, shook his head. "Bloody damn, but I miss Will. Things were so… uncomplicated with him." He grimaced in apology, inclined his head against hers. "For me, anyway."

"Well, they were fairly straightforward with me, also." Marion shrugged, tucked her arm in closer to his. "And still are. This waint last forever."

"Neither will we," Rob said. "If we wait too long, then surely it'll pass us by. Look at what's happening even now."

She tucked in closer, closed her eyes tight. It was true. True, and even though the Lady had filled her with hope, Her name was also Sorrow.

"Surely there's a world where we can be together," Rob murmured. "You and Will, me and Gamelyn… all of us."

"Does such a place even exist?"

"Aye, it does. It's around us," he continued, slow, and as his eyes lifted, took in the Wode, there was a gleam that warmed Marion, even more than Gamelyn's body heat. "It takes us in, cares for us. It's all around us, Mari, and hardly a one bothers to see it. "But *I* see it, and I canna look away."

Silence, again, only this time it was less than comfortable.

"Something's happening, Mari. I can feel it."

Marion stole an arm about his ribs; she could feel his heart against her forearm, hammering quick as a bird trammeled to ground. His breath was shallow, coming in tiny pants. He had always felt things before Seeing them, always been more prey to his instincts and senses; it had not dulled with age and time, merely sharpened.

She was glad it wasn't so with her. "Shh," she coaxed. "What'll happen will happen, if we but wait for it."

"Sometimes," he said, "the waiting is *not* good."

ꟹ

HE WAS barely aware of the waiting. Barely aware of anything but the press of stone and the half arch of sky and green just beyond.

The moon had risen, was sinking into the west. Gamelyn watched it, desolate and dry-eyed, felt the light of it spill over him, cold and pure. He was curled up on the wide stones of his narrow window ledge, legs folded and propped against the opposite side from where he sat, arms wrapped close. His eyes and mind roamed where his body could not: up into the cloud-wreathed stars, across the fields, into the trees, every thought and feeling he possessed fanning outward, a mixed swath of terror and longing.

What he hoped for, he had no idea. The moon's light traced pewter ghosts across the black trees. The bailey below was quiet, not even a fire's crackle to break the stillness. The guards stood idle on the gatehouse and walls. There was something in him, tiny and forlorn, hoping for an answer to a question he could not bring himself to ask, yet there was nothing. No curl of breath, no deep, enervating heat-stoke of flame-tinged voice. No feelings of belonging, of completion… of escape. Even the forest spirits had deserted him.

It was all he was worthy of, surely.

"I'm sorry, Papa," Gamelyn whispered. "I never meant to hurt you. I never meant it to happen like this. If only"—he hesitated, kept going—"if only you knew him. If only you could... understand *why*."

He could see them both when he closed his eyes. Rob and Marion would have eaten by now and piled into the furs, back to back like comrades-in-arms.

He hoped they slept.

He had to get word to them. Somehow.

He had to convince them to stay away until this was all over.

He could only hope… pray… that it *would* be over.

Oh, God. He laid his head back against the stone, mute. If only he could pray. If only he could find answers.

There is no sin that He does not know…. To despair is to turn your back on God….

"Which one?" he half laughed, half choked, and knew, then, that he was truly damned no matter which way he turned.

Why had he expected anything different? He had come into this world through the death of his mother; why should it be surprising that ill fortune should dog his steps, that the demon upon his left shoulder should have a more powerful whisper than the angel upon his right? Even the dreams he'd had, portents of destruction and pain more powerful than any Eden could seek to conquer. Too sullied for a fae son of the Shire Wode. Certainly, by now, too sullied for the God's son of his own kind.

Eden, out of reach. He had been rived from it by force, thrown and tied down upon the stones of his own place, his own people. They loved him, they wanted to save him from himself; his father was dying while he himself had only just learned to live. He revered and feared them as he revered and feared the treacherous shoal of his own new-wakened self. They meant him no harm, only good, only what was true and honorable and Godly.

He had eaten of the tree of knowledge and found sustenance only fit for the son of God, had drunk in the forbidden enchantment of the garden, had found a love that seared his soul and filled his heart and *could... not... be.* He had committed sin after sin, mortal and venial and everything in between; he had not been shriven from any of those. He deserved nothing more than this chamber and whatever privations his lord saw fit to cleanse him, and….

And all he could think upon was how to *get back.*

ଓଃ

TWO more mornings dawned, and still no sign of Gamelyn.

On the third morning, Rob came back from the hillside altar with a strange hesitation to his gait. His face was ashen, and he held one arm against his chest. He seemed dazed.

"Rob?" Marion knew her voice was somewhat shrill. She didn't care.

He waited until he gained her side, held out his hand. Dangling from his fingers was the leather cord of a making-charm… or it had been. The charm was unrecognizable, bits of clay crumbled against the crushed wooden core.

Marion cradled it in her hands. Even destroyed, it had tiny, lost vibrations of magic wisping about it. Instinctively, she reached for them with her own talent, untangled them as she untangled the lanyard from Rob's trembling fingers, grounded and set them free….

Recognized them. She raised her face, met Rob's white-rimmed ebon eyes, and understood. "Gamelyn."

Rob nodded, slowly. "One of John's house-bound friends found it when they were sweeping out Sir Ian's solar. She knew it as John's work, brought it to him."

"John?"

"He's the one made it. He's a stable lad."

This John held the *tynged* for such making after a more powerful fashion than any Marion had seen, including their father. Rob nodded, as if discerning her thought.

"John said he was told Gamelyn's locked in his chambers. Talk is he was found wandering. The nobles are talking sorcery."

"Oh, Rob…."

"He said he'd help."

"Who? John?"

Rob nodded. His face was just as leached of color as before, only now it was grim, set. His eyes were blazing.

She knew that look. "Nay, Hob-Robyn. You'll never get into the castle… and if you do," she said, overriding what comment he was going to make, "you'll never get Gamelyn out."

"So I just leave him there?"

"Rob." She had to go carefully with this; he wasn't going to take it well no matter how she phrased it. "It's his *family*, Rob. He's part of them—"

"His brother doesn't need any excuse to knock shit out of him—"

"I understand… believe me, I do. But he's no stroppy peasant in danger of being whipped." She raised her hand to his back, traced the scars there. "He's not some villein who'll have his hand lopped off for poaching where he's no rights."

"Their kind *burns* witches, Marion!"

"They waint turn on their own—"

"You think? D'you really think the nobles waint rend their own young, that they just save it up for us and never use it otherwise?"

"Oh, Rob." She kept tracing her hand along his back—this was going to be even harder to say. "Are you more afraid they'll punish him for going against their ways, or that he'll decide they're *right*?"

And Rob… crumpled. Head down, eyes dimming, just curled in on himself until Marion wished she'd kept her tongue behind her teeth, possibility or no.

"You don't understand," he said, miserable.

"I *do*—"

"You've not heard all the things he's said to me, all the ways he's cut little pieces from himself. Every time we lie together, even… he feels he doesn't deserve any of it. Like it's wrong. Like he canna have an honest feeling in his soul without some price exacted—"

"Nothing's free, little brother—"

"But not like this! It's twisted all wrong. They've raised our Summerlord in a *cage*, Marion, feeding him rotten meat and moldy bread like they've the right… and now they've bunged him up again, set to poison him anew!"

"Rob, what's in Gamelyn's heart is a lovely thing; his faith is part of what we love about him."

"His faith. What's in his heart, not what they'd twist his heart into." Rob shook his head, paced over to the cavern, and shrugged into his overtunic, his fingers lingering on the nubs and dips of coarse-woven wool. "He was sleeping. I woke him. And now I'm just to let them sing him back to sleep, and him screaming while they do it? Not bloody likely."

Marion followed him. "You canna go off half-cocked to that castle. If they know what Gamelyn has been up to, then they likely know with who! They'll *kill* you!"

Rob smiled, fleeting and dangerous. "They'll have to catch me first, aye?"

ଔ

GAMELYN knew he *was* waiting—for what, he wasn't sure—but when the knowledge paused before him, would inform him, it almost immediately whirled past and out of reach. Time was passing him up, things happening around him of which he had little to no grasp.

He hadn't been paying attention, and the lack was swamping him now. His thoughts, usually so pristine and orderly, were chaotic, unbiddable. Had been since he had scanned every inch of his chambers and realized that he was thoroughly and completely buggered. If someone set a fire alight at his door there was only one way out—straight down, out the window, four stories down to the stone cobbles. He didn't even have a rope.

It was then he started to stalk the floor akin to a caged beast.

The sun was beginning to set as the bolts were thrown and the door creaked open. Gamelyn stopped pacing as the Abbess entered, her acolyte, as ever, behind her. This time the novice bore food on a tray.

"The servants say they bring you food, yet you do not eat," the Abbess said, softly. "Your father is worried. You need to eat, and keep up your strength."

Gamelyn wasn't hungry. His every nerve was twitching, rasped raw akin to a blade being whetted with a too coarse stone. Everything seemed… slow. As if he had been kicked slightly askew of time's normal flow. It made him alternately feverish-frantic and leaden-sick. In fact, the sight of the relatively simple fare on the tray made him as queasy as contemplating the rich sight of a full banquet.

Instead Gamelyn forced himself back within the happenstance of *now*. "How is he?"

"He is not well, Gamelyn. I am sorry. I counseled your brother to be cautious in this matter, that it was unwise to disturb your father so, but he was determined—"

"As were you," Gamelyn retorted, just as softly. "Neither of you were thinking of anyone but your own designs. With Johan, it was shaming me. With you?" He considered her. "What do you want, Reverend Lady? What can you possibly gain from all this?"

She peered at him for a moment, compassion gone cold. "It was not I who dishonored my father and my family by bellying a peasant boy."

And so, she was not as untouchable as he'd imagined. It was strangely comforting. "I thought," Gamelyn replied, "that I was under a spell."

"There was weakness in you, else you would not have fallen prey to such a spell."

The statement scraped too close to his own insecurities to be lightly heard; Gamelyn gritted his teeth and looked aside.

Toward the window.

He closed his eyes.

"I am disappointed in you, lad. There was a… light about you. A faith, a strength. A purity that any of us would long to have nestled in our souls. And you… you merely cast it aside! Treated it as cheap and unholy as the sins you sunk yourself into. Tell me again, Gamelyn Boundys, that *I* was the one thinking only of my own designs."

Again, the words didn't just pink, they scored blooded furrows. This time Gamelyn looked down at his hands. "Will my father recover?"

"He has refused to have the leech attend him. I will not lie to you, Gamelyn, it does not bode well."

"I want to see him."

"And you shall. After you make your confession." She seemed nonplussed as he backed a step. "That is why I'm here, lad. At your father's request. He wants to know you have had confessional and taken Holy Communion. He wants this purged from you. Only then will he consider seeing you."

It was as though Gamelyn was breaking into tens of tiny, friable pieces. "I have a confessor. Brother Dolfin."

"And he has done such an exemplary job so far." The sneer was slight, but all the more cutting for it.

"I will make my confession, as my lord father requests. But *I* have the right to request my own confessor."

"That you do." The Abbess seemed unperturbed. "But your father has requested this of me, Gamelyn. Are you so lost in the spell of this creature?"

Creature. It jabbed Gamelyn in every soft place he possessed. "If I was as bewitched as you say, then surely God will understand." He could scarce believe the words were coming from his mouth even as they escaped.

"*Gamelyn.*" It was stern. She walked over to him, and there was something in her demeanor that suggested caution.

Of course. He was not any mere sodomite, but an enchanted one. And the odd thing? Only over a fortnight ago, he might have agreed with her.

"It is plain you are not yourself. The lad I have come to know, he never would have even had the desire to dishonor his father's wishes."

But then, you don't know me. At this moment, I *don't know me….*

"Do you really intend that I should leave this room, go to your ill father and tell him his most-beloved son has not only lied to him and committed sodomy, but refused confessional of it?"

He gritted his teeth and looked out the window, felt tears inexplicably burn behind his eyes. "No," he whispered.

"Gamelyn, it's all right. It will be *all right.*" A hand laid on his head, a grave, compassionate weight.

Nay, it won't. Can't you understand? Things will never be all right again.

"It wasn't your fault. I'm sure it wasn't, and Sir Ian will come to an understanding with that. I know that you never would have done such a thing on your own."

Remorse swamped him, took his footing from him and battered him with doubts.

You deserved this. You asked for it. You knew it was wrong... not only wrong but evil... *and you dove in headfirst into one sin after another. He's a pagan. He doesn't know any better, but you do. You. Do.*

"But I would suggest that, being a disobedient and wayward son as of late, you do your father's bidding in this." The black-veiled head tilted. "It is, after all, most possible that Brother Dolfin will not be here much longer."

"You cannot!"

"I?" the Abbess shrugged. "It is not I who am responsible for any of this. *Your* actions are what have brought many things to heel." She leaned just that much too close. "How many more lives must be set askew by your weakness, Gamelyn?"

Had she been a wily poacher, she could not have garroted him with a more skillful hand. He literally had no words, just stood there, quivering and staring at her and feeling the bottom drop out from beneath him....

"We will bring you back." Her whisper wafted across his cheeks, a faint scent of almonds. "You have wandered far, but not so far that you cannot repent. We will glean the poison from your veins just as we took the poison from your father's bedside—"

Words came, suddenly and furious. "That's a lie. You know it's a lie. Eluned never would have poisoned him. He was doing well enough. If you had just *left* it, let him have the comfort of the simples Eluned brought for him—"

"The enchantment is strong, I see." Tucking her skirts about her, Elisabeth turned, moved over to the chair against the far wall, and seated herself. Poised, she smiled. "I feared destroying the charm might not be enough. So. You will confess, and take Communion, and cleave to your father as you ought.

"But first, you must eat. You will need your strength."

Gamelyn shook his head. Backed away.

The Abbess rose. "It is of no matter. I can wait." She motioned to the acolyte, who picked up the tray. "Perhaps a bit more hunger is what you need, after all."

☙ ENTR'ACTE ❧

"THREE days," Otho said with little preamble, walking into Johan's solar. "He's not eaten for three days, now."

"Our brother must be punished." Johan was only now dressing, with the aid of the old man who'd been his body servant since childhood. He was still hung over with lack of sleep, having spent the night keeping watch on said brother, as agreed. The Abbess was hoping something would break, soon, convinced that peasant whoreson who'd cozened Gamelyn into such madness would show up, try to take him back.

Johan doubted it. No peasant would dare the walls of a castle merely for some light tumble. And Johan had already decided their Reverend Cousin was altogether nigh to madness herself in her conviction that some Heathen cult was stalking the woods, all in itself a seditious danger to Christendom.

Likely just a bunch of jumped-up perverts full of mead and sin, thinking themselves more than what they were. Magic, pah! But Johan had committed himself and so would see it through, no matter how paranoid Her Holier-Than-Thou-ness acted on the way.

"Gamelyn has to be punished," Otho agreed. "He's flouted commandments—which I still can hardly believe—and he's brought a lot of trouble to squat at our gates. You can't believe he meant any of it. Even the wortwife… the medicine did help. It was foolish to discontinue it." Otho grumbled a sigh. "Papa's not exactly in his right mind now, and the Abbess is overly strong with her convictions… well. She means well."

"Otho, you've always been beneath the mistaken apprehension that everyone *means* well."

"Gamelyn certainly meant no harm, Johan. He's the baby, Papa's sheltered him because of it, and when his balls finally did drop, he went a little mad. We all have."

"Sodomy?" Johan sneered. "I think not."

"Only truly sodomy if he was the one poked instead of doing the poking."

Johan glared at his brother.

"I actually pay attention in mass, Brother," Otho pointed out. "Bloody hell, Johan, every lad including you has stuck his knob into something he shouldn't at some time or other. I know what you do at night without the benefit of matrimony—"

"With a *woman*—"

"Several, sometimes. Quite a sin, that. And I know damn well you, like every lad born, has had a quick and dirty wank with his mates. If we didn't have some horrific thing to confess, the priests would die of boredom."

"You're forgetting the tiny matter of consorting with witches—"

"I'm forgetting nothing, and neither am I saying he doesn't deserve a good beating for all of this. All I'm saying is that Alais is convinced he's set to starve himself before confessing to the Abbess, and I'm not sure I blame him."

In a twist of temper, Johan shrugged off his servant and snapped at him, "Get out! I'll manage!"

The servant threw a look of long-suffering at Otho then obeyed. Otho leaned one hip against the table by the entry.

"Johan. Let Gamelyn have his own confessor. It's the right thing to do and you know it. Neither of you likes the other much, and each of you has your reasons, but Papa's too ill for this nonsense."

"Illness that was perpetrated by Gamelyn's idiocy." Johan frowned at Otho.

"So the family hardheadedness continues! Think of Papa, curse you! Gamelyn's already making his prayers when he's not pacing the floor. Papa wants to see him, but he won't see him until he's had Communion. Both of them, stubborn as mules. And I know damn well the Abbess is taking liberties with what Papa said. He confesses to her because she's family and of higher rank. Never bad to hedge your bets when you're getting close to Heaven. Papa likes Brother Dolfin quite a lot and did he know Gamelyn requested him, he'd respect that right. Then it would be done."

"The Abbess seems to think the pagans aren't done with Blyth."

"The Abbess sees evil lurking everywhere. That's her job, but it doesn't have to be ours. See it done, Johan. See it done and let's get on with our lives, eh? See Papa through his last days with some dignity and grace, not this… nonsense."

☙ XXIV ❧

"ALMS. Alms fer a cripple… thank'ee, sor, bless you!"

The voice floated upward, cracked and coarse and just that much over the top. Even an hour ago, Gamelyn might have thought he was imagining it. But Alais had come in not long ago with a tray of food and more sympathy than he'd yet had, and the news that Brother Dolfin would be in not long after to give him absolution and Communion so he could go and see his father.

He'd not wanted to believe it, at first. But she had insisted, and sat with him, ensured that he'd eaten every scrap of the simple meal she'd brought him—not too much, as she'd said, else his empty stomach would just puke it back up again. And she'd told him how his father was, made it clear that, no matter what had happened, she forgave him and there was no doubt in her mind but that the wortwife had helped Sir Ian.

He'd waited, after Alais had left. Sat in his window and watched a baby wolf spider spin a web in one corner, expecting the Abbess to descend at any moment and tangle him up in another sort of web. He knew, before she came and after she had left, that she had wrapped him tight in his own culpability, sunk her words like venom in his veins… and he knew, deep down, that it wouldn't affect him so if there wasn't some truth to it.

"Alms! A palm of grain, sor, would surely feed an 'ungry man…."

Gamelyn looked down, saw a wide hat, tattered braies that barely came to mud-encrusted ankles, and a filthy hand holding out a wooden bowl warped from ill use. Some traveler, Gamelyn would wager, rather than one of the peasantry who looked to Blyth; one who knew how to use that bathetic tone to full effect. Perhaps some jongleur who'd lost his trade when he'd lost the use of whatever limb had crippled him. Perhaps a former tumbler—that right arm extending the bowl looked fairly muscular beneath the overmended sleeve.

The wolf spider lost its footing, dropped a good hand-length and saved itself with a silken thread just before it reached Gamelyn's bent knee. Relentlessly it began climbing back up.

Usually the beggars didn't hunch down beneath his window. Usually they didn't hunch nigh to any window, never being sure when the pisspots would be dumped.

"You there! Gi' off!"

And sure enough, one of the guardsmen was descending upon the hapless beggar.

"You're not t' be here! Hie y'rself to th' gate or the back wall, where y' belong!"

The beggar seemed to be either deaf or not heeding. Gamelyn leaned outward slightly, wondering if he should drop something on the fellow's head. Perhaps he was deaf... but nay. He was getting to his feet, quite slowly.

"Clear off, I say!" The guard grabbed the beggar's tunic; he wobbled and Gamelyn could see he had a twisted foot. "Look up there!" the guard was blustering. "His lordship's quarters are in this turret! You're not to disturb him." The guardsman saw Gamelyn, gave a quick bow, and grabbed the beggar again, shook him. The beggar cringed, throwing up the hand without the bowl. The guardsman pointed. "See? You've disturbed one of my lords already! Your pardon, milord, I'll see this 'un on his way."

The beggar looked up then. Straightened slightly, and met Gamelyn's gaze, a mop of wheat hair that seemed totally incongruous with the dark brows. Those brows were angled quite fiercely over large, ebon eyes. One was held in a squint, which relaxed as the beggar met Gamelyn's gaze, held it.

It was *Rob.*

"Oh, God." It hissed through Gamelyn's teeth. He shook his head violently. *No. Get out of here. Go....*

"Go on, get out of here!" Unconsciously aping Gamelyn's very thoughts, the guardsman aimed a halfhearted boot at the beggar's rump. With a nimbleness that belied any lameness, the beggar dodged the kick and scuttered around the corner.

Yes, Gamelyn prayed. *Get out of here, Rob, what in Hell are you* thinking*?—you bloody fool!*

ଓଃ

"HE SAW me, I'm sure of it," Rob murmured.

John smiled, but it slid into a grimace as he scrubbed at the grime on Rob's nape. From over the wall of his cot, the horse occupying the next stall stopped chewing, gave a stomp and a snort, then resumed chewing.

Rob was also trying to undo some of the damage of disguise—plus some extra achieved during his act. "Some lads thought a cripple was fair game for improving their aim with a dried horse turd. Wankers. Me mam would have their guts for garters, were they her boys." He turned and peered at John. "You're sure of this, are you? I can climb the wall—"

A shake of the dark brown head, quite adamant.

"I don't want no trouble for you."

John met his eyes, still frowning. Clearly chiding.

Rob smiled, reached out, and ran his fingers along John's cheek, then angled forward and gave him a kiss. It started as a brief intimacy; John leaned into it, with parted mouth and tongue and a hint of a nip to Rob's bottom lip, then broke the kiss and nuzzled into Rob's neck.

"He is ours, lord," John whispered. "Even as you."

"I only hope he believes that."

"You must," John's grin was cheeky, lopsided, "convince him."

"Aye," Rob muttered. "There's only been one way I've been able for that. In the middle of a bloody castle full of bloody murderous swine who'd as soon see me shot as walking, no doubt."

ᴄᴚᴤᴐ

BROTHER Dolfin came to hear Gamelyn's confession, reassuring Gamelyn that Otho was standing outside the door to see to their privacy. He was subdued, his robes properly hanging about his ankles and his sandals on his feet, which suggested that, after all, there had been some chastisement his way. But he had brought several books, and didn't, as usual, demand that Gamelyn return ones he already had on loan to keep the new ones.

Gamelyn asked for absolution and Communion. When Dolfin canted an eyebrow at him and muttered something about young men who weren't sorry they'd done something, only very sorry they'd got caught, Gamelyn shook his head and asked, half choked, whether Dolfin really thought Gamelyn had any intention whatsoever of starting it all over again.

Dolfin gave him a long, troubled look. Then he leaned forward, kissed Gamelyn's forehead, and began the words of absolution.

After that, Gamelyn padded across the hallway, beneath the watchful eye of Johan and surely more guards than even a well-grown lad should need.

The Abbess was coming from his father's solar; she halted before him, compassionate. Of course, even when she was sitting in his room, spinning the web, she had reeked of compassion….

"Please, you must understand," the Abbess laid a gentle hand on Gamelyn's shoulder, and it was all he could do to not flinch away. "I meant you no harm, only help. You've trained as soldier as well as scholar, and you know the sense of a good sweat to release all the ill humors. Suffering is often the only way to release ill spirits trapped within. Sister Deirdre can attest to that, isn't that true?"

Deirdre had joined them as they stood there, and her eyes were flat upon Gamelyn. Gauging, as if she could all but smell the rebellion, nearly boiled dry but still simmering, beneath the regret and shame. The latter should have left him with Brother Dolfin's absolution but hadn't; it was merely scabbed over, a pus-laced sore that he couldn't help but pick at.

For he believed the Abbess. He didn't want to, but he did and worse, he *knew* it.

"Your father is waiting for you," the Abbess said, and dipped her head as she got out of his way.

Sir Ian looked horrible. Wilted and lank against the cushions, nearly the same color as the bleached linen sheets despite that Alais had assured they were not bleeding him. Gamelyn sped to the bedside, took his father's hand, and fell to his knees beside the bed.

"Please," he begged. "Forgive me."

"It's done, my boy. Forgiven. Forgotten."

No, never forgotten. Gamelyn would never forget. Any of it.

"I've made arrangements," Sir Ian whispered against his hair. "The Abbess has agreed, in light of your penitence, to see to it. I have given her the proper donations to ensure your place, and she has sent the marks on to the monastery at Ely. It's so far away; I'd hoped you could stay close, but this is better. Considering...."

Considering that within Ely's walls bided one of the richest and scholastic monasteries in all of England, one that Gamelyn had once sworn he would kill to study with.

Considering the Abbess's likely irritation over his rejection of her over the past days.

Considering Johan's certain ire when he heard how much money had been disbursed.

Considering the very real fact that Sir Ian was dying.

Considering... *Rob.*

It was a dream, he willed, mute torment, as he laid his head in his father's hand and begged his forgiveness. *A wild, lovely dream that I'll never forget. But you cannot come for me, you must go and never come back. I've lost you. It's over. It* has *to be.*

Rob, they'll kill you and I'm not sure I can live with myself now as it is....

"Thank you, Papa. It is more than I ever dreamed of."

Sir Ian smiled. "I think it would be best." He closed his eyes, hesitated.

"Papa?"

"Perhaps you should not wait overlong to take your leave, eh? We both know that I have such a short time left."

"*Papa.*"

"When your brother is mesne lord...." Sir Ian went silent again, with Gamelyn reliving every silent agony he possessed. But when Sir Ian spoke again, it was firm. "You must go, son. Take what is yours. I have given the order; your paxman will go with you at the time of your choosing. But...." The old man wavered, "Will you stay close? Until your departure?"

"I will stay close," Gamelyn said. "That I swear to you."

ଓଃ୧ଠ

JOHN'S friend, a lass named Anne, came down to the stables to inform them that the overabundance of guards in the lord's turret had been dispersed. There were only the normal ones, parading back and forth, easy enough to avoid if one knew the way of it.

"And I do." Anne gave Rob a critical eye. "You're sure the height of Dunstan, though awful shaggy and way too skinny. He's off t' see his ma in Thurcroft, though *they* aren't knowing that." She rolled her eyes and shrugged. "We can pad you up a bit, give you a shave. You can likely braid that hair up, cover it with a coif. Dunstan wears one when he's stacking wood in th' chambers."

"A white rag cap?" Rob couldn't help the protest. "I'll look like me old granda just before he fell dead over his plow. As to shaving…." He grimaced and rubbed a hand over his chin, where stubble was giving way to serious beard. "I do look a proper wild man, I guess. We'd best have it over with so the nicks'll be gone by tonight."

"I'll leave no nicks," Anne promised, and went to get supplies. John began watering the horses.

Rob stood there, chewing at a thumbnail and contemplating his options. They looked better than ever. Even considering a kerchief on the head.

"When you take the horses to pasture," he told John, "m' sister will be watching out for you. Tell her we're set for tonight."

ଓଃ୧ଠ

THE back stair was dark and narrow and had a distinct draft that more than once fluttered the edges of the coif about Rob's ears. Just as well Anne had fastened it down with some hairpins, even if Rob's humiliation was thusly complete.

Gamelyn had best bend his lovely arse over more than the once for this night's work.

His ankle twisted beneath him; the stone steps were amazingly uneven for a supposed 'mastery of Frankish architecture'. Rob gave a muttered curse and Anne thwapped him with the end of her besom for his pains.

For some reason she didn't treat him with the least bit of reverence, and it was bloody refreshing.

He nearly ran into her at the top of the stair—not paying attention, trying to decide what he was going to tell Gamelyn when he laid eyes on him—and Anne glared at him, mouthed, *Wait*.

Better to go in without any encounters, brief or otherwise, and rely on the disguise only for emergency. Anne had sworn at the curls hanging down his back—they had kept evading even the tightest braids and now were giving him a skull ache that a staff knock would envy—but she was handy with a sharp dagger and had given him a better shave than even his mam could tender.

"Quit foolin' with that cap and come on!"

They stepped out into the hallway, and as luck would have it, straight into the path of the patrolling soldier. Rob threw Anne a querying glance. She shrugged and walked over to the guard. "I've linens for the lord's dining chamber."

The night hours weren't a factor, as Anne had earlier confessed; they were expected to do their work when it wouldn't have to be seen or endured by their masters.

The guard nodded, shot Rob a sour glance, then blinked. "Hoy. You aren't Dunstan—"

Rob acted on sheer adrenaline and instinct. He whirled on the guard and, instead of the expected blow, sidled up beside him.

"What're—"

Bringing up both hands before him, Rob opened them with a flourish that set the guard back on his heels. It gave him the necessary instant to breathe across his palms once and then again, first with intent, then a whisper: "*Cysgwch yn dawel.*"

The guard crumpled. Rob caught him just before he hit the floor—not without a grunt; the man was bloody heavy in all that mail.

"You killed him," Anne whimpered, cowering back. "With nobbut a word!"

He grabbed her, shook her. "Nay. Was a bid to set him sound t' sleeping, nowt more. Help me!"

She got hold of herself and helped him drag the guard to the narrow, winding stable stair and prop him on a step. Rob looked down at him, thoughts as twisted as the stair, looking for the out. He straightened. "Anne. Is there…." and trailed off at the look on her face.

"M… m'lord?" Suddenly there was reverence, hot and nearly terrified, in Anne's eyes, and Rob mourned the coming of it as if he'd lost a limb.

"Will there be another coming for a while?"

She shook her head. "Th-the one who g-guards my lord's chambers around the curve will stay there, and none else to relieve this one 'til the dawn."

"Then on with you, lass. I'll either be fine or I waint; either way there's no use to you getting amidst it any more than you have." She hesitated, frowning, and Rob shook his head. "Go on, then."

With a quick nod, Anne turned and hurried away.

ଓଃ

IT WAS a mercy that Anne had shown him precisely which door was Gamelyn's chamber—they all looked as like as the fancy archery butts in Sheffield's common before any arrows had pricked them.

And the bloody door *creaked.* Rob shoved at it—better a quick sound than one that lasted ages—and then shut it just as quickly behind him. For a mercy it didn't creak again, and the bolt was well-oiled, nigh silent as he slid it home.

The chamber was bloody huge. His family's entire cottage could have fit with room to spare. Rob didn't see anyone, was coming close to panic until a familiar silhouette moved from the shadows of the far wall and into the nearly full moonlight of the one window, ruddy-fair hair glinting like silver.

Gamelyn peered at him in the dim. "What do you want?"

Of course. He was thicker, dressed wrong, all tarted up like some old farmer….

Rob stepped forward into the one stream of candlelight. "It's me," he hissed.

Gamelyn's eyes widened, at first, it seemed, in shock. Then his eyebrows furrowed. One side of his mouth gave a quiver, tilted upward.

It was that bloody codger's cap. Rob yanked it off, sending pins flying. It didn't help. Gamelyn closed his eyes and looked away. His shoulders shook, and it wasn't fear. Rob looked down: his clothes were dirty, but on straight, his knob wasn't hanging out or anything… but a quick recce of hands over face and skull told him the braids with which Anne had fastened his hair were sticking out at all angles. With a growl he yanked at the worst offenders, left the rest straggling, and came to a decision.

For *this* his poncy ginger paramour was going to owe him a bit more than just *one* bend-over of that lovely arse.

Instead the poncy ginger paramour stiffened quite suddenly, rounded back on him, and hissed, "What in Heaven's name are you *doing* here?"

Rob grinned, shrugged from the too-big coat, and threaded the coiled rope from over his shoulder. He proffered it with a small bow. "I'm here to rescue you, Sir Gamelyn."

"This is not funny!" It was nearly—nearly, despite their necessary spate of whispers—a growl. "You have to leave, Rob. Now. If they catch you—"

"Aye, they'll kill me 'n' all of that." Rob came closer. "Fair enough, but I'm not leavin' without you."

Surely it was not good that Gamelyn tottered back, out of reach. Even less that he shook his head. "I can't leave."

"Gamelyn—"

"You don't understand. You never have, have you?" There was an odd expression on Gamelyn's face. It seemed altogether akin to… pity.

It sent all sorts of alarm tingling up and down Rob's spine.

"You have to go. It's over, what we did. It wasn't real, don't you see?"

"Nay, I canna see a thing you're...." Rob trailed off. It was true. He saw nothing. *Saw* nothing. Only the weave of *tynged* to the mere reach of his arm, threads chopped off and blackness beyond....

He blinked. Shook his head. Reached out with mind-magic only to hit that blackness. It wasn't as Cernun had said, a rent in time's fabric.

It was a wall. An *ending*.

"You have your world, and I have mine—"

"What have they told you?" It was barely a whisper, choking at Rob's throat. "What did they do?"

Gamelyn was still looking at him, that strange, indefinable chill behind his eyes. "They've only told me what we both knew they would. Rob, I promised. I promised my father." It choked off, and Rob stiffened.

"Is he all right? Is he worse?"

"He's much worse. He's stopped taking your mother's medicines—"

"Sweet Lady, *why*?"

"Because he thinks your mother's a witch!" It was a scream, all packed and smothered into a bare whimper. "He thinks all of you are witches and he thinks your mother used her magics on him, on all of us. He thinks you enchanted me. They *know*, Rob. They know what we've done, and I warned you, warned you more than the once what would happen to us and *you have to get out of here*."

"Not without you."

"I'll be fine. Don't you understand? This is my place. This is where I belong, where I'm supposed to be. What I have to... be." Gamelyn shook his head then went over to the window, looked out. "Use the rope. Lash it to...." He started looking around. "If nothing else, I'll belay it—"

"I'm not"—Rob realized that his voice was starting to crack above the muted whispers they were using, stifled it back—"leaving without you."

"Rob, you don't—uh!" A small grunt as Rob grabbed his sleeve, yanked him close.

"I'm not leaving without you," Rob said, and kissed him.

Gamelyn uttered a noise against his teeth, broke it off and sent Rob sprawling against the wall beside the window with a shove, merely to end up staggering after him when Rob didn't loose his sleeve. "Are you out of your bloody mind?" Gamelyn hissed.

"Happens I am." Rob yanked the sleeve again. *Convince him*, John had said, and Rob had joked about what persuasions he'd have to use. Joked.

Hear me laughin', little stable lad? Ha.

So he curled one hand about Gamelyn's nape, pulled him closer for another kiss. Gamelyn wrenched sideways, tried to wrest free. The action merely allowed Rob to curl his arm around Gamelyn's throat and pull him back. "So." It was a breath against Gamelyn's nape. "Is this a 'don't'?—or a 'don't stop'?"

Because, oddly enough, he didn't know. Couldn't read Gamelyn's body like his own—couldn't parse the sudden… *strangeness* of it—and it sent alarm from a tingling into sharp little bells jangling in the back of his skull, faint but there.

Then Gamelyn sent it all wheeling sideways by giving a little shudder and moan, then twisting in his arms to take Rob's mouth with his own, lips parting, hungry and desperate as a man starving for a se'nnight. Rob's spine knocked hard against the wall as Gamelyn shoved him there, framed his face with his hands then slid fingers up into Rob's hair, at first thwarted by the tiny braids there then grabbing at them, using them to pull himself even tighter against Rob.

Aye, then. "Don't stop." Definitely.

Rob wrapped his arms around the small of Gamelyn's back, slid one hand down to Gamelyn's haunch, dug his fingers in and pulled, gave a slow, grindy shove that made Gamelyn gasp into his mouth.

Only then Gamelyn was tearing away, staggering back, sucking in air and shaking his head. "Rob—"

Enough was enough. Rob still had that sleeve-grip; he gave another yank, a twist and shove, and not for the first time thanked those brawny pub lads who'd taught their skinny mate the proper uses of leverage when outweighed and overmuscled.

And all of it still in that eerie, heavy quiet. With the broken-threaded blackness beyond his Sight….

"My turn," Rob said against Gamelyn's ear. "You'll stop this."

"You *have* to—"

"I warned you, love. I told you I'd come for you. I told you, you're worth the catching and there's nowt any of your kind can do to convince me otherwise. Nowt *you* can do 'less you're planning on dragging me out to the gibbets and let your soldiers hang me—"

"My father said he'll have you hung, he'll—"

"He'll have to catch me first."

"I can't—*Oh*!" This as Rob sidled against him—hard.

"And if rutting you stupid is the only way I can get it through your bloody thick skull, then I'll do it."

"You… daft clot… if we're found… if you're *caught*…."

"Well, you're so good at confessing, I've one to make to you," Rob murmured. "Sometimes it takes a little wank beneath the eyes of the black to make you know what it is to be *alive*."

Gamelyn was shivering between him and the wall, gave a grunt, a lurch, and a shudder as Rob snaked his hand down beneath Gamelyn's braies.

"Just what I thought. Look at that soldier, all at attention." Rob lipped at Gamelyn's earlobe, fisted him tight, pushed then pulled. "I'm thinking he's also liking the raw nerve of it all—"

"You're… absolutely… mad." The breaths came in bursts, truncated to the rhythm of Rob's fist.

"And you're mad to think I'll just leave you here." Rob skated murmurs over freckled skin, from copper-scruffed jaw to the arch of throat, down his breastbone and over to one hard-ruched nipple. Gamelyn leaned back, hips lurching with every jerk of Rob's hand; he had one hand at Rob's skull, tangled in braids and curls and pulling him down, mouth trailing over breast then belly, tongue dipping at his navel.

Rob snatched Gamelyn's braies down; Gamelyn kicked one leg free. Rob knelt on the crumpled fabric, met the gleam of Gamelyn's eyes beneath the fall of ruddy silk, saw his chest rise and fall beneath pale muslin, the flush of his cheeks and lips brilliant and dark.

"Nay, you're no dog… yet no wolf either," Rob whispered against the down of Gamelyn's belly as if it were a minstrel's love song. "You're more a hawk they've tried to break, jessed and hooded and never set to fly save to a lure."

Hooded.

Hooded….

You are not meant to wear a hood, my last-born son. You are meant to wear the sun and spread your wings across the Summering….

Rob heard it as if spoken, a memory not his own; the voice steaming deep within Gamelyn, velvet as the wet nap of Rob's tongue curling about him, as deep as the sudden twist-*push* of Rob's fingers inside him. Felt Gamelyn's shudder as if it were his own, took him deeper, slid his fingers harder and Gamelyn twisted, cried out.

It echoed in the stillness of the room.

They both froze, trembling. Waiting.

Like Gamelyn had ever figured out how to hold anything back once he got going, including those lovely cries that Rob usually ached to hear….

A fist in his hair, dragging Rob rather unwilling to his feet, and Gamelyn panting against his cheek. "The bed. Quiet. *Cushions.*"

Madness?

Aye, well, then.

Who dragged whom across the flooring was immaterial, and there was a brief struggle when they arrived at the bed. But once Gamelyn had twisted around, back to front, his hands tugging at Rob's breeks, once Rob curled fingers about him and started mocking hand rhythm with his hips, it became very clear who wanted what, and how.

Rob bent Gamelyn over the bed. He spat in his palm twice, sent a breath across it, slicked himself with it and slid through his hand, then pushed inward, slow. Gamelyn propped against him with a hoarse grunt, then arched his back and gave another shivery cry as Rob pushed deeper. Mid-cry, Rob grabbed at thick, ruddy hair, shoved Gamelyn's face down into the cushions, stifling it into a whimper.

Not that he could lay blame; it was all Rob could do to bite back his own voice. Instead he leaned over Gamelyn, held him down and went at him, at first slow then building as Gamelyn writhed beneath him in an obvious demand for more… and when Rob couldn't keep his voice stilled any longer, spent it in whispers along Gamelyn's spine, into the freckled hollows straining between his ribs. "Give it to me. All their damnation, and hate and scorn; let 'em say what they want. I can take it for you. I can take it. The only thing I'll not be able to take is leaving you here in hell—"

And Rob Saw it: *tynged* rippling into being, no longer frayed, no longer *ending*, but chasing after the black and taking Gamelyn's with it, knotting fast even as Gamelyn knotted the sheets in white-knuckled fists, smothered his cries into the ticking, and shuddered to another ending.

Saw it, still rippling in green eyes as Gamelyn tilted his head to suck in hoarse breaths, to peer at Rob as he pulled back, then snuggled along his back and laid his cheek to Gamelyn's arm.

No longer fear, somewhat gentled, but still.

Gamelyn rolled over, pulled Rob onto the bed with him, curled close to him… and Rob had never felt a bed so soft, never felt bedding against his skin that was more akin to the gossamer of a spider's web, or the first milky fur of a newborn foal.

He rubbed his face into the cushion where Gamelyn had smothered his pleasured cries, and sighed.

Gamelyn was smiling at him, a curious thing that could have been derisive but instead was gentle bemusement. He took a handful of bedding, stroked it across Rob's forehead then trailed it down his breast.

"You'd better take care," Rob murmured, "or there'll be rutting again. How can you *sleep* in all this? I just want to wallow like a happy sow."

Gamelyn smothered a laugh against his shoulder, then stayed there, nestling down. Rob smiled, wrapped arms about him, breathed the sweated silk of hair, watched the skeins of *tynged* light his lover's eyes.

But he could feel the dawn approaching—only a matter of hours. They were running out of time.

"Gamelyn. Please. Come with me. Be with me."

"I can't." Gamelyn sat up and rubbed his hands over his face. *Tynged* faded, replaced by something dark and cold. "And you have to go, Rob. It's impossible. We were dreaming like children. We *can't*—"

"You've said this before. More than the once."

"Yes, well, I mean it this time. I *have* to."

"Gamelyn, please."

Fingers tautened, dug into the freckled forehead. "You have to understand. I promised my father. I promised him I'd stay close. Rob, he's *dying*."

And that Rob did understand. He leaned forward, pulled stiff fingers from Gamelyn's brow and nuzzled the spray of gilt forelock out of his eyes. "There has to be a way. Somehow."

Gamelyn lay silent, then said, very slowly, "Papa. He said a place had been made for me at the monastery at Ely. He said he had made the arrangements, and that the time of leaving would be my choice." Rob saw him swallow, hard. "He said I might be better off leaving. Before he…."

Rob tucked closer to him. "Where is Ely?"

"In Cambridgeshire."

"I… dunno where that is, either."

Gamelyn frowned. "It's on the other border of Huntingdon. About… a hundred miles?"

"Bloody damn," Rob whispered. "That's the other end of the world."

"But I'd be free to go."

Rob propped on one elbow. "When could you leave, then? If… if you could go in two days, you could come to t' Fête, to Beltain." He nodded to himself, thinking aloud. "You could clear y'rself of these lies. Come see what we are. And after Beltain…." He hesitated and peered at Gamelyn; it was no less a huge jump for Rob than Gamelyn contemplating leaving his dying father. Taking a breath, he held it, then let it out. "After, I'd be free to come with you."

And his voice didn't so much as quaver.

Gamelyn was equally grave, quiet, looking away. "Where is it held?"

"I'll wait for you in our caverns. Take you there."

"But…." Gamelyn was adamant. "Where?" Then, softer, "What if we miss each other? If something happens. If you have to go on… if you want me to follow…."

There was a ban against telling outsiders where the rite was held, but it wasn't exactly a secret, either. "Of course I want you to follow. It's the old dolman circle to the southeast of Loxley Chase, between Hathersage and Dronfield. Mam Tor, remember it? We've ridden through it a time or two when you came to visit."

Gamelyn nodded, still not looking at him. He swallowed, then said, slowly, "It's just… hard. Do you understand?"

"I do." Rob curled a hand at his chin, lifted it. "Perhaps your da's pain will be over, anon, and you'll truly be free."

A sudden light flickered behind Gamelyn's eyes, soft answer, then dulled again. "It could only be a blessing, now, an end to his pain," Gamelyn murmured. "And I've done nothing but make it worse."

"Worse?"

"All of it." Gamelyn turned into the cushions for a second, and when he turned back to Rob his eyes were as reddened as his lips and cheeks. "*This*," he furthered as he reached out and stroked Rob's cheek.

"Was it you that told him, then?"

Gamelyn blinked, shook his head. "I'd never have—"

"Then seems to me 'tis more a blame on the head of who told a sick man sommat he didna need to hear."

Gamelyn gritted his teeth, hissed, "That's what I told the Abbess—"

And every nerve on Rob's body drew up. "*She* was the one who—?"

Voices, outside the door. Raised in consternation, then hissed into quiet.

Both of them froze. Rob gave a soft growl, made an agile roll to his feet. Nigh silent, he crept over, snatched up Gamelyn's discarded braies. Gamelyn's recovery was not as practiced or swift, but he was upright in time to catch the braies as Rob pitched them to him. As he straightened from yanking them on, Rob padded back over and spoke against his ear.

"I'm thinking they found the guard I made to sleep."

"You *what*?" Gamelyn hissed

More voices, muted and urgent, from the door.

"It was s'posed to—"

A tap on the door, and they both stilled. "Gamelyn?"

"I bolted the door," Rob said, just as it shook.

"It's my brother… You have to get out of here!" Gamelyn gritted, half whisper and half hoarse plea. "He can't find you here—"

"Gamelyn, are you in there?"

Rob watched the wish to panic flirt itself dry in Gamelyn's expression, replaced by a scary-cold reserve as Gamelyn lifted his chin and spoke. "I am. What do you want?"

"Aye, *that's* my poncy ginger paramour," Rob purred in his ear, and for a moment, Gamelyn nearly laughed.

Instead he snatched up the rope. "Check below," he murmured back. "Now."

Rob padded across, looked down as Gamelyn uncoiled the rope, tossed it to him.

"Open up, Gamelyn. It's about Papa."

Gamelyn paled, but gave the rope two wraps about his waist. "I'll be right there!" he called. Then, to Rob, a bare whisper, "Get out of here. I'll hold you, throw the rope after you."

Rob tested his grip, arched an eyebrow at Gamelyn. "Can you, then?"

Gamelyn snorted. "You and two others just as skinny. Go *on*, damn it!"

Rob hopped into the window, took a firm grip on the rope, and swung out into the air with his feet braced against the sill. Stopped, groped around his belt.

"Rob!" Gamelyn hissed. "What in Hell are you—?"

Rob held up the quillion dagger, and saw him pale, go mute. "D'you…." He almost couldn't say it, was afraid to hear the answer. "D'you want it now?"

The freckled cheeks suddenly flushed dark, and Gamelyn took in a thick breath. "Keep it," he growled, low. "I'll come for it. We'll go. Together." And set himself against the rope.

Rob bounced, slid, and toed himself down the stone turret, landed straddled and bent-kneed, tugged the rope. He paused only long enough to snatch at the rope as it came soaring down after him, then fled.

ЖЖЖ

GAMELYN threw the rope down, watched the dark figure scoop it up then melt into the shadows outside like a shade. He leaned heavily against the window, touched three fingers to his lips, and blew a kiss after. Only then did he walk over and open the door.

Johan came bursting in, with two guards right behind him. "What were you doing, taking a piss?"

"It's my chamber, Johan, and perhaps I was…." Gamelyn trailed off as the guard began looking: in the clothes press, under the bed, behind the hanging in the corner. He was afraid he knew what—who—they were looking for. But there had been no alarm raised. Surely there would have been if they thought…. "Johan, what's happened? You said Papa—"

"He's well enough. No thanks to you." Johan was watching the guards, his ire growing by the second. They looked at him and shrugged; he jerked his head. "Get out."

They bowed, obeyed—but not without wary looks at Gamelyn. None of it made *sense*. "Johan, you said you were here about Papa? Is he—?"

Johan strode over, quick as a snake, and struck. The backhand blow caught Gamelyn unprepared, snapped his head sideways and sent him staggering back.

"Where is he?"

A thrill along Gamelyn's nerves—active fear. He allowed none of it to show on his expression, shook his head. "I don't know what you—"

Johan hit him again. It was almost casual, the method behind it, but of the power there was no question, even open-handed. "Keep quiet, *petit frêre*. You have been loud enough this night; if you wake our father, the consequences will not be pleasant."

Gamelyn hit the floor sprawling, then rocked up to his hands and knees with a curse and lunged.

He got several silent, brutal blows in before Johan swore and punched him, a heavy fist into the gut that drove the breath from Gamelyn as well as what was left of his dinner. Gamelyn dropped to hands and knees, and once he started retching he couldn't stop, and heaved until his ears were ringing and his vision red-soaked.

Only then did a hand tangle in his hair, haul him to his feet and shove him backward until he hit the stone wall. Johan held him there, nearly dangling.

"It is over, little *gadelyng*." The old taunt held even more bile than usual; in this place and moment struck home all the more. "Don't lie to me. I know he was here." Johan stuck his face into Gamelyn's. "A castle such as this has secrets, ones that only the lord and his heir might know. There are passageways in the walls, ways to safety. Ways to observe nearly every room here. I was watching you, just in case. I saw the peasant whore-son come in here. I saw you talking, and *then?*" His eyes gleamed, furious. "All this time, I thought you were acting the man. I scoffed at the Abbess's talk of witches and enchantments, but I was wrong. You are enchanted. You *have* to be."

The fear was filling him, as if he were submerged in water, flooding into his eyes, nose, throat. "Johan, you don't—"

"I saw you. Saw you… *with* that scrawny *cuivert maleis*." The oath was as vulgar as Johan's tone was abnormally quiet. He preferred shouting, striking, throwing things—this stillness was disturbing. "It turned my stomach, but I watched you with him, and you liked it, what he did. You *begged* that filthy peasant scum to fuck you. Like a dog. Like a *woman*."

"You…." Fury and disgust were so mixed up they were choking him. "… *bastard*!"

Johan clapped a hand over his mouth. "Keep your voice down!" he hissed. "Our father is ill enough without knowing the full details of your sins."

Gamelyn jerked away, hissed back, "You showed such tender regard for his health before, when you dragged me before him for no better reason than to shame me!"

"It was a mistake I do not plan to make again. I will confess I was willing to show him you're not the untouched saint he thinks you… *non*, I was more than willing. But *this*." Johan shook his head. "He is weak and this would kill him. You are out of your mind with this… this *thing* that has enchanted you, and our father does not need to know that… that the son he loves above all else"—he spat it like the bitter dregs it must have been—"has been made slave to an animal."

Johan was not the only one swallowing fury's acid; Gamelyn was nigh choking on the taste of it, his words muddled into near incoherence. "You don't… know… *anything*!"

"I know enough." Johan stepped back, released Gamelyn to totter and stagger against the wall. He raised his voice, ever so slightly. "Gervais!"

"Aye, my lord?" The largest of the two guards stuck his head in, followed by the other as Johan motioned.

"My brother has become… irrational again. We must guard him carefully, for his own protection."

"Johan," Gamelyn growled, "*don't—*"

"You give me no choice, *petit frêre*." Johan motioned the guards in, and they advanced.

Gamelyn backed away from them, shaking his head. Pinwheels still hung, red whirlwinds, behind his gaze. "And what of Papa?" he demanded.

"I myself or Otho will bring you up to see him, should it be necessary. But until your little sodomite friend and his demon-worshipping family are dealt with, it is plain you cannot be trusted to act rationally."

"Dealt with?" Gamelyn struggled almost perfunctorily as the guard took hold of him, spent an almost rabid focus on Johan's words. "What do you mean, *dealt with*?"

"Oh, *gadelyng*. Truly, you are raving." Johan tsked with a pitying frown. "Do you really think that some peasant witch-cult can be allowed to take liberties with a lord? Or that lord's son?"

"*Johan—!*"

"Silence him." Johan made a gesture, and the larger guardsman twisted Gamelyn's arm up behind him. A meaty arm snapped about Gamelyn's neck, mail and leather stifling the surprised cry it drove from him.

"Take him," Johan ordered, "to the undercroft."

☙ XXV ❧

HE HIT the floor hard, slid then skittered across the hard dirt of the passageway and lay on his back for valuable seconds.

Shocked. Still stunned.

Furious.

Gamelyn staggered to his feet, leapt for the door just as it shut and he slammed against it.

There was the sound of the heavy lock tumblers clunking home as he bounced off the door; it was the impetus to renew the fight. He lunged up against the door, banged his fists against it.

Kept banging. Shouted. Ordered. Finally screamed abuse into the thick wood, his throat tightening, scraping, and burning.

There was no reply. He could hear nothing beyond, and behind him….

He turned, looked down the narrow, meter-long passageway. There was a torch burning at the end, and beyond it, a dark hole.

The undercroft was in the very bowels of the castle, sided with rock and masonry, the arches and foundations of which supported the bastion above clearly visible. There was but one way out; this passage and this locked door.

Gamelyn bent, picked up the sack that had been flung in with him, and trod forward, into the black. He took the torch from its sconce as he entered the undercroft chamber, held it aloft. It was dank, deathly quiet, the only sound that of the fire in his hand, hissing and crackling along the pitch-fueled surface of the torch. There was the smell of ferment, mold and compost; the back wall abutted the stables, with gratings that, when he inspected them, were too small to contemplate wriggling through had they led anywhere but more darkness. Moisture abetted the growth of moss and fungus in the cracks and corners, and there were casks of wine aging against the western wall. There were also several other sconces, with torches; Gamelyn made a circuit of the chamber, setting them alight and settling the one he held in an iron stand at the undercroft's center.

Then he inspected the bag. He had been left with a promise of a good meal in several hours, a candle and flint against the dark, a thick fur to ward the damp chill, and a warning not to attempt to drink any of the wine—it was surely still vinegar at this point.

It seemed… impossible. Impossible that he was here, impossible that it had all gone *so bloody wrong.* Gamelyn leaned against one enormous arch, put his head in his hands and wanted to weep. Instead, he let out one solid howl and kicked the emptied sack against the far wall.

Put his face in his hands again. Considered his options.

There had to be options.

Had to be.

He was to be locked up until they'd dealt with Rob and his family.

Dealt with, how?

Gamelyn's hands clenched in his forelock, chased back to his nape, threaded together.

It was obvious what Johan had seen… and even now that had the power to send a cold fury coursing through Gamelyn's veins.

Mine. It's mine, damn you, you had no right!

Only Johan did. He had every right, and it was Gamelyn that had walked every wrong that existed….

"No." It was a hoarse growl. "No, no, *no*!"

There had to be a way. As impossible as it seemed. Yet if he was down here, he couldn't stop whatever it was Johan intended to do. Couldn't meet Rob. Couldn't go with him for the Fête… Beltain. Couldn't stop what Johan intended to do. He'd once sworn that if Rob went to Hell, he wouldn't go alone… was Hell now stalking Eden, its fires to burn through the green Wode?

He didn't know. He *didn't know*, and he should.

Hadn't Rob already come after him, risked capture and death just to give Gamelyn a *choice*?

And how craven was he, if he refused to even reach for it?

For it was his. *His*. Everything he had done over the past month, everything he had felt, every light he had seen shining in Rob's eyes, pain or passion or defiance, it was a living thing, lit between them like an artifact. Part of him. They couldn't take it from him without his own consent. Only God could take it from him.

ꕥ

MARION was waiting by the rock. She wasn't sure what to feel when she saw Rob coming up the hillock—alone. She'd had doubts, certainly. Rob's expectations had been as foolish as reckless and romantic. But she'd also hoped.

Perhaps if there was some chance for Rob and Gamelyn, there'd be one for her and Will.

She was wearied of this strange, unsettled limbo they seemed to be walking in, neither one nor the other, forward or back.

You are meant to walk the road together, wherever that road might lead. If all else is forgotten, remember that, and it will illuminate the darkness....

She was here, then. They were together. Beyond that, she wasn't sure what else to do.

Rob gathered her in by gaze alone, somber. It wasn't exactly reassuring. But there were no alarms from the castle, and he wasn't being pursued, so that much was well enough.

She followed him back to the cave in silence.

*

THE clunk of the lock tumblers echoed down the short passage and ricocheted around the walls of the undercroft.

No possibility of sneaking up on him in here, at least. Gamelyn didn't move from where he was propped up against an arched beam, didn't raise his head, merely slid his eyes up to see who had entered.

It was Abbess Elisabeth. With, of course, the gray-clad novice, who held a large wooden supper tray.

Gamelyn gave an embarrassing stagger as he lurched to his feet, and realized how long he had been sitting there, wheeling between furious and dumbfounded; the cold and damp had penetrated nearly bone-deep.

"A cold place," the Abbess said, her graceful halt seeming to chide Gamelyn's awkwardness, her gaze taking him in. "I am sorry for the necessity of this."

Necessity. He threw a look over to the novice holding the tray, then peered back at the Abbess. "I am allowed food this time?"

"Gamelyn." Her look was chiding. "I know you cannot help yourself, but this obstinacy is unappealing. It merely convinces me that your brother is altogether correct in confining you. When you hold your own safety so lightly, others must see to it for you."

It was tempting to make some pithy comment. Unfortunately, he didn't have any. Instead Gamelyn went over to the tray and looked down at it. Eels and sturgeon, a slice of pigeon pie with sauced apples.

Rob would have called it a rich man's portion.

Gamelyn wanted to smile; instead he let the warmth of the thought wax through him. There was a resounding strength in it.

Mine. Mine, and you shan't have it.

He had spent enough time in numb confusion and disbelief, in self-indulgent flailing, in waiting for things to happen. All any of it had done was see him locked up. He was no longer skirting the borders, no longer "the afterthought." Things were happening, ones that concerned him and his lover….

His lover.

This time the smile did quirk at his mouth. Just as quickly, it vanished, and his eyes flattened.

He needed to know what was going on. Why. How. He had to be self-possessed, collected. Had to be that cold and insensitive nobleman's son that Rob had once condemned.

Had to think. *Plan.*

"I am sorry," he murmured, and the apology echoed against cool stone. "I… sometimes don't know what I mean. Things… are very confusing right now."

Silence. It was difficult to not turn, gauge the Abbess's response. Instead he put a hand out, ran it around the edge of the tray. "I don't mean to be…," and he trailed off again. Waited.

"I warned you." Her reply was soft, but echoed and carried through the hollows and arches. "Remember? I warned you of the danger. Not only from the outside, but within yourself. Your pride. Your insolence. All of it, weakness ripe for the poison of enchantment."

The words quivered, acute weapons against new-laid defenses. Gamelyn closed his eyes, swallowed hard, hardened his heart.

It was not easy. She advanced, step by step, wielding poisons with sharp-honed skill.

"I greatly feared the enchantment ran deep, and I was right. Everything you've done: the lies, the insolence, the unnatural… acts. And you thought a rumpled monk could cleanse you!" A hand came to rest on his shoulder; with no small effort he did not pull away, merely slumped against it. Offered the appearance of capitulation.

You can touch me, but I'm not here.

Defenses held.

"Ah, lovely Gamelyn, could it be that you finally see? This demon boy has taken your heart and pierced it with a thin, long bodkin. He would have you for his horned master, and you lying in your blood upon their altar."

The stag. The hooded figure, waiting. The voice, like sharp tines swathed in spring's velvet, feral and ferocious….

Flowers on the altar. Flowers in Rob's hair; the smell of lake silt, mint, and foxglove. Beauty to stop one's heart….

"You must turn from them. But it will take more than a one-time soldier masquerading as a priest to give you peace. To grant you lasting absolution."

"Then," Gamelyn took a deep breath. "If I asked it of *you*?"

Again, the Abbess was silent.

He turned suddenly and dropped to his knees before her, clutched at the hem of her robe with one hand and brought it to his cheek. "Please. If I asked you for absolution, would you let me out of here? Would you set me free?"

This time she rested her hand atop of his head. "I *am* going to set you free," she murmured. "Set this *shire* free. And it is needed, Gamelyn, badly needed; don't you think?"

"I… I think it's all… confusing. I don't understand."

"It's quite simple. Shall I enlighten you?"

Please. Do just that, and I swear I'll pray for your *absolution.*

Her fingertips started smoothing over his hair, catching in the tangles and knots. The caress made Gamelyn's skin crawl in a visceral almost-pain. He wasn't sure he understood that either; nevertheless, he stifled any reaction.

You can touch me. But I'm... not... here.

"After all, it is you who has given us the method by which we will see them destroyed."

That not only touched him, it slammed into him as powerfully as Johan's fist. He shuddered with it. Her hand stilled, and only by sheer force of will did he regain control of his body and escape the urge to look up, lurch up, grab her and shake the truth from her.

"I have?" he whispered, and by some miracle it was level, unshaken.

"Your brother was, of course, dismayed by what he saw take place in your room. It certainly brought home to him the seriousness of your situation, but thankfully, it did not affect his hearing."

He knew what Johan had seen… what had Johan *heard*? What had they said to each other?

The Fête. Beltain.

"Come with me."

God! Oh, *God*! What Rob had said, while they lay curled about each other, gentled foolish by loving….

"... the old dolman circle to the southeast of Loxley Chase, between Hathersage and Dronfield. Mam Tor...

And Gamelyn had been the one to *ask* it.

"See? Even beneath such a pernicious influence, you are a good and righteous son. God is still fighting for your heart, has given you cause to set in motion the machinery to your own freedom. Thanks to you cozening the witch to tell you where his kind will gather, I have sent word to Nottingham. He and I have both waited for the chance to weed out the chancre in his shire, and we did not have to wait overlong, after all. Upon May Eve, his soldiers will ride to Loxley Chase and despoil their ritual. You will stay here, safe, forevermore out of their grasp."

Gamelyn was so hung upon the horror of what she was telling him that he lost balance, had to steady himself against the floor with one hand. Only then did he become aware he was shuddering, curling in on himself, and all but hanging by the hand clutching to her robes. "You're… going to kill them. Ride on them and cut them down while they're gathered, celebrating a holy festival—"

"Celebrating a *demon's* rite. Oh, my dear." She slipped her hand beneath his chin, raised his face to meet hers. "Despite God's voice within you, you would still stoop to the cunning of those beasts. You would speak any lie, make any pose, to gain your freedom and go to them." Her hand upon him was suddenly malleable as lace slipped over a gauntlet of steel, her eyes blazing. "Yes, I know why you want to be freed, lovely cousin. But you even *smell* of that demon boy. Do you think me such a fool?"

"No," he groaned. "You cannot do this!"

"You will see, cousin. When I take you to see what work we have wrought killing those pagan monsters, you will thank me. You will be in your right mind once more, and take your place in God's plan. Where you belong."

She twitched her skirts from his hold and walked away, the novice quick after. And such was the grip of his horror that Gamelyn couldn't even make a move to stay her, only sprawled there, panting, on hands and knees as the door slammed shut and the lock shot home.

ഗ്ദ

"HE WAS so… strange," Rob confessed.

"If I'd been locked up by me own family, I'd be acting strange too."

Rob nodded, dropped his chin nearly to his chest, was still and silent for so long that Marion scooted closer and put her arms around him.

"You know, you canna tup him into submission *every* time, Hob-Robyn."

Her sly tease made him smile, ever so slightly. "Well. It's always worked so far."

The fire crackled at their feet, flickered over the walls and roof of the little cavern. It had been such a lovely time. Their own place. Their own… kingdom.

Admittedly, it had been a bit more than frustrating to watch the two of them feeling each other up constantly. She was pretty good at taking care of her own needs, but a lover would be nice.

"He did say he would come with us to Beltain."

"He did." Rob inclined his head against hers. "And after that—"

"After that, we have choices to make," Marion agreed.

ഗ്ദ

"MILORD."

Gamelyn blinked.

He was cross-legged on the dank floor, fingers folded together, elbows propped on his knees. He'd resorted to Psalms, over and over, for he'd long ago run out of prayers. He wasn't sure they would be heard, did he have any more in him, but the familiar cadences were a comfort.

He'd considered the ultimate blasphemy of praying to Rob's god, but realized he didn't know the first thing about it. Or if the Heathen even prayed as Christians did. It had made him want to weep… surely he should have known that. It was *important*.

But the psalms' rhythm helped him think, instead of "greetin' and wailin'," as Rob would say. He had to *warn* Rob and his family; he could not start thinking about what would happen if he didn't get out of here and warn them….

The chapel bells had given him some aspect of time. Matins had rung and they'd brought him breakfast, Sext had sounded not long ago but they wouldn't bring him dinner until Nones: May Eve was already a third over. Rob and Marion wouldn't wait for him much longer, if they hadn't already gone on. He could likely take out whoever next brought him his meal, but there would be guards at the door. He didn't have his weapons on him. He had no hope of getting anywhere did he chance to break free!

No. He couldn't think like that. He had to do it. Failure was not an option, even if it was a likely outcome….

"*Milord*!"

The voice returned. It was no velvet-dark god's voice. It was rather high-pitched, half hissed, and coming from his knee. Or, rather, the grating near his knee.

Gamelyn frowned, then angled forward on knees and elbows. "Who are you?"

"'Tis Anne."

Anne. He didn't know any Anne.

"I do th' linens in your family's chambers, milord."

Inconceivable. "What do you want? Why—?"

"I'm John's friend, milord. He and I, we're the ones as helped sneak the Hunter in t' you. We never thought 'twould come t' *this*—"

"John, are you there? Where are you?"

"He's here. He en't one for talkin', as you might've guessed. He heard you were being kept in th' undercroft, and John, he knows every bit of these stables."

It came from Gamelyn before he could choke it back. "*Help me*. Please."

Silence. It made him panicky.

"Listen. You have to listen to me. I have to get out of here. They're taking soldiers to the Fête! I have to warn them, before it's too late!"

More silence. Gamelyn wallowed down onto his belly, grabbing at the grating, slick and rusted against his clutching fingers.

"Please, don't go… listen! She's going to raid Beltain. They're going to *kill* them!"

"Lord." It was John. "What must I do?"

The soft, steady *surety* of it… that all Gamelyn had to do was ask and John would see it done….

Gamelyn clenched his fists, put his forehead against them, thinking.

"Lord?"

"All right." Gamelyn took in a sharp breath, huffed it out. "Have Much be ready to ride at a moment's notice."

"Much is gone, lord. He's gone."

"Gone?"

"Lord Johan was goin' to have 'im arrested for aiding you, milord." Anne, again. "He ran."

"God." The consequences of his sins were indeed adding up. "He got away?"

"S'far as we know."

Gamelyn closed his eyes, recited the psalm. It was the Thirty-Fifth. Apropos.

"Contend, o God, with those who contend with me…."

Thought, hard.

"Lord?" John, again. "What must I do?"

"Sext has passed?"

"An hour ago, at least," Anne said.

"They won't bring me anything else until Nones… John. Is Diamant still in his box?"

"Aye, lord."

"You'll need to have him saddled and bridled by the bells for Nones. If anyone asks, say he's in need of exercise. I've seen you do that before."

Silence, with John, was assent.

"Anne, can you get into my chambers?"

"I think so, m'lord."

"I'll need you to bring my sword and mail to John, to pack on Diamant. They're in the press at the foot of my bed. And a warm cape."

"D'you have a knife?"

"They left me a knife to eat with." The psalm kept echoing, behind the possibilities in his mind. "I've some silver pennies there, as well, if you can find it."

"Without cause they have hidden their net in a pit for me. Without cause they have dug a pit for my soul…."

There was a scraping sound, and the sheathed edge of a long, slender knife peeked through the dark. It had a narrow guard, and fit through the grating easily once Gamelyn took it.

"John's knife, milord. He'd appreciate it back sometime, but if not, he'll understand."

It proved strong and razor sharp to Gamelyn's inspection, and light enough to easily hide in his tunic. "The guards. How many are there between me and the stable?"

"We'll find out," Anne said. "From what I've heard, some guards have orders from your lord father t' let you leave. And then others have their orders from your brother t' the opposite. It's right confusing in the guard's bunk now, I'll tell you. How many's too many?"

"Now that I've a knife, I can handle a few," Gamelyn said, grim.

"Let destruction come on him unawares. Let his net that he has hidden catch himself. Let him fall into that destruction...."

ଔଓ

"HE'S not coming."

"I don't believe that."

"Rob—"

"I *don't believe* that, Marion!"

They sat doubled on Arawn, at the crossroads just past the line of forest overlooking Blyth Castle. They'd waited as long as they could at the caverns, come this far only to wait a while longer.

Rob didn't want to tell her that the... nothingness had returned.

He didn't want to believe that, either. But it was here, *tynged* shaping itself into a void gone thick and clotted-black, like blood. It was *here*.

And Gamelyn was not.

"It could be something as simple as his brother caught him trying to sneak out. His da could have had a turn for the worst."

"His da told him to go."

"We made a promise to *our* da, Rob," Marion reminded softly. "We're going to be arriving after dark as it is. We can come back. And if nowt else, we know where his father's sending him."

Rob growled, deep in his chest, then whirled Arawn on his haunches and pointed his nose for Loxley.

ଔଓ

THE chapel bells rang Nones. Christ's death had supposedly happened at this, the third hour after midday. And here Gamelyn stood, in his own tomb, leaning against the wall beside the entry passage and reciting another psalm in a litany of cold, discerning serenity. Waiting. The heavy pewter tray that had brought his breakfast was in his hands, and John's knife.

You can touch me, but I'm not here....

The heavy tumblers to the door clacked and creaked. Gamelyn softened his knees, put the knife in his teeth, brandished the tray.

The door opened, and the sound of boots, a long stride, down the short corridor. First hands holding the tray, then a dark head... Gamelyn swung.

Johan got out only the first syllable of Gamelyn's name before he fell face-first into the dirt, the tray he held clanging over the hard floor, food spilling into the dirt.

"You," Gamelyn whispered, then smiled.

"My lord?" A voice from the door.

Gamelyn dragged Johan out of sight of the doorway, put a quick hand over his mouth; while Gamelyn was heartily thankful for whatever impulse had made Johan decide to bring his lunch and given Gamelyn a chance to whack him one, he didn't actually wish him dead. He felt a shallow breath and nodded then rose, unsheathing the knife.

He took the tray. And Johan's sword, just in case. Arrogant clot, to wear his sword into a gaol. Of course, Johan had never imagined the "little rabbit" much of a threat.

"My lord?" Hesitant, coming into the passage.

Not here. I'm not here. And I'm not going to let *you touch me.*

Two guards, Anne had conveyed to him, and one more on the way around to the stable that they would try to divert—but be ready just in case they hadn't. And, of course, the ones patrolling the back bailey....

"My lord—? Uhn!"

It took two blows with the tray to dispatch him, and the second guard rushed in just as his fellow hit the dirt. Gamelyn used an elbow to the face then, when it only staggered him, employed the knife.

Then he said a quick prayer—this time, in thanks for Roberto's tutorials—and slipped from the undercroft.

ଔ

GAMELYN had managed to avoid much notice by snagging a basket of roots from a doorway and a shawl hanging to dry from a ledge. The latter he wrapped about his head, the former he hunched over, holding Johan's sword against his body, and sneaked in the side aisle of the stable.

Diamant was tied in his box, dancing. He knew what full packs and a sword athwart his saddle meant: a good, hard gallop. John came trotting over, seemingly from nowhere, and untied the stallion, bringing him out into the aisle and whispering into his ear. Diamant just danced harder.

"Good boy." Gamelyn patted Diamant's sleek neck and slipped him a root from the pilfered basket. "We're going to need it." He quickly checked the girth and fastenings, started to step up then hesitated. Took precious seconds to hold John's knife out to him.

John shook his head, pushed it back toward him. "*Bendith, Arglwydd.*"

Blessings, Lord. The velvet-deep voice rumbled what he knew was a translation.

You haven't forsaken me, Gamelyn returned desperately.

You must stop them, or not only you will be forsaken.

There was… fear in it.

"No fear, Gamelyn," he muttered, then swung up. John patted his boot, smiling up at him, and Gamelyn smiled back, touched his fingers to his lips and then placed them against John's forehead. "*Bendith,*" he said, softly, then, "God be with you."

Hoofs clattered on the cobbles as Diamant burst into the light, rumbling low in his chest like a demon from the underworld.

No one stayed Gamelyn. No one. Everyone merely got out of his way, and the only visible guards were across the wide bailey, on the front wall and gate. Gamelyn still held his brother's sword, just in case. He kept Diamant to a slow canter; the stallion was round and drawn as a loaded trebuchet, his hoofs pounding a collected cadence. They made it halfway across the bailey without so much as a question, and Gamelyn was beginning to think they were going to make it.

"Stop him! Hold him!"

Johan's voice. Hellfire!—he hadn't hit him hard enough.

Gamelyn spurred Diamant, and the stallion responded mightily, blowing a challenge as he leapt forward and galloped across the bailey.

"After him! The gates! *Close the gates*!"

The alarm bell began to toll, flat and loud and anxious. Diamant felt the spur again, and this time the stallion hunkered down, surging forward with a speed that proved he'd only been out for a romp before. The gates were closing ahead of them—slowly, they were heavy—as Gamelyn leaned forward. The guards who did run up were dispatched either by the sheer mass of Diamant's charge or the flat of Johan's sword.

"Stop him! The *gate*!" Gamelyn heard someone scream, and archers gathered up on the ramparts, taking aim.

"Mother of God—don't shoot! Don't—!" A few arrows came whizzing anyway, loosed before the order, and one buzzed past his head like an angry bee. Gamelyn had no time to thank God it wasn't Rob shooting at him—Rob would have bloody well *hit* him—but he did it anyway, spurred Diamant. Pandemonium ensued about him, more screams, shouts, and the gate still closing….

Diamant came clattering down the bridge and out the gates with a tail's-length of spare. There were shouts and curses; people leapt out of the stallion's charge right and left, some into the moat and some hanging onto the rails. Diamant slipped once on the wood, regathered himself, and thundered out into freedom.

"Thick darkness was under his feet. He rode on a cherub, and flew. Yes, he soared on the wings of the wind."

Gamelyn let out a whoop and sat down to ride.

ଔଷ

"MAM is going to give us both sides of her tongue, y'know."

"I know." For the third time, Rob tried to thread the two leather pieces together, then growled and flung the bridle on the ground.

Arawn snorted and angled back. Marion gave him a steadying pat, eyed her brother.

"It's just old and worn out," Rob said. "I should've found leather to make another a while back, but I like that bridle. Well, that's torn it; we'll have to make a rope bridle for him."

"And you have rope."

"Enough, I think. I might have to knot the bridle rein to it. I think our lovely lad would carry me without the bridle, but not both of us, and not on a full moon. Too much madness in th' air—we'd end up running crazed as the Wild Hunt."

Marion picked up the bridle and began unknotting the rein from the bit. Rob went to the packs to search for rope.

ଔଷ

THEY were following him.

Gamelyn had stopped at a stream to let Diamant take some air, to offer him several sips of water—not too much, they still had a ways to go—to take several sips for himself from the water skin hung on his pommel.

There was a distinct presence coming from the northeast—a larger one, surely, than an escaped third son guilty of sodomy would merit. Why would they bother?

"Perhaps," he told Diamant, "they aren't really after me. Perhaps *she* just wants to be in on it."

"Does the smell of blood just make you want more?"

He could believe that. He could still remember the chill it had given him, the light in the Abbess's eyes when she had talked about "saving" him. "Saving" the shire….

Either way, he had to get there first. Gamelyn mounted and Diamant settled back on his haunches, once more ready to be off. He scratched the stallion's withers and gave him his head.

৩৪৩

THEY were still as stones in the trees, dark against the darkening forest. Rob held the makeshift rope bridle with a hand on Arawn's nose; Marion held his tail, ready to pull at it should he start to lift it, whinny.

It was a medium body of horse, but they were soldiers, armed to the teeth, trotting and cantering like they had somewhere to be. The rumble of them had carried across the land like thunder across a stormy sky, and Rob and Marion had heard them, hidden away long before they had appeared on the horizon.

No good consequence had ever come of any peasant traveler staying on a road to meet a company of horse.

"What are they doing out? Where are they going?"

"I don't like it," Rob said. "This is the third patrol we've come across…." His breath sucked in. "Look at this one's banner."

It fluttered, shadowed with the dusk, with a deep hue dark as clotted blood. As dark and Sight-less as the futures he could no longer sense, only feared.

"That abbess," he gritted. "'Tis hers. I'm not understanding it, but we have to get home, Mari."

ENTR'ACTE

THEY should be here by now.

"Horned One protect us!"

"Protect us... protect us... protect us...."

They would have been here by now. Something must have happened.

"Lady be with us!"

"Be with us... be with us... with us...."

Her worries did not reflect in her face as Eluned raised her arms to the cloudy night sky. The chanting continued about her, a gathering of nearly the whole of Loxley, as well as those, serf and freeman alike, who had traveled across the shire. They circled about her in groups, even as she walked a small circuit within the ancient stones. Cernun crouched, naked and hair unbound, upon the middle altar stone. When Adam appeared, Cernun would disappear, descending into the caverns. The fire flickered at his feet, reflected in the faces of the watchers, against the stones, down from the low-hanging clouds.

She saw the questions in Cernun's eyes, the worry carefully disguised. The Horned One would appear; did their followers also wonder where the Maiden and Hunter were? Her children, who were supposed to have arrived over an hour ago, in plenty of time for the Fête of Beltain.

It could not occupy her now. Eluned took a staff of wood from an acolyte, raised it high. The chanting ceased. Silence ruled, echoing back from the stones as powerful as any sounds of the throat. No fire. No sound. Yet they all started to sway, first Eluned then the gathering, as if in thrall of the music held beneath the silence. The wind rose, small gusts swirling her hair about her.

She walked forward, thrusting her unlit staff into the small pyre, and the bit of chaff at its end sparked, blazed, broke the silence with a rush and popping. "Dance!" she cried. "Make the power! Call the Hunt!"

Cernun did not move, head bowed, still kneeling in almost fetal position, as if he had no life. As was so. The people must weave the life-spell, raise the power.

Call the god to life.

"Raise the magic." Eluned began the chant, stepping onto the altar. "Rise. Rise.... *Rise!*"

The fire leapt into the air, a showering of sparks and a plume of smoke… and Cernun was gone.

"It is *time*!" Adam's deep voice rang out. As one, they all turned to find him standing at the key stones, bronze-tipped antlers on his head, clad in deerskin armlets and breeches. Beside him, the horse gathered on its powerful haunches, rearing and plunging, eager.

"The Hunt!" a woman cried out, then another, and soon the glade was alive with gleeful shouts, clapping, voices ringing out with encouragement. "The Hunt! The Lord of the Wode to the Hunt!"

"To the Hunt!" Adam bellowed out in return, and swung up on the horse. With a shout, he whirled the beast beneath him and took off

"Why does he go, Lady?" It was a lad only several years younger than Rob. She felt the fret and pang of absence once again—where were they?—then straightened. The vessel of the Lady must not appear worried, or frail.

"The Horned One rides to Hunt the vision of his *tynged*. He must chase it, seek the way of it. Only then can he return to his people and his Maiden, drink of the cup then bless the fires in the heat of blood-rut."

The boy blushed and turned away. Then he jerked backward, stumbled, and fell across Eluned, a crossbow bolt through his throat.

☙ XXVI ❧

GAMELYN overtook them not far from the crossroads, and would have missed them had Diamant not whinnied and had there not been an answer from the thick cover of trees an ell west.

Arawn. And Rob and Marion sidling out of the trees, and every wary, slow step twinged Gamelyn's nerves all the tighter.

He had found them. Found them, and now they had to go and warn….

"Loxley!" he shouted. "Get up—we have to go, we have to ride, *now*!"

Rob was making motions for him to come on. "Get off the road! The soldiers—"

Gamelyn sent Diamant cantering over to the tree line. "Mount up! I know! We have to stay ahead of them!"

Rob's face went pale. With no more words, he swung up on Arawn's back, offered an arm for Marion to mount, and as soon as she was pillion, he drummed his heels on Arawn's ribs and took off.

Diamant spun on his haunches and followed with hardly a word from Gamelyn.

"What is happening?" Marion was shouting above the rush of wind.

"They're following me!" Gamelyn shouted back

Rob slid him a confused gaze, said nothing. Instead he bent lower on Arawn's neck.

It wasn't much farther to the village, but farther yet to the stones. The two horses thundered down the road, toward the crossroads that would take them more swiftly toward Loxley. Arawn was faster, lighter; he'd obviously not galloped much of the way and was fresher; Diamant would go until he dropped, but Gamelyn could feel the great horse was starting to tire, was falling back slightly.

Rob noticed the slowing of Diamant's pace as well, threw Gamelyn a sharp look.

Then a small company of horse came bearing down upon them from the east branch of the crossroads.

More of the Abbess's soldiers—no more than four or five—but more than enough to head them off. Crossbows leveled, swords at ready, the small company descended upon them. Rob started to drive Arawn on; Gamelyn grabbed at his rein, halting him.

"What are you—?" Rob rounded on him.

"Trying to not get us shot at!" Gamelyn snapped back as he shoved the scarf from his head and demanded of the outriders, "I am Gamelyn Boundys, son to the mesne lord of Blyth. By what right do you delay us?"

"I beg your pardon, milord, but we have orders to stop and identify any heading toward the border."

"And you have done so. Let us pass, at once."

From the north came rumbling, closer than Gamelyn had thought possible. The soldier hesitated.

"I said, let us pass."

"Stop them!" came the shout from the approaching riders. "Stop them!"

Gamelyn met Marion's eyes, then Rob's. "Go!" he hissed.

Rob kicked Arawn, but it was too late. The soldiers closed in. One grabbed Arawn's cobbled-together rein; the others leveled their weapons, crossbows and lances, on the riders.

"Let us pass!" Gamelyn growled, brandishing his brother's sword. "Or I'll—"

Again, it was too late. The small body of horse came galloping up, slowing and circling behind. A few soldiers from Blyth. And Johan. And the Abbess Elisabeth.

Rob's breath escaped him in a low, purling growl.

"Rob," Marion moaned out. "*Gamelyn*—what is happening?"

"*Excellente, petit frêre*. Your foolishness has saved us some work after all. Now." Johan rode over to Gamelyn and held out his hand. "My sword, *s'il te plaît.*"

Gamelyn was prepared to give him his sword, all right. He drew up, ready to knock Johan into the next shire. Froze before he could even begin the motion.

Rob was watching him. *Watching* him, and the expression on his face was raw, disbelieving; as if Gamelyn had taken the sword and thrust it deep into Rob's belly.

And Gamelyn processed, abruptly, all that had been done, and said—more, what Rob had *heard* in it.

Johan rode between them, breaking the stunned contact. "I said, give me my sword."

Numbly, Gamelyn let him reach over and take it. All he cared about was catching Rob's eyes again

He had no chance. Rob had bent forward, reaching up Arawn's neck. There was a hissing sound, and Arawn suddenly reared up, black head bare and bridleless, front hoofs flailing. The guardsmen beginning to ring him fell back; one who had dismounted was flung aside, face blooded from a hoof strike. Rob was making the hissing noise, with several murmurs peppering it, and it seemed to make Arawn mad; he plunged forward, kicking and striking, with Rob hanging tight to his neck and Marion clinging to him like a limpet. Darting sideways, they whirled and galloped away.

"They're escaping, you fools!" the Abbess cried. "Stop them!"

The report of crossbow quarrels broke just as Gamelyn spurred Diamant. With a grunt, the stallion leapt in pursuit of Arawn. More bolts chased past Gamelyn's ears.

"Don't keep shooting, you idiots!" Johan's voice rang out. "You'll hit Gamelyn!"

Why do you care? Why...? Of course. They thought him mad. Enchanted. And Johan was many things, but he did not want the curse of kin-slayer upon his head any more than Gamelyn had wanted him dead in the undercroft....

Arawn took an abrupt detour, heading into the trees.

Gamelyn didn't stop to think; all that mattered was that look of sudden suspicion he'd seen flickering on Rob's face, the disbelief on Marion's. Diamant veered off after Arawn; Gamelyn let the stallion follow. His pursuers were foiled for long moments, enough to him to get a headlong start into the forest on Arawn's heels. Calls resounded behind him—varied expressions of panic at having to ride into the dense growth. But Gamelyn knew Rob would know a horse-safe path, Rob knew Loxley Chase like he knew the backs of his brown, bow-hardened hands.

Gamelyn didn't consider that his path would be a beacon to the others just as Rob's was to him... and by the time he did consider it, it was too late. They were following him.

And then he saw the orange glow lighting the trees.

ଔ

"HANG on, Mari, we're going!" Rob saw the path leading into the Chase and instinctively leaned, used hands and weight and voice to guide Arawn into the forest's shelter.

Marion didn't waste any breath on words, just burrowed in tighter against his back. There was an odd tremor in the normal wiry strength of her arms, but her thighs were firm against his, following his movements since she couldn't see what was going on. Like the games they'd played as children, one blindfolded pillion on the horse, while the other guided them headlong through the Wode.

This was no lark.

And... *Gamelyn....*

Rob didn't believe it. Wouldn't believe it. Yet every time Rob asked the question there was nothing in answer but the ending; the frayed soot of *tynged* behind his Sight, curling and cowling him. Everything rational pointed to rightful suspicion; everything in his heart wanted to explain it away, to find that core of belief that had been so firm in him only days earlier. To let it envelop him, wrap him close, murmur love words in his ear and tell him it was a mistake, had to be.

Had to be….

Rob smelled it before he saw it; the sweet-thick tang of wood smoke, the sweet thickness of green wood and foliage mixing in with the sharper, dry taste of straw and wattle-daub. It sent suspicious tendrils into his mind just as he saw the orange glow rising, lighting the lake clearing just east of the village, slatting angry light through the far copse.

Several people burst from the undergrowth into the clearing, sending Arawn backward and snorting.

"Run! They're burning Loxley!" a man cried, running past them to disappear into the trees.

"Burning?" Marion's voice was slurred all thick, like clotted blood; she gave a hard shudder against him, tipped sideways.

Rob barely caught her before she fell from Arawn's back and was nearly pulled over himself. He grabbed to the black mane just in time, turned tumble into slide and twist, landed mostly on his feet with one arm still around…. "Marion?"

Her head lolled against him. Rob clutched her, started to shake her. "Mari!" His voice castrated itself into a choke as his hands came across the arrow in her back. She shuddered back into consciousness as the accidental touch jostled the shaft, let out a raw and smothered cry.

Rob's knees went weak. He almost fell again, managed by some miracle to keep upright long enough to lower her to the ground. "Marion, *please….*"

There was a loud, soaring rush of air—wind past the copse, bringing with it ash and heat and the crackle of wildfire. And then soldiers started pouring into the clearing.

Rob let Marion down, swift but gentle, and threaded his bow over his head. There was only one thing to do, and he had to make sure he'd the time to do it.

You must listen, little pwca. *You must hear the breath beneath the words.*

He was listening. Finally.

An *ending*.

Thankfully Arawn was still beside them, croup hunched and shivering; Rob snatched his quiver and spared a few more precious seconds to put his cheek against Arawn's nose. "Wait for her, Arawn-*bach*," he whispered. The words would give him the power, but it wasn't just words—horses knew words, but they more understood feeling, body cant, mind-pictures. "Wait in the trees for her, I'll send her to you. *Go*!"

The black bolted for cover.

... make the pact: wed yourself soul and heart's blood to our sweet green Wode, defend the virtue of our Lady, give our body to our challenge....

Rob turned on his pursuers, a smile on his face, and put an arrow to nock. Beltain was the time of the Great Marriage—this would be its own giving, its own taking and submission. Drawing in a deep breath, he drew his bow. Drew down the moon of Beltain. Drew the blood rite, this time with fire and death, and poured the moon's silver light into the fading life of his Maiden.

ଓଃଚ

IN THE few seconds that Gamelyn lost sight of Arawn and he was searching madly ahead, a tree seemed to rise up out of the ground before them. Diamant went right and Gamelyn went left; Diamant kept going and Gamelyn ended up against the tree.

This time, Loxley Chase didn't keep him. He peeled himself off the tree, staggered to his feet, and kept running. Diamant's pale croup was disappearing into the trees before him; he set his sight on that and gave pursuit.

He wasn't sure why, anymore, only that he had to catch Rob. Make him see. Help Marion. Save them all from this mad and horrific catastrophe that had somehow come crashing down on Eden.

The soldiers were all about now. He ended up in a brief and brutal hand-to-hand with a guardsman who had neither Gamelyn's skill nor a knife; only the sword that was useless in the close quarters Gamelyn forced upon him.

His own sword was still on Diamant, so Gamelyn took the soldier's blade. An inferior weapon, but it would do.

He lurched into the clearing, saw the mere shining orange, the sky burnished with flame, the smoke starting to hang in thick hanks through the trees. People were running, screaming, being slaughtered like cattle by soldiers wearing the colors of Nottingham's sheriff.

But the Abbess herself was there, riding upon the clearing, two soldiers at her stirrups. She looked as if she were observing a picnic. Johan was there, as well, cursing and looking frantically about.

Rob was on the opposite side of the clearing. Marion was lying at his feet. It seemed that there was a vibrating, thick darkness shifting about him, and when Gamelyn looked, Rob's lips were moving. Every arrow he shot was sent off with a word, and he never missed. He looked to be some darkling angel—surely Lucifer had not been so terrifying leading the rebellion into Hell—cold and systematic, standing over Marion and daring them to come and get her, black hair haloed with the glow of the burning, and the wind blowing it like fire.

ଓଃଚ

ROB was running out of arrows and he knew it. He was running out of spells; he'd sucked every last bit of light and air from the still place about him, pouring it—*breathing it*—into Marion, willing her heart to keep beating. It was working. He could feel it in his own pulse, feel his knees wobbling from the draw of the bow, the draw of Moonsilver and Maiden.

A glint of gold impinged, more in Sight than vision, and he turned, saw his rival stagger into the clearing. Saw him *See*: the magic of Beltain, the blood and breath.

Lover. It pulsed between them, blood coursing thick-hot through a struggling heart. *Rival.*

A shiver of consciousness still young and human screamed within Rob—*I loved you, I* believed *in you…! Did you do it? Did you?* Why *did you?*

Rival. The deep obsidian *place* that had Hooded itself upon his shoulders quivered and sang. *Betrayer.*

Rob turned, aimed the arrow between Gamelyn's wide green eyes, pulled the arrow halfway to nock.

Then Rob saw *her*. The Abbess, hovering against the trees like a raven upon the dead-fields, and knew what his last arrow would cost him. He lowered his bow, shook his head at Gamelyn.

You win, my Summerlord. Beltain is your birth, your time. Take our Maiden into your stone gaol, protect her and love her as you could not me.

Stay, o King, and watch the King die.

Rob dispatched two more foes almost casually, then curled his fingers about the last arrow from his quiver, hurled the quiver aside. Licked the fletching and put it to nock. Spun the magic tight about it.

It pulled the air from him, set already starved lungs heaving like a broken bellows, danced crimson behind his eyes. His knees wobbled, tried to buckle; Rob bit his tongue and tasted blood, held them rigid by sheer will.

It was the last breath in him, but it was the only one that mattered anymore.

"*Anadlu eich* tynged, you bitch," he whispered, and pushed against the longbow. "*Marwolaeth yn canf—!*"

Something thumped against his chest, hard, breaking the rhythm of the spell-words and staggering him back. Taken aback, he looked down and saw it: a thick crossbow quarrel buried halfway into his pectoral.

It was then the pain hit. It flowered fire into his entire being, sucked the last of that final breath from him. Sent him to his knees, the spelled arrow dangling from a limp string and the bow falling—so slow, ever so slow—from numb and useless fingers.

"*Rob*!"

A scream. It sounded like a scream, anyway, a word rasped all raw and horrified… but thick and slow, as if he were hearing it from underwater. Rob blinked, put a hand to the quarrel to pull it out. Couldn't. His fingers were thick, fumbling and numb. Instead he looked up as his name sounded again—more ragged, more horror—and, almost in puzzlement, saw a familiar, broad, and ruddy-haired figure sprinting for him.

Saw the raven, gliding forth.

Saw the trees making a slow, blurry arc as he fell forward.

The quarrel splintered and shattered as Rob fell atop it, and the indescribable flare of pain sent him hurtling… the last thing he saw was black robes, and the glittering spin of a huge, pectoral cross dangling before his eyes before it all… went… *away*.

ઉ૪ઌ

GAMELYN had run halfway across the clearing after Rob had turned from him—he'd almost wanted him to shoot, almost wanted to fall to his knees in some prayer-filled, sacrificial submission. But Rob had seen the Abbess at the same time Johan had seen him, and Gamelyn had lurched into a run. Rob was running out of arrows, and if Gamelyn was in the way, at least Johan wouldn't let them shoot at him.

He saw the bolt hit Rob, and as if it had struck him as well, Gamelyn staggered to a halt, tottering. Horror-struck. Saw Rob fall forward, limp and sprawling. Screamed his name.

Then something slammed into his own temple and sent him sprawling, nearly unconscious, full out onto the forest floor.

No, he told himself. *Don't… go. You can't. You have to….*

To what?

Hands upon him, holding him down, and he fought. Fought against the ones holding him down, fought against the black with screams and kicks. It slowed around him, everything seemed to be floating, and suddenly Gamelyn heard Johan's voice, wavering in and out of the threatening black. And then a female voice.

"Bring him here. He needs to see this. We need to make sure."

He was muscled up, woozy and half conscious, and half dragged over where Marion was lying, where the Abbess had crouched over Rob like a carrion bird and tangled claws in his black hair, pulling his head up.

"See?" It was calm, almost gentle. Her cross reflected against the dark of Rob's flat, staring eyes. "This is how a demon dies, Cousin. This is how we've freed you."

Gamelyn didn't say a word, merely lunged at her snarling like a rabid wolf, nearly won free of the soldiers holding him.

"Idiot!" Johan swore. "Do you just not know when to stay down?"

Another blow came stinging from the dark, and Gamelyn slumped, heard no more.

ଔଓ

MARION came back to consciousness and into hell. Fire in the sky, licking up to the gravid moon. And she could *breathe*, breathe deep into her lungs without pain, though she remembered she had been shot. They had been riding away from the horses—*Gamelyn*! a deep place within her mourned, *What happened? Why?*—And she had clung to Rob even when the quarrel had hit her in the back, because they had to run and couldn't stop.

Only now the quarrel lay beside her, bloodied, not in her back. And Rob was standing over her, the black streaks of sucked-dry *tynged* tightening about him, almost like a cowl.

Like a *hood*.

Marion tried to speak, stop him. Then she saw Rob stagger back, an ebon shaft blooding and blossoming from his chest, and tried to reach toward him. But her limbs were not her own yet, and she couldn't.

She saw Gamelyn hurtling toward Rob, saw how it took several soldiers to stop him, shoving him down into the dirt as he screamed and struggled and fought them.

It wasn't his fault. It couldn't have been. She had never heard anyone keen with such pain as that.

Saw a black, cowled figure rise from Rob's body, step over it as if it was nothing.

Hooded One... His power is taken... taken....

Saw Gamelyn's brother club him like a mad dog not once, but twice.

Again, she tried to crawl toward Rob, couldn't. Saw his face, pale streaked by sweat-wet inked curls, his ribs, shuddering and heaving with a breath he no longer possessed, his eyes, deep and staring, lit by the flames lighting the night sky.

Saw the black figure lean over her.

"No...," Marion said. "My... brother...."

"Your brother is well now, *ma petit*," the black figure said, warping and fading. "You will be with him anon... *Sacre Jesu*!"

There was sudden fear and wonder in the voice, and as Marion looked up at the figure, she could see a raven. Knowing eyes, head cocking back and forth, a huge, sleek raven sitting fat and cheeky on the shoulders of Death, only the moon had drawn down another aspect, another face, very familiar: Hope and Sorrow....

Marion reached out, touched the chill face, and whispered, "Mother?"

Then sank into the black and knew no more.

☙ ENTR'ACTE ❧

HE'D come late, detained but for very good reasons. Had sneaked a ride on a covered cart most of the way, had been eager to see what an afternoon's efforts had wrought, the magic that might had resulted.

Instead, John found the magic murdered.

The moon was still high in the sky, illuminating everything as if by daylight. In the north, sullen orange lit the sky: more light. Yet it was not a scene anyone would have wanted to see in such brutal detail. The sacred stones lay upturned and broken; the ones who'd thought to do honor to them had not even had the decency of any kind of burial, lying scattered, bloody and bloodied. Those who had somehow survived had no doubt already crawled away.

Upon the altar was the worst sacrilege. She had been beheaded, this vessel for their Lady….

Once she had been the *si* woman. Eluned of the March. Rob's mother. Now she was merely another unrecognizable corpse.

John drew his tattered cloak tighter and hurried away.

He had to find them.

He hadn't gone very far before another body greeted his eyes; a huddled ball of mangled flesh from which carrion eaters scurried away as they were disturbed. Also beheaded, the only thing to identify Adam of Loxley lay a few feet away: the great headdress of the Horned One. It was broken, and stripped of its gold trimmings by another type of carrion. He started to bend down, take it up, then shook his head.

It was finished.

And he still had not found what he sought.

He stood there, head down, breath warming his chilled hands. Then he took in a deep, cleansing breath, opened his palms, let the breath out over them.

"Show me," John whispered, with every warp and weft of mind-magic he possessed, then closed his eyes and breathed again, "*Anadl fy tynged.*"

And stood there, throat and chest thrown wide, hands outstretched, quivering and seeking any tiny vibration of the magic, any hint.

The answer came, in a faint and faltering echo. He opened his eyes, nodded, and broke into a run toward the crimson sky.

It was a lengthy run, but he was used to running even more than riding. The sky was a beacon, glowing sullen threat; smoke hung thick in the trees, and it was silent. Too silent.

A crashing in the brush; he alerted, then smiled as a forlorn nicker sounded. A black rouncey came forward, glad to see a friendly face. It was obvious the black one had waited, and waited… yet none had ever come for him until now. John rubbed at the gelding's face and captured him with his name.

"Arawn."

Arawn willingly carried him the rest of the way.

Trees grew thinner, gave way to a clearing. Bodies littered the ground here, too, and torn-up earth.

Arawn knew what he was looking for, went to stand beside the prone figure. John slid down, wobbling; his legs almost didn't want to carry him. It was… impossible.

What had happened? Where was the Knight? The Maiden?

For here lay the Hunter….

He gave a groan as he knelt beside the fallen one. Turned him over—gently, ever so gently. There was a broken-off crossbow quarrel still piercing the Hunter's breast; wisely John did not touch it, but laid his head upon the Hunter's breast. Thought he heard a slow, sullen thump, but was not sure. Rocking back and forth on his haunches, a finger in his mouth as he thought, suddenly he nodded and dug into his purse.

He had found it at the glassblower's; a lovely, flat piece of robin's-egg blue that, in a pinch, had a decent cutting edge. He held it to the slack lips, waited.

The glass misted, faint but undeniably there.

Tears rose to his eyes, grateful and sudden.

Beside him, Arawn grunted. A shadow fell over them, and John started, peered up to see an old man, white hair streaming from a bloodied forehead, leaning heavily upon a staff.

"Ah, the Hooded One cannot die from an *arrow*," Cernun said, and knelt down with them. "Nay, we will not let him."

John smoothed the hair back from Rob's face, and wiped his eyes, and nodded. "Aye, lord."

☙ END BOOK ONE ❧

ACKNOWLEDGMENTS

THERE can be numerous things that go into writing a book, and books either based on or set into historical timeframes have their own challenges and joys. *Greenwode* and its immediate sequel, *Shirewode*, have led me on an amazing journey.

Over thirty years ago, I wrote the first novel of a trilogy: what would become the precursor to this project. I had the opportunity to travel to England and research the stomping ground of Robyn Hode (aka Robin Hood)—his time and place, companions and precursors and successors. I spent hours hunched amongst ancient tomes in the closed stacks of libraries and ignoring my ever-patient spouse; on the other hand, he and I together made the most romantic of pilgrimages (and yes, he does consider such things romantic) to cairns and priapic chalk giants, stone circles, and the eye of the White Horse. We crawled castles and churches, both ruined and intact, hid 'neath the bracken of Sherwood Forest (what remains, anyway), and slid as if ice-skating on sheep dung whilst climbing Glastonbury Tor. In short, we got to touch a depth of history that, in the Americas, has been long destroyed by white invaders. Bliss!

The first incarnation of *Greenwode* nearly went to contract twice but was felled by various strokes of ill luck. I put it away in my files, thinking the matter finished... yet it was never forgotten. The soul-breath of these books—*tynged anadl*, as the Heathen of the Wode no doubt would say—has been swirling and morphing for all that time and, in the manner of all magics, has exhaled with its own new life. I thought I was merely giving the manuscript a good stiff edit; instead, a valiant and freshman effort remade itself into something deeper. *Greenwode* kept growing into a duology that explored the ways myths can be birthed and how legends, both on paper and in the collective of the unconscious, cannot help but intertwine. I ended up digging even deeper into the old ballads than before, giving honor to the original sources while taking a new tack, setting for the horizon of an authentic, earthy, and affective story. *Greenwode* is about the origins of Robyn Hood, companioned by the other characters that had the making of him, not just Marion but an oft-forgotten precursor to the outlaw tales: Gamelyn Boundys. Not nearly so notorious as Robyn, but often regarded as one of the earlier faces of the Robyn legend, Gamelyn was inspiration for another bard who wrote a play based on a fifteenth-century retelling of *The Tale of Gamelyn*—a play called *As You Like It*. He is also suspected to be the Gandelyn of "Robyn and Gandelyn," a ballad that easily slides into the myth of the brother/lover kings who do battle for the May Queen. It seems to me as of late that the mythic romance (in the oldest, truest sense of the word) of Robyn's world seems to be falling by the wayside. There's plenty of gritty militaristic "reality," plenty of safe retellings in a world that craves formula and extremes of marketability, but the myth and magic of Robyn's truest love—the "swete grenwode"—has been missing.

It is past time to revive it!

So here we are. As nothing is created in a vacuum, from ancient ballads to the most far-out, speculative SF or fantasy world, I must give due to some of the sparks that kindled *Greenwode* (Yes! Go read them!):

There are so many wonderful examples of English medieval ballads and texts, but of particular help to this project were: "A Gest of Robyn Hode," "The Tale of Gamelyn," "Robyn Hode and Guy of Gisborne," "Robyn and Gandelyn," "The Wanderer," *Sir Gawain and the Green Knight*, *Perceval*, *The Canterbury Tales*. Many thanks go to the translators and essayists, too numerous to name, who have done and continue to deconstruct and decode and discuss these tales.

The books which were never far from my keyboard: *Rymes of Robyn Hode* by R.B. Dobson; *The Golden Bough* by James George Frazier; *The White Goddess* by Robert Graves; Margaret Murray's *The Divine King in England* and *The God of the Witches*; *The Fairy-faith in Celtic Countries* by W. Y. Evans-Wentz; *Robin Hood* by J.C. Holt; *Medieval Roads and Tracks* by Paul Hindle. Others that I read for mythic and historical texture were *Holy Blood, Holy Grail* by Beigent, Leith, and Lincoln; *The Templars* by Michael Haag; *Medieval Masculinities: Regarding Men in the Middle Ages* edited by Clara Lees; *The Templars: Knights of God* by Edward Burman; *The Knights Templar* by Stephen Howarth; numerous and valuable medieval histories by not only Joseph & Frances Geis but also Barbara Tuchman, as well as various books by Mircea Eliade. A book I first read at least forty years ago, which led to much more study, was Margot Adler's *Drawing Down the Moon*. A childhood mainstay (with illustrations by the amazing N.C. Wyeth) was Paul Creswick's *Robin Hood* and, of course, *The Adventures of Robin Hood* by Howard Pyle.

Credit must of course go to my draft readers, Carole and Rosina. The former is a remarkable friend who has read more of my writing in primitive stages than anyone should have to endure, kicked my arse on a regular basis, and is solely responsible for nagging me into trying publishing again. The latter has reminded me of such things as "knob" being a much more appropriate term than the one (oft overused to much hilarity) that denotes both a rooster and a certain bit of male anatomy; she also reassured me that my grasp of Yorkshire sound and dialect was "no' so bad, pet." And of course there is *my* lovely John, who is actually quite chatty and gregarious, puts up with his mad and obsessive writer spouse, can push a longbow, and looks *really* good in tights.

The Internet did not exist when I first wrote this book. No, really, it didn't. A weekly trip to the library was my staple then; as to now, I have a love/hate relationship with the initials WWW. It has proven both invaluable resource and irritating distraction. When one enjoys research as much as I, to have the possibility of finding a picture of That Remote Barrow Mound, or a map of the wapentakes of Yorkshire, or a resource about the Templars that does *not* rely on some unfathomably popular and thoroughly unreadable work of fiction... well, it is often irresistible. I must salute The Robin Hood Project at the University of Rochester (lib.rochester.edu) and British History Online (british-history.ac.uk) for being invaluable and easily accessed sources of texts and historical references.

It is also impossible nowadays to discount the effects of TV/movie influences. *Robin of Sherwood*, a brilliant mythos in its own right, a mystical and thankfully British retelling from the '80s that will *always* be one of the quintessential Hoods. *The Lion in Winter*, because, well, how not? Douglas Fairbanks, yowza! Errol Flynn and Basil Rathbone with their sped-up action, bendy swords, and neon tights. The black-and-white TV series *The Adventures of Robin Hood* starring Richard Green, which I adored as a child. *Robin and Marian.* Daffy Duck and Friar Porky. *Men In Tights*! *Monty Python and the Holy Grail*!

And the caveat? (Come now, you knew there must be one somewhere....)

While *Greenwode* and *Shirewode* are both lovingly researched and historically based, this duology is above all else speculative, and therefore firmly in the realm of Fantasy. I have done my damnedest not to let very malleable facts obfuscate the purpose of the magic and the myth. Any retelling of history is a fantasy—and that's as it should be, for we live in a wonderful and terrible chaos of scattered viewpoints and unfortunate crusades. Archeological evidence rests on the interpretations of individuals, all of whom have their own agenda. Papers can be forged and languages lost. And if a people has a mostly oral transmission of their language and are subsequently wiped out....

I am a history geek, no question, but all of us history buffs have to remember this very important fact:

History is chronicled by conquerors.

At best we have a narrow and polarized viewpoint of any given event. Which is, sort of, what good storytelling is about anyway.

Questioning any source is a fine thing. Questioning an “authority” is *always* a fine thing.

I think Robyn Hood would agree.

—JTH

Autumn 2012

❧ NIGHT BEFORE ACRE ❧

A TALE OF THE WODE

"SWEET Lady, *listen* to it! It's *breathing*."

"Breathing." Said with a hint of skepticism; Gamelyn knows his eyebrows are disappearing upward and into his coppery bang even as a slow, indulgent smile tugs at his lips.

At times like this, Rob is more child and wild, more ingenuous than anything he's ever claimed of Gamelyn.

But Rob doesn't answer, standing... no, *swaying* with every rush and ebb of foam and wave. The beach is endless, fathomless pale against dark gray sea. The cliffs reach up so high behind, even Rob couldn't tickle an arrow to crest them—but Rob has no mind for archery now. His bare toes clench against the wet sand, and pressure marks of silt and wet shimmer, ripple outward. Those traces remain, stray shadows as Rob lurches forward, running for the surf.... Nay, it's more half-trip and stumble as he peels from what remains of his clothing, and Gamelyn is laughing, bending down beside the footprints, arms wrapped around his knees. Watching.

A yip as cold waves hit, a laugh slapped with salt as Rob throws his arms wide and welcomes it. Dives in.

How odd that still, between Gamelyn's own bare toes, Rob's footprints remain, marking where he's been. An aura. A wish.

A *memory*.

Gamelyn bends to trace them, light and curious. A memory? They have never been to the storm-tossed English coast....

The laugh dies in his throat. Apprehensive, he peeks upward.

Yet Rob is *there*, sporting in the foam, diving and fetching like some sea creature. Yips and yowls of pure joy rise and merge with the rush and roar of surf; somehow Rob is one with an element he's never before experienced. But it's *cold*, the wild water, and it isn't long before Rob retreats, rising from the waves all blowing and shriveled and shivering, ebon hair hanging like seaweed trails over skin tinged distinctly blue. He looks nothing less than a kelpie from the depths, sleek and windswept, eyes all brassy-bright.

"It's *breathing*, I tell you!" Rob manages between chattering teeth. "Like t' breath of a stag blowing fierce, but also hummin' sweet."

It's Gamelyn's, this time, to yip as fully over six feet of wet-cold and naked lad curls against him.

"*Christ*, Rob—!"

"Warm me up, then," Rob purrs, then sighs. "Mm, you're warm as a good hearth, y' allus are." Then, like a dog worrying a bone, "Surely you could hear 't, did you try."

"I do try."

Rob's fingers are trailing at his breastbone, making Gamelyn squirm. A crooked, wayward smile tilts Rob's narrow face, quite impenitent as he leans in closer for a kiss. He tastes of brine and mist, heat within a chill, fresh wind. "Not half hard enough... or happens you are." This, as those fingers trail even lower. "Hard enough, leastways."

And they're bloody *cold*—but indeed, it doesn't seem to matter. "You never play fair," Gamelyn protests.

"'Tis only unfair if you ent fetching what you want." A chuckle, and fingers exploring light enough to tease Gamelyn *mad*. "Seems plain t' me you are." A pat to his belly as Rob rolls to crouch on his haunches, gestures outward. "But this ent. Plain, that is. Close your eyes. *Listen*."

Not without a sigh, Gamelyn tucks his chin and obeys—slowly, for to watch Rob is always a pleasure. The footprints are *still* there, between his knees and next to Rob's haunches. The sight fills him, nigh to bursting, with sudden yearning and a foreign-delicious pain. Riveting. He cannot close his eyes to it.

"Quit staring at my arse, you. You ent half *tryin*—"

"Shut up, Hob-Robyn!" Gamelyn snaps, squeezing his eyes shut, and thinks, *Not all of us are forest spirits. Sea serpents. What*ever *you are.*

The thoughts fade away as he finds it: the wonderful necessity/escape of silence and self where nothing can reach—*can't touch me, I'm not here*—the fierce inner focus that is his alone. His own breaths slow, commingle with Rob's against the sand and sea, then that, too, fades. Only the water, roaring and churning. Only the water....

And Gamelyn hears.

Hears it: coupled with and beneath the fierce roil of water, of shifting sand. Feels it: ebb and flow, intake and exhale, as if some giant sleeps in the cliffs, to rise only when the full moon calls. Surf furls in, foaming at his knees and tickling the sand from beneath them.

It licks the long toes of Rob's footprints with luminescence, wet and gleaming in the last rays of sunlight.

Gamelyn's legs quiver; he shakes his head, gives himself fully to the great breath gusting against his being, leans back on his heels. The vast bowl of sky presses down upon him, but it is a weight he can bear, a held breath in his belly, a mirror against the sea. There is nothing but him and the sand, the water and the sky....

"See?" Rob whispers, reaching out to stroke his arm. "'Tis time y' understood, aye?" The words turn teasing. "Past time, 'milord'—"

NIGHT BEFORE ACRE

"—PAST time, milord."

And the sky... *shuddered.* Shivered from sunset into a night pocked with stars. Chill, yet the sand was... dry. Desiccated. Gamelyn half opened his eyes, gluey with matter and dust. The footprints were still between his hands—a ghost of what was—yet the more he opened his eyes, the more those footprints began to shrivel and dry, swirl away on a heated breath. The hand was still on his arm; it tightened, slight but insistent. Gamelyn shut his eyes, clenched his teeth—sand and grit—and splayed his hands, clutched, *dug* into the sand. Searching for the wet, and the spray, and—

The *memory*....

"AYE, *feel* it breathing." The voice—the *voice*—and wet, goose-pimpled flesh curling against his back, and quick, excited breaths heating his nape; sensation brings him *back*, tilts the sky into sunrise once again. A callused hand, stealing around his waist to nestle in the curve of his belly. A low plea, burring homely-soft upon his shoulder, and tendrils of ebon hair tickling his collarbones. "We could swim in the sound of it... come on, then. Come with me. I won't let y' drown, I promise. Just come with me."

He wants to go. Somehow he wants to dive—dive *deep*—and never surface again.

"Please, come with me. *Please*, Gamelyn...?"

"...*GAMELYN*?"

He shuddered, still lured by the call of the surf, the hope of that slender figure trailing kisses down his back, the sand mirroring wet ghosts against his reaching fingers....

And woke to darkness.

Waves broke and spilled over the sand; they had never stopped, only grown more distant. Commingled with watery breath of impact and retreat, roar and hiss, was the insistent rhythm of predawn preparation: low voices snapping orders, the dull, metallic susurrus of chainmail, the jingle of spurs and bits, the snorts and nickers of excited horses, the dance of hoofs against shale and beach-pan. A murmur lost into the vast, starry night, dreams insubstantial beneath the thrum of tension, and waiting.

This land breathes. Aye, it breathes warm water to foam, exhausts chill air to turn upon a sunrise, whispers with ice-white stars, pants with heat-shimmered sun. It kisses his cheeks, murmurs through his close-cropped hair, tastes of salt, baked ash, and grit.

And leaves no footprints that wind and wave cannot wash away.

A hand at his back, nearly as familiar to him now as Rob's had once been. Gamelyn shuddered again, though he tried not to.

"'M sorry, milord." The voice was soft, concerned, slurred with home. Only they weren't. *Home*. "They're callin' us t' arms," Much furthered. "'Tis time."

Time. The surf, breathing, and hot sand folding, slipping beneath his hands. The *shuss*-grind of his sweat-stained white habit, its bloody cross imprinted into the sand like a forlorn, futile prayer. No more lasting than those footprints in the sand, swirling away with the wind to shimmer on the horizon, beckoning....

Then, gone.

'Tis time. Aye, past time.

To arms. To battle.

And Acre, waiting.

"I'm all right," Gamelyn took a deep breath, held it, let it out as his heart began to slow to normal. He rocked up slowly, to hands then knees.

"Another nightmare, then." Much phrased it like a question—yet not. He squeezed Gamelyn's shoulder, released him, and stood.

"Nay," Gamelyn answered nonetheless, a faulty whisper as he stared across the black and blood-warm expanse of the Sea of Faith. "Waking is the nightmare."

And his breath rose into the star-pocked desert sky, a frosty cloud which tore itself into silence beneath pounding surf.

Read this excerpt from

Book Two of the Wode

The King of the Shire Wode. That is what they will call you.

Years ago, a pagan commoner named Rob of Loxley befriended Gamelyn Boundys, a nobleman's son, against seemingly insurmountable odds—and with horrific consequences. His home razed by order of the Church, Rob was left for dead, believing his sister, Marion, and his lover, Gamelyn, had perished.

But Gamelyn yet lives. Guilt-ridden by his unwitting betrayal of Loxley, one of the last bastions of the Old Religion, Gamelyn rides off to seek absolution in the Holy Land. Rob vanishes into the greenwode and emerges as leader of a tight-knit band of outcasts who revolt against the powers that be.

When the two lovers meet again, it will be in a brutal, blindfolded game of foxes and hounds that pits Templar assassin against Heathen outlaw. Yet the past cannot be denied, and when Rob discovers Marion is also still alive, the game turns. History will chronicle Robyn Hood and Guy of Gisbourne as the deadliest of enemies, but the reality is more complicated—and infinitely more tragic.

http://www.dsppublications.com

☙ PRELUDE ❧

Deep in the Shire Wode
Waning of Beltain, 1190 ACE

"I AM a stag of seven tines."

The old man sits at the fire, breathing smoke, invoking flame. Humming an elder bard's song of island magic, old when he was young.

"I am a tear the sun lets fall."

The young Hunter is flung at the old man's feet, sacrifice to the rocks, to the earth, to Mother. Nearly bled white, there is a great and gaping hole breaking the usual line of tensile muscle along his breast. The arrow has been cut out, but the damage is great. The poultice has been replaced, over and over, furs laid and the fire drawn hot.

"You are a hawk above the cliff."

But his *tynged* lies still-quiet. A skein spinning outward, vivid sparks of warmth amidst the violated aubergine of viscera, into indigo and then fraying into the black against moonlight. The moon is waning; Her dance now has him, tripped and tangled, Her voice drawing him down into the death spiral. She would take him back, set him free.

The Horned Lord would foil Her, have his weapon back. And Cernun is the Horned Lord's: spirit and body.

"I am the womb of every holt."

Cernun uses every wile, every healing mantra and simple, every bit of magic in his aging frame. Twice already has he drawn the shroud over the Hunter's face, sung the death song. Twice has the thin flax lay still then, impossibly, sucked inward, breath still stirring, faint.

Blooded. Broken. Yet still the Hunter fights, knowing his fight is not yet begun. The magic would take him down and he would seem to have no choice but to let it swamp him—Death breathes his name even as She heats him with fever and infection.

Part of him welcomes Her....

...all of them dead... lost... mam!da!mari!... burning... hanging on the cross... death of me, deathofme... loved him... loved *him!*

...treachery... betrayer... murderer....

And despair leads to pain leads to rage back to pain... but rage is always the stronger, and pain but feeds the fury in his blood. The Hunter refuses to bow, to bend. Incites the darkness. Shows throat, but with a snarl.

So the old man snarls back. Touches death. Tries to weather the squall. Breathes the spells to set the Hunter back into thisworld.

"Take my life for his," Cernun chants. "Mine for his. He is our future, our purpose, our hope. All that is left. You have his blood, Lady, my life is forfeit. I am but Your Hermit, old and spent. This boy has purpose, yet; he would be Your Darken King."

He is wounded too grave, heart and body. The Lady's voice is a soft echo within the caverns. *Would you countenance a crippled King?*

"Who walks unburdened, in thislife?" is Cernun's quick riposte. "Together, we can make him whole."

Are you so sure? Nay, my own, it is finished. All things must end.

It is not yet Our time! Her consort protests, muted thunder in the depths. *It is not yet* Our *ending!*

I am Death—

And I am Your spear roaring for blood. I am Time, the meaning *of Death. The meaning of—*

Life, She must concede.

"His blood is Yours, the teind paid, Holly King fallen beneath the Oak King's sword," Cernun murmurs. "He has been broken, bound, the Sacrifice endured. If You must hold a spirit's hem, grasp mine."

She turns great, luminous eyes upon him. *I shall. Never doubt that.*

Silence falls, truncated softly by the drip of water against rock, the crackle of the flames, the hoarse, faint breaths of the wounded. Even the presence of the lad who sits watch outside is magnified, held in thrall of the magic. Then:

What of the others? She asks. *The Pale Knight and the Maiden?*

They are taken by Our enemies, flung to wind and water, to barren stone. They are lost to Us. The Horned Lord pauses, then says, fecund with meaning, *He is the only one who can bring them back.*

The Lady Huntress concedes, bows Her bright head, turns aside. And the Horned Lord grabs his Hunter by the hair, kisses him, all passion and cold fire and indomitable will.

Breathe the fire. Breathe your destiny. Breathe, *Hob-Robyn.*

I am the tomb of every hope, comes the answer, teased wavering from the black. *I have no breath. I am a ghost, howling in the night, disappearing in the trees, dreams of hope and love twisted into betrayal and nightmares....*

You are. Breathe them. Anadl tynged, *my own. You are all of those, and more.*

You told me. Told me... told me *he would betray us all. And I didna listen. And now... I canna See....*

Cannot, or will not?

It is... gone. All I See is the ending. The precipice. I hang with bloodied fingers over a thick, black void, and tynged *is frayed, burnt beyond any hope. Burnt like Loxley. Like my heart. He... he let us fall, his Maiden and his lover both....*

And you will take your vengeance. That I promise you. You will have what is yours by rights, and see the traitors writhing at your feet. The cowl upon your heart will also shroud your head. It will be your protection, your being. It will be how your people will know Hob-Robyn is not dead. The Hunter will never die. He is resurrected into the Hooded One.

The Hooded One is a spirit.

Aye, as you will be a spectre, a cry in the night, fae green Wode sprite, breath of nightmares and dreams. The Hooded One is Mine, My soul, you are *Me. My avatar and all of ours is both spirit and flesh, blood of the King who has bled and died and lives again through the love and tears of his people.*

The King....

The King of the Shire Wode. It is what they will call you. Rob in th' Hode.

Robyn Hode. Aye. That *is who we are.*

☙❧

The coast of Normandy
End of May 1190, ACE

"SO THIS is the new one, eh?"

Dead. They're all dead. While he is alive.

There is an irony in it. Something twisted and injured, like an animal in a trap waiting for the coup de grace, *the hand to break its neck, the edge to open an artery. The relief of* ending....

He does not deserve relief.

"*Sacre tête*, boy, you look like Hell. Your trip across the Channel was not so kind, eh?"

Gamelyn bowed his head lower, gave a small shrug. It had in truth been miserable; a high wind filling the sails and heaving waves slamming the bow, which in turn had him heaving his guts over the railing for nearly the entire trip.

"I imagine once the *mal du mer* passes, you will be glad to finally see the land of your people." A grim chuckle. "Not that we will have much time to entertain the sights of Normandy."

Gamelyn should be awed. Respectful. His father had come from here, and some of his dam's people; they had traveled across the English Channel in the wake of Hastings and the one Rob's people still called Willy Bastard....

Rob. Marion. Their... people, dead. All of them, cut down like animals and none to mourn their passing, none to even express regret....

Even his own remorse was a silent and castrated hollow place within, one he had dug himself and kept backfilling with rage and grief. Over and over and *over.*

Now there was only a queasy gratitude that his feet were once more on solid land, Norman or no. Even if a sadistic little pig of a guard captain had nigh dragged a tottering Gamelyn from the gangplank and quick-stepped him, horse and all, from the portside to the encampment. Once there, Gamelyn had been marched through the chaos of soldiers sparring, shouting and armoring, to this tent where he now knelt in the chill, stomped-down mud to meet *chevalier* de Gisborough, his new master.

Who just happened to be a Templar Knight.

Gamelyn had heard stories of the Templars. They were uncompromising fanatics, zealots. They put entire towns of Jews and Saracens to the torch: men, women, children—it didn't matter. If they were deemed to have offended God, the last sight beheld would be the white tabard and crimson cross. It was said Lionheart himself owed much of his working capital to what funds had been passed to him by the Templars: they held power over a *king....*

"Uncover before your lord!" The sadistic little pig, still behind Gamelyn, tangled hard fingers in the woolen scarf about his ears and yanked it away. Gamelyn grabbed it just before it throttled him; the captain seemed satisfied, did not press the matter. Damp oozed down his nape, and Gamelyn caught a whiff of vomit; he had worn the wrap first to ward away the damp Channel passage and now against the crisp wind rattling the tent flaps.

A snort from the Templar. "Well, there's no doubt he fits the physical description here." He brandished the parchment; Gamelyn's eyes rose to it then chased away. "The hair alone.... Leave us, Etienne."

"My lord, he came with a horse. A fine courser."

"And this is my concern how? Other than he's well equipped and I am grateful for it."

"He's a mere squire—"

"Who will likely earn his knight's spurs anon, as he is not baseborn. You are covetous, Etienne, and you will see the chaplain for it before night's end." There was an almost-lazy threat beneath the words, merely emphasized by the opulent baritone; Gamelyn snuck a look at the sadistic little... at Etienne... and saw the threat blossom apprehension in the narrow face. "I will myself come and ensure that you give such a valuable animal into the care of my own groom. *Va t'en. Vite!*" the Templar added as Etienne hesitated further.

Etienne obeyed, retreating from the tent. Gamelyn breathed a bit easier; he had not liked leaving Diamant tied outside all packed up like a charcoal burner's nag. But only a bit, as he was left, kneeling alone, before the Templar.

"You're a quiet one."

Ah, but Rob would have laughed himself sick at that one....

And the great, aching hole opened up again, making Gamelyn sway sideways and put a hand to the chill, well-trodden mud to steady himself.

Enough. He would not do this anymore. *Enough.*

"Get up, lad. You will be my squire, not my serf."

Gamelyn resumed the relentless backfilling of the despairing rent in his soul, got up. Slow, wary, he watched his new master the entire while. The Templar was some inches taller than Gamelyn, his frame lean but built up into a power that gave suitable promise beneath the white tunic with its bloody cross. His brown hair was cropped short, beginning to grizzle; his beard similarly grayed and trimmed. He met Gamelyn's gaze and matched it, edged keen and glinting pale by the flickers of lantern light.

But his eyebrows were drawn together, considering. He seemed... nonplussed.

"Well. No doubt I'll talk enough for the both of us." Once again the Templar consulted the roll of parchment Gamelyn had presented him. "It says here your father has but recently died. Your brother has given you a proper writ of lineage, stating you are Gamelyn Boundys de Blyth, third son to Sir Ian, mesne lord of Blyth and noble vassal to Huntingdon and King Richard. He states, here, your intent to pledge yourself to Crusade for absolution of your sins." The eyebrows drew together even tighter, then relaxed. One climbed upward. "Hard to know what sins a sixteen-year-old lad can truly claim."

Gamelyn clenched his jaw, said nothing.

"Hm. I see that none of this *amour fraternel* kept your brother from sending you in lieu of the scutage he could have paid for your service."

Brotherly love? Again, Gamelyn clenched his jaw....

"You were the one who cozened our father to send so many marks to Ely's monastery; now you will make up for that lack. Our king demands scutage; instead he shall have you. If we want to keep these lands our father worked so hard to gain, then sacrifices must be made...."

Sacrifice. What will you *sacrifice, Summerling?* The velvet-deep voice of Rob's god had queried... then had not sounded again, not even in the depths of nightmare.

He was, truly, bereft.

The Templar was still watching him, still seemed... curious? "No doubt, however you inconvenienced your brother, the worst of those sins was likely mere proximity."

Ah, yes. Sins.

If he lived to see ninety-nine, he would never atone for what sins the fires of Beltain had wrought. Nightmare had become reality: all of them, dead.

Even his father. The illness had taken him that same night, and Gamelyn hadn't been there. Hadn't said good-bye. Everything was lost, had in truth been wiped from Gamelyn's existence in that moment when Rob's hot, dark eyes had leveled down the arrow he aimed at Gamelyn and screamed: *Rival. Lover.* Betrayer.

They had dragged Gamelyn's unconscious body back to Blyth; he had woke, chained like a mad dog to the first convenient barrier—a buttress in the main hall. Otho had been the one to explain, painstaking and patient, how when they'd brought Gamelyn back to the castle and managed to revive him, he had, indeed, gone a little mad. Drawn a dagger on the Abbess, taken out several guards and nearly Johan as well.

Under the circumstances, what choice was Johan to make?

"The church might be loathe to take in a madman; the Crusade, however, is full of them. Otho has insisted you be given a choice, petit frêre*: this is your choice. You can either ride to your new appointment of your own will, or I can deliver you there tied hand and foot. But you will go and be gone...."*

"Well," the Templar said. "Not an uncommon predicament in these troubled times; you are one of many secondary sons marching with us. It is no cause for shame."

His throat still too tight and thick to speak, Gamelyn bowed his head, acknowledging the kind words.

"I knew your father, lad. Sir Ian was brave, fought in Palestine like a tiger. You could do worse than emulate him."

Strangely, this unclenched Gamelyn's throat, made it possible to say, quiet, "Thank you, my lord *Chevalier*."

The Templar blinked, taken aback, and Gamelyn realized it was the first thing he'd actually said. Then the Templar shrugged. "I would hazard you've heard more than a few tales about your new master... or his Order, I should say."

It was Gamelyn's turn to blink.

"Eh, boy? Have you heard we sacrifice virgins upon the full moon, eat the hearts of our enemies? That we worship Heathen idols and lie with each other instead of women?"

Well, Gamelyn considered grimly, the last two should suit him just fine....

Enough! He slapped misery mid-whine and tipped it into the never-ending hollow; began, again, to backfill.

"The women which, I assume, we sacrifice." The Templar gave a derisive snort. "Hear me, Gamelyn Boundys de Blyth, you are now squire to *Chevalier* Hubert de Gisborough, *Templier*, Master and Commander to Hirst Preceptory of Yorkshire. I do not answer to Church, Crown, or any idle gossip. I deny nothing. I admit nothing. It is no one's business but our own, and if you have the leanings insinuated in this letter, then you might have the Holy Orders within your grasp should you act with humility and prudence. You will do well to keep your mouth shut. Which I assume," the Templar rolled up the parchment with a swift twist, "from these past moments we have spent in each other's company, will not be a hardship for you.

"So. I know enough of why you're here in Normandy—"

Actually, you really don't, and that's just fine.

"You've been sent to me because, as it happens, my junior squire was killed in a bizarre accident. Run over by a loose tourney horse. He was a good lad, but stupid. Clumsy. And couldn't write a blessed word… can you write, boy?"

"Yes, my lord *Chevalier*."

The Templar's gray eyes lit up. "Really? Can it be possible you achieve more than a pathetic scrawl?"

"Yes, my lord *Chevalier*." Gamelyn was beginning to take note of more than the minimalist details of tent and Templar. All about, on tables and stacked in open trunks, were an assortment of tomes and parchments being packed. It loosened his voice even more. "I can write Latin as well as both *Langue d'oc* and *Langue d'oïl*. I used to pen letters for my father. He often remarked upon my steady and legible hand."

Pride, Gamelyn. Pride will be your death....

If only. Now, 'twas all that was left.

"Bloody marvelous!" the Templar exclaimed, his voice a smooth power of accompaniment to the slap of his hand against the table. "And you seem to know words of more than one syllable. Dare I hope your reading is as easy as your spoken vocabulary?"

"I can read, my lord *Chevalier*."

"But do you *like* it, lad?"

"Never liked reading. Too many thoughts gathered all ripe in one place, too many scrawls and marks t' make anyone's head full to bursting. You and Marion can have it, and welcome...."

"I…." And bugger and piss, but his throat was trying to close up again. "I do, my lord *Chevalier*."

"*Excellent*. You'll be a goodly improvement over my last squire—rest his soul." The Templar peered at him, searching. Gamelyn dropped his own gaze, uncertain. "Well. You've come far from home, and will be farther yet, anon."

"I'll go. Of my own will. There's nothing left for me here...."

"We'll see what you're made of. A few cautions, then. When you do address me, it will be as 'Commander', or 'my lord Commander'. In actuality, I prefer you not address me unless I speak directly to you; again, I assume this will not be undue hardship. You seem not overly made of chatter."

"Yes, my lord *Cheva*… my lord Commander."

"Go, then. See that your horse and baggage is tended to, and report to Etienne. He is the sergeant in charge of the squires. He has taken up the duties of *Confanonier* since that unfortunate man was killed in a sortie north of here, but he is not of noble blood, so you will address him merely as Sergeant. It annoys him, but we all have gadflies we must endure. If you have questions, Etienne or your fellow squires are the ones you will ask. I am not your nursemaid. You are no peasant, so we will find a boy to see to your basic needs, but you are new and shall work your way into favor no less than anyone. You are not one of us yet, mind."

And may never be. What Holy Order would take me now?

"*Va t'en.*"

"Yes, my lord Commander," Gamelyn said and bowed out of the tent into the wind and the rain.

ꕥ

Worksop Abbey

Autumn of 1190, ACE

YOU will find the abbey a safe and holy place, the Reverend Lady had promised, and so she had found it. The stone walls had enclosed and clothed the mother-naked bairn that she was. Her life had truly started anew. No doubt for the better, or so Sister Deirdre would say; even if there was something about Sister Deirdre that was somehow unsound, tainted.

No doubt it was due to such feeling that she had not quite trusted to drink the draughts Sister Deirdre had provided when she had first been brought to the abbey from the castle, bundled up and taken away in a cart not unlike the one used for the dead. The secrecy was necessary; there was an evil spirit loose in the castle, the Reverend Lady had explained, an unfortunate man driven mad by the same evil ones who had tried to sacrifice her to their demon, and her spirit could not be contaminated with his. She had heard howling, like a demented wolf... and it followed her into dreams when she poured Sister Deirdre's draught into the piss pot instead of drinking it.

No, not just dreams. Nightmares. Of horned demons and naked worshippers, of blood and fire and a hooded figure leaning over her in the dark, as if to steal her, breath and spirit....

From that night forward, she took the draught, and the dreams stopped.

There had been talk of traveling, since she had recovered so quickly—a miracle, the Reverend Lady said, when they had found her in the forest. God Himself had smote the filthy pagans about her and it had been the Reverend Lady who had first put hands upon her, found her not dead, but healed of her grievous wounds. A miracle. Traveling had been an exciting thought. But when she went too far from stone walls, too close to the tangled horrors of the woodland surround, the headaches would start, and the half-memory/half-nightmarish *things* would swirl about her, as if she held some sort of recognition for them.

As if she were unclean.

It would get better, Sister Deirdre promised. Once the spirits had found her unassailable by anything but God, they would cease their caterwauling, the Reverend Lady insisted. She should stay cloistered, and pray.

The barren stone would protect her.

She was eager to do so. The abbey of Worksop was a proud edifice to do God's work, but also held a private chapel for those who did not choose to open themselves to secular scrutiny, and a separate dormitory to the same ends. She was given a tiny cell, and a simple white shift to wear until the Bishop could come and witness her case. It was not so simple as taking oaths or vows, the Reverend Lady had explained; a novitiate needed to be in a state of grace to take communion, and considering the miracle, surely she was, but.... It was a man's world, at the end of it, and the Archbishop wanted to see this wondrous nearly martyred victim for himself, to judge.

And when she asked for a name, at least—a name with which to cloak herself to meet this uncompromising Archbishop—the Reverend Lady told her she might choose herself. When she spoke the first name that rose to her tongue, it seemed to give them pause, but it... fit. Was hers, in a world where nowt belonged save the sound and feel of it upon her tongue.

"Marion," she said. "My name is Marion."

ꕥ

Coming in 2015

Winterwode

Book Three of the Wode

Robyn Hood is the undisputed ruler of the wild, green Wode. Reunited with his sister Marion and his lover Gamelyn, Robyn and his band of outlaws seek to raise the Ceugant—the magical trine of the Old Religion—against the tyranny of Church and Crown. Yet their forest kingdom is roiling with conflict. Marion has been made welcome, but old shackles and new fears hamper her true promise. Gamelyn is torn between oaths of heart and head—and the outlaws never let him forget he was but recently Guy of Gisbourne, defrocked Templar and Robyn's fiercest enemy.

When a lone traveler is waylaid on the road, a common occurrence quickly proves uncommon. Knight and Maiden, Archer and Men, all are conscripted to aid a Queen's—and ultimately a King's—ransom. For beneath winter's chill is awakening the deepest of magics, and there are those who seek the power of Robyn Hood and his Shire Wode for their own ends.

J TULLOS HENNIG has had varied professions over a lifetime—artist, dancer, teacher, equestrian—but has never successfully managed to not be a writer. J Tullos is blessed with an understanding spouse, kids, and grandkids, is alternately plagued and blessed with a small herd of horses and a teenaged borzoi who alternates leaping over the furniture with lounging on it.

And has, for the entirety of that lifetime, been possessed by a press gang of invisible "friends" who Will. Not. S.T.F.U.

Correspondence welcomed through the website: jtulloshennig.net and e-mail: JTH@jtulloshennig.net.

DSP PUBLICATIONS

visit us online.
WWW.DSPPUBLICATIONS.COM

CPSIA information can be obtained
at www.ICGtesting.com
Printed in the USA
FSOW03n1156040417
32707FS